“Amanda … most satisfying … people that I have ever read. Like Patrick O’Brien’s sea stories, they are funny, humane novels of character and manners, as well as excellent adventures.”

Ursula K. Le Guin

Flute Dog had been married for the space of one warm spring night when the Horse Searchers came home. No one had really thought they would come back.

Spotted Colt and Mud Turtle looked different now, Flute Dog thought, while she stood on the edge of the crowd that gathered around them. They looked like people who had been to the edge of the world, and she wondered what they had seen.

It came to her very suddenly that there could be anything in the world . . . things she had never seen, things so far away and strange that they didn’t have names.

Pale men. Horses with ears like rabbits. Stone that could be melted and sticks that shot flame and small stones.

If all those things could be, then any other thing was possible, too.

Other Books in
The Horse Catchers ***Trilogy by***
Amanda Cockrell

WHEN THE HORSES CAME
CHILDREN OF THE HORSE

The Deer Dancers ***Series***

DAUGHTER OF THE SKY
WIND CALLER'S CHILDREN
THE LONG WALK

ATTENTION: ORGANIZATIONS AND CORPORATIONS
Most Avon Books paperbacks are available at special quantity discounts for bulk purchases for sales promotions, premiums, or fund-raising. For information, please call or write:

Special Markets Department, HarperCollins Publishers, Inc.,
10 East 53rd Street, New York, N.Y. 10022-5299.
Telephone: (212) 207-7528. Fax: (212) 207-7222.

THE HORSE CATCHERS

TRILOGY

BOOK THREE

The Rain Child

AMANDA COCKRELL

AVON BOOKS
An Imprint of HarperCollins*Publishers*

This is a work of fiction. Names, characters, places, and incidents are products of the author's imagination or are used fictitiously and are not to be construed as real. Any resemblance to actual events, locales, organizations, or persons, living or dead, is entirely coincidental.

AVON BOOKS
An Imprint of HarperCollins*Publishers*
10 East 53rd Street
New York, New York 10022-5299

Copyright © 2001 by Book Creations Inc. and Amanda Cockrell
ISBN: 0-380-79551-5
www.avonbooks.com

All rights reserved. No part of this book may be used or reproduced in any manner whatsoever without written permission, except in the case of brief quotations embodied in critical articles and reviews. For information address Avon Books, an Imprint of HarperCollins Publishers.

First Avon Books paperback printing: February 2001

Avon Trademark Reg. U.S. Pat. Off. and in Other Countries, Marca Registrada, Hecho en U.S.A.
HarperCollins® is a trademark of HarperCollins Publishers Inc.

Printed in the U.S.A.

10 9 8 7 6 5 4 3 2 1

If you purchased this book without a cover, you should be aware that this book is stolen property. It was reported as "unsold and destroyed" to the publisher, and neither the author nor the publisher has received any payment for this "stripped book."

For Tim Dunbar

INTRODUCTION

THE PEOPLE YOU WILL MEET BETWEEN THESE PAGES were never real, nor were their tribes. That said, they are always real, the folk of myth and legend. So while you will not find in these novels any real tribe of the Plains people who for a short and shining time wandered the Grass on horseback, neither, I hope, will you find people who could not have lived there.

Imagine, if you will, a time of upheaval, of rumors on the wind, of horror stories from the west. Into that stew steps a magical new animal who can change the world by measuring its distance out with his long legs. On his back, food is easy to find, and leisure is born for art and dancing, for thinking more deeply about the ways of the Universe. Who can know what might follow next? Perhaps more things no one has seen before; the lure of the new is very strong. You embrace these magic things. Now you are actually watching your world change. Not so fast as it changes now while you are reading this page, but steadily and surely, fast enough to frighten you; at times comically, upending people with the capriciousness of the wind; at other times tragically, that which was lost never to be regained. And all around your campfire are the pawprints of Coyote.

PROLOGUE

Coyote Dreams

THE SQUARE WAS IN THE SPANISH PART OF TOWN, WITH the Courthouse at one end of the plaza and the old mission at the other. In between were galleries and restaurants, and, at the center of a bed of blue-purple lilies of the Nile, a fountain that burbled green water into the air. There were wet footprints in the sand around the fountain that might have been a dog and might not, and two girls soaking their feet in the water.

In spring the rain falls suddenly, and the desert blooms overnight, as if all the beauty of the world has been sleeping under the sand. The air feels like silk on the skin and Coyote dreams come into everyone's heads at night.

Restless dreams of wandering, of riding in boxcars or the thin silver airplanes needling through the sky overhead. Dreams of sleeping in hammocks under arbors made of grapevines, in old, walled, Spanish haciendas.

Dreams of walking through the desert at night when the borders between the worlds are thin and the old rock carvings come alive, and dancing with the little hump-backed flute player down the long valleys into another time. Since dreams are only another level among the many levels of the world, it is not surprising if a dream dreamed on a spring night sometimes calls something of itself into the daylight.

The girls were in the early years of their adolescence, when they could feel themselves stretching, growing like the grapevine tendrils, getting ready to bloom like the lilies of the Nile. *Be careful*, the nuns warned them, sensing this green yearning, *Don't talk to strangers*.

They were still in their blue-and-white school uniforms when they met Coyote in the park. This time she was an old bag lady with a red feather in her gray hair and a long brown skirt held together with safety pins. She sat on a bench with a basket at her feet, putting things into it and taking things out. The girls saw her as they were drying their feet, Coyote Grandma with golden eyes. The brush of her tail just showed under her long skirt.

"Sister Catherine said we weren't supposed to talk to you," one of the girls said, although the old woman hadn't spoken to them yet.

"I'll tell you a story Sister Catherine doesn't know." The old woman took a string of glass beads out of her basket. The sun poured through them, red and orange and yellow, with bits of bright blue in between like drops of water.

The other girl picked up her shoes and walked barefoot over the warm bricks to the bench beside the fountain. She had gold hoops in her ears and a gold cross around her neck on the breast of her blue-and-white uniform, but she yearned toward the red and orange beads.

"What kind of a story?"

"Well, what do you like?"

"I like horses."

"Not boys?" The old woman put the beads back and got out a little white leather horse with white feathers for a mane.

"Well, boys, too," the girl said. "But I don't know many. We go to a girls' school."

Her friend stood at the other end of the bench behind the old woman's back, making faces at her, grimacing and beckoning. The other girl ignored her.

"Well, this is a story with horses *and* boys," the old woman said. "Tell your friend to sit down, she is making it hard for me to think."

The friend sat gingerly on the corner of the bench.

"There was this chief's daughter," the old woman said. "She was beautiful."

The girls nodded. All fairy-tale princesses were beautiful if they were good. Only the mean ones were ugly.

"Beautiful but stupid," the old woman added thoughtfully. "All the young men were courting her."

The second girl sighed. Sister Catherine was always telling her what a fine mind she had, but when the school had a dance with the boys from St. Andrew's, the boys all danced with Graciela, who was stupid as an adobe brick, but beautiful.

"Well, boys are stupid, too," the old woman said. "There's no getting around that. Anyway, this chief's daughter had all the young men courting her, sitting outside her house playing the flute all night long. She would sit inside and listen and smile. Her widowed sister-in-law lived with her and *she* was getting tired of it and wished the chief's daughter would marry someone . . .

Well, Coyote saw her and he thought that he would like to marry her. But she wouldn't look at him any more than she would say yes to any of the other young men. So Coyote thought about that, and he remembered the new people he had seen. Now, this was a long time ago and there weren't any white people here yet, just a few over on the coast bothering the people there. But Coyote can go anywhere and time doesn't matter much to him. So he went over to the coast to see what was going on. He nearly got shot, but he came back with some things nobody here had ever seen before.

Then he built him a house right next to the chief's daughter's house where she lived with her sister-in-law. And he started making noise in the night, howling and carrying on and banging with sticks on the walls. He made so much noise that the chief's daughter couldn't hear all the other young men playing their flutes. He made so much noise she couldn't sleep. She put her hands over her ears, but he kept on howling and banging. Finally she said to her sister-in-law, "Go over there and see who's making all this racket and make them stop."

So the sister-in-law got up and went next door in her nightgown and told Coyote, "Stop that. Don't you know people are trying to sleep?"

"Oh, I can't help it," Coyote said. "I am making some wonderful new things and it takes a lot of noise to make them."

"Well, why don't you make them in the daytime, then?"

"I can't. These things can only be made at night." And he went back to howling and banging on the walls.

Now, the sister-in-law didn't know he was Coyote. She thought he was just a crazy-looking young man with kind of pointy ears. So she went back and told the chief's daughter what he had said and they both put cotton in their ears and tried to sleep. In the morning the chief's daughter told her, "That young man certainly made a lot of noise last night. Go over there and see what it was he was making and bring him here with it. I want to see it."

The sister-in-law went next door and pretty soon she came back with Coyote.

The chief's daughter said, "Well? What is this wonderful thing you made? It had better be worth all the noise you were making."

The old woman rummaged in her basket and got the beads out again. The string seemed longer this time. The red and orange ones flowed over her fingers like little drops of lava and the blue ones hissed and spat when they touched the red ones. The whole string shimmered in the sun with a whispering like taffeta cloth. "This is what he had."

"The chief's daughter wanted it," the first girl said with conviction.

The chief's daughter wanted it. She said, "I have never seen anything so beautiful. What do you want for it?"

"Oh, I don't want much," Coyote said. "Just a kiss."

"A kiss?" The chief's daughter looked at him dubiously. He was wild-eyed and hairy. She whispered to her sister-in-law, "What do you think I should do?"

"Well, a kiss isn't much," the sister-in-law said. "I can't imagine him giving away a thing like that for a kiss. I'd kiss him before he changes his mind."

So she kissed him and Coyote thanked her many times and gave her the necklace of beads. She was very happy with the bargain, and that night, when he began howling and making noise again, she wasn't as angry as before. "He must be making something wonderful," she said to her sister-in-law. "In the morning, you go over and see what it is."

In the morning the sister-in-law went next door, yawning and rubbing her eyes. She hadn't slept at all, but Coyote looked happy and rested. He doesn't need much sleep. She brought him back to the chief's daughter, and the chief's daughter said, "Well? What have you made now?"

The old woman poked around in her basket, mumbling, while the girls watched. She took out a small lizard and put him back again so quickly the girls couldn't tell if he was rubber or not. Then she pulled out a mushroom and a feather and put those back, too, digging deeper and deeper like a terrier, scattering odd bits of things that caught the light as they flew out of the basket and melted in the air.

"Here it is." To their disappointment, she held up a small dark-gray pot, the right size for a doll's house. When the girls looked bored, she smiled. "A good cook pot is a valuable thing. You go home and ask your mothers. And in any case there had never been anything to cook with before but baskets and clay. You try boiling your stew with hot rocks in a basket and see how hungry you get." She poked a finger into the little pot as if she were stirring it and they caught the faintest whiff of a smell. It might have been fresh-baked bread, or chicken soup, or roast corn. Their stomachs growled and they looked at the pot longingly now.

Coyote's new thing was an iron kettle. No one had ever seen iron before. The chief's daughter ran her fingers over its cold surface and rapped it with her knuckles. It sang the way a plucked bowstring does, but a deeper note.

"It cannot be broken," Coyote said proudly.

"I want it," the chief's daughter said. "With a pot like that I can marry any man I want and he will bring me six blankets, not one. What do you want for it, another kiss?"

She puckered up and got ready to kiss him, but he said, "No, I had a kiss. This time I want to fondle one of your breasts."

"What?"

"Well, just one, and very quickly." Coyote looked hopeful.

The chief's daughter looked at her sister-in-law. "Do you think I should?"

"I don't see the harm in it," the sister-in-law said.

"Well, just one. And quickly!"

So Coyote reached down the neck of her dress and fondled one breast a little and went off whistling.

The sister-in-law rapped the pot with her knuckles. "I think you got a bargain."

"I hope so," the chief's daughter said. Her breast tingled strangely where his fingers had touched it.

That night the chief's daughter didn't even try to sleep. She sat up listening to all the howling and banging from the house next door and imagining what wonderful thing he could be making now. Wings, maybe. Or a loom that wove cloth by itself. In the morning she sent her sister-in-law over there as soon as it was light.

She brushed her hair and rebraided it quickly and sat down to wait for whatever he was bringing.

The old lady lifted the lid of the basket and took the little white horse out again. He balanced in her palm, the breeze ruffling his white feather mane. He looked real and both girls sighed.

"I would let a boy touch my breast if he gave me a horse," the first girl whispered.

Her friend glared at her. "That isn't nice!"

"You would do it, too," the first girl said with conviction.

Coyote was leading the horse when he came to the chief's daughter's house. (And no, I don't know where he had been hiding it.) The chief's daughter and her sister-in-law stared, mouths open like fish.

The chief's daughter put out her hand and touched the horse's nose. It was warm and silky and she could feel his breath on her palm. She rubbed his head between his ears where his white forelock stirred in the breeze. He blew down his nose and snorted at her and she laughed.

"He's tame! What is he called?"

"He's called Horse," Coyote said. "You ride on his back to hunt or pick berries, and he can run a long time and take you very far and back in a day."

"Oh, I want him. I will let you fondle my other breast if

you will give him to me." She leaned forward invitingly, closing her eyes.

"Mmmm," Coyote said. "I already did that. Now I want to fondle your backside."

"My backside!"

"Oh, very quickly," Coyote assured her. "Just a feel."

"What do you think?" the chief's daughter whispered to her sister-in-law.

"Well, he already got a kiss," the sister-in-law said. "And he already felt your breast. What difference is a buttock going to make?"

"I suppose so. All right, then, you can feel it. Just once."

Coyote put his hand up her dress and felt her backside. His fingers were warm. He squeezed her buttock. Then he thanked her and went away.

The chief's daughter rubbed her bottom thoughtfully. With her other hand she scratched the horse between his white ears. He whickered and blew down her neck.

That afternoon she went for a ride on the horse's back. It felt like flying. It is *wings, she thought. The wind blew her hair out of its braids and it streamed out behind her like the tail of a comet. That night she slept, even though Coyote was next door banging and howling again. She dreamed that she was at a Green Corn Dance and all the drums were beating and she was dancing, dancing, her feet never touching the floor of the plaza, dancing just a handspan above the ground. Someone was dancing with her, but every time she looked up at his face, the moon went behind the clouds or other dancers passed between her partner and the firelight and she never could quite see him. Sometimes she thought it was the horse, and sometimes she thought it might be a dog with big pointy ears. They danced and danced.*

When she woke up, she felt wonderfully rested, but the sister-in-law was sitting at the table holding a cold cloth to her forehead.

"I have such a headache," she moaned. "All that banging and noise."

"Oh!" The chief's daughter said. "Hurry! Go bring him here and let's see what it is. It must be something marvelous."

The girls watched expectantly to see what the old woman would pull out next. Like the chief's daughter, they too felt that it must be something wonderful. She made a production of it, muttering and fussing. While she scrabbled in the basket, the lizard climbed out and ran across the plaza, his green and gold skin winking in the sunlight. He climbed a paloverde tree and began to bask on its limb. Finally the old woman sat up, holding the last treasure between her fingertips.

It was a tiny mirror, the length of her thumb. Its case was a squash blossom of hammered silver set with turquoise chips around the edge. The sun flashed from its glass like sparklers. The girls looked into it. It seemed to them that they could see things behind their reflected faces that weren't really in the plaza: horses running across a wide plain, and wild yellow eyes in a wild dark face behind their own.

The old woman cackled. "No one had ever seen a mirror. It's one thing to look at your face in the rain jar, all watery and not too clear. It's another to see it in a glass, like looking at your own fetch. Mirrors show you things you didn't know were there. Maybe things you don't want to know. That's what makes them magic."

When Coyote came to the chief's daughter's house he was grinning like he knew she wanted to see him.

"I don't care what you've got," she said. "I know I want it. Show it to me!"

Coyote gave her the mirror. It was a white man's hand glass, Spanish work with a heavy silver back and symbols she didn't recognize on it. The cold silver was as strange to her as the iron pot, but when she turned it over and a face looked back out at her, she nearly dropped it.

"Who is that in there? Sister-in-law, look, there's a person inside. Is she magic?"

The sister-in-law came over to look and suddenly there were two faces in the mirror. The chief's daughter gasped. "That's you!" She looked quickly from the mirror to the sister-in-law to be sure it hadn't sucked her inside it.

"It's a reflection. Like in water," the sister-in-law said. "That other one is you, Stupid."

"Oh." The chief's daughter looked again, for a long while this time, turning the mirror this way and that in her hand, beginning to admire herself. "I am really very beautiful," she said finally. "No wonder all the young men come around."

"Oh, very beautiful," Coyote assured her. He sidled closer and looked over her shoulder, just resting his chin on her shoulder. She saw a flash of yellow eyes and hairy ears in the mirror.

"Don't do that!" The chief's daughter posed in front of the mirror a while longer, unable to tear her eyes away. "I want this," she said finally, licking her lips. "I will let you fondle my other breast and *my other buttock if you will give me this."*

Coyote thought. It was his last magic thing, although the chief's daughter didn't know that. "No, I don't want that. I will give it to you if you will let me look up between your legs."

The chief's daughter put her knees together. Then she snuck another look at the mirror. "Well . . ."

"It's just a look," Coyote said.

"Only a look," the sister-in-law agreed. "He's behaved himself so far."

The chief's daughter made up her mind. "All right." She spread her legs out and hiked her skirt up past her calves. "One look. A quick one."

"Of course, Most Beautiful." Coyote got down on his

hands and knees and peered up her skirt. "Oh!" he said, distressed.

"What? What?" the chief's daughter said.

"Oh, that's too bad." Coyote backed out from under her skirt and stood up. "What a shame. It's in there upside down. You'll have to have it remade, it can't stay like that. But thank you very much anyway."

He went out the door whistling and the chief's daughter sat down on the floor and started to cry.

"What is it?" asked the sister-in-law, who had been looking in the mirror.

"Oh! Oh! He says it is in upside down! He says I have to have it remade! Who is there who is capable of a thing like that?"

The sister-in-law looked at the miraculous pot and the fiery beads and the horse munching grass in the plaza, and finally at the magical reflecting glass that could show you your own face. "No one," she said. "Except the man who could make things like this. Why did you let him leave?"

"Oh, you're right." The chief's daughter leaped up. "Go get him right away. Tell him I am begging him to come and fix it. Oh, I hope he will do it. I know it will take a lot of magic. What do you think he will want?"

She was very surprised and grateful when he did it for free.

"She was stupid," the girl on the end of the bench said.

"Well, I did tell you that," the old woman said. "But everyone is stupid when they want something badly enough. So be careful what you want."

"I wouldn't want anything like that," the girl said primly. "We are only to want God. Sister says that."

The old woman smiled. She had very yellow teeth. "Wanting makes things happen. That's why people do it. Because nothing would happen if people didn't want things."

"Even things like the chief's daughter wanted?"

"Things have a shadow. When you call up a thing you get its shadow too, and the shadow is what makes time happen. I will tell you some more about that girl . . ."

1

The Fool Dancers

FLUTE DOG HAD BEEN MARRIED FOR THE SPACE OF ONE warm spring night when the Horse Searchers came home. First, Young Owl gave her father a black-and-white horse, and then there was a feast and she went to live in Young Owl's tent. When they fell asleep the sky was wheeling toward dawn and Toad Nose, the Night Watcher, was yawning by his campfire. And then Toad Nose was stamping and dancing through the camp, howling and pointing, and they fell out of their tent into the morning, rubbing their eyes, to see the cloud of dust coming over the Grass.

No one had really thought they would come back. All the horses that the Dry River people owned were descended from the same two, who had come to the Buffalo Horn people in the days of the grandmothers, and made more horses. Anyone could see how horses would shift the ground between people and the buffalo so that there would be meat all the time, and so the Dry River people had stolen some. Finally, the Dry River people and the Buffalo Horn had been fighting over horses for so long that there were ghosts in the air. Both chiefs knew something had to be done. That was when they sent two Dry River riders, and a brother and sister from the Buffalo Horn, to look for new horses in the Cities-in-the-West.

Anyone knew that the Cities-in-the-West were full of hive people who lived indoors all year and never saw the sun, and that was where First Horse was said to have come from. There were rumors out of the west of new, strange monster people, who might have come with the horses or brought them. It was a daring thing for the four to do, like trying to climb the sky, and everyone thought they had ridden into legend. No one really expected them to come back.

But it couldn't be anyone else. There were four on horseback, amid a herd of loose horses and a pair of dogs. A black horsetail flew from the lead rider's spear and his shield was painted with the spiral suns of the Buffalo Horn. The Dry River chief sent a fast rider south to the Buffalo Horn camp to tell them, and Toad Nose, who was head of the Horse Clan, and Howler, the tall, wild-eyed chief of the Holy Clowns, put on horse heads and went out to meet the riders.

Spotted Colt and Mud Turtle looked different now, was the first thing Flute Dog thought, while she stood on the edge of the crowd that gathered around them. They looked like people who had been to the edge of the world, and she wondered what they had seen.

Everyone talked at once until the Dry River chief, who was Spotted Colt's father, roared at them to be quiet. He was trying to keep his dignity, but he couldn't help dancing in the grass in his delight. The new horses whickered at the smell of the Dry River horses and seemed happy to be there.

The new horses had hard gray shoes like crescent moons pounded onto their hooves with spines of the same stony stuff. It was something made by the monsters who were living in the Cities-in-the-West now, Spotted Colt said. The Buffalo Horn girl had died there and no one from the Grass should go back there again.

Flute Dog could see now that the woman with them wasn't the Buffalo Horn girl after all, but another one who, it turned out, had run away from the Cities with Spotted Colt. Spotted Colt's mother looked at this girl suspiciously and the children clustered around her, patting her to see if she felt like ordinary people.

Young Owl was more interested in the new horses. He dug with his fingernail at the half moon of hard stuff on a buckskin mare's hoof. "It's like stone." He beckoned Flute Dog over.

"That woman who came with them says the pale people make it by melting rocks," Toad Nose said, bending over, too.

"Nobody can melt rocks."

"Somebody did once. That's what made obsidian. Rabbit Dancer says," he added. Rabbit Dancer was a shaman and knew things that weren't told to other people.

"This isn't obsidian." The mare snorted in Young Owl's ear and he let her foot down.

Toad Nose rubbed his chin. "They all have to be taken off. Their hooves are growing and these stone things don't grow. Mud Turtle says he pried some of them loose with a stone, but he says it takes a long time." Toad Nose looked important. Mud Turtle was his youngest aunt's son, and now a man whose name would mean things, whose journey would be painted on the calendar hide of the Dry River to mark a hinge year in the history of his people.

Flute Dog rubbed the buckskin mare's nose while they talked about how to get the things off her feet. The new horses seemed just like any others, but Spotted Colt and Mud Turtle had stolen them from a camp of pale people, and now they knew it was pale people who had brought horses into the world. That seemed as odd as any creation story of breath blown into mud. And what had brought the pale people no one knew.

It was the horse with the long ears that convinced her of their reality, their actual habitation in the world she lived in too. The buckskin mare whickered and he lifted his head, like a rabbit with a horse nose on his face. Flute Dog's eyes went wide. If there could be a horse like that, then there could be men with pale skin.

Mud Turtle was unloading the packs on the long-eared horse's back. "We don't know what he is, either," he told her. "But he is strong. He can carry more than the others."

It came to Flute Dog very suddenly, with that, that there could be anything in the world. There could be things she had never seen, things even Rabbit Dancer didn't know of, things so far away and strange that they didn't have names. She listed some of them in her head:

Pale men. (No one had ever seen a pale woman. Maybe there weren't any.)

Horses with ears like rabbits.

Stone that could be melted, and molded like mud or a wet hide.

Sticks that shot flame and small stones. (That story was circulating around the camp already; Spotted Colt and the rest had seen them.)

If all those things could be, then any other thing was possible, too.

"Antler," Young Owl said, practical. "The tip of an antler worked under there will pry those things off."

"What are they made of?" Flute Dog whispered to the buckskin mare, but she didn't answer.

That night the Dry River people and the Buffalo Horn danced the Horse Dance together, and told the ritual story of First Horse. The Buffalo Horn's Horse Clan chief wore the yellowed head of First Horse, and Howler and the other clowns danced along behind him, imitating the dance, leaping goofily from foot to foot, fingers up to their heads to make horse ears. Everyone laughed and the Horse Clan chief pretended not to see them. The Fool Dancers were as important to the dance as he was—they made people see their own ridiculousness, pried them open, and let their self-importance out. When that happened, and a person was laughing, real power might come in.

Flute Dog clapped her hands to the drumbeat, watching Young Owl whirl into the pattern with Mud Turtle and Spotted Colt and the Buffalo Horn men, pulling the rest in too, leading their horses at first, then up on their backs, wild hair tied with sweetgrass and horsehair tassels. Howler winked at her as he cavorted by, hopping and yelping, pretending to be a horse.

In the morning Red-and-Yellow-Dog, chief of the Buffalo Horn, and the chief of the Dry River people, who wasn't named Horse Stealer for nothing, divided up the new horses, solemnly putting pebbles in two piles, and smoking in between to assure each other of their complete honesty. The Dry River men kept the long-eared horse and three of the six mares. Young Owl got the buckskin mare, which pleased Flute Dog. He was the best horse trainer the Dry River had, except for Mud Turtle.

They pried the strange shoes off their feet and the new horses mingled with the Dry River herd while the strangeness slowly slid out of them, like meal poured from a pot. Horse Stealer and Mud Turtle, Spotted Colt and Young Owl began to talk of how to breed them, which horse to whose, and made bargains with the Buffalo Horn men to trade stallions at certain times. All horses had been descended from two, until these. Now the Buffalo Horn and the Dry River arranged their marriages more carefully than those of any chief's daughters.

Blacktail Horse, the buckskin mare, was with foal by Flute Dog's father's black and white stallion, Magpie

Horse, and among all the mares there were more foals born in the next spring than ever before. The gray coyotes who lived in the Grass hung around the edges of the herd, watching them and pretending to catch mice. They knew better than to try to steal a foal—horses had hard hooves and bigger teeth than the coyotes thought appropriate for a grass-eater. But foolish horse children who strayed from their mothers were another matter. The Dry River people saw the coyotes and assigned watchers with dogs to the herd at night until the foals were too big to be tempting.

Blacktail Horse's foal was a colt spotted in three colors: magic, lucky markings, Young Owl said. He named it Painted Water Horse. The next year she had another, a buckskin filly with white socks, and the third year another filly with a white blaze on her face. By then Young Owl had begun to ride Painted Water Horse.

Flute Dog watched Blacktail Horse and her foals enviously. She had not had any children herself so far and it didn't seem fair. It was as if all the fertility magic had gone out of her tent into the new mare and left the human woman bereft.

"They will come." Spotted Colt's foreign wife, who was called Green Gourd Vine, patted her hand. When the second year had gone by, she gave Flute Dog a charm made out of maize husks that she had brought from the Cities-in-the-West.

Howler made her a tea of herbs, and one for Young Owl, and stood grinning over him until he drank it.

Mud Turtle gave her one of his dog, Laugher's, puppies to practice on. When Laugher came in season she would growl at the camp dogs and go off into the Grass.

"You are a slut," Mud Turtle would tell her. "One day something will eat you afterward." But Laugher was bigger than a coyote and had a temper, so they didn't try. And her pups were smart, craftier than the camp dogs, and loyal.

"Raise this and then Mother Earth will see you are good at it and need one of your own," Mud Turtle told Flute Dog, handing her the pup. It was a bitch pup with blue eyes turning a muddy yellow and eye teeth like needles. It sank one of them into her thumb, but it didn't seem vicious. It was only looking for something to suck on. Flute Dog gave it a knuckle bone.

She named the pup Hungry because it ate anything: glue, leather shoes, spiders. As soon as it could walk, it followed Flute Dog everywhere and she let it sleep in the quill-embroidered cradleboard that had been her mother's and then her own, so that the cradleboard would want a baby, too.

In the summer, her father died and they put his body up on a bier with horsehair flags tied to the four corners. When the eagle people had cleaned his bones, Flute Dog took the skull and set it in a skull ring in the valley to the west, where her mother and her two younger sisters were, so that they could talk to each other, and she could come tell them all the news whenever she passed that way.

"Next year I will bring my baby for you to see," she told them.

At the start of winter, Flute Dog and Young Owl packed their tent and belongings on a horse travois and went to make their Winter Camp. Young Owl's parents were both dead, and with her father gone, it was just the two of them this year and the empty earth lodge seemed barren and forlorn.

But the squash vines she had planted beside it in the spring were a tangle of withered leaves, with bright yellow squashes among them, most of them good. Flute Dog sat down and gathered them into her lap, feeling the sun in their skin.

Once she had swept out the lodge and Young Owl had put up new poles for the roof, to replace the ones the bugs had eaten, and Flute Dog had arranged all their baskets and boxes and their bed to her liking, it was homier. The squashes glowed in their basket by the door. The horses and dog helped keep the lodge warm, and she thought that by spring she would be pregnant.

In the spring Blacktail Horse was pregnant instead, and so was Hungry. Flute Dog had no idea how Hungry had managed it and Hungry didn't tell her. They packed all their belongings onto the horse travoises again and Flute Dog swept out the earth lodge and planted some squash seeds by the door so that maybe there would be squashes in the fall if the coyotes and the kit foxes didn't eat them.

Young Owl painted Flute Dog's face and she washed her long black hair and braided feathers into the ends, and put on her best dress, of soft doeskin grown white with many cleanings, embroidered red and black with porcupine quills, to ride with Young Owl to Gathering Camp. The first camp of spring was always a flurry of old friends, of new babies, of winter deaths recounted to the people who would want to know. The old died in the cold of midwinter and their bones were brought back to the skull ring so they would have someone to talk to. The young emerged from their winter cocoon unfurling like fern heads. The boys sat outside Boys' House and watched the girls as they carried their waterskins down to the stream and came back balancing them on their heads, slender wet feet leaving prints in the dirt.

At the spring equinox everyone danced the New Buffalo Dance and the men tightened the lashings on their spears and restrung bows that had gone slack over the winter. By Spring Grass Moon the buffalo were on the move to their summer graze.

"I'm going to ride Painted Water Horse this year," Young Owl told Flute Dog, when she set his breakfast in front of him on Full Moon Morning. He scooped two fingers into the hide pot and stuck them in his mouth. It was mush spiced with new cress from the stream, but it was still mush. "I dreamed about eating hump meat and backfat last night," he told her, grinning. "I shot a buffalo and the arrow went clean through it and killed another and another, and we had a feast."

"Painted Water Horse is too young," Flute Dog said. "He hasn't seen buffalo."

"I've been showing him their hides all winter."

"Hide isn't hoof." Flute Dog swatted Hungry's head out of the mush pot. "Take him, but ride Magpie Horse. Let him see buffalo before you get on his back."

Young Owl shook his head stubbornly. He had been training Painted Water Horse all winter, and wanted to show him off. She said "Don't" again, but it wasn't going to do any good. When the men left for the hunt, he was riding Painted Water Horse.

The hunt was almost like a dance, solemn in preparation, jubilant in its expectation. Rabbit Dancer put his buffalo mask on, the huge head so big it came down over his shoulders, and shook a rattle made of horsetails and buffalo hooves at the riders. Boys too young to hunt rode imaginary horses through the trampled grass and told everyone how many buffalo they would kill next year.

All the horses were decorated with paint and feathers. Painted Water Horse's tail was tied with red leather thong and his hide marked with Young Owl's handprints between the spots. He looked very fine, his bi-colored mane rippling in the sun like the water of his name. Flute Dog thought he looked unreliable as water, too.

When the men left, the women broke camp and followed, slowly, herding human and horse children along. They would catch up to the hunt, butcher what the men had killed, tan the hides and dry the meat, and feast on the fresh humps. Flute Dog's stomach growled at the thought. All winter everyone grew lean on strings of dried meat that pulled loose teeth out, on shriveled fly-blown onions, and lumps of fat mixed with withered berries and meat dried and pounded to a powder. Fresh humpmeat was a taste in her mouth so sharp she could smell it.

All around them, ahead and behind, the other women of the Dry River folk were spread across the Grass, babies in cradleboards on their backs, toddlers sitting solemnly on travoises, older ones running naked and joyful along the trail, their arms spread to the warmth of the sun. They stitched the pattern of the Dry River people through the Grass like a needle going in and out of a hide.

Blacktail Horse's yearling filly and her new one trotted after the travois, and Hungry waddled beside them. The spring air felt like old soft doeskin on Flute Dog's arms. The new grass was full of green juice that the horses bit off in mouthfuls as they walked. Hungry wriggled her way through in bounding leaps like a fish, her ears popping up over the waving blades and vanishing again in a ripple of watery stalks. She looked like the Fool Dancers when they danced in the Spring Grass Moon. A grasshopper zoomed past Flute Dog's ear. High in the sky a hawk was circling like a dark spot across a plane of turquoise air. The men's trail veered south and the women followed it, weaving their pattern in the Grass.

Coyote sat on a hillock and watched the buffalo hunters crossing like a knot of shiny threads and bright stones on the Grass. He felt pleased with the horses, and that satisfaction was very pleasant in his stomach. It had been a long time since he had given human people anything new and exciting. Not since he had thought of Art. Before that there had been maize, and before that, fire. All brand new ideas. Now horses were another entirely new thing. Only a genius could think up horses.

The Spring Grass Moon dipped a little lower to see what he was looking so smug about. Her round face was disapproving. "Did you think up those things that came with them?"

"What things?" Coyote looked as if he didn't know what she was talking about.

"You're so irresponsible." In the bright sun she was ethereal and nearly transparent. "You asked Grandmother if she couldn't get rid of them," she said. "I heard you."

"Oh, those." Coyote scratched behind his left ear. "Well, you know Grandmother. 'All thread gets woven,' that's what she said."

"You've changed everything again," Full Moon said resentfully.

"If I didn't, where would we be? Everyone back under the ground, and you shut up in a bag."

"It was a nice bag. It was restful in there."

"You shot out fast enough when I opened it."

Full Moon sniffed. "You don't understand pattern. You can't go on opening bags whenever you feel like it. If *I* did that, the tides would be all over everywhere and women wouldn't know which end was up."

"Isn't this sun bad for you?" Coyote asked her. "I can hardly see you."

She pulled her blanket over her head. It was wispy, woven out of clouds. "Now I can't see," she said fretfully.

"That's a shame," Coyote said. "I'll watch for you and tell you what's happening."

The buffalo were a moving, living river flowing from side to side of the plain of Grass. Spring herds were groups of youngsters and blunt-horned two-year-olds and cows with their new calves; the bachelor bulls stayed away until the summer breeding season, when they grew dangerous. But even in spring, their numbers were uncounted, like the stars in the sky. They walked and ate, ate and walked, covering the earth with their footprints.

Each herd in its wanderings passed through the hunting grounds of several bands, like the advance of a storm, moving slowly and with ponderous purpose. The Dry

River buffalo scouts knew where they were, had heard their heavy footsteps in the ground. Coyote felt the dogs stiffen as they caught the scent, and the horses toss their heads and blow down their nostrils. Horse and Buffalo had things to say to each other, a language spoken through the wind of their passing, and danced out in the movement of hoof and horn.

The riders circled the herd, careful to stay downwind of the cows until they were ready to charge, stripped to a breechclout and a handful of arrows in quivers slung over their backs. Only a fast horse was faster than a buffalo, so weight and encumbrances mattered. Coyote knew about Buffalo's horns. Sometimes he ate a new calf that was orphaned but he wasn't so foolish as to cross a buffalo cow. He waited until human people had killed her and then he ate the bones.

Human people killed Buffalo with an arrow behind the last rib or just back of the left shoulder. They rode close to shoot from a bow's length away. If the arrow wasn't good, Buffalo turned her head and hooked horse and rider into the next world.

Coyote watched the riders bearing down on the herd now, the lumbering buffalo cows beginning to run, the flash of sun on arrowheads and skin, on the spotted hide of Painted Water Horse. Young Owl's hair, tied behind his back in two bundles, came loose from its thongs and flew out behind him like dark rain. There was more rain in the distance, walking across the Grass out of the west, too far away from the riders to see it, but Coyote saw it, saw the things that happened beyond the curve of the earth.

It all happened at once, the dark curtain of rain, the angry clap and boom like lightning in the west, the thundering buffalo, the water roiling down a dry wash, filling it with gray foam, leaving behind it strange debris. Everything happened on top of everything else without time to lay across them like a measuring stick. Coyote could see the pattern, rain over river over buffalo, just as he could see Painted Water Horse rearing on his hind legs at the sight of the herd, rearing and leaping like a fish, until he stuck his foot in a ground squirrel's hole and Young Owl went flying off his back under the thundering hooves.

2

The Rain

IN THE CITIES-IN-THE-WEST THE RAIN WASHED AWAY the way things had been. It filled the kivas with black water and where they had been people that no one wanted built houses where they put their own gods. The new gods were a dead man and his mother.

The new people were pale as toads and their skin burned bright pink in the desert sun. But there were a lot of them and even the ones that Coyote ate came back again. No one would have let them stay except that they owned sticks that shot flame and small stones that could go clear through a man and kill him. Those stones and the pale men's knives were made of something new that the Cities' Old Men said were pieces of a fallen star. It was harder than stone and as sharp as obsidian.

The rain washed the pale people into every city in the valley of Water Old Man and west to the Endless Water and south to the jade traders and the people of the spotted cat. And it washed their dead god and his mother with them. When people fought them, they were slaughtered and some were burned alive, so they didn't fight anymore.

3

The First Wonderful Thing

IT WAS HARD TO TELL THAT IT HAD BEEN YOUNG OWL. They brought his body back to Flute Dog tactfully wrapped in a buffalo hide, a buffalo he had killed the year before and had been using for a horse blanket.

Flute Dog howled and cut her hair off short with her belt knife, and chopped the tip off the little finger of her left hand because that was what she was supposed to do, but inside herself she kept waiting for Young Owl to come home and mourn with her, under the bier of some other young man. She sat and stared at the end of her finger, trying to make it grow again.

Spotted Colt's foreign wife, Green Gourd Vine, brought her a bowl of soup, and Howler brought his medicine kit to smear salve on her fingertip. Then he wrapped a piece of skin around it.

"Rabbit Dancer is painting his face," Howler said, to encourage her. The ghosts might not recognize Young Owl in the Hunting Ground of the Dead if his face wasn't painted, and it was hard to do when he had been so badly trampled.

"My father-in-law Horse Stealer has given his best tent hide to wrap him in," Green Gourd Vine said.

"Mud Turtle and Spotted Colt and Toad Nose are putting up the bier."

"Everyone is giving him honor."

Flute Dog didn't answer. She was trying to think how Young Owl might come back and explain to all these people that he wasn't dead. Howler's salve stung her finger, worse than cutting it off had done.

Green Gourd Vine and Howler looked at each other over Flute Dog's head. It was sad.

"Where is Painted Water Horse?" Flute Dog asked them.

"You don't want that horse," Green Gourd Vine said.

"Yes, I do. He can tell me what happened to my husband."

Green Gourd Vine and Howler looked at each other again with concern. She was not right in the head because of grief. "The horse ran away," they told her.

Flute Dog didn't say anything else about the horse until Rabbit Dancer had painted Young Owl's body and she had dressed him in his best shirt and leggings, and shoes embroidered with porcupine quills. Rabbit Dancer wrapped him in wet buffalo hides, and wrapped him again in Horse Stealer's tent, which had yellow suns and red running horses painted on it. Spotted Colt and Mud Turtle tied the whole bundle with sinew and put it on a travois hitched to Magpie Horse. They had painted Magpie Horse's spotted hide with red mourning blotches and cut his mane and tail short like Flute Dog's.

Flute Dog walked beside Young Owl while Magpie Horse dragged him to his bier. Hungry trotted beside her, swollen with pups and whining. Flute Dog tried to see that it was Young Owl inside those wrappings, because she knew everyone thought she had gone mad, and it was important to remember that. Her finger stung in its bandage. It hadn't seemed real when she had spread her hand out on a stone and brought the ax blade down on it, but now it ached and her hand throbbed.

Everyone from the Dry River camp followed them. Buffalo sometimes took somebody when you hunted him, and that person deserved honor. Outside the camp, the rotting carcasses lay in the sun, black with flies. The human people had taken every piece of Buffalo that they could use, from his hide to his bladder to his sinews and his long bones. His liver had been eaten raw by the man who had killed him, and the bones would be drilled and shaped into flutes with which a Dry River boy might court a girl in the long dusk of a summer evening. What was left was for Coyote and the eagles and the insect people. Nothing was wasted, nothing left unused.

Young Owl's life had not been wasted. He had gone to Buffalo, and Dry River people must not begrudge him because he had been brave and it was only right that sometimes Buffalo took someone in return. The women said this to Flute Dog as she walked beside his body. Howler hopped beside her like a flea, with two fingers to his head making buffalo horns, to show her that Young Owl would live in the buffalo now.

The procession stopped at the bier, which stood on the windy, open plain, its platform lowered to knee height between its poles. Mud Turtle and Spotted Colt and Toad Nose had cut four saplings from a grove of trees up the valley and dragged them to this spot, where they had set them into the ground and lashed them together with sinew. The platform of branches suspended between them looked to Flute Dog like a raft, to sail Death on.

Mud Turtle and Toad Nose lifted the wrapped body onto the bier and tied it down, while Flute Dog and the women wailed. Then, with Spotted Colt and Horse Stealer, they loosed the ropes from their pegs in the ground, and pulled. The platform rose slowly, swaying, until it came to rest at the top of the poles. They tied off the ropes and wedged braces beneath the platform for support. Rabbit Dancer hung Young Owl's pipe, his bow and quiver, and his spear and shield from the corner posts, with bundles of the hair cut from Magpie Horse's mane and tail.

Flute Dog stared up at the bier. She could see the dark oblong shape of the shroud between the branches of the platform. After her people had moved on, Young Owl would lie there on the open Grass, through the summer and the winter snow, while his body decayed and the bier fell to pieces. In a year or two, she could come back for his skull and put it in the skull ring and talk to it, and maybe he would return from the Hunting Ground of the Dead to listen. The women clustered around her now, patting her, making comforting noises. She shook her head. It felt strangely light without the weight of her hair.

"Now I am going to find the horse," she said.

They stopped patting her and began to argue, but Flute Dog ignored them. Their voices chirped around her head like birds or grasshoppers.

"That was a good horse. I want it back."

Mud Turtle looked at her severely. "Then we will go and find it for you."

"No. I want to talk to it."

"I will talk to it for you," Mud Turtle said.

Everyone nodded in agreement at that. Horses told Mud Turtle things, and they heard his voice when he whispered things to them. If anyone could talk to a horse, it was Mud Turtle.

"It's my horse." Flute Dog looked stubborn.

"She is mad," they whispered. "She is mad with grief." Spotted Colt's mother, Prairie Hen, nodded, clucking her tongue. She had had a sister who had gone mad and gone into the Grass by herself and never come back. Madness was something no one could do anything about. Howler hopped over to Flute Dog and peered into her face, as if to confirm that. Flute Dog stared at him stubbornly. Her short hair stood out from her face as if it had been lifted by lightning.

Howler balanced on all fours like a frog, looking up at her. "Maybe she will find the horse," he said finally. "She will find something."

Or something would find her. They all made gestures to keep away spirits, at that. But if Howler said they had to let her go, then they had to let her go, especially since they couldn't keep her tied up.

"Take plenty of water," Green Gourd Vine said.

"Take a spare knife," Toad Nose said.

"Take someone with you," Spotted Colt said.

Flute Dog packed a journey bag with meat, and two skins with water, and loaded her tent on a travois behind Magpie Horse. She left Blacktail Horse and the rest of her small herd with Mud Turtle. She tried to leave Hungry, but Hungry wouldn't listen.

Flute Dog pushed at her, shoving her toward Mud Turtle's tent. "You look like a melon. Stay here with Mud Turtle's dogs. You will have your pups on the trail and I'm not going to carry them for you!"

Hungry got up on the travois behind Magpie Horse and sat on the bundled tent.

Flute Dog glared at her from the curtain of her shorn hair.

"Take her with you," Howler said. She hadn't seen him coming up soft-foot behind her. "I will go with you, too." He looked hopeful.

"I will not be eaten by wolves," Flute Dog said. "And it is not the season for the Red Bow people to be raiding. And I do not need help to catch a horse."

Howler's eyes rested on her thoughtfully. He had a bony face and a nose that bent to the side a little where he had broken it climbing a tree after an eagle's eggs when he was a boy. He had been born the same year as Flute Dog, and always thought he knew what she ought to do. "Well, be careful who you talk to out there," he told her.

There was no one to talk to in the Grass, just the wind that whispered endlessly through its hair. Flute Dog thought of trying to talk to Young Owl, but that was ill luck just now, while his spirit was still so close to home. It might make him want to come back and she knew that would be bad. So she would have to ask the horse what had happened instead. She had hiked her doeskin dress up around her thighs to ride and Magpie Horse's black and white back was warm under her. What was left of his cropped mane stood up raggedly along his neck.

She found the place where the hunters had picked up Young Owl's body, after the herd had passed. The grass was trampled into dust and the bare ground where he had lain was dark with his dried blood. She got down off Magpie Horse for a moment and knelt beside the spot. She put her hand on the ground, palm flat to the earth, to see if there was any of Young Owl left there, but he had gone. Hungry nosed the ground and whined.

Flute Dog got back on Magpie Horse and looked south, away from the trail that the buffalo herd had left in its flight, thinking that Painted Water Horse, frightened, would have run the other way. She didn't know how far he would go, but he wasn't wild. At some point he would be more afraid of being alone on the Grass than he was of the buffalo. If he didn't panic and get eaten by wolves or a cat, he might try to come back.

Hungry sniffed the ground again and looked expectantly at Flute Dog.

"Do you smell him?"

Hungry didn't answer but she didn't get back on the travois. Instead she waddled away through the flattened grass, nose to some trail. She looked like a dog who knew what she was doing, although dogs always looked that way. Flute Dog decided maybe she *could* smell Painted Water Horse, so she followed her.

The Dry River tents had disappeared in the tall waves of rippling grass and she felt now as if she were on the lip of some other way of living, that she might come suddenly to one of the deep gulches that criss-crossed the plains unseen until one was on their edge, and topple over it into another world. Young Owl was going to the Hunting Ground of the Dead, but Flute Dog was going somewhere too.

At late afternoon she came to the edge of the Dry River people's graze and made camp in the lee of a bluff above a stream called Where the Girl Saved Her Brother. The bluff was eaten away at the bottom by wind-carved caves and fissures that looked as if they might lead underground to the place where Green Gourd Vine said her people had come up from under the earth. Flute Dog felt suffocated at the thought of that. Her own kind had been put on the world by Grandfather, He Who Always Is. Grandfather had set them down in the sunlight on the plains, in the open air, and given them the buffalo to hunt. Maybe it was having been underground that made city people want to live in boxes now. Mud Turtle had seen houses made of mud, stacked one on top of the next, three and four houses high. Flute Dog pitched her tent outside the caves in the shelter of the bluff. A dead tree lay beside the ford that crossed Where the Girl Saved Her Brother, and she hitched it to Magpie Horse's travois harness and dragged it up to her tent. She made a fire with her slowburner, packed in a buffalo horn, and fed it with bits of dry moss and twigs from the brush that studded the base of the bluff. The tree's wood burned with a blue-green glow where the river water had left strange substances on its surface.

When she had eaten some of her journey cake and

given the other half to Hungry, Flute Dog made a bed of brush and lay down with the tent flap open so she could see the stars and listen to Magpie Horse, pegged to a tether outside, munching grass. Hungry curled herself at the foot of the bed, but she was restless, getting up to turn around and lie down again, never for long.

In the morning, Flute Dog saw that she had had her pups, and they were all dead but one.

"I told you not to follow me," she said, crying for the pups because there were too many things dead just now and their still bodies made her think of Young Owl.

Hungry looked sorrowful. The last pup was sucking at her teat and Flute Dog couldn't see anything wrong with it.

"I'll make it a bed on the travois," she said to Hungry, doing what she had said she wouldn't. She folded a tent hide into a nest, and tied it down so Magpie Horse's gait wouldn't jolt it loose. She lined it with grass and put the puppy in it, carrying it carefully. It was another she-dog, eyes shut, tiny claws digging at her palm.

Flute Dog turned Magpie Horse toward where they had left Painted Water Horse's trail, and when they got there Hungry stuck her nose in the grass, businesslike. Flute Dog hoped he was near. The air had grown still, warm and overcast. It felt as if they were pushing their way through it. Something was coming, she thought. A storm. She marked the cliffs in the bluff with her eye in case they had to run back to them. Storms blew across the Grass like a roaring herd—dark and wild, water horses thundering over the earth. They could turn dry washes into torrents in an instant. Their winds could upend a solitary tent and send it tumbling and rain-soaked across the ground, when the wind could catch it again and fling it like an arrow into some other place. Flute Dog had seen it happen.

The sky darkened more as they moved south, but they found a pile of horse droppings, not a day old, and so they kept going. At noon the sun pried the clouds apart and shone through them, yellow-gray. "Thank you, Grandfather," Flute Dog said to it, so he would know she was appreciative.

She sat on the edge of the travois and ate another piece of journey cake while Hungry nursed the pup. Hungry had found two jumping mice and eaten them, but Flute Dog gave her a piece of the journey cake anyway. They had enough for a handspan of days. If she couldn't find Painted Water Horse in one more day she would have to give up.

They went on, following the signs that led from the pile of fresh droppings—broken stems of grass and another spot where he had pissed and the ground was still wet with it. Flute Dog whistled between her teeth every now and then. Painted Water Horse had been trained to come to that. Hungry got down from the travois and trotted ahead of Magpie Horse, her tail cutting through the grass like a hairy flag. Flute Dog shaded her eyes. The plain of grass rippled all around them, yellow-green, with the shadowed blue ridges of hills to the north and a snake of trees to the south that meant a river.

A hawk circled lazily above them on the thermals but nothing else moved. She knew that if she got off Magpie Horse and looked closely, she would see the things Hungry did—mice and bug people going about their business, the yellow eye of a burrowing owl peering from its doorway—but from where she sat everything was stopped and shimmery, opalescent, like looking in a pool of water.

Then as if a rock had dropped into the pool, the stillness cracked open. The hawk fell from the sky with a scream and rose again with a rabbit in its talons. Hungry barked. The ground dipped away suddenly before them. It tumbled into a gulch with a stream at the bottom, and there at the foot of the buffalo trail that led slantwise down its bank, was Painted Water Horse eating grass.

Painted Water Horse threw his head up at their approach and danced nervously along the water's edge.

Flute Dog could still see the faded red smears of Young Owl's handprints on his flanks. She put her fingers in her mouth and whistled and Painted Water Horse's ears swiveled toward her.

"Foolish," Flute Dog said softly. "Wait there for me." She slid off Magpie Horse and dropped his rein on the ground so he would stand still.

Painted Water Horse sidled toward the stream and snorted while Flute Dog slid a coil of rope out of her packs on the travois. He watched as she came down the bank toward him, picking her way through the litter of rounded stones along the stream bed. He moved uneasily along the bank as if he were going to run. The water burbled just beyond him, a small, busy sound.

"Sh-sh, Foolish." Flute Dog clucked softly to him. His ears pricked toward her. He snorted again. People who talked to him like that gave him things to eat; Painted Water Horse began to remember that. She came close and stroked his nose. He bobbed his head into her hand.

"I told him not to ride you when you hadn't seen buffalo." Her voice caught in her throat as she slipped the rope around his neck. The storm-still air hung about them like a curtain. In its enclosure she thought she might be able to hear Painted Water Horse. "How was it," she whispered to him, "when my husband fell under the buffalo's feet?"

Painted Water Horse bobbed his head again and said, *Big hairy smelling awful horns*. Or something did. The voice echoed in her head.

"And you thought they were on your back?" she whispered.

Eat me.

"Buffalo eat grass."

Eat me. The voice was insistent. *Eat me. Jump away fast they can't catch me.*

"He's dead. The one who was on your back is dead now."

Painted Water Horse snorted. He bobbed his head up and down so she would scratch between his ears some more. He was a horse. He didn't know about death, only fear.

Flute Dog leaned her head against his neck, tears stinging her eyes. "You are stupid," she said mournfully.

The sky, which had lightened earlier, was growing dark again now, a heavy yellow-gray light that deadened to black, and she knotted the rope around Painted Water Horse's neck. A flash of lightning crackled over the mountains behind them. Hungry got up on the travois and Flute Dog swung onto Magpie Horse's back. She could see the dark hump of the bluffs across the prairie, and kicked Magpie Horse into a trot.

The motionless air had begun to move. They passed a clump of cottonwoods, leaves dancing at the ends of their stems, pale undersides rippling in the wind. A spatter of rain brushed her face.

Now the sun had gone entirely. The Grass was lowering, dark as an open mouth. Flute Dog thought for a moment that something was running through it beside them—she saw it frozen in a flash of lightning, a dark movement through the windblown stalks. Then whatever it was disappeared into the storm.

The grass lay flat along the ground now, blades bent into the wind like the current on water. Flute Dog's shorn hair blew about her head, ends snapping in her eyes. She bent her face over Magpie Horse's neck as a clap of thunder cut the air, and he began to run, the travois thumping wildly behind him.

The pup bounced out of its nest. Hungry jumped after it and Flute Dog dragged on Magpie Horse's rein, but the wind was howling around Magpie Horse's ears now and Painted Water Horse was shrieking with fear, and they didn't want to stop. Ahead, the distant bluffs rose in a dark blur.

* * *

The storm picked up everything in its path and flung it aside. It uprooted trees and sent them flying like arrows. It picked up Hungry with the pup in her mouth and rolled her end over end, until both vanished in the wind. It tipped the travois sideways and the packs spilled out behind Magpie Horse as he ran.

The shadow in the grass saw the horses and cowered away, wailing as the wind buffeted her. She staggered, howling, into the storm's eye while it bit at her heels like a dog. In the boiling gray stormlight she thought it *was* a dog, a gray shape with yellow eyes and white teeth driving her on. She lashed out at it with her walking stick and it disappeared in a whirlwind of blown sticks and leaves.

Coyote hopped back out of the whirlwind and bit her ankles again and she kept running. He had seen her leave the city to the west where the new people were, slipping out between the walls at dusk, weeping, and he had watched her cut through the bean fields and take the trade trail east, with nothing but a pack on her back, a bow and quiver, and her belt knife. Coyote watched her as she went, belly growing bigger and face more gaunt, eating wild onions and bearberries, and once a ground squirrel she had killed with an arrow. She wasn't a very good shot.

Coyote watched her at the same time he was watching Young Owl fall under the buffalo's hooves, and things that were going on in the terraced stone cities to the south. Once he was shot in the backside by a pale newcomer with a stick thing while he was nosing around the new person's camp, and he dug out the lump of stuff it threw and took it with him to taste it and see what it was made of.

The storm boiled around the bluffs and the sky opened with a pouring rain, a curtain of water that flattened grass and lashed at skin and hide. Coyote saw that it was driving her toward the caves, so he stopped biting her and disappeared into the storm, until he was just a pair of yellow eyes glittering in the black clouds.

Flute Dog saw the eyes as she slid off Magpie Horse and staggered toward the bluff, leading the horses, the travois bumping empty behind them. She cowered, one arm up to shield her face, and the horses danced at the ends of their leads. She plunged through the driving rain to a cave mouth deep enough to hide in and dragged the horses in after her.

The horses snorted and stamped their feet, ears swiveling at the storm, but they quieted inside the cave. She dropped their reins to the cave floor, trusting them to remember that that meant they were tied to the ground. Outside the air was black and the wind roared. The water lashed the cave walls and splattered on the ground outside. Little runnels came through its open mouth. She couldn't see anything through the wind-blown rain.

She wished she had been more careful with the wood she had cut last night. Now it would be wet, if the storm hadn't scattered it. When the wind seemed to die for a moment, she darted out and scrabbled in the water and mud for the wood. She found a few pieces and brought them back, splashing through an ankle-deep stream. Her slowburner was in the spilled packs, but maybe she could start a spark with a fire drill when the cave dried out. Shivering, she leaned against Magpie Horse's flank, trying to soak up horse warmth through the wet hide.

Magpie Horse snuffled at her ear. The wind whirled the rain into a waterspout just outside the cave and she cringed as the cold water spat something out of it. The horses snorted and jumped, but Flute Dog saw that it was Hungry, with the pup in her mouth.

Flute Dog pried the pup out of Hungry's jaws. It lay in her hand, inert and cold as bone, but she could feel its heart through the wet skin. She sat down and cradled it between her breasts. Hungry crawled in her lap, whining, and they huddled together under Magpie Horse's feet.

"How did you get here?" Flute Dog said to Hungry.

Hungry got up and shook, sending a spray of cold water across the cave. She shook again and lay down with her head in Flute Dog's lap, watching her pup. The pup began to move. Its feet dug into Flute Dog's skin.

"Here." Flute Dog pulled Hungry back into her lap, and tucked the pup against her flank. It whimpered and nosed blindly at Hungry's teats. Flute Dog poked one of them into its mouth and bent over them both to keep it warm.

They sat, sodden and miserable, while the storm howled outside. Flute Dog thought about her slowburner, and her tent, scattered in the mud. She didn't know what Hungry was thinking about. Rabbits, maybe. Dog thoughts. Flute Dog shivered and wondered if Young Owl's spirit had got to the Hunting Ground of the Dead before the storm broke, or if the storm would bother a spirit. Maybe it *was* his spirit, looking for Painted Water Horse. The wind shrieked and they all jumped. Something was at the cave mouth, trying to get in. Flute Dog pushed Hungry out of her lap and stood, her hand on Painted Water Horse's lead.

Whatever was at the cave mouth fell inside and lay in the water on the floor. Flute Dog peered out of the shadows. Hungry made a low growl in her throat and Flute Dog shushed her. It was a person, and it wasn't moving.

She left the horses and picked up a rock from the floor of the cave, just in case. "Good fortune on the stranger in the lodge." The person didn't move. Flute Dog tiptoed forward, clutching the rock.

It was a woman, in clothes of woven cloth such as they wore in the Cities-in-the-West, but they were torn and shredded as if she had worn them to pieces. Her long hair was a sodden, tangled mat of burrs and twigs. But the thing that was important about her, the thing that Flute Dog saw first, was her belly. She lay on her side, barely breathing, the wet cloth plastered to her swollen stomach, and Flute Dog could see the ripple of the child inside.

The rain was still coming down, flowing in little streams into the cave, parting around the woman's inert form, channeling around her to pool in a shallow hollow at the center. Flute Dog took the woman by the arms and dragged her to the back of the cave. Her skin was cold as ice, colder than Hungry's pup. She whimpered once like the pup, and was silent.

When Flute Dog had dragged her out of the water, she knelt and peered into the stranger's face, touching a forefinger to an icy cheek. The woman's eyes opened. She looked at Flute Dog, and at the interested horse faces behind her, and shrieked. She writhed on the floor, trying to get up.

Flute Dog held her down. "No one will hurt you. The maize bids you welcome," she added. It was a greeting that Green Gourd Vine had taught her. She thought maybe this woman came from Green Gourd Vine's people.

The woman didn't answer, just flailed her arms and legs harder, eyes wide. Then she stopped fighting as suddenly as she had started. Her eyes closed and her head lolled to the side.

Flute Dog said "The maize bids you welcome" again, but the woman didn't hear her. Her chest heaved and she spit up a mouthful of muddy water. Flute Dog turned her on her side again so she wouldn't choke.

Flute Dog sat and stared at the woman. What was she doing alone on the Grass, with a child due? Maybe they had driven her out. The people of the Cities were not like Grass people. Maybe living crowded together like that made them crazy and capable of wickedness. Maybe they had plenty of children.

The rain was still pouring down outside, broken by sharp flashes of lightning that lit the landscape for an instant in cold white light, but the cave had begun to warm with the heat of the horses and Hungry. It was a late spring storm, almost summer, full of the booming of the Thunder Being's wings, but not as cold as winter rain. Flute Dog was afraid that wouldn't matter to the woman on the cave floor if she was dying anyway. The woman moaned and her hands clutched at her belly. A contraction rippled across the skin, beneath the wet cloth, and Flute Dog knew the baby was coming no matter what.

She tore the shredded clothing away and put it under the woman's backside her to keep the baby out of the dirt. Then she pulled the woman's knees apart and stared between them. There was nothing to be seen but dark hair and a trickle of water. The woman groaned and more water came out.

Hungry got up and came to look too, the pup complaining blindly where she had left it on the cave floor.

"What should I do?" Flute Dog said.

Hungry didn't know. Dogs didn't do anything. They just had babies. Sometimes they lived and sometimes they didn't. Since there was nothing to see, she went back to the pup and moved it to where the horses wouldn't step on it. It was warmer now, its belly rounded with milk, and it went back to sleep when she lay down beside it.

Flute Dog looked out through the cave mouth into the storm. The woman had come out of the storm. Maybe she belonged to it. "What should I do?" she asked the storm.

The eyes looked back at her. "I thought you would know," they said.

Flute Dog's own eyes widened. She had never talked to the weather before, although Rabbit Dancer spoke with the Thunder Being. "Are you the Thunder Being?" she asked it as respectfully as she could.

"Hah! Old Noisy? *He* doesn't know anything about babies!"

"I don't either," Flute Dog told it.

"You don't expect *me* to know, do you?" The eyes narrowed, and then they closed and weren't there anymore, just the black sky boiling over the Grass to the south. Flute Dog wasn't entirely sure they had been there to start with, although Howler said everyone should always pay attention to visions.

The woman moaned and Flute Dog turned back to her. Her lips were stretched back from her mouth in a grimace, like a skull. She was nearly all bone under her skin, except for her belly. Her hands, digging into the rubble of small stones and debris on the cave floor, were skeletal, the nails split and worn away, the fleshless fingers clawlike. She shrieked as if something was tearing her open. When the contraction passed, she clenched her teeth and ground them together. Flute Dog knelt between her legs. This wasn't how it was supposed to be. She took the woman's hands and tried to get her to stand up. The Grandmothers always said that helped, that you shouldn't lie down like a log and try to push a baby out sideways. The woman sat halfway up, and pulled her hands away. Another contraction came, and she lay back down, moaning. There was blood on the ground under her now. Flute Dog looked between her legs and thought she could see the baby's head, a dark, wet ball protruding between stretched lips.

The woman had fallen silent, as if she were too weak even to scream. Flute Dog tried to get her hands around the baby's head and pull it out. She gave that up and pressed on the woman's belly, and it came a little further. She put both her hands on either side of the head and tugged gently.

It was a big baby, and the woman's flesh tore as it came out. She didn't scream again and Flute Dog looked at her anxiously, the baby cradled in both hands, its cord still stretching up inside the mother, into that vast and mysterious place where babies grew. The baby twitched in her hands and she lifted it quickly to make sure it was breathing. It looked back at her, wide-eyed and solemn, and opened its mouth in a wail.

Flute Dog pulled a hair out of Painted Water Horse's tail to tie around the cord before she cut it. Painted Water Horse snorted indignantly.

"Nobody has any hair but you," Flute Dog told him. She gave her attention to the cord, and after she had cut it with her belt knife, she tied a knot in it to be sure. The baby was a girl child, covered in blood and a film of waxy stuff. Flute Dog couldn't find anything dry to wrap her in, so she scooted over to Hungry with the baby in the crook of her arm and put it against Hungry's hairy side, next to the puppy.

She looked back at the mother dubiously. The afterbirth had to come out, she knew that, but she wasn't sure how you got it out. Most women just expelled it naturally, but this one wasn't doing that. Flute Dog tugged at the cord experimentally, but it didn't pull anything out. The woman's skin was clammy and Flute Dog bent over her and peered into her face. She didn't think she was breathing.

Flute Dog put her head next to the woman's mouth but she couldn't feel anything. No breath whispered past her ear.

Flute Dog sat back on her heels. "Don't die!" she commanded the woman.

The woman's eyes were half open, her jaw slack. The rain was still lashing the bluff outside the cave mouth. Flute Dog saw what she thought were faint shapes blown past it on the wind, ghosts maybe, come to get this woman and take her to the City of the Dead where Green Gourd Vine said those people lived after they died. It was under a lake, Green Gourd Vine said, and maybe you had to go there through water.

Flute Dog pushed down on the woman's stomach again, the way she had seen the Grandmothers do, but nothing more came out, and when she laid her head against the woman's chest she could hear no heartbeat. The breasts, swollen with milk, were clammy to the touch, like fish.

Flute Dog looked at the baby despairingly. What was it going to eat? She saw that Hungry was licking it, her long red tongue making efficient swipes along its back and legs. It didn't seem to mind. Rosy fingers curled and uncurled like little worms, and when they brushed Hungry's flank they grabbed a handful of gray fur.

Flute Dog knelt beside them. Someone had given her a baby, if she could keep it alive. She turned the baby around and put its face to one of Hungry's swollen teats. The baby's mouth closed around it with a grunt.

4

Flute Music

THERE WAS NO DOUBT ABOUT IT, HOWLER THOUGHT, that child was funny looking. Maybe it came of being suckled by a dog. Her eyes were very wide, as if she were always startled. Her hair was an odd brownish color and the little tendrils around her face curled like a buffalo's fur. In the winter her skin got paler than anyone else's.

Rain Child didn't know she was funny looking. She followed her mother, Flute Dog, solemnly carrying little armfuls of firewood or a water skin nearly bigger than she was. It had been three summers since Flute Dog had found her. When she was two they had passed by Young Owl's bier, and Flute Dog had taken his skull to the skull ring and shown him Rain Child and told him he had a daughter.

Flute Dog hadn't married again, although Howler had asked her. The Dry River grandmothers said she ought to marry again and have more children. Proper children who weren't funny-looking, they thought, but no one said that. Flute Dog had a temper.

"If you married me," Howler said, sitting cross-legged on the grass beside her while she scraped a buffalo skin he had brought her, "they would quit bothering you." He had already tried all the other reasons he could think of.

"And what makes you think I would have any more babies?" Flute Dog asked curtly, working the bone scraper over the hide. "I never did before. I had to get Green Gourd Vine to nurse this one for me."

Howler's eyes rested on Rain Child, who was rolling on the ground with Hungry's newest litter. Like all Dry River babies, she wore no clothes in fine weather, and her pink feet waved in the air above the pile of puppies.

"All children from the Cities look like that," Flute Dog said angrily. "I asked Green Gourd Vine."

"They don't," Howler said. "I asked her too."

"Then I don't see how I can marry you, when you say things like that about my daughter."

"I didn't," Howler said. "But you can't say she looks normal."

Flute Dog glared at him. "That does not matter to me. She's mine."

"Certainly. But saying she doesn't look different is like saying a dog is a buffalo. You can say it, but it goes on being a dog."

"She isn't a dog!"

"I didn't say she was." Howler said patiently. "I just said it was like that."

"It's not like that."

"I was giving you an example."

"You are Most Wise," Flute Dog said sullenly.

Howler still came and sat outside her tent at night and played his flute. It was an elaborate love flute, painted all over with flowers and stars, and tied with tassels of doe-skin dyed red and yellow.

Rain Child poked her mother in the darkness. "He's playing again."

"I can hear him," Flute Dog said. If she were going to marry anyone, it might be Howler. But he wasn't Young Owl and it was hard to forget that. "We don't need a husband," she said to Rain Child.

"Why not?"

"Because we have plenty of horses."

Rain Child knew that. Blacktail Horse's foals were worth enough meat to feed them all year.

"And we can make Winter Camp with my brother."

"Do you think Uncle Head Carrier likes having us there?"

"I'm sure he does."

"Auntie Soft Foot doesn't," Rain Child said astutely.

Flute Dog giggled. Outside the tent, Howler heard her and paused hopefully. Flute Dog put her hand over her mouth, eyes crinkling at Rain Child. After a while, Howler began to play again, a soft whispering melody like spring rain, yearning, hopeful.

"Auntie Soft Foot is just jealous," Flute Dog whispered to Rain Child. "Uncle Head Carrier snores like a buffalo and grinds his teeth at night. I expect she would much rather I slept with him and she got to sleep with you and the dogs."

She snuggled Rain Child into the crook of her arm and stuck her toes under the pile of warm puppies. Outside, Howler's flute made a soothing ripple of sound. It was very pleasant to listen to. If she married him, he would probably quit playing for her.

By now Rain Child had learned that on the Grass the seasons turned in a circle, always moving, but they always came back to summer. For Rain Child, summer was the heart of the year.

In summer the new foals were old enough to run on their wobbly legs and eat berries out of her hand, held very flat while their stiff whiskers tickled her palm. Now that she was too big to be carried in her cradleboard—the fine embroidered one that Mother's mother and grandmother had used—she could sit on the travois behind Blacktail Horse while they moved on to a new camp, and sing to the foals that trotted behind. They had six horses now: Painted Water Horse, whom Flute Dog mostly rode, and Magpie Horse, and four mares, Blacktail Horse and her daughters Whitetail Horse, Sun-up Horse and Blue Squirrel Horse.

Besides their own horses, Rain Child liked best Rabbit Horse, the long-eared animal that belonged to Uncle Mud Turtle. Nobody knew exactly what he was and he never got any foals, although he tried. Uncle Mud Turtle said he was the only one there was and he had come from the Cities-in-the-West. He didn't run as fast as the other horses, but he was stronger, and he never tripped or skidded on the stones on the riverbank or a narrow trail. Mud Turtle's wife and babies rode him when they traveled, but when the Dry River people all camped together, Mud Turtle let Rain Child ride him.

Besides riding Rabbit Horse, here were some of the things you could do in summer: pick berries and eat them so you came home with your face and hands stained red. Dig up camas bulbs with a stick. Collect buffalo dung for the fires. Watch the Horse Dance on the night of the Longest Day. Draw on your stomach with the paint Uncle Howler used on his face. Lead the foals around with a rope so that they got used to it. Teach Hungry's puppies to come when you called them so they would have manners when they went to live with other people. Look for bee trees with Only, Hungry's daughter who had been born when you were. Have Mother tell you the story of how she found you in a cave. (That was important, because Hungry had fed you and so you must always be kind to dogs, and to wolves and coyotes, too, because they were sisters.)

Summer achieved a rhythm that was like being rocked in the cradleboard that Rain Child had outgrown, dangling and swaying gently at the end of a branch—warm days and warm nights, punctuated by the terrifying thrill of a summer storm roaring across the Grass, its dark amorphous form lit from inside by the Thunder Being's lightning, making the hair stand up on Rain Child's arms.

Then the days grew shorter, tilting toward the hinge point of the fall equinox, when it was time for the autumn buffalo hunt. That was when the whole of the Dry River band, together with the Buffalo Horn, hunted the vast herds that flowed like a living river over the plains on the way to their winter graze. Autumn buffalo were fat, their coats thick and soft. Autumn camps were full of drying racks with strips of meat curing in the sun. Someone always gave Flute Dog and Rain Child a buffalo in exchange for one of the foals, and Flute Dog soaked the hide and smeared it with buffalo brains and rolled it up to be tanned during the long winter.

After the hunt the Dry River people went to their Winter Camps, sometimes two or three related families to a camp, sometimes just one. Flute Dog and Rain Child always camped with Young Owl's brother Uncle Head Carrier and his wife Auntie Soft Foot and their children, a boy and a girl named Beaver and Willow. In the spring Beaver would go to live in the Boys' House and go on his first buffalo hunt. Girls didn't have to leave until they got married. Rain Child thought that was a much better idea, although Willow, who was old enough to be married, argued all winter with Auntie Soft Foot over a boy she liked and Auntie Soft Foot didn't.

When they got to Winter Camp there were bright yellow squashes growing by the door, where they had planted seeds last spring, and Flute Dog and Auntie Soft Foot and Willow picked them and put them in the deep, cool storage pits inside the lodge. The earth lodge was dug into the ground, waist deep, and lined with poles. They always made a new roof each winter, of more poles laid crossways and thatched with willow mats and grass.

Then Uncle Head Carrier piled dirt over the whole house so that it looked like a hillock in the ground, with a smokehole in the center and an entrance corridor sloping down into it from the front. Uncle Head Carrier and Auntie Soft Foot slept in the bed in the middle, nearest the hearth, and everyone else slept in beds around the sides. The dogs all slept on the floor, and when it was very cold, they brought the horses inside, and they made a warm horsy-doggy-smoky smell that Rain Child found comforting.

When the snow came, Flute Dog and Rain Child sat inside the warm lodge and sewed their buffalo skin into new fringed dresses that they embroidered with porcupine quills. Flute Dog and Auntie Soft Foot dyed the quills in hide vats of red and yellow and brown that filled the lodge with an acrid scent. The leavings, poured out, made bright splashes of color in the crusted snow. Rain Child put her hands in the red dye and made a pattern of handprints on her own calfskin, the first she had tanned. The hands made a circle, fingers pointing outward, that she found very satisfactory.

Sometimes Uncle Head Carrier and Beaver went out on snowshoes and brought back a deer, and once a buffalo cow, who had got stuck in a snowdrift. At the solstice Uncle Head Carrier danced the Dog Dance by himself, very solemnly marching around the fire, to turn the sun around and show him the way back to summer. When he wasn't dancing or hunting Uncle Head Carrier sat and thought about things. Rain Child sat beside him and thought, too.

At first Beaver didn't like that. "You're a girl," Beaver said, looking disgusted. "You can't think about things."

"I have thought about three things," Rain Child said. "I have thought about why squashes grow out of seeds, and whether Uncle Mud Turtle's Rabbit Horse is really another kind of animal and not a horse at all, the way Big

Cat and Bobcat look like each other but aren't. And I have thought about why you are so ugly."

"I am not ugly!" Beaver bent down and glared at her. "*You* are ugly."

"No, I'm not," Rain Child said positively. Beaver had a face like his namesake, and buck teeth.

"You are ugly," Beaver said. "Everybody knows it. Your skin is a funny color and so is your hair. Your eyes are weird, too," he added, considering her carefully.

Rain Child was only four and a half, but she knew what men considered important. She peered up under his breechclout. "Your balls are little," she told him.

Beaver backed away from her. "Father should not let you be here. You'll grow up and be a witch." He stomped away to where his snowshoes hung from a peg on the lodge wall and snatched them down.

Head Carrier bent down to look at Rain Child solemnly. "Small children should not be rude to their elders."

"He was rude to me first," Rain Child protested. "He said I was a girl and couldn't think about things."

"Women have other work to do," Head Carrier said. "It is true that it is men's work to think about things." That was the business of a man, in the winter, to think about the Universe and how the world was made and how people ought to be living in it.

"The Grandmothers think about things," Rain Child said. "The men ask for their blessing when they hunt, and give them presents afterward, for thinking about the buffalo."

"They are old. You are not. You should be sewing your new shoes."

"We have finished. Mother and Auntie Soft Foot are making black dye and they won't let me help."

"Then grind acorn meal."

"I did that. I'm not strong enough to grind it fine.

Mother has to do the second grinding." She smiled up at him. "I like to sit here with you."

Her strange hair curled in little tendrils like new squash vines around her face. Her round, surprised eyes rested on him with affection. Head Carrier sighed. Soft Foot thought she was a strange child and resented having her and Flute Dog in their lodge. "Your sister-in-law ought to marry again," Soft Foot said. "It isn't respectable."

"Many widows don't marry again," Head Carrier had said.

"They are old. She isn't."

"She was heart to heart with Young Owl."

Soft Foot turned her nose up. "She only cut off one finger. What kind of respect is that?"

"She wasn't married very long."

"You said she was heart to heart," Soft Foot retorted resentfully. "And she ought to marry again now. If any-one wants her, with that peculiar child."

Head Carrier looked down now at the peculiar child. "What do you think about?" he asked her.

"I think about the woman who had me in that cave," Rain Child said, surprising him.

"And what do you think about her?"

Rain Child shook her head. "That something bad hap-pened to her. I think that maybe if I think about her enough, I will dream about her."

Head Carrier nodded. There were regular dreams and there were vision dreams. Regular dreams were the wisps of daytime events that had got caught in your head. Vision dreams came when you crossed over into the spirit world and a spirit came to tell you things.

"Mother says she left her in the cave," Rain Child said. "I suppose coyotes ate her."

Head Carrier nodded. In that case she probably wan-dered the Grass as an echo, since no one had been there to show her the way. It was hard to say where she might have gone. If she was of Green Gourd Vine's people, maybe she went to their City of the Dead. Or maybe the coyotes had showed her the way up the Backbone of the Universe, across the sky to the place where the Grass peoples went to hunt after death, since her daughter had been adopted by Grass people.

"I think about why people go on two legs and everybody else goes on four," Rain Child added.

"Bears walk on two legs," Head Carrier said, happy to change the subject.

"Not all the time."

"Neither do we," Head Carrier said triumphantly. "When we are little, we go on four."

"Birds walk on two, also, when they are not flying."

"And snakes don't have any."

"Maybe it isn't simple," Rain Child said.

"Nothing is simple." Head Carrier smiled. The child was not simple, either. "You may sit and think with me if you want to," he told her, "until your mother needs you." If Soft Foot got angry, he could threaten to marry Flute Dog himself. A lot of people thought he ought to anyway, since she had been his brother's wife. Head Carrier himself thought she was too willful, and as things were, he had her to work in his lodge in the winter without having to be married to her and wonder when he lay down with her if she was thinking about his brother. That might not bother some men, but Head Carrier, who thought about things, thought it would bother him.

There were other things to do in the winter, besides think and turn the sun around. At night Mother told stories or Uncle Head Carrier did. These were the winter stories that you told after the season of the thunderstorms. Rain Child wasn't sure why, but there was a season for stories just the way there was for squash and buffalo.

Many of Mother's stories were about Coyote, who was always doing stupid, braggy things and getting in trouble, but who had also made the world, and thought up human people after the animals were made. When Rain Child asked how someone smart enough to make the world could go around playing mean tricks on people and getting caught in his own jokes, Mother said that being talented didn't mean you were a nice person. Rain Child understood that. Won't Smile, for instance, made such beautiful drawings on hide that everyone wanted one of her tents, but she was always mean as a snake. Rain Child wondered if unpleasant people were given a talent gift to make up for their personality. Maybe that was something Coyote did.

There were lots of stories about Coyote. Mother told the world-making ones, too, but the ones Rain Child really loved were the tricksy ones, where he lured Buffalo off a cliff so he could eat him, or dressed up like girls with Fox and pretended to marry the Wolf Brothers.

There was a ritual to the storytelling, which made it seem even more wonderful and important. When the lodge was dark except for the glow of the fire, Mother would settle herself beside it, making a big production of having Rain Child spread a robe for her to sit on, and then fetch her a cup of acorn beer. Beaver and Willow would settle themselves beside her, while Rain Child cuddled in her lap, and then Mother would need a hot stone to warm her hands. Someone would get that, and then finally Uncle Head Carrier would sit down too, on the other side of the fire. Even Auntie Soft Foot would come and listen. Then Mother would think for a long time, while everyone tried to be quiet. Sometimes she would brush out her hair while she thought. It had mostly grown out by now and fell halfway down her back. Sometimes Rain Child, impatient, would brush it for her so she would start. The hair crackled and made a soft singing through the brush that seemed to go with the story. Rain Child liked standing behind her, feeling the warmth of Mother's back through the dress and the buffalo robe around her shoulders, while the hair gleamed in the firelight and crackled in her hands.

"A long time ago this didn't happen," Mother would start, which was how a storyteller let you know that a story was not true and true at the same time. "A long time ago, Coyote was coming along . . ."

The stories lasted all winter, until one day there was a sniff of something new outside, a green smell that warmed the air, and they would hear the sky begin to shake while the Thunder Being woke up. "Time to put away the stories," Mother would say, packing them away in her head like clothes. There were some stories you could tell in the spring, but not Coyote ones. The Thunder Being didn't like him, Mother said, so you had to talk about him while the Thunder Being slept.

Uncle Head Carrier and Beaver would become very busy, testing the bindings on their spears and fletching their new arrows. Auntie Soft Foot would make a stew with the last but a bit of the dried meat, talking about how good fresh buffalo humpmeat was going to taste. Willow picked her way through the slush and frozen mud to the stream for the new cress that grew as soon as the ice melted. When she came back with a handful, everyone had a bite, the taste sharp and hot on the tongue, and cold at the same time.

Then it was time to load the travoises, the big ones for the horses and little ones for the dogs. In the days before horse days, Mother said, everyone carried their things on dog travoises, like the Red Bow people did now. Only the Buffalo Horn and the Dry River people had horses. They were a gift of the spirits to a Buffalo Horn chieftain of the Grandmother Days, and then the Dry River people had got some too, by being clever. Being clever meant stealing them, Rain Child knew. Even now when they were supposed to be at peace with each other, the Buffalo Horn and Dry River young men made reputations for themselves by stealing each other's horses.

Rain Child couldn't imagine being a people without horses. She was lucky that Mother had come to find her in the cave. This spring Mother said she was old enough to ride to Gathering Camp, instead of sitting on a travois, and Mother boosted her up onto Whitetail Horse's back.

Whitetail Horse's hide was furry and warm and her belly was stretched wide under Rain Child's legs with the foal she would have soon. Rain Child thought she could feel its knees and feet through Whitetail Horse's skin. It made Whitetail Horse waddle from side to side like a duck when she walked. Rain Child pulled her skirt up around her thighs (it was still too cold not to wear clothes) and let her bare legs swing in the cold sun. "Summer, we're riding to summer, we're going to summer," she sang as they went.

By the time Rain Child had twelve summers she rode better than any of the Dry River girls, and most of the boys. Since Flute Dog had refused to marry again, despite everyone's good advice, she and her daughter trained their horses themselves. At twelve, Rain Child could jump onto a horse's back from behind or either side, ride with no rein, and bend down and pick up a stone from the ground at a gallop. Uncle Mud Turtle had taught her to talk to them, and listen to what they had to say back, and sometimes when a horse was ill or crazy, Rain Child knew why when nobody else did.

She spent most of her days lying along Blacktail Horse's broad back, watching the sky, while her mother's horse herd grazed and Only, who had taken Hungry's place and was getting old and gray herself now, snoozed in the grass. Flute Dog had made sure Rain Child knew how to sew clothes and tan leather and make baskets, and all the other things women did, but Rain Child was the only girl who was a horse boy. The other horse boys teased her when she first began to go out with the herd, but after she pulled one off his horse and rolled him in an anthill, they let her alone.

"My grandsons will watch your horses," Uncle Head Carrier said to Flute Dog.

"They can graze with mine," Uncle Howler said.

"They are our horses, we will watch them," Flute Dog told them.

"Does that child know how to dry meat?" Auntie Soft Foot demanded.

"Yes."

"Can she make quillwork?"

Flute Dog considered the toes of her new shoes, which Rain Child had made. They had a pattern of the Thunder Being's lightning, surrounded by the circle of the Sun, so that somebody would always guide Flute Dog's feet. The left lightning bolt was only a little longer than the right. "She made these," Flute Dog said.

Auntie Soft Foot sucked a tooth irritably. The quill ends weren't properly tucked down. They would unravel in a moon. She knew it.

Many other people had advice for Flute Dog. She listened respectfully to them and then did what she wanted, just as she always had. So they gave up and left Rain Child to watch clouds on Blacktail Horse's back and go about in dresses that had one side longer than the other.

When she began to bleed like the other girls, the summer she was twelve, everyone thought it was a good sign, because Flute Dog had been secretly afraid she might not, she was so odd looking, and the other women had not been secret at all about *their* predictions.

Rain Child went to sit in the Girls' House for eight days with two other girls who had just started. The Girls' House was made of brush with the leaves still on, like a journey hut. It was built on a hillock away from the rest of the camp because women's magic was very powerful and could cloud men's magic so that they couldn't hunt or see clear visions. Rain Child liked the idea of that power.

The other two girls, Crane and Hopeful, had been there for a day already when Rain Child came, and they looked superior, as if that had given them a head start on something.

"It's Buffalo Girl!" Crane said, clapping her hands.

"Don't call me that." Rain Child drew back a fist.

"She doesn't mean any harm." Hopeful frowned at Crane. "It's just the way your hair curls. Nobody else's does that, except Buffalo."

"Everybody's does, in the Cities-in-the-West," Rain Child told her.

"That's not what Green Gourd Vine says. Hers doesn't." Spotted Colt's wife had hair like normal people.

"The woman in the cave where Mother found me came from a different city from her," Rain Child said. She didn't know, but she was tired of having her differences discussed. She made a point of staying in the sun as much as she could, so that her skin got dark like everyone else's. The only trouble was, that made her hair lighter. No doubt in the Cities-in-the-West there were lots of different kinds of people, even if Spotted Colt and Mud Turtle hadn't seen them.

Rain Child glared at Crane and Crane didn't say anything else until the Grandmothers arrived to get Rain Child properly settled. They took her dress away and gave her another one of woven rushes, like the ones Crane and Hopeful were wearing, and unbraided her hair so that it hung down her back. They gave her a pad of cattail fluff to stick between her legs.

"This is a time of importance, and for thinking on being grown up," old Grandmother Lizard, who was the oldest person of the Dry River people, so old her hair was gray, told her sternly. Grandmother Lizard had been widowed twice, she was so old, and only had two fingers on each hand. She made love spells for young men, and all the girls were afraid of her. After she had left, Crane whispered that if a girl wasn't good, Grandmother Lizard could make her fall in love with an ugly old man.

The Grandmothers made sure the girls had plenty to do. They left them a bag of rushes to make a basket each, and three grinding stones and an enormous hide bucket of acorns to grind. They came back every morning to see how they were getting on with it. In the Girls' House you weren't allowed to eat meat, but the other women brought them water and herbs and camas bulbs, and Flute Dog picked them a basket of berries. When Rain Child's stomach cramped with the bleeding, Flute Dog made her sage tea and rubbed her back. Flute Dog and the other mothers could come to see their daughters in the Girls' House, but the girls couldn't leave it.

When the older women had gone, the girls tried hard to think solemn thoughts about being grown up, but it always came to talk about boys. What would it be like to marry one of them? There was very little privacy inside a tent, so the girls knew a lot, but the idea of actually doing these things themselves evoked wild speculation.

"Do you think it gets hard when he tells it to?" Crane asked. They were grinding acorn meal, which was so boring it was hard not to think about other things. "Northwind Boy says his has a mind of its own and doesn't listen to him."

"That Northwind Boy has been playing his flute outside your father's tent since the last full moon," Hopeful said. "I think *it* listens to the flute."

Rain Child leaned her weight on the handstone, working it back and forth across the meal in the grindstone bowl, thinking of Uncle Howler playing his flute for Mother. Sometimes he still did that, but not every night now. Mother wasn't going to marry him. "It wouldn't be hard to find out," she said. It struck her as funny. "I think the boys would show us."

"Out in the tall grass!" Hopeful said.

"*I'm* not going to go with any boy who won't bring my father horses," Crane said primly.

"Then how do you know you'll like being married to him?" Rain Child asked her.

"Rain Child! That's disgraceful!" Hopeful made a face, but she laughed anyway. Men made a big point of wanting virtuous wives, but most people tried things out anyway, and girls whispered among themselves about this young man or that. Hopeful had heard her older sister and Willow talking.

"I'm going to marry Northwind Boy as soon as he gets a reputation," Crane said. A boy had to steal some horses or raid the Red Bow people and kill one—or even better, touch him with the spearpoint and then run away laughing while he was ashamed—to be thought of as an adult, a man with a reputation. Then he could marry a girl and have the right to paint her face. If your face wasn't painted, it meant your husband was of no account.

"What if he didn't get a reputation? Would you marry him anyway?" Rain Child asked.

"Certainly not! And go around like your mother with my face bare?"

"My mother's face was painted when she was married!" Rain Child said fiercely.

"It would be sad to love a boy who didn't have a reputation." Hopeful looked mournful at the thought. There were stories about doomed loves like that.

"It would be sadder to stop loving him because he didn't," Rain Child said.

Crane looked exasperated. "You don't know anything. You grew up with us, but you don't act like it. It must be from whatever funny-looking people you come from."

Rain Child balled up her fist again. "If you call me funny-looking again, I'll break your nose and then *you'll* be funny-looking!"

"Crane didn't mean *you* were—" Hopeful started to say, but Crane had, and Rain Child knew it.

"May your babies all look like frogs," Rain Child said to Crane.

"*You* had better marry whoever asks you," Crane sniffed. "It's a good thing your mother has a lot of horses, because no one will give her any for you. Maybe you can marry a poor young man who needs horses."

"Stop it," Hopeful said unhappily. "The Grandmothers will be angry at us."

"The Grandmothers don't think she'll have any babies," Crane said. "I heard my old Granny talking to Granny Lizard. They say she's like that Rabbit Horse of Mud Turtle's. Anyone who wants her will have to have another wife too, and she's not even pretty, so what good is she?"

Rain Child leaped at her, tipping her grindstone and its meal into the dirt. Hopeful shrieked as Rain Child pushed Crane over backward, upsetting her grindstone too. "Nobody would marry *you*, Poison Lips!" Rain Child said, as she pounded her fist in Crane's face. Her other hand was around Crane's throat.

Crane shoved her away, raking Rain Child's face with her fingernails. She grabbed Rain Child by the hair and tried to hit her with the handstone. Hopeful was trying to pull them apart.

"Stop it!" Hopeful pushed her face between them, and Crane nearly hit her instead. "Stop!"

Rain Child stopped, panting. She knelt over Crane, her knees on either side of Crane's hips while Crane clutched the handstone. She could feel the blood seeping out between her legs where it had filled the pad of cattail fluff. She backed away from Crane while Hopeful tried to sweep up the spilled meal with her hand.

"I'm going to tell Grandmother Lizard," Crane said venomously.

"Yah, go ahead." Rain Child crossed her eyes at her. She pulled the pad away and rolled it up to put in the hide box at the back of the hut. When they left they would take the box and bury it and the Grandmothers would dance around it and make magics so that the girls would have their babies easily. *Like my mother did in the cave*, Rain Child thought. It wasn't the birth that had killed the stranger woman, Flute Dog had told her. The woman had been thin as bones as if she had been wandering alone a long time. Rain Child wondered how she had got lost in the Grass.

The warm blood made her thighs itch. She stuffed more padding into the hide strip and tied it back between her legs. Her rush dress was shredding. Whenever she moved, it shed bits of itself as if it were turning back into reeds. Rain Child wondered what would happen if they didn't stay in the Girls' House, if they just went out and walked naked all through the camp. She eyed Crane and Hopeful thoughtfully. Neither one of them would do it. Rain Child wasn't sure she would either, but she wanted to. She wanted to see what would happen, if the men would fall down sick before her terrible new power.

Crane was patting the skin around her eye where Rain Child had hit her. She was going to have a black eye, Rain Child thought with satisfaction.

"I'm going to tell Grandmother!" Crane hissed again.

"You'll make a bad magic, fighting," Hopeful said. Her eyes filled with tears. "Stop, please. Both of you."

Rain Child sighed. Hopeful had always been nice to her. Hopeful was nice to everybody. Rain Child said to Crane, "If you tell, I'll tell Grandmother Lizard and your Granny you were snooping on them, Big Ears."

"I was not. I just happened to be there."

"It doesn't matter," Hopeful said.

She looked so distressed that Rain Child patted her. "It's all right. We'll be good and the Grannies will make a good magic and you'll marry a handsome boy with a big reputation, and we'll all dance at the feast."

Hopeful smiled. "I just don't like to see you fight." She took Crane by one hand and Rain Child by the other.

"Now, sit down and we'll grind meal together, and we'll sing. You can't argue if we're singing."

Rain Child chuckled, but she sat down and straightened her upended grindstone. She blew the spilled meal away into the breeze that fluttered the leaves around the doorway. Maybe the spirits would like to have it.

Hopeful began to sing the Grinding Song. Green Gourd Vine had taught it to them. It was what the women sang when they ground maize in the Cities-in-the-West, she said. Green Gourd Vine always looked wistful when she talked about that, although Rain Child couldn't see how anyone would miss grinding meal. Hopeful had a high, lilting voice, like butterflies. Crane and Rain Child joined in grudgingly at first, but then the tempo picked up and it started to carry them along, faster and faster, until finally they slipped down the song like an otter slide, into the rhythm of the grindstone, handstone on grindstone, back and forth, side to side. Rain Child wondered if her first mother, the stranger woman, had ground meal to that tune.

By the time they had ground all the acorns and made their baskets, Rain Child's flow had stopped. She and Crane had not made friends, but had at the least achieved a truce based on Hopeful's intervention. The Grandmothers and the girls' mothers came to get them early in the morning just as the sun was spilling over the horizon in the east, carrying folded buffalo blankets, new dresses made of quilled and fringed cowskin, and new shoes. They stripped the girls of their disintegrating reeds, wrapped them in the blankets, and took them to the river. There the Grandmothers stood them in a pool where willow trees overhung the water, washed them from head to toe, and brought them dripping to their mothers, who dressed them in their new clothes, and braided their hair with fringes of red-dyed cowhide.

When she was dressed, Flute Dog let Rain Child go back to the pool and peer into its surface, dappled with sun and shade beneath the willow fronds. Rain Child thought she looked very fine. The water made her hair as dark as everyone else's, and plastered it flat to her head. She stared into the face in the water while little brown fish swam through it. A bug-eyed frog looked back at her from a stone on the water's edge and she laughed and flicked a drop of water at him. He fell with a plop into the pool and sculled away.

The mothers led their daughters back to the camp, and paraded them proudly among the tents, while the men and boys eyed them with interest and the younger girls tried to pretend they weren't jealous. Flute Dog sat Rain Child down outside their tent, on an upturned hide bucket, and took out her paints. "Sit still," she said.

Flute Dog painted a red stripe down the part in Rain Child's hair, just like the one in her own. Rain Child could see Hopeful's mother painting her head too, outside their tent. Flute Dog held the paint stick in her right hand and the pot in the three fingers of her left. Rain Child looked at her mother's chin as she worked, and wondered if she minded not being able to paint the rest of her face, like the married ladies. If a woman was very old, like Grandmother Lizard, she might paint her own face, but Mother had been young when she was widowed and no one had given her permission to do that.

When their heads were painted, the Grandmothers went back to the Girls' House for the hide box, since they couldn't bring it among the tents. The girls and their mothers met them there and they walked in a procession to a hummock north of the camp, with the rest of the Dry River women following them.

It was like a funeral, Rain Child thought. Grandmother Lizard started to dig a hole with a digging stick made from a shoulder blade, but after a few chops at the thick grass, she handed the stick to Flute Dog, and chanted while Flute Dog dug. The roots of the grass were like fingers knotted together and it took a long time to cut them out. After a while Hopeful's mother took a turn, and then Crane's. When the grass was cleared, they dug a hole into the damp earth and Grandmother Lizard put the hide box in it. She sprinkled the top of it with acorn meal and put a piece of each girl's rush dress beside it. The three mothers took turns scooping the dirt back into the hole.

Rain Child watched with some sense that they were burying a piece of herself. Now that she had bled, she was old enough to marry, although most girls waited a while. But there was something in that box that had come out of her that she couldn't put back. The other women all seemed to approve. They sang softly while Flute Dog patted the dirt down on top of the box. Green Gourd Vine was smiling at her, with her arm around her middle daughter, who was a year younger than Rain Child. Even Auntie Soft Foot looked as if she thought Rain Child and Flute Dog had done something right for a change.

When the Grandmothers were through chanting, the women all marched back to the camp, in groups this time, laughing and talking about whose daughter would be next, and how tall they all had grown. Their voices were like birds, or dance flutes, or water falling, not like the voices of the men, which sounded to Rain Child like stones being poured. The men all watched them, Crane and Hopeful's fathers and Uncle Head Carrier feigning disinterest in this woman business, but all the others with a taut attention, like drawn bow strings. Rain Child saw Northwind Boy looking at Crane. He was painting a new war shield and only looked at her sideways, his eyes sliding along her skin. He upended his paint pot when he turned his head to follow her.

At dusk, on the Night of New Women, there was a feast. A minor feast, not like the one a boy had after he went out to the Grass to find his vision spirit, but a girl feast. Rain Child was gratified by any feast at all. There was a freshly killed buffalo, and stew made with antelope meat and the acorn meal the girls had ground. Onions and wild squash cooked in the embers of the fire. Grandmother Lizard brought out a skin of acorn beer, a fermented sour drink that made Rain Child dizzy. When everyone had eaten, the girls danced, just the three of them, to the drumming of the Grandmothers. Rain Child felt the bare earth of the dance ground meet her feet as if it were stepping up while she was stepping down. Somebody was watching her from the shadows just beyond the light. She saw the silhouettes of the Dry River men, their scalp locks standing up like little trees on their heads, their long braids red-black in the firelight. The Somebody was behind them. Sometimes she thought he was in the air. His eyes seemed to float above Uncle Head Carrier's shoulder, where he couldn't see him.

"It's a shame my niece is so ugly," she heard Uncle Head Carrier say regretfully to Uncle Howler next to him.

Rain Child locked her eyes on the Something beyond them, on the eyes like pinpricks of fire. She spun in a tighter and tighter circle, making her own dance within the dance, pulling it around her until the hair on her arms stood up the way it did when the Thunder Being was going to throw lightning. She danced past Uncle Head Carrier and knew that he felt it flowing off her like sparks. She felt his uneasiness and heard Uncle Howler chuckle softly in the darkness. She danced on, conscious of new power.

5

The Second Wonderful Thing

By the summer after the summer after Rain Child started to bleed, Hopeful was married, and so was Green Gourd Vine's middle daughter. Crane had married Northwind Boy the year before that, right after he had killed a warrior of the Red Bow people and come home with his hair. No one had brought a horse to Flute Dog and asked her for Rain Child.

That didn't mean no one had asked Rain Child to go walking with him in the tall grass. Northwind Boy had asked her that, before he had married Crane. So had Long Face and Little Striped Bird. She hadn't gone with Northwind Boy because Flute Dog said it was better to be a good person than a vengeful one. After that Rain Child didn't tell Flute Dog things like that. She went walking with Long Face, and the next day he pretended he didn't know her. Stiff with shame, she found a scorpion and put it in his shoe. When Little Striped Bird asked her to go walking, she said he hadn't courted her yet, and waited until he had played his flute outside her tent for three nights. Then she went with him. In the morning he told her he had no horses to bring her mother, but her mother could give him a horse for marrying her, because no one else would.

Rain Child thought about Long Face and Little Striped Bird fumbling with her body in the grass, and how it had hurt more than it had really been any fun.

"Little Striped Bird wants you to give him a horse for marrying me," she told Flute Dog.

"Hmmmph!" Flute Dog said. But then she said, "Do you want him?"

"I don't think so," Rain Child said. "I don't know. How did you know you wanted Father?"

"Your father gave *my* father Magpie Horse. And when I didn't have any babies, he didn't marry another wife."

"You didn't know that beforehand," Rain Child pointed out.

"No. Well, you can decide this way. Do you want to wake up and look at this boy's face every morning for the rest of your life?"

"Little Striped Bird's? No."

"Then don't marry him. You aren't going to like his face any better when he is old than you do now."

"Would you really give him a horse to marry me, if I wanted to, though?"

Flute Dog put her sewing down and put her arms around Rain Child. "I would give you what you want."

"Even though I'm ugly." Rain Child snuffled. "If I'm ugly, why do they want to walk in the tall grass with me?"

"First of all, you are not ugly. Different is not ugly. Second, because boys follow their cock wherever it is pointing first, and listen to their mothers afterward."

"Little Striped Bird says his mother thinks I won't have babies."

"I didn't have babies," Flute Dog said. "It is my fault they think you won't." She picked up her sewing sorrowfully, willing to shoulder the blame.

"Crane says I'm like Rabbit Horse was. Made wrong."

"Yah, they are fools. Does it matter what they think?" Flute Dog knotted her thread, snapped it taut, and bit it off.

"Won't it matter if no one marries me?"

Flute Dog smiled, her head bent. Rain Child could hardly see it. "You have horses. More horses than those boys. Would you rather have horses or a husband?"

"Horses," Rain Child said. "You know where you are with a horse."

Flute Dog chuckled. "Yes." Flute Dog was a skillful breeder; she knew whose stallion to take her mares to, which bloodline to insert here, what strain to cross there. Sometimes she took a mare to the Buffalo Horn people and traded a man there a new set of leggings to have her mounted by a stallion she picked out. When, in all those matings and crossings, Flute Dog had the urge to do it again herself, it was a much simpler matter than being married. Rain Child might find that out, too.

"Little Striped Bird will be angry," Rain Child said. "He is counting on you giving him a horse."

"Let him be," Flute Dog said. "Why should we give away a horse to buy you something you don't want?"

Everyone else among the Dry River people could answer that question: because a girl ought to be married. Because it was shameful not to be. Because it was even more shameful not to care. Because it wasn't right for two women to own more horses than anyone else.

"Take her to the Trade Fair where the traders go every spring," Grandmother Lizard told Flute Dog. "Maybe you can find her a husband from those people."

"That is in the Cities-in-the-West! No one goes there anymore. The traders say those places are all full of monsters now."

Grandmother Lizard looked as if she thought monsters might be willing to marry Rain Child, but she didn't say any more.

"Take her to the buffalo feast when we hunt with the Buffalo Horn people," Auntie Soft Foot said. "Maybe one of them—"

Every woman had advice, except Green Gourd Vine. Green Gourd Vine looked at Rain Child with an odd, thoughtful expression, but she didn't say anything.

Rain Child went on minding the herd with the horse boys, while she grew older and they younger. Soon she was riding out in the morning with the little brothers of boys she had grown up with. They regarded her as some strange apparition, like a walking fish, but since she was bigger than they were, these horse boys let her alone. She taught Flute Dog's yearlings to follow on a lead and the two-year-olds to carry first a blanket, then a pack, and then a person on their backs. Only had grown old and grizzled around the muzzle, and deaf as a stone, but her daughter Clever helped Rain Child herd the horses. It was easy to lose a horse in a summer storm if you weren't careful. They were frightened of loud noises and the Thunder Being's booming. When a storm was brewing, you had to tie them up in a line and watch them, and talk baby talk in their big stupid ears so they didn't grow afraid and run away.

There were a few wild horses living on the Grass now, who had run away from someone and wouldn't be caught. The Red Bow people had begun to trap them sometimes, which no one liked. The Red Bow people were slave raiders, and it was not a good thing for them to have horses. That was information drilled into the horse boys' heads every morning when they went out with the herd, and so when Spotted Colt's new brown mare ran away in a storm, it seemed like a good idea at the time to blame Rain Child.

Rain Child saw the wind kicking up and the dark thunderheads building to the west, but they had let the horses spread out too far on the Grass and there wasn't time to round them up. Rain Child had told them not to let the herd wander so far, but she was only a girl and so they hadn't listened.

She whistled to Clever and they swung wide around the edge of the herd, Rain Child on Whitetail Horse and Clever on her four fast gray feet. The horses in the herd tossed their heads and whinnied nervously. The air made the hair stand up on Rain Child's arms. The herd began to run, tails high, eyes wild. Rain Child could see the foam flying from their lips. Clever nipped at a bay stallion's heels and he kicked her but he turned, and some of the mares turned with him. At the far end of the herd the other horse boys were trying frantically to swing a knot of frightened horses back away from the river, where the slope dropped sharply to the water in a scree of loose stone. Upriver, where the ground was level, the tents in the camp bobbed on their poles, bouncing in the wind. A loose blanket flapped past them like a lumbering bird. Rain Child saw a mother run from her tent and pull her child's cradleboard off the tree branch where it had been swinging.

Clever went one way around the horses and Rain Child went the other, while the boys and their dogs drove them away from the river. The sky lit with a sudden flash and the Thunder Being's voice cracked through it. The rain began to come down, drenching the camp, plastering Rain Child's hair to her head. The horses slithered in the mud. Clever nipped at old Magpie Horse and drove him toward the center of the herd, and Flute Dog's mares and young stallions bunched around him. They stood there, shivering, while the thunder boomed again. Clever trotted around and around them in a circle, weaving dog magic. They looked at her with wild white-rimmed eyes, but they stood still.

Then the boys came out of the storm with the rest of the herd. Two of them were limping when the boys drove them into a circle with Flute Dog's horses. The boys positioned themselves around the perimeter to hold them. The water poured down their necks and splattered on the sodden animals standing shoulder-hunched and miserable in the rain. The ground beneath them ran with rivulets where the water dug even the fingers of the Grass away. The dogs, half drowned and mournful, nipped at the heels of any horse that started to break from the bunched herd.

"Go and get the tether line," Rain Child said.

"We were just going to," Spotted Colt's son, Evening Bat, retorted, lest she think she was telling him what to do. He kicked his horse toward the camp and slogged back with a coil of rope and a bundle of stakes. Rain Child and the boys drove the stakes into the ground with mallets and strung the rope between them to make a circle around the horses. The flightiest ones they tied by the neck to the rope while the rain sheeted down around them. Evening Bat sneezed unhappily.

Eventually the rain stopped. The sun edged from the dark clouds and water began to steam from the horses' backs. The stakes that held the rope corral were leaning dizzily to the side, the wet rope slack. The horse boys began to pull them up. They counted the herd and found Spotted Colt's mare gone.

"That is her fault." Evening Bat pointed at Rain Child. "She let the herd scatter."

Rain Child glared at him, outraged. "I did not. I told you they were going too far down the riverbank."

Evening Bat looked greatly surprised. "I didn't hear you say that. Did you?" He looked at the other boys.

"We didn't hear that."

"I'm going to tell my father it was your fault."

Rain Child slid off Whitetail Horse. "Watch them," she told Clever, and Clever nudged Whitetail Horse into the rest of Flute Dog's herd and watched them. Rain Child started for the camp. Her cowskin dress was sodden and her shoes squelched mud when she walked. She could hear Evening Bat and the other boys trotting after her, to get the first word in.

As it happened, Spotted Colt was busy worrying about his father, Horse Stealer, who was very old and getting ready to go to the Hunting Ground of the Dead. He was not interested in who had let the herd scatter, despite Evening Bat's shrill assertion that it had been that girl.

"Go tell your mother," he said, not looking over his shoulder. "And go find my horse." Horse Stealer's labored breath heaved in and out of his chest as Spotted Colt bent over him. Rabbit Dancer sat cross-legged on the other side of the bed, in the smoky shadows of the hearth. The tent smelled of wet ashes and sickness. Rain dripped down the outsides of the tent and crept in under the edges, wetting the rushes on the floor and the buffalo rugs that cushioned Horse Stealer's thin body. Spotted Colt had put back the flaps that shielded the smokehole, to let in the light, and water dripped slowly from them too. Each drop hissed in the fire as it fell. Horse Stealer's shield and spear hung from the tent poles above him, with a bundle of tobacco and a medicine bag of charms to ease his way. Evening Bat stood looking at them, biting his lip, but his father didn't say anything else. The only sound was his grandfather's labored breathing and the quiet, sibilant chant that came from Rabbit Dancer's lips, like the whisper of the Grass. Evening Bat thought of ghosts and left.

Rain Child stood outside the tent, arms folded. "I have enough manners not to bother your father at a time like this," she hissed at him. "Why don't you?"

"He said for you to find his horse," Evening Bat told her.

Rain Child looked down at him. "He did not." She studied him further as Evening Bat's lip trembled. Evening Bat was too little to go out in the Grass and look for a horse. Certainly his mother would think so, and Spotted Colt wouldn't have told him to, if he had been thinking clearly. "What will you give me if *I* find the horse?" she asked Evening Bat craftily.

Evening Bat thought, fingering the protection that hung around his neck on a leather cord—the little bag that every Dry River child wore, with a piece of his umbilical cord inside.

"Give me that!" Rain Child said suddenly, pointing at it.

Evening Bat looked as if she might pounce on him. He closed the bag in his fingers. "You can't have that."

Cord bags were sacred. Now that she was grown, Rain Child's was tucked into a box among Flute Dog's treasures. She grinned evilly at Evening Bat. "It won't protect you from the water spirits. You know how they like to come out after a storm and swim in the rain water. I think I saw one just now."

"It won't protect you either."

"I was born in the rain. Water spirits can't hurt me."

"I'll tell Mother."

"I'm sure that horse has gone to the west. All the dry washes there will be full of water now."

"I'll give you something else. I'll give you my eagle feather and my turquoise beads." He kept his fingers closed around his cord bag. No telling what she could do to him if she got hold of that.

"If I find your father's horse?"

Evening Bat folded his arms. "I could find it myself, of course. But with Grandfather getting ready to leave, I should be here."

"Of course." Everybody had been waiting for the old man to die for days. When he did they would elect a new chief, not necessarily Spotted Colt, although a lot of people thought he would be the one. It didn't matter much to Rain Child; no one was going to ask for her vote. She pointed a long finger in Evening Bat's face. "I will go and find your father's horse that *you* let get loose. If you ever lay blame on me for something like that again, I will bring the water spirits back to camp with me and put them in your bed!"

She turned away from him and splashed through the mud to Flute Dog's tent. She thought she heard the faint sound of Horse Stealer leaving behind her. Maybe he had decided to take the brown mare with him. In that case, no one would find her.

"Shame," Flute Dog said, biting her lip so she wouldn't laugh. "He's just a little boy."

Rain Child stuck her chin out. "I told him not to let the herd get so far downriver." Now they were grazing beside the camp, as if they had never heard there were monsters in the storm and tried to run into the next world. Clever lay at Flute Dog's feet, dripping muddy dog water on her shoes.

"Then why did you say you would go?"

Rain Child dug her toe in the dirt floor. "Because he didn't know what to do. He couldn't disobey his father."

"Oho, Most Thoughtful."

In the distance they could hear Horse Stealer's widow Prairie Hen wailing. She had cut off four of her fingers.

Rain Child looked rebellious. "And because I thought I might see a vision spirit in the Grass, the way the boys do."

Flute Dog smiled. "I will make you a journey bag and you can ride Red Sandstone Horse." Red Sandstone Horse was Flute Dog's favorite, more reliable than Painted Water Horse. She touched Rain Child's cheek. "It's hard to say what you might see on the Grass, but it wouldn't surprise me if you saw something. That is where I found you."

"Absolutely ill-advised to let that girl go out alone." Toad Nose looked exasperated. "My cousin Mud Turtle taught her to talk to horses. Now she thinks she's a boy. It's all a bad idea."

"She'll be back," Flute Dog said placidly.

"More likely to lose another horse." Toad Nose was

pessimistic. "What comes of not marrying," he said pointedly. "Bad example. Evening Bat says she let the horse loose in the first place."

"That boy needs to understand the difference between the easy way and truth," Flute Dog said.

Howler looked at Flute Dog thoughtfully. He had on his Fool Dancer costume of cattails and rushes, with a cap of feathers, to dance at Horse Stealer's funeral and send him away in the right direction. A chief who didn't go the right way was a dangerous ghost. Too much undirected power could fold in on itself and blacken people and tents like lightning.

Toad Nose didn't know what Howler was doing here; you'd think the woman had had the sense to marry him, when she hadn't. "She's upsetting the balance," he said to Howler, since he was there. "Tell her."

"Maybe she's a contrary," Howler suggested. Contraries did everything backward, which was powerful because it showed the opposite reality that people couldn't see but which existed.

"She's a woman," Toad Nose said.

"That's contrary," Howler said. Contraries were men. No one had heard of a woman doing that.

"She's going anyway," Flute Dog said. She sounded proud, and pleased with Rain Child.

"It's a bad idea," Toad Nose said glumly.

Howler wasn't sure, watching Rain Child ride off on Flute Dog's best horse. Clever trotted at her heels, ears pricked and tongue hanging past her teeth, a dog smile, like someone going to do something exciting. The grass here was knee high where the herd hadn't grazed it over, and it waved gracefully as they rode into it. Rain Child sat very tall on Red Sandstone Horse's back, her bow and quiver slung over her shoulder, her spear erect. She had tied a bundle of hawk's feathers to it. Whatever she found would do well to watch out for the spear, Howler decided. Dry River women didn't hunt except in emergencies, but there wasn't one among them who couldn't defend herself.

The bier they had raised for Horse Stealer cast a long angular shadow across the grass behind Rain Child. Strange days were upon them, Howler thought. The death of a powerful man always skewed the universe a little, but Horse Stealer's had come on the heels of odder news. A trader up from the south had said he had been afraid this season to go near the cities of the jade carvers. There were monsters living in those cities, stranger and even more dangerous than the spotted cat people to whom the jade carvers belonged; and the jaguar people were like beings who lived in the Moon to a Grass dweller's eyes. Their faces were flat and they drank blood. Mothers hushed troublesome children with tales of the jaguar folk.

What could be worse than jaguar people? The trader said the new monsters were pale, like toads' bellies, and had sticks that could call down the Thunder Being. Howler wouldn't have believed in that if Spotted Colt and Mud Turtle hadn't said the same. The pale monsters had come to Green Gourd Vine's city, and that was why she had run away with Spotted Colt. No one had seen them in the Grass, though. The Grass would swallow them up, Howler thought, if they tried to come here. It was perilously easy to get lost in the Grass if you hadn't been born to it. The Grass ate strangers. The traders taught their children and their apprentices the trade trails, and marked them in secret ways, but no one else but those born to it traveled there.

Howler watched Rain Child's and Clever's forms diminish, shrinking to nothing like stars winking out in the dawn. He thought something contrary might have sent Rain Child on this journey, but if there was something waiting to be found, then shouldn't you find it? If the person who was supposed to find it didn't, someone would, which might be worse. The Fool Dancers knew that not everything that was supposed to happen would please people.

Rain Child herself hoped for the ghost of the stranger woman. Was she still out there, a perilous, thin echo, carried on the wind that blew through the stalks? Rain Child didn't really think of the stranger woman as her mother, but as a sort of kinswoman. There were many ways to be someone's child and the Dry River people didn't distinguish between them. Childless people adopted orphaned or stolen babies. In the genealogy of the Dry River people, Flute Dog was Rain Child's mother and Young Owl her father.

All the same Rain Child wanted to see what the stranger woman looked like. She knew enough to know that while who had birthed you didn't always have anything to do with whose child you were, it did have something to do with what you looked like. You only had to look at Toad Nose's children to see that.

Of course it was possible that Spotted Colt's brown mare had run away for no reason, or just for horse reasons like the thunder banging in her ears or wanting to go back to the Buffalo Horn camp that Spotted Colt had stolen her from. But all this spring and summer, Rain Child had been thinking that something was out there that she needed to find, something waiting for her. She remembered the eyes that had watched her while she danced the Dance of New Women. Maybe that had been the stranger woman, trying to see her daughter. The brown mare had been handy, but she might not have much to do with it at all.

The first night Rain Child camped beside a dry wash where she had seen hoofprints. There was mud in the bottom from the rain, but the water had all run out again, leaving little puddles in the hoofprints. At least she knew the mare hadn't drowned in the wash. She didn't worry about water spirits. Any that could live in a hoofprint were too small to bother with.

Red Sandstone Horse snorted in her ear, nuzzling the last of the grass she had cut for him. She hadn't wanted to stake him out to graze. Earlier they had heard coyotes warbling in the near distance and their hungry song had made Red Sandstone Horse nervous, even though he was too big for a coyote. His warm horse breath blew down the back of her neck as she curled herself in a buffalo robe by the dying fire. Clever was curled inside the robe on Rain Child's feet, her dark nose sticking out a fold at the bottom. Red Sandstone Horse lay down with a thud, and Rain Child yawned. It was warm between the horse and the dog, like being in Mother's tent. Sometimes they kept a foal that had come early and wasn't doing well inside their tent by the fire, and Flute Dog and Rain Child and Only and Clever all slept with it to keep it warm. Rain Child closed her eyes. Red Sandstone Horse snuffled in the darkness and Clever snored.

When the light began to bleed over the horizon in the east, Rain Child sat up and stretched and yawned. The sky was pale and watery looking, like the inside of a shell. Clever came out from under the buffalo robe and stretched too, curving her back and spreading her toes. She yawned, making a high whine past white teeth, ending with a *yowp* as her jaws closed around them again in a snap. She looked hopefully at Rain Child.

"You could catch a rabbit," Rain Child told her.

Clever looked around, swiveling her head like an owl. *Do you see rabbits?* her expression said. She trotted a little way off to squat and piss, and then came back and nosed in Rain Child's packs.

Red Sandstone Horse stood up, and Rain Child grabbed his tether before he could piss too and drown them, and led him away from the fire. There were no coyotes to be seen in the daylight so she staked him to graze at a little distance, where she could still see him. There had been coyotes, though, she discovered. Brazen little beasts. There was a set of pawprints down the mud of the wash, not twenty paces from where they had slept.

She looked sternly at Clever. "You might have said something."

Clever looked innocent. *Coyotes?*

Rain Child inspected the tracks, triangular pads with four splayed toes. They came down the wash from up-water at a purposeful trot. The ground had still been damp and they were neat, perfect impressions, each with a drop of water in the bottom. Rain Child peered into one, looking for water spirits. If they were in a coyote print, it might not matter how small they were. Only her own face looked back at her, egg-shaped and distorted in the single drop. She stood up again and began to follow the prints down the wash. Clever bounded over the lip and went with her. The sun was already baking the mud into hard-pan, cracking it into random, jagged pieces like shattered stone. The tracks, embedded in the cracking mud, went in a straight line. They didn't deviate even when they crossed those of a jumping mouse. Around a bend, they stopped.

Summer storms could fill empty stream beds in a heartbeat, and the roiling brown water was fast and vicious. Once Rain Child had found old bones, too big to be anything recognizable, jutting from a carved-out bank after a storm. There were no bones here, but the water had tumbled rocks loose from the channel and upended small trees that had taken root there. The tracks halted abruptly in the middle of the mud. They ran four times around something, and then leaped up the bank of the wash and were gone.

At first Rain Child thought it was another boulder dug from the wash bottom by the water. But when she got closer, she saw it wasn't. It was round and black. The coyote tracks went all around it in a circle, and she could see where the animals had stopped to dig it further from the earth. Rain Child knelt down and stared at it. Clever sat beside her and looked, too. Rain Child touched the thing with a fingertip. It was cold and hard. And it was hollow. It had been filled with dirt, but the coyotes had dug some of that out. Rain Child could see the scrapes of their nails inside.

She picked the thing up with an effort and shook it, and more dirt fell out. It was heavy. She set it down again with a thud. Something banged against the side and she saw that the thing had a handle, worked through holes in its edge. Once it had had feet on the bottom, but two of them were gone.

It was a pot. A pot made of strange material. Rain Child knocked her knuckles against its side and it hummed. She scraped the surface with her fingernail. That made the hair stand up on her arm. She stared at it while Clever stuck her nose inside and sneezed at whatever scent was left there.

It must have come from upstream, washed downriver on the current in this storm or another one. Rain Child tapped its side again with a fingernail. No one had seen anything like this before, not even Rabbit Dancer or Uncle Howler. She put a hand on its round contour, possessively. This was hers. The coyotes had dug it up for her.

6

How to Cook Magic

THE POT FOUND SPOTTED COLT'S BROWN MARE. AS soon as Rain Child stuffed it into the bottom of her pack and slung it over Red Sandstone Horse's back, the brown mare came walking over a hillock. Rain Child put a rope around the mare's neck and held on tight to it while she packed the rest of her gear, but the brown mare just stood there, docile, like a horse who was wondering why Rain Child had taken so long to come and get her.

When Rain Child swung up on Red Sandstone Horse, the mare nuzzled her ankle. The pot in the bottom of the pack bounced comfortably against her hip.

The Dry River people had moved camp after Horse Stealer's funeral; it was not a good idea to live beside a bier while the ghost decided which way to go. Rain Child found their tracks and set off after them with the brown mare trotting beside her.

When she caught up with the Dry River camp in the next valley, Evening Bat came out of his father's tent and sullenly gave her his eagle feather and string of turquoise beads.

"I don't want those anymore," Rain Child said loftily. She handed him the brown mare's rope. "The water spirits you were so afraid of brought me something else. If you hadn't been scared, you could have had it instead."

"What?" Evening Bat demanded. Other people were gathering around them now, lured by some whisper of news in the air. Spotted Colt and Uncle Howler appeared, and Flute Dog looked satisfied and expectant, as if she had known Rain Child would come home with something wonderful.

Rain Child made a show of untying her pack and rooting in it, as if she were looking for something small. She could feel the pot in the bottom, under her hand. It felt warm now, like a stone that had been in the sun. Once she knew they were all watching her, she took it out and turned to face them, cradling it in her arms.

Evening Bat squinted at it. "What is it? A rock?"

"No, Mannerless. It's a pot." Rain Child held it under his nose, so he could see it was hollow. "It has a handle."

"Where did you get it?"

"The rain dug it out of a wash." Rain Child knocked her knuckles against it and it made a deep humming sound.

Everyone stood stock still, as if the sound had caught them in a snare. "Do that again," Spotted Colt said.

Rain Child picked up a stone instead and tapped it against the pot. The stone made the same note, a shiny sound like insects too large to imagine.

Hopeful stood on her tiptoes, round-eyed, to stare over Mud Turtle's shoulder. "Is it magic?"

"I expect so," Flute Dog said, pleased.

Crane pushed her way past her through the other women, and peered at the pot. The Grandmothers glared at her for rudeness, and she bit her lip and flushed. "It doesn't look like much to me," she sniffed. "Is it clay?"

"No." Rain Child thought of dropping it on her foot to show her that.

"Well, what is it good for?"

"You can cook in it. It holds water. And it doesn't break." Rain Child had tried it out on the trail. You could set it right in the fire and it didn't melt or crack either.

"And you *found* it?" Crane sounded suspicious.

"Some coyotes showed it to me." Rain Child smiled, baring her teeth a little, dogwise. "They had been digging it out of the wash. We frightened them off and found it together, Clever and me."

Old Rabbit Dancer had been standing on the edge of the crowd, on the inside ring of the circle of Dry River people. Now he stepped forward carefully and put his hands on the pot, both palms pressed against its surface. After a while he took them away and put his ear to it. Then he straightened up.

"It doesn't say anything to me. It doesn't speak." He looked at Howler, crouching beside Flute Dog, staring up at the bottom of the pot. "Whatever lives in it doesn't talk."

"Or we don't hear," Howler said thoughtfully. "Did you cook in it, child?"

"It is very good for that." Rain Child put both arms around the pot in case they decided that it was therefore too important for her to have.

Howler cocked an eye at Spotted Colt.

"It seems like a fair trade for my mare," Spotted Colt agreed. He had just been elected chief in his father's place, and could afford to be generous—was obliged to, in fact. He put his hand on Evening Bat's head. "But I think you had better give her one of those blue beads anyway. And the feather."

Evening Bat looked rebellious—Rain Child had a magic pot already—but his father prodded him forward and he bit a bead off the string and stuck his hand out with the feather and the bead on his palm. Rain Child put them in her pot. Everyone heard the note as the bead struck the bottom.

"A musical cook pot." Howler looked amused. "I will play my flute to it in the evening and see if it answers."

"The pot's more like to answer you than the woman," Toad Nose chortled, liking the joke. Everyone knew Flute Dog had been ignoring Howler's love flute for years.

"Some things take time," Howler said gently. He picked the pot out of Rain Child's hands and stood hefting it. "May I carry it, child?"

"Yes."

Howler held it in both hands—it was heavy—and Flute Dog and Rain Child followed him to Flute Dog's tent, one behind the other, like a procession.

He set it on the floor of the tent and they waited to see if it was going to do anything, but it didn't. Rain Child yawned. She curled up on her bed beside the place where Howler had set the pot and watched it sleepily. It looked misty in the dim light from the smokehole. Mother and Uncle Howler were talking softly, and she could hear the rest of the Dry River people outside the tent, like a murmuring of birds. The pot seemed to settle itself beside the fire, like a dog curling up. Or maybe that was Clever. It was a long ride from where the Dry River camp had been before, to where she had found the mare, and back, and then to this camp. Her legs felt heavy, as if they were made out of rocks.

"You should find out what this pot is made of," Clever said to her.

"You're a dog," Rain Child said sleepily.

"If you could make stuff like this pot is made of, you could make wonderful things with it," Clever said.

"Well, what is it?"

Clever sniffed the pot. "Stones."

"Stones?"

"Partly. Broken up stones. They say someone melted them."

"I'm sleepy," Rain Child said irritably. "Leave me alone. You can't melt stones."

"You could try," Clever said.

In the morning, Rain Child thought she had probably dreamed that. Clever didn't have anything to say now. Rain Child went down to the river to get water, and when she got back there were people outside the tent waiting to watch Rain Child cook in the magic pot. Rain Child ignored them and poked up the ashes of last night's fire and fed it little pieces of kindling. She left the tent's door-flap open so they could see. Howler was squatting under the smokehole. Flute Dog had let him in because he said he heard the pot talking to him.

"What does it say?" Flute Dog demanded.

Howler cocked his ear at it. "It isn't saying anything now."

"You said it was."

"That was earlier. Maybe I heard a bird instead."

"Maybe you wanted to come in my tent."

Howler smiled. His smile was childlike, dreamy and peaceful. He put his ear to the side of the pot. Rain Child poured water into it from a skin and splashed him but he didn't seem to mind. She picked the pot up and set it on a stone in the middle of the fire.

"Put your ear back on it," Flute Dog told him.

Howler smiled and tugged his earlobe.

Rain Child ignored them both. She was used to her mother and Uncle Howler. She put a scoop of acorn meal in the water and stirred the mush with a bone spoon. When it thickened she chopped six little wild onions and threw them in, wiping her knife with a handful of grass. It was a fine knife that Uncle Howler had made for her long ago, the blade chipped from obsidian, sharp as puppy teeth. The mush bubbled in the pot. The people outside the tent stared in at it, waiting for the pot to crack in the heat or burn up or melt. The pot just sat there in the fire.

It was a magic pot, there was no doubt about it. When the mush was done, Rain Child fed it to Mother and Uncle Howler, and ate her share thoughtfully, trying out the taste that the pot gave it. Then she picked it up by its handle and took it down to the river to wash it out.

"Can I come with you?" Hopeful fell into step beside her. She had her baby in a cradleboard on her back.

"If you don't bring Crane," Rain Child said ungraciously.

"She's just jealous because she doesn't have a magic pot. I wish I had one, too," Hopeful admitted.

"When something is magic, there is probably only one," Rain Child said.

"That's a shame." Hopeful looked wistful.

"If there were a lot of them, they wouldn't be magic." Rain Child knelt by the water and put the pot's mouth to the current. Little bits of mush floated downstream. A fish leaped up from the deeper heart of the river and snapped one from the surface. Rain Child rubbed the inside of the pot clean with her hand and set it on the riverbank. It listed sideways where it was missing two feet, lopsided and mysterious.

Hopeful took the baby out of the cradleboard and set her on her bottom in the sand beside the pot. She wobbled, overbalancing, and steadied herself, small hands outflung, eyes bright with the river's reflection.

The three of them stared at the pot. It stared back, blank-eyed, enigmatic. While they were sitting there, Grandmother Lizard came down the path from the camp, hobbling on a stick. Rain Child and Hopeful stood up politely. Grandmother Lizard stopped in front of the pot. Her back was bent and she had to peer up at Rain Child. Rain Child tried to make herself as short as she could, out of politeness.

"Ask it if I may boil medicine in it," Grandmother Lizard said.

"In my pot?"

"Yes."

"Well, I'll ask." Rain Child didn't know how to tell what the pot answered. She glanced at Hopeful and Hopeful gave her a nod. It was certainly a new thing to have Grandmother Lizard asking Rain Child for things. Rain Child knelt down by the pot again, feeling uneasy.

"This grandmother would like to boil her medicine in you," Rain Child told it. "Her bones hurt." She put her ear to the pot. When it answered her, she jumped back as if it was still hot.

Rain Child blinked, trying to pretend she had meant to do that. Grandmother Lizard and Hopeful seemed not to have heard anything. "You will be important now because you own a wonderful pot." That was what the pot had said to her. It seemed to be quite pleased with itself. Rain Child narrowed her eyes. She stared suspiciously into its mouth and two yellow eyes stared back. Then they blinked out and all she could see was water in the bottom of the pot.

"It says you may boil your medicine in it, Eldest," she told Grandmother Lizard. *You'd better watch out*, she thought at whatever was in the pot.

"You may bring it to my fire," Grandmother Lizard informed her, as if that were a privilege for them both. She stumped back up the path.

The baby was patting the sides of the pot with chubby fingers. "Maybe some of its magic will go into her," Hopeful said.

"I don't know what kind of magic it has," Rain Child said. "Besides not breaking."

"It makes Grandmother Lizard come to you and talk as if you were Most Important. That is magical."

Rain Child giggled. She picked up the pot and kissed Hopeful's baby on the head. "Maybe it will make you strong, Smallest."

Hopeful put her back in the cradleboard and they hung

her from a branch by Grandmother Lizard's tent while Grandmother Lizard heated water in the pot. The wind swung the cradleboard back and forth and the baby sang a little crooning song to it. After a while she went to sleep. The brew in the pot smelled like swamp water, but it was always the bad-smelling medicines that worked the most good for you.

Grandmother Lizard muttered over it, dropping things in and stirring them with a long bone spoon, while little puffs of steam drifted off its surface.

"What did she put in it?" Hopeful whispered to Rain Child.

"I don't know."

Hopeful wrinkled her nose. "Dead toads."

"Mouse tails." Rain Child giggled.

"Skunk eyes."

Grandmother Lizard peered into the pot where a kind of brown-green scum was now floating on the water. She tasted it with her spoon and long slurping noises, while Rain Child and Hopeful made faces at each other behind her back, crossing their eyes, tongues protruding as if poisoned.

Grandmother Lizard smacked her lips. "Go get me a skin to put this in," she told Rain Child.

Rain Child got up grumpily—she had already lent her magical pot—and rummaged in Grandmother Lizard's tent until she found a buffalo bladder with a stopper in the end. There was a hide funnel in the box with it, and she brought them both to Grandmother Lizard.

Grandmother Lizard poked the end of the funnel down into the bladder's neck. "You hold it." She handed the bladder to Hopeful. "And you pour from the pot." She nodded briskly at Rain Child, conferring another privilege.

I was doing you *a favor*, Rain Child thought rebelliously, but she picked up the pot, using the hem of her dress to hold its edges, which were hot. The medicine sloshed into the funnel, looking like the run-off from a hard rain, afloat with twigs and nameless gobs of something. *I hope my bones never get that old,* Rain Child thought. *Not old enough to drink that.*

When the bladder was full, Grandmother Lizard took the pot, still holding its edges with Rain Child's dress, and upended the rest into her mouth, nearly taking Rain Child's dress over her head. Hopeful stifled a snort of laughter. Grandmother Lizard was older than the mountains, no one could remember her being born, and she was getting old in her mind, too, although no one would tell her that. Last moon she had scraped out a hole in the ground and tried to make a bed in it instead of putting up her tent, until Uncle Howler and Spotted Colt had come along and put up her tent for her and led her into it. In the morning she had stuck the cut stems of flowers in the hole and patted the dirt around them, but they didn't grow.

Now she put down the magical pot, her chin dripping with medicine, and wiped the drips on her arm. "When you have washed the pot out, you may take it home," she told Rain Child, and disappeared into her tent.

They were washing it again in the river when Green Gourd Vine came up to them. Rain Child smiled at her. Green Gourd Vine was still beautiful, even with the lines around her mouth and eyes that the wind and years had cut into her face. She was big-bellied again and comical about it. "We are sisters, your pot and I," she said cheerfully to Rain Child, easing herself down onto the ground beside the flowing water, to hold her water basket in its current.

"Maybe your pot will make Grandmother Lizard pregnant!" Hopeful said with a hoot of laughter.

"Respect your elders," Green Gourd Vine said, but she grinned as she sat down. "Oof! See? I lean to one side, just like it does. And why should it make Grandmother Lizard pregnant?"

"She boiled her medicine in it," Rain Child said.

"I see." Green Gourd Vine studied the pot, brows knitted. "May I touch it?"

Rain Child held it out.

Green Gourd Vine touched it with her fingertip. Rain Child waited to see if the pot would say anything else, but it was silent. "Do you think it came from the Cities-in-the-West?" she asked Green Gourd Vine.

"Not from my people. I saw a cup made of something hard like this once, but it wasn't dark, it was shiny—just like a little piece of the moon." Green Gourd Vine squinted her eyes, remembering.

"Maybe it is only dirty." Rain Child rubbed the pot with the hem of her dress.

"You just washed it," Hopeful told her.

"This thing I saw." Green Gourd Vine looked away across the Grass. "It was in Red Earth City, but it came with the pale people. Just before I ran away."

"The monsters?" Hopeful put a hand to her mouth.

"I thought they were monsters." Green Gourd Vine looked dubious now. Her eyes slid to Rain Child.

"Why did you run away?" Rain Child had heard the stories about how Spotted Colt had fallen in love with the girl from the Cities-in-the-West and stolen her away. They were romantic stories, something to make a flute song about.

"I was afraid," Green Gourd Vine told them. "One of the pale men put his hands on me, and I ran off like a silly girl, thinking to go home later when they were gone. And then I found another one in the desert. I gave it some water but it died anyway, and I knew they would think I had killed it.

"But what about Spotted Colt?"

"Oh, he was there." Green Gourd Vine smiled to herself. "He wanted me to come away with him, before that. It was just that the pale thing's dying made it easier. I was afraid of the Grass."

"What is it like in the Cities-in-the-West?"

"Now? I don't know. I have heard that my people are slaves now." Her smile faded and she got up abruptly, pushing herself off the riverbank with her hands, the water basket balanced between her feet.

"Of the monsters?"

"Of whatever they are." Green Gourd Vine shot a quick look at Rain Child. The shadow of the pot fell across Rain Child's lap and seemed to give her an odd shimmer like someone backlit with the sun. "All the stories tell us there were monsters in the far-off times, who lived among us. Why not now?"

Hopeful watched Green Gourd Vine trudge up the trail to the camp, balancing her water basket on her head. "That was strange."

"She is always strange." Rain Child shrugged and hugged her pot to her in her lap. "It comes of being born to Other people in an Other place."

Hopeful gave Rain Child a sharp look. Tendrils of pale brown hair curled around her face like a buffalo calf's. The pot in her lap made her look as big-bellied as Green Gourd Vine, pregnant with who knew what.

"You were born in an Other place," Hopeful pointed out.

"I was born for Flute Dog," Rain Child said indignantly. "That is different."

Hopeful knew there was no arguing with her when she was in that mood. She picked up the baby's cradleboard and slung it on her back and they went back up the path to the camp, carrying pot and baby. The baby was singing some small babygirl song to herself, like a bird on a branch.

All the people who had been watching Rain Child cook in the pot had gotten bored and left. Only Howler was still there, braiding a coil of rope and watching Flute Dog sew him new shoes. Rain Child thought Flute Dog might as well be married to Howler. She packed the pot away at the foot of her bed and went out to take the horses to graze.

It was a warm day, drowsy with the hum of bugs and the occasional zing of a bumblebee past her ear. Rain Child lay down on Whitetail Horse's back and stared at the clouds while Red Sandstone Horse paced around the mares, snorting, pausing now and then to pull a tuft of grass and chew it watchfully, ears pricked. When he was younger, Red Sandstone Horse and Magpie Horse had fought, but now Magpie Horse had given it up, and let Red Sandstone Horse lord it over the mares.

Rain Child was asleep when Grandmother Lizard started to shriek, and at first she thought it was bugs in the grass, cicadas whirring out their long, whistley notes like the Fool Dancers' flutes. Then she heard other people shouting and she sat up, turning groggily on Whitetail Horse's back to stare at the camp. Everyone there was running back and forth, dark scurrying figures like ants in an upset hill. Rain Child gathered up Whitetail Horse's rein. "You stay with the herd," she shouted at the horse boys.

"You aren't chief of us," Evening Bat shouted back.

"I'm bigger than you are," Rain Child said, balling up her fist. She kicked Whitetail Horse toward camp.

Flute Dog and Uncle Howler met her, hurrying toward Grandmother Lizard's tent. Uncle Howler was hopping on one foot, turning backward, hoping to distract whatever evil it was with his dance. Grandmother Lizard's shrieks dissolved into a choking gurgle and then gagging noises as if she were trying to vomit. Uncle Howler flipped onto his hands and shook the rattles around his ankles. When he saw Rain Child, he flipped back and said, "Take me up, child." She stopped and he vaulted onto Whitetail Horse, sitting backward. They left Flute Dog hurrying behind them.

Outside Grandmother Lizard's tent, Rabbit Dancer knelt on the ground where Grandmother Lizard was moaning and rolling her eyes up into her head. Her face was pasty gray, as if someone had smeared it with ashes; spittle ran from the corners of her lips. Rabbit Dancer put his finger to Grandmother Lizard's lips and then to his own, tasting and frowning.

Uncle Howler jumped off the horse and danced around them on his hands, but whatever spirits were in her didn't seem interested in him. People were pushing around them, trying to see over each other's heads. Spotted Colt shouldered his way through them and tried to push them back.

"She has eaten something," Rabbit Dancer said, still frowning. "Does anyone know what?"

"She boiled her medicine in Rain Child's pot," Crane said.

Rabbit Dancer cocked his head at her.

"This morning," Crane said, pleased. "I thought it smelled bad."

"You weren't there!" Rain Child said hotly.

"I could smell it all the way across camp." Crane looked superior. "It was a poison smell."

"I cooked my breakfast in my pot," Rain Child said.

"Maybe you will die next."

"Quiet!" Rabbit Dancer pointed a finger at Crane. "That is ill spoken to talk of dying."

But everyone could see that Grandmother Lizard was dying. Her breathing was shallow, and stopped and started as if her lungs were a wind fading out across the Grass. Her gnarled fingers clutched the tufts of dry weeds that grew from the ground outside her tent, and her hands shook with palsy. Her belly was distended, swollen as a cocoon under her cowskin dress, ready to split open and hatch death. While they watched, her feet drummed the hard ground and stopped. Her fingers loosened their grasp and her bowels let go in a vile-smelling pool.

Uncle Howler flipped down off his hands and stood, head bent, beside her.

"Where is what she cooked in that pot?" Rabbit Dancer asked.

Rain Child slid off Whitetail Horse and went into Grandmother Lizard's tent. She brought out the medicine bladder, carrying it carefully, and gave it to Rabbit Dancer. "She made the medicine herself," she told him. "Ask Hopeful."

Rabbit Dancer took out the stopper and sniffed. He wrinkled his nose.

"What is in it?" Howler asked him quietly.

"I don't know. But go and bury it where the dogs won't get it." Rabbit Dancer put it gingerly into Howler's hands.

"It was the pot," Crane said with satisfaction.

"I ate from that pot!" Rain Child turned on her, furious. "My mother ate from that pot. Uncle Howler ate."

"I did," Howler said.

"So did I," Flute Dog added indignantly.

"She was old," Rain Child said. "She forgot things. I don't know what she put in that medicine."

The others looked at her uneasily. Rain Child folded her arms across her stomach as if she were clutching the pot to her. "It is my pot. And it was Grandmother's time, maybe," she said to Howler.

"Maybe. But maybe also it would be a good idea to be quiet just now and come and help me with this." Howler held up the bladder.

Rain Child looked aggrieved, but she went with him, leaving Whitetail Horse with Flute Dog. "It wasn't the pot," she said stubbornly, when they were out of earshot.

"I am not dead, that is true." Howler stopped by his own tent and got a shovel, made from a buffalo shoulder blade lashed to a long handle. "But there is magic in that pot all the same, and people are afraid of magics they don't understand."

"It wouldn't be magic if you understood it," Rain Child retorted as he started for the midden. Her jaw stuck out and her eyes narrowed obstinately at him.

"You have it backward," Howler said. "The more you understand, the more magical a magical thing becomes." They skirted the edge of the midden and Howler laid the bladder carefully on the ground downhill from it, on the side away from the stream. He began to dig a hole.

Rain Child watched him, lips compressed. There was nothing the matter with her pot. *She* felt fine since she had begun to cook in the pot. Better than ever. The pot was a tonic. Grandmother Lizard had just put something bad in her own medicine because her mind was wandering. That was what had happened.

Howler laid the medicine bladder at the bottom of the hole and pushed dirt over it. He piled a little cairn of stones on the dirt and eyed the camp dogs, who were watching him with interest. When people buried something that usually meant someone could have eaten it. People were wasteful. Rain Child saw that Clever, who had been on some errand of her own, had joined them.

Howler knelt down until he was on all fours, at dog-level. "That is bad potion. If you dig it up and eat it, you will fall down dead. Like this." He rolled over on his back, legs stiff in the air. The dogs looked at him thoughtfully. Howler growled at them and said something else that sounded to Rain Child as if it was in dog language, and they turned away to investigate the midden instead.

As Rain Child walked back to the camp, Clever caught up to her. A piece of bone stuck out of the corner of Clever's mouth and she held her head high, prancing with it, while Only trailed her.

"Shame," Rain Child said. "Give your mother a bone."

Clever looked abashed and laid the bone down. Only picked it up and lay in a patch of sun with it.

Rain Child went back to Flute Dog's tent and checked to make sure that no one had taken her pot. Clever stuck her nose inside it and snuffled.

"I washed it," Rain Child said. "Maybe I ought to wash it again." She picked it up by the handle and started for the river. She would scrub it out with sand, just to be sure that whatever Grandmother Lizard had put in it was gone.

Grandmother Lizard's granddaughters were laying her out, painting her old face with red and blue lines, and sewing up a hide to put her in. They glared at Rain Child as she walked past.

"It wasn't the pot," Rain Child said.

"Tchah!" The oldest granddaughter, who was a grandmother herself, spat on the grass. "Not a sick day in her life, and now this."

"Did you think she wasn't ever going to die?"

"Take that pot away!" They all turned around and pointed their fingers at Rain Child, and she hurried away from them.

"It wasn't the pot," she said to Clever, her eyes filling with tears. She knelt down on the stream bank and scooped up a handful of sand.

"They're just jealous," Clever said. "If you found out what the pot is made of, you could make more of them and then everybody could have one."

Rain Child turned around to stare at her, but Clever just yawned, showing a long pink tongue and white teeth. She looked bigger than she had. Her ears stuck up and they were bigger, too. A yellow eye closed and opened again, in a wink.

Rain Child set the pot down. The air around them was odd, gray-green, as if a storm was coming, but there was no wind, and the sky overhead was still blue.

"Go away," she said uneasily.

"No, really, you should find out what that pot is made of."

"Go away. I don't want to talk to you. Get out of my dog."

Coyote smiled. It was an odd effect, on a dog. "Pooh. I showed you that pot. I've been watching it for a long time, ever since it washed downriver. Waiting for the right person to show it to." She stuck her nose in it and sniffed again. "It's clean now. If you're afraid to eat out of it, I will."

"I'm not afraid!" Rain Child said indignantly. "And I'm not going to feed you, either."

"Everybody feeds me," Coyote said, "one way or another."

Rain Child edged away uneasily. The yellow eyes followed her movements in the green air. Coyote ate whatever fell into his jaws. Rain Child didn't think Coyote-Woman inhabiting a bitch would be any different.

"Grandmother Lizard fed me," Coyote said, speaking Rain Child's thoughts aloud. If you got so old you didn't know poison root from boneset, Coyote was bound to eat you. "If you're afraid of that pot, I'll give it to someone else."

"I'm not afraid of it. It's my pot." Rain Child clutched it possessively.

"Then what are you going to do with it?"

"It's magic. It doesn't break and it doesn't burn." Wasn't that enough?

"Yah, you don't think! What if you could make more of these?"

"How?" Rain Child remembered what Clever had said to her before. "I can't melt stones."

"How do you know?"

"Because *nobody* can melt stones," Rain Child said. "Not even you," she added astutely, "or you would have done it."

"What if you could make knives of this stuff?" Coyote asked her.

"Knives?"

"Notch the rim of that pot with your belt knife."

"Why?"

"Don't ask so many questions," Coyote said, exasperated. "I will show you why."

Rain Child took out her obsidian knife and sawed at

the rim of the pot. It made no mark. She dug harder and the blade chipped. "Yah! Look what you made me do!"

"What if you could make a knife as hard as this pot? Or a spearpoint?"

What if the mountains were in the river and fish in the sky? Rain Child started to retort, but someone was coming down the path. The greenish air faded away into a greenish mist and Clever shrank back into herself.

"Who were you talking to?" Flute Dog demanded.

"No one." Rain Child wasn't entirely sure anyway.

"Well, don't stay down here by yourself." Flute Dog bit her lip. "Not with that pot. People are saying things."

"They always have plenty say. Yap, yap, this person is lazy, and that person ought to train his horses better, and yap, yap, did you hear about this other person?"

"That is what makes it not a good idea to give them things to say."

Rain Child tried, but it was so easy to set the Dry River people talking. If the rain was late in coming in the Spring Rain Moon, they talked about why. If the buffalo moved their graze, it was the subject of speculation. If the bug people came up from their winter underground in greater or smaller numbers than usual, old Rabbit Dancer talked to the spirits about it and everyone else talked to each other. These things were important, of course, but the Dry River people, so Green Gourd Vine had said, talked more than any other people she had met. When they didn't have anything new to talk about, they talked about why the sky stayed up and why water ran downhill, and what the Great Mystery, Old Grandfather, had put them in the world to do.

"That is the proper business of a person, to think about things," Howler explained to Rain Child when she complained. "It happens that just now they are thinking about you."

"Grandmother Lizard is bones in the ground now," Rain Child said grumpily. "Her granddaughters have divided up her blankets and her clothes, and they are still making noise. Old Rabbit Dancer came by yesterday to put his head inside my pot again and see if it was cursed. It wasn't cursed the last three times he did that."

"No." Howler smiled. "But he is old, and one of his apprentices has been hinting that his mind wanders like Grandmother Lizard's. It is a brave thing to put one's head inside your pot."

Rain Child snorted. "Maybe all the boys will want to come and put their heads in my pot. As a test of bravery. Or to see if they can see something. Like the vision quest, only not so uncomfortable," she added sarcastically, because the vision quest was supposed to be uncomfortable.

"Maybe," Uncle Howler said. "In any case, now that it is time for the Horse Dance, you and they will have something else to do."

All the horses had to be painted for the Horse Dances, held at the spring and fall equinoxes, and at the summer solstice. The Spring Dance was about the new foals, the Summer Dance about the coming of First Horse, and the Fall Dance about hunting the buffalo.

Only men danced the Horse Dance, but everyone got the horses ready. Rain Child and the horse boys took them down to the river, under the elders' supervision, and washed their backs and broad flanks with balls of yucca soap, and rinsed their manes and tails with sage water. Then she tied them to a tree so they couldn't pull loose to roll in the dirt while Rain Child and Flute Dog brushed them with quill brushes until they gleamed.

Flute Dog brought out her pots of paint and they painted all the hooves red and drew red circles around each eye. Uncle Howler was going to take Flute Dog's horses into the dance for her, so she painted figures walking upside down to honor him. Then she and Rain Child dipped their own hands into the black paint and pressed the palms to the horses' shoulders, in a circle pattern, fingers pointing out, like rays of a dark sun. They added more sun faces in yellow, and blue lines for water, so they and the horses would always have enough to drink, and crescent moons to symbolize the buffalo's horns. Rain Child made strings of feathers and blue stone beads and tied them into the manes and tails. Old Magpie Horse looked very pleased, like a chieftain with a new ornament in his scalp lock.

At sundown Rain Child and Flute Dog brushed their own newly washed hair and painted red lines down the parts. Every Dry River person wore the red part line, but other women would be sitting still now while their husbands painted their faces, too. It irked Rain Child that Flute Dog couldn't do that.

"Your father painted my face while he was alive," Flute Dog said. "That is enough for me."

"It isn't fair," Rain Child said sulkily.

"Do you want me to marry Uncle Howler so you won't be embarrassed?" Flute Dog's voice was tart.

"No! I just meant—I don't know what I meant."

"You meant that life is not fair. That is a notion that has crossed most people's minds from time to time. Ask the fish caught in the weir."

"Things would be more fair if you knew how to make what is in that pot," a voice said behind her and Rain Child jumped up.

"Come along, Mother, we'll be late. Uncle Howler has already come for the horses."

The Horse Dance was danced by firelight, flames leaping and flickering on the painted hides, the men riding round and round the fire in circles, spinning tighter and tighter, driving the loose horses with them. Only Mud Turtle and Toad Nose were on foot, but they wore horse heads over their own, which made them taller than the ridden horses.

The crested heads, with their empty eye sockets and taut skin, baring yellowed teeth, looked like ghost horses in the flare of the firelight, almost as old as First Horse, whose head belonged to the Buffalo Horn people. Mud Turtle and Toad Nose pranced along the inner ring of the dance, just inches from the fire, their great heads bobbing over the flames. Then Howler began to dog Toad Nose's footsteps, prancing and whinnying until everyone giggled. The rest of the Fool Dancers ran out then, diving, spinning, ducking past the horses' hooves, popping up under their noses, making them snort and shy.

"He'll get stepped on!" Rain Child said, as she always did.

"No, he won't," Flute Dog said, as she always did. It was their part of the Horse Dance—mutual worry for Uncle Howler, combined with the reassuring knowledge of his skill, the dexterity of his feet, his power. Rain Child suspected that Uncle Howler talked to the spirits more clearly than old Rabbit Dancer.

Spotted Colt, the chief, was at the heart of the mounted dancers, his face painted like his horse's flanks, while Green Gourd Vine, his foreign wife, stood in the ring of women, big-bellied as a melon now. It was her baby's birth time, past due, and she leaned backward, feet braced against the weight and droop of her belly. She saw Rain Child and smiled at her, making a face as if to say, no, she didn't know when it would come, but it was certainly time, wasn't it?

Hopeful's little brother, a boy with his scalp lock sticking up from his head like a tree, stood nearby with Evening Bat, both of them a year too young for the Horse Dance. Rain Child could see them yearning toward it. They envisioned themselves on thundering hooves, hair decorated with feathers and strings of bone beads, the hot fire wind rushing past their cheeks. She could see their thoughts in the air. In the spring they would move into the

Boys' House and never live in their mother's house again. They wouldn't mind.

Rain Child saw Green Gourd Vine knit her brows and run her hands along her belly, and wondered if she would mind, if she would miss Evening Bat. Rain Child didn't see how anyone could miss a child like that, but then, she wasn't his mother. No doubt it was a good thing Green Gourd Vine had this new baby to take his place.

Flute Dog elbowed Rain Child and she stopped looking at Green Gourd Vine and looked back at the Horse Dancers and Uncle Howler. It was mannerless to let your attention wander during a dance, and the spirits, as Rain Child had been thoroughly instructed, did not like mannerless behavior. Their displeasure was likely to show up in next year's crop of colts or the fall buffalo hunt if you weren't respectful.

Rabbit Dancer was saying the prayers now, with Uncle Howler cavorting giddily around him. The rest of the Fool Dancers circled the ring of watching women and children, shaking fingers at their noses, making faces. Hopeful's daughter howled and Hopeful scooped her up in her arms. A Fool Dancer stopped in front of Rain Child. He made stirring motions, as if he were cooking something, and tasted it with an imaginary spoon. He smacked his belly and danced away, chortling.

When Rabbit Dancer had finished, Spotted Colt lifted his arm in the air to signify that the dance was done. He reined his horse over to where his wife and son were standing and picked Evening Bat up under the arms and set him on the horse in front of him. Evening Bat looked proud, but he didn't say anything, because no one could talk to a Horse Dancer until he had washed the paint from his face.

Green Gourd Vine's brow was still furrowed and Rain Child could see that she carried both hands pressed over her belly as if it hurt. Maybe the baby wouldn't come out.

"That Fool Dancer blessed your pot," she said to Rain Child, as the men rode away toward the river. "I saw him. Will you let me touch it?"

"Of course," Flute Dog said. "You honor us and my daughter's magic pot." She looked as if she didn't really want to say that, but there was no polite way to refuse. When medicine wasn't working and you wanted a charm, the first principle was that like called to like. If something wouldn't open, you showed it something that was open, like a pot or a box.

"I will come with you now," Green Gourd Vine said, with a swift look over her shoulder.

"Does your husband know it isn't well with you?" Flute Dog demanded.

Green Gourd Vine shook her head. "He thinks monsters made your daughter's pot, but I have seen them, and they are just ugly people, who know things we don't. Maybe it will help me. I nursed her when she was a baby. Surely her pot will help me."

And that settled that. When someone has given you life and reminded you of it, you cannot refuse what they ask. Rain Child and Flute Dog took Green Gourd Vine back to their tent and let her put her arms around the pot, breathing deep of whatever emanated from its heart. They looked to see if the baby felt it, moving under her skin, but the taut curve of her belly was still.

"When did it move last?" Flute Dog asked her, voicing the question that neither of them really wanted answered.

"This morning," Green Gourd Vine said. "The Grandmothers say it's just resting, but . . ."

"I'm sure that it is," Flute Dog said soothingly. She looked at Rain Child over Green Gourd Vine's head. Green Gourd Vine had her arms around the pot and was weeping silently into it.

7

Dog Night

GREEN GOURD VINE'S BABY CAME THAT NIGHT, DEEP into the darkest hours when anything that happens will make you afraid. She had gone home and lain down by Spotted Colt, who was snoring in harmony with Evening Bat on the other side of their tent. While they slept, she lay tensed, waiting to feel something, but nothing inside her moved until the pains started.

Spotted Colt sent Evening Bat running for the Grandmothers. They knelt in a circle around her, while Spotted Colt and Evening Bat waited outside the tent and made a fire to drive the dark away and welcome the baby into this world.

Green Gourd Vine knelt in the dark inside and gave birth to the baby she had known would be stillborn since the morning. The dawn came down the smokehole and she watched the Grandmothers try to breath life into it anyway, but the cord was wrapped around the neck, two tight loops, and anyone could see there was no use.

"It didn't work," she said tearfully to Spotted Colt

when the Grandmothers called him into the tent to give the dead baby his blessing.

"It's all right, Heart." Spotted Colt held her in the crook of his shoulder. "Maybe there will be more."

"I am too old," she said sorrowfully. "I tried to make him come out. Everything felt tight inside, strangled." She choked back a sob. "I went to Rain Child's tent after the Horse Dance, but even the pale men's pot didn't have enough magic."

"You touched that thing?"

"They could do wonderful things," Green Gourd Vine sobbed into his shoulder. "You didn't see them."

"I did," Spotted Colt said grimly.

"Not in our city. I saw the things they had in their sack, and their sticks that shot fire. I saw one of the sticks throw a rock through a water jar. Surely if they can do that, they could have brought my baby out before he died!"

"She touched the pot," one of the Grandmothers said to the rest.

"She did." They all nodded their heads, satisfied that now there was an explanation.

"It wasn't the pot!" Green Gourd Vine wailed. "He was dead before. You saw he hadn't moved. I thought the pot could help!"

"You were ignorant," the Grandmothers said with satisfaction. "It is because you are foreign."

Green Gourd Vine continued to protest that it wasn't the pot, while they buried her baby, but Spotted Colt appeared to be of two minds about it. He didn't stop Rabbit Dancer and Toad Nose and the Grandmothers when they went to Flute Dog's tent in a delegation and said that Rain Child had to be purified, and had to get rid of the pot.

"It would be best if it was left on the top of a mountain for the Thunder Being to take," Rabbit Dancer said. He leaned on his staff. The top was crested with a horse's foreleg and hoof, painted red. "It would be best if *she* took it up there." He nodded at Rain Child.

"Well, I won't," Rain Child said.

"Hush!" Flute Dog stepped on Rain Child's foot.

"I won't," Rain Child said again.

The Grandmothers shook their heads. Flute Dog had always been a willful girl. That was what happened when you left a woman like that alone to bring up another: disrespect for old men and women who knew more than you did.

"There has been something wrong with that girl since you found her," Grandmother Whooping Crane, who was eldest now that Grandmother Lizard was dead, said to Flute Dog.

"There is nothing wrong with my daughter!" Flute Dog said. "And mind your manners!" she added to Rain Child.

"That is *my* pot," Rain Child said.

"We know this." Uncle Howler had somehow slipped past Rabbit Dancer and the Grandmothers and whispered in Rain Child's ear. "But there are ways and ways to say a thing, and you are being rude."

"That thing has killed two people," Grandmother Whooping Crane told him.

"An old woman and a babe with a cord around its neck!" Flute Dog retorted.

"It is ill-intentioned, anyone can see that. It shouldn't be among us."

"It will poison the horses," Toad Nose said.

"It comes from the same place *she* comes from, most likely!" Little Grandmother Jumping Mouse pointed a tiny finger at Rain Child.

Rain Child's face glistened with tears. "I come from here!"

"Hush," Uncle Howler said into her ear. He looked sternly at the Grandmothers. "Whatever this thing is she has found, it is ill-natured to speak so of Flute Dog's daughter. When have the Dry River people abandoned a foundling?"

"Foreign people are dangerous." Grandmother Jumping Mouse's little mouth was a thin line. "That Green Gourd Vine didn't know enough not to touch that thing and she killed her baby with it!"

"You had best not let Spotted Colt hear you say that." Howler looked at her sternly.

"Let Grandmother Jumping Mouse ask *her* mother where *she* came from." Flute Dog looked sullen. "I heard a story from *my* grandmother about the mother of this one and a little trader man, while her husband was on a buffalo hunt!"

"That is enough!" Howler spun around and glared at Flute Dog. "We are not going to dig up people's grandmothers and ask them who they went walking with. Shame!"

Flute Dog looked abashed. Grandmother Jumping Mouse was livid with fury. She hopped from foot to foot like her namesake, fists clenched.

Toad Nose made an important face. He pushed forward and held out his hand. "I will take the thing to the mountain," he said gruffly. "Someone must."

Rain Child still stood stubbornly in front of the tent door, with Clever peering between her ankles. Just her long gray nose showed under the fringes of Rain Child's dress.

"Go away," Flute Dog said. "You have made my daughter cry and made me speak disrespectfully to Grandmother Jumping Mouse. Leave us alone."

"What about that pot thing?" Grandmother Whooping Crane demanded, not ready to be distracted.

Rabbit Dancer lifted a hand as if about to make a pronouncement.

"What do the Holy Clowns say?" Flute Dog demanded of Howler, before he could.

Howler scratched his chin. "The Holy Clowns speak in

riddles, and play. They don't test magic to see if it is bad or good. They only show you what you ought to think on."

"They are wise, nevertheless."

Rabbit Dancer had stopped, hand still lifted in pronouncement, to see what Howler would do. The Holy Clowns didn't often interfere in individual cases.

"We will think on it," Howler said finally. He knew no one would be happy with that, so it must be fair. "We will think on it by moonlight and we will tell you what the moon tells us."

"When?" Toad Nose demanded.

"Why, ask the moon. Now—" he pointed at the Grandmothers "—go make a stew for Green Gourd Vine, and remember that we are all foreigners that the Great Mystery has sent to this place. Shame."

They skulked away, mumbling, and he shooed Toad Nose after them.

"There had better not be anything wrong with the horses," Toad Nose grumbled.

"Nothing more than swayback from hunters who are growing fat," Howler said cheerfully.

When they had gone, he looked grave and made Rain Child hand him the pot.

"What are you going to do with it?"

"What is it going to do with me? That is the question." He held it to his ear. When he had finished listening, he bit the edge of it. Then he ran his fingers over its surface, eyes closed, and finally bent down and smelled it. Then he took it away without telling them anything.

Coyote watched the moon come up in Rain Child's pot. The Holy Clowns had painted themselves white and danced around it, while the moon lifted over the eastern horizon and her spirit coalesced in the pot.

From his spot on the ridge above the Dry River camp Coyote could see her climbing over the hills. She was round-bottomed and ample-breasted tonight, and he grinned at her out of the stars, making himself an attractive young man, such as a girl like herself might want.

"Good evening, Beautiful," he said, dangling his paws over the edge of the Star Road.

"Oho, it's you." The Moon paused to survey him.

He leaned back, swinging his legs, noticed the paws and changed them into a pair of russet feet. His hair was long and unbraided, and it blew around his face.

The Moon thought him handsome. This time of the month she was always susceptible to beauty. She cast a quick look back at her own face, reflected on the gray ridges of the sea beyond the horizon, and patted her starry hair.

"Look down there if you want to see yourself," Coyote suggested. He pointed downward, where the Holy Clowns had stopped dancing and were peering at her face in Rain Child's pot.

The Moon chuckled. "Where did they get that?"

"Do you know what it is?"

"Dear boy." She sighed. "I know things you have never heard of, on the other side of the world."

"I have seen both edges of the world," Coyote said. "There are some very wonderful things coming along. I just don't happen to have seen this one before, that's all."

"Both sides of the world." The Moon looked scornful. "Men always think they have seen everything."

"Sit down here and tell me about it," Coyote suggested.

She hesitated, coyly. His yellow eyes floated above the stars like topaz planets. "Well," she said, settling herself on the edge of the Star Road beside him. She let her cloudy draperies trail, fluttering in the night wind, tickling his feet. "Over the Water, everything is different."

"The Endless Water?"

"Nothing is endless."

"The sky is," Coyote said hopefully. "The stars are."

"Bosh. There have been four worlds already, just here on the Grass. You talk like one of them." She pointed down at the little ant people running in and out of tents in the Dry River camp.

"I know," Coyote said, slyly sorrowful. "I don't know what's come over me."

"Well." The Moon patted his knee in a comforting way. "Change is nothing to be afraid of. Look at me. I change every night. If I didn't, women wouldn't know how to behave, or the fish in the sea."

"I suppose that's true." Coyote edged closer, so that his thigh brushed hers. His hand just happened to be on it. His eyes were wistful. "You must be able to see farther than anyone."

"Oh, I could tell you stories."

"Tell me a story." He rested his chin on her shoulder.

"There are people to the south of here with flat faces, who count things."

"I've seen them," he said.

"And people in the east who live in forests, in houses made of bark."

"I've seen them, too," Coyote said irritably. "Those are all regular people. I thought you would tell me something magical about Over the Water."

"Well. Over the Water there are people as dark as an obsidian knife, and people as pale as I am. And sand-colored people, and people with hair like fire, and others whose hair curls like the buffalo. Have you seen them?"

"No. I think you are making that up. People as magical as that would have magical things."

"Oh, they do. They have elephants and cathedrals for their gods and arquebuses and silk robes made out of worms' cocoons."

"Now I know you're making things up."

"Well, I'm not!" The Moon was indignant. Her ample bosom heaved, luminescent in the starry darkness.

"I don't imagine you even know what that is." Coyote pointed at Rain Child's pot on the ground below them. Now the clowns were sitting around it in a ring.

The Moon peered down. "That? That's just an old iron cookpot."

"What is iron?"

"The thing it's made of. I've seen lots of that."

"Where?" Coyote demanded.

"Over the Water." She looked bored. "I was going to tell you about the Emperor of China, who built a wall across his whole country."

"Why would anyone want to do that?" Coyote asked her, sidetracked. "The buffalo would come to the wall and bump their noses and then they would turn around and go away. That's silly."

"They don't have buffalo." She frowned, thinking how to explain it. Coyote was part of this place, like the rocks and the prairie. Once it had all been one land but that was so many years ago she had lost count. When it had separated, the spirits that came along to make the worlds had made them out of the lands they knew, because they were part of the land themselves. As well try to explain buffalo to an Arctic ice sprite.

"Tell me this, Most Beautiful, and I will believe you: what is that iron pot made of?"

The Moon tried to remember what she had seen. "It is made by heating stone with iron ore in it, heating it very hot, and the iron comes out of it. It is a metal, like the copper that the people in the southeast work, but very much harder."

"Melting stones. It told the truth."

"What did?"

"The pot. I half didn't believe it."

The Moon patted his knee again, maternally. "You land spirits are all the same. You think every place must be like your place."

"How do I know this iron ore?"

The Moon thought. She noted the pointed ears pricking through his black hair, and the twitch of his long nose. "I imagine you could smell it."

Coyote filed that thought away. It was clear that he would have to find it. Or maybe that dog, the little gray bitch that the girl owned, could, if he helped her. "How do you heat it?" he asked.

"Am I World-Maker?" The Moon was beginning to be a little irritated.

He nuzzled her neck. His hair blew around her face in a dark cloud. "No, I am. You are World-Instructor. I will sit at your feet."

She relented. "The fire has to be very hot, hotter than wood will burn."

"Charcoal? Charcoal!" Coyote said happily. "Thank you, Most Luminous." He licked her ear.

"Dear boy. You're really very nice." She could feel his hands slipping up under her dress, and she thought, *Well, why not?* as he put his mouth on one round, glowing breast, his cold nose pressed between them.

Clever watched her two-legged person's pot. That was her job, to watch things that belonged to Rain Child. She had watched it all night from behind a bush while the Holy Clowns were dancing and howling around it, and while they were sitting in a circle watching it themselves. It never did anything, that night or the next day, and finally they had given it back to Rain Child, so now Clever was watching it in the tent again while Rain Child slept.

Clever put her nose on her paws and blew out a long, snorty breath. Uncle Howler had carried the pot to the fire in the central camp where the Dry River people came to tell stories and sing, and said to Spotted Colt, "The Moon says the pot doesn't know how that happened to your baby."

Clever hadn't really understood him because Uncle Howler didn't speak Dog—at least, not very often—but she could tell that Spotted Colt wasn't sure about what he had heard. But they had let Rain Child take the pot home again in the afternoon, so here they were with it. It didn't seem like anything to make a fuss about to Clever. You couldn't eat it and it had a funny smell. You could cook in it, but dogs didn't see the point in cooking things anyway. Food was much better for you raw and whole, and then later you could throw up the parts that didn't agree with you.

An owl *hoo-hooed* somewhere outside and there were faint whisperings of field mice and shrews in the grass. Clever's nose twitched. Somebody else was outside, too. All the human people in the Dry River camp were asleep now—except for old Grandmother Whooping Crane, whose legs hurt her at night, and Rabbit Dancer, who was sitting up late talking to spirits. Clever stood up and stretched, forepaws extended, back end in the air. She spread her toes wide, and opened her jaws in a long yawn. When everything went back in place, she shook herself and padded to the tent door, nosing past the flap.

She peered out, black nose sniffing the dark. Some four-legged person was in the camp. At first she thought she didn't know him, and then she thought she did. She examined the scent, sifting it from the smells of mice and water and a hunting snake and the newly dug ground where they had buried the dead baby. It was familiar. At first she thought it was her mother, and then she thought it was Toad Nose's dog that she had mated with last fall. And then the wind shifted a little, and there was a wild scent, like the underside of a downed tree, or an otter's den in the riverbank. Then her hackles went up because threaded in with the others was a strong scent of coyote.

Clever lifted her lips and bared her teeth. The camp dogs, who were mostly half coyote themselves, maintained a wary truce with the wild ones. The coyotes were allowed to pick through the midden when the camp dogs were through with it, and the dogs knew better than to go into the wild ones' territory alone. But a coyote trotting straight through the Dry River camp as if he owned it—

that was not allowed. Clever gave a short bark to let the other dogs know what was going on, and went out to tell him so.

But it wasn't a coyote. It was sitting by the fire in the center camp (the fire which had been out earlier when everyone had gone to bed), its dark shape looming against the glow of the embers, bigger than two coyotes. She thought at first it was a wolf, and braced herself, waiting for the other dogs to come out and help her drive it off. But nobody came. And now it smelled like a human person, which made her head spin.

Clever felt uneasy in her skin and remembered the thing that had come twice and sat inside her head. "Go away," she said to the wolf, or person, or whatever it was.

"Oh, come and play with me," it said in Dog. It seemed to ripple in the firelight, like a fish flashing in water, and then the other scents blew off it, and all she could smell was dog smell, friendly and enticing.

"I have to watch my person's pot," she said dubiously. True, it was night, and all the other two-legged people were asleep, so no one was going to bother that pot.

"It won't go anywhere," the dog said. Or maybe it *was* a coyote. It was very hard to tell. "In fact, that's what I came to see you about."

"I'm busy," Clever said. Maybe she was coming into season, but she didn't feel in the mood.

"Smell that air!" the strange dog said.

Clever sniffed.

"Who could stay inside all night, ruining their nose with woodsmoke, when they could be chasing rabbits? I know where their warren is. Not far from here."

"Really? Rabbits?"

"Lots of them."

"Well . . ."

"Oh, come on."

"Where did you come from?"

"Oh, just the next valley over." He cocked his head,

yellow eyes gleaming. She could see rabbits in them, bounding through the brush under a bank."Come on." The big dog stood up, looked toward the north side of the camp, and then back over his shoulder at her. He cocked one ear up and one down and wagged his tail.

Clever sniffed. There was just the faintest scent of rabbits in the air. "I have to be back by morning."

"Of course." The big dog grinned at her. "We're always back by morning. What two-leggeds don't know won't hurt them."

He bounded away from her, flowing through the camp like fast smoke, dodging around tents, leaping over fire pits. Clever followed him, running hard to keep up. A few horses, tethered outside the tents, half raised sleepy heads as they passed. The horses in the herd beyond the camp dozed in the moonlight and didn't seem to see them. The big dog galloped past them, and slowed to let Clever catch up to him on the other side.

"Sorry." His tongue hung out mischievously from one side of his mouth. "I don't like to upset the horses."

He began to run again and Clever found that now she could keep pace with him. They ran through the wild grass and through the rabbit brush and the greasewood bushes, past stands of cottonwood and sycamore, ghostly in the thin moonlight. The moon glazed the rustling surface of the Grass and the faces of the distant mountains, leaving them milky and mysterious.

They ran through the buffalo grass and through folded valleys hidden in its glimmering expanse. The stars wheeled over their heads and flickered in the big dog's eyes as they loped side by side down a dry wash, the sand scattering beneath their paws in a white spray. Clever's tongue hung from the side of her mouth and the scents of the night filled her head. The big dog leaped over the side of the wash and Clever scrambled after him, digging into the bank with her back feet.

He stopped to wait for her, eyes bright. "Come on!"

They ran again, down a narrow valley with a stream at its heart, and a tumble of low hillocks above it. The scent of rabbits came as clear and sharp as a flash of light.

They were feeding in the moonlight, many rabbits, moon-washed rabbits, flickers of movement, of ears and eyes, many rabbits, many many many rabbits.

Clever and the big dog plunged together into the herd, careening joyously through the grass as the rabbits scattered around them. They ran, drinking in the night air, the rabbit scent, the wet grass as it tore under their feet. In a frenzy they circled, reversed course, skidded on their hind legs, zigzagging with their prey, blood pounding in Clever's heart, rabbit smell, glorious, delicious rabbit smell in every hollow and passage of her skull.

The rabbit ran and she was gaining on it, faster, closer, smell of it dizzying, hot rabbit taste in her mouth, a quick shake and it hung from her jaws, and now she was ravenous, she wanted to eat it *now*.

The big dog had caught a rabbit, too, and grinned at her around its limp form. They grinned at each other and trotted to the stream bank to eat. When there was nothing much left except feet, they drank at the stream, blood and grease drifting from their muzzles into the current, the cold water lapping around their paws.

The big dog lifted his head, his snout dripping, and sniffed the air.

"What are you looking for now?" Clever asked him. Maybe there were more rabbits somewhere else. These here wouldn't come out of their dens again tonight.

"Rocks," the big dog said. "Magic rocks."

"Who wants rocks?"

"Two-legged people want rocks."

"That's not dog business." Clever was uninterested. "Two-legged people make life hard for themselves wanting things like rocks."

"These rocks would make your person very happy," the big dog suggested.

"Next time I come here, I'll bring her a rabbit. That will make her happy."

"You'll forget. You'll eat the rabbit."

"Maybe," Clever conceded.

"You wouldn't want to eat the rocks."

It was complicated and it was making her head spin.

"These rocks smell like that pot thing your person has," the big dog said confidentially. "Have you ever smelled rocks like that?"

"I don't think so." Clever yawned. Rocks weren't interesting.

"If you do, you must tell me right away."

Clever was sleepy, and full of rabbit. She closed her eyes. She was dreaming rabbits when the big dog beside her said, "Uh oh."

Clever sat up, nostrils widening. The big dog's nose twitched and he had swiveled his head northward. There was no question what he was smelling now. In an instant the air was heavy with it, the sulphurous smell of a storm coming. As Clever watched, the first crack of lightning split the black sky to the north, and his face flashed in front of her, huge ears pricked, coat star-spangled like the sky. His afterimage wavered bluely, four-legged, two-legged, four-legged. Sparks formed around it. He shouted something at the sky.

"I have to go home!" Clever looked around her, panicked. How had they got to this place?

"This way." The big dog leaped forward into the night and she followed him. The storm crashed around them, and lightning struck the place they had been. She could just see him ahead of her, his coat limned with a faint radiance, sparks flowing from the brush of his tail.

"This way!" He jumped up, into the black air, and she followed him. Lightning struck again, singeing her tail, and they ran faster through the darkness, while the storm beat around them. A crow blew by on the wind, its tumbled black wings flapping uselessly. The water battered her head and filled her nose, until she couldn't smell anything but the storm. Lightning crackled, illuminating the sky, strange shapes riding the wind.

The big dog shouted something angrily over his shoulder again at the sky and the Thunder Being answered him with a crack and a boom that exploded under their feet.

"Hurry!" The big dog nipped at Clever's flanks, driving her through the rain. She couldn't see him now, but she could hear him behind her, arguing with someone as they ran.

Clever ran faster and with a leap they fell out of the storm into the Dry River camp. Clever tumbled head over tail, bruising her nose, and ended sitting and snorting water at the edge of the Dry River midden.

When she looked around, the big dog had gone. The horses in the herd were stamping their feet and tossing their heads at the sky. The trees turned inside out, showing the pale undersides of their leaves in the wind. The storm was coming. She had only outrun it. The air banged behind her like rocks crashing together and she shot across the camp toward Flute Dog's tent.

8

A Box Full of Fleas

MUD TURTLE, SERVING HIS TURN AS NIGHT WATCHER, saw the clouds that had swept across the stars like a closing fist and thought that he must have slept. Shamed and horrified, he shouted a warning as the sky broke open and water poured down. The Dry River people woke and floundered out of their tents. The horses were screaming and thundering across the open grass, trying to outrun the banging in the sky.

Clever flattened her ears to her head and dived in through the doorflap just as Rain Child stumbled out. Rain Child pitched headfirst over her and Clever yelped and spun around, snapping at the air. The ground was a sodden mess of mud already and Rain Child picked herself out of it, spitting wet dirt. A river of mud flowed under the tent while Flute Dog, rain pouring from her face, tried to lash it to the ground. It swayed and buckled in the wind. Above the howling of the wind and the crack and boom of thunder they could hear another sound, a roaring voice that came from the stream bed. Water pooled around Rain Child's ankles as she staggered into the darkness, looking for the horses.

The water came down between the stream banks and washed Grandmother Jumping Mouse into the brush below the midden. It filled the tents and floated them away, uprooting their tethers from the dissolving earth. It lapped around Rabbit Dancer's knees while he held his horseleg staff and his basket of holy things above his head. It flowed into Howler's tent and sucked away his stores of herbs and fouled all his medicines with black mud. It swirled through the camp, growing faster and deeper, driving the people to higher ground, trailing their sodden possessions with them.

Spotted Colt put Evening Bat on his shoulders and with Green Gourd Vine they slogged and fought their way up onto the ridge behind the camp. All around them the Dry River people were clambering up the slope, driving the horses ahead of them, dogs swimming at their sides.

Howler found old Grandmother Jumping Mouse clinging to a thorn bush, screaming while the current tried to drag her away, and he put her over his shoulder and carried her up the ridge. Hopeful and her husband wallowed through the muddy water, carrying their baby in her cradleboard between them. The baby watched the sky lighting up with wide black eyes, too frightened to cry. The water pulled Auntie Soft Foot away from Uncle Head Carrier as they staggered out of their tent, their arms full of boxes and bags of clothes and tools. She stumbled under her burden and toppled, and he abandoned his load to catch her as the water rolled her head over heels into its muddy current.

Crane and Northwind Boy fought the wind and the rain for their tent and finally, cursing and crying, watched it tumble away, floating with the wreckage of the camp. A box floated by in its wake, lid askew, followed by a spear and a beaded shoe. The haunch of a deer came next, bobbing on the surface in the rising water. Northwind Boy and Crane began to swim.

Mud Turtle, the Night Watcher, stood on the riverbank, transfixed with shame, staring into the water as rain poured into his ears and the current rose. It was up to his chin before Toad Nose came by on a horse and pulled him out with a rope.

Flute Dog and Rain Child had caught Red Sandstone Horse and rode double on his back into the storm, looking for the others. Everywhere they turned the rain came like water poured out of a pot. On higher ground they could see, in the lightning flash, the river rising over its banks, inundating the remains of the camp, flowing outward in muddy torrents, drowning trees and bushes. The willows on the bank were a topknot of fronds that floated like river weeds in the current.

"They'll have gone to high ground," Flute Dog gasped.

"They'll have gone into next year," Rain Child said. "I never saw a storm come up so fast. Old Mud Turtle never smelled it coming."

"They'll be back," Flute Dog said. "We'll find them in sunlight."

"Maybe," Rain Child said pessimistically.

The rain plastered their hair to their faces as Red Sandstone Horse lurched up the muddy slope of the ridge, his hooves sliding in the deepening quagmire to which the rain had turned the trail. Rain Child clenched her fingers in his wet mane and Flute Dog wrapped her arms around Rain Child's middle as they lumbered up the slope. The wind howled around their ears and blew into their eyes and mouths.

At the top of the ridge, the Dry River people huddled together, horses, dogs and humans, with barely room to turn around. They cowered for fear of the lightning, and watched the water carry off their camp. With each flash they could see the brown water surging higher, and the wailing of mothers who had lost children rose above the sound of the wind and rain and the river's angry roar.

Flute Dog looped Red Sandstone Horse's rein through her arm and they stood beside him, letting his tall back hide them a little from the rain. Rain Child felt something cold and wet under her hand and saw that it was Clever, mud-caked and mournful, apologizing for snapping at her.

"Where is your mother?"

Clever leaned her sodden face against Rain Child's leg.

Rain Child sighed. Only was deaf now and her eyes were milky, and the river had probably gotten her. She was the same age as Rain Child. Only's mother Hungry had fed them both for three days when they were born. Hungry had died the year that Rain Child was ten. *If I was a dog, I'd be dying*, she thought. Did ten years seem longer to a dog than it did to a human? People said that dogs didn't know about death, but she thought Clever knew.

A hand touched her arm, and she saw Howler standing there, his dripping face slack with relief. He wouldn't reach over and touch Flute Dog, but Rain Child knew he wanted to. He had thought she had drowned. Howler had found a horse, too: his brown and white stallion, Mud-Spattered Horse, snuffling dejectedly at the wet ground, with a rope tied around his neck.

"I caught Most Foolish because he was afraid of a rag flapping on a tree limb and turned and ran back to me. I don't know where the others have gone." He made a gentle fist and smacked Mud-Spattered Horse on the neck.

"Ours are all gone," Rain Child sniffled. "And I can't find Only."

"Poor old bitch. She should have gone away lying by the fire, with a full belly."

A woman behind them screamed at him, a shriek like a hawk-torn bird. "My daughter is gone and you're talking about a dog?" She beat on his back with her fists.

"Hush! Hush now!" Other women pulled her away with uneasy looks at Howler. "Her husband is missing, too. He went to look for the child," they said, patting her. "She means no harm."

"I am not angry," Howler said mildly. "That the dog matters does not mean that the child does not. We are all alive in this place."

They led her away, wailing. Rain Child looked after her, while the hair prickled on the back of her neck. Lightning flashed, an explosion of fire that froze them all, limned in charged air, and thunder that left them deaf and speechless. Its blow threw Rain Child against Red Sandstone Horse's flank and Red Sandstone Horse to his knees in the mud. Afterimages flashed green fire in her eyes, burning into the rain. Howler and Flute Dog sprawled beside her. The woman who had beaten at Howler's back lay on the ground, her body hissing in the rain. Another flash came and they flattened themselves in the mud, but not before Rain Child saw her face. It was burned away by the lightning, a black charred path that ran down one side and left her foot blackened, too. Rain Child sat up in the mud and began to weep.

The storm slackened at morning, as the lightning seemed to fade before the sun's glare. The rain slowed from a downpour to a thin, gray curtain and then lifted, leaving a drowned land behind it. The brown water of the river covered the camp, strange bits of clothing and unidentifiable garbage floating on it. Above the level of the water were downed tree limbs and boulders washed from the hillside by the rain. The river roared its way down its widened channel, taking what was left of the camp with it. Beyond the ridge, on the far side, they could see another distant sodden land, but no standing water. A few moving black shapes on the horizon might have been horses. Except for the few that had been coaxed to take refuge on the ridge, there were no others.

Spotted Colt walked up and down the ridge line, counting noses, giving orders, whispering to the grieving. He paused beside the lightning-struck woman's body and said a few words into the sky for her.

"The water is going down," Howler said quietly, and they looked where he pointed. The river had begun to drop again, as if it were being sucked up by a giant face beyond the valley.

People began to move down the slope, and Spotted Colt put out a hand. "Wait. Not yet." He motioned for Toad Nose and Mud Turtle, whose face was wild with misery, to go and see, and they slithered down the trail, catching hold of the sodden brush for balance.

The others watched, whimpering and yearning like tethered dogs, while Toad Nose and Mud Turtle prodded with sticks at the mud to see if it would hold their weight. They bent over, poking in the sludge left behind, picking up small objects.

When the river dropped some more, three children and an old man and Only were left behind it. Mud Turtle and Toad Nose carried them up the slope, and their parents and relatives howled.

Howler picked up Only. "I will bury her," he said, and went down the other side of the ridge. Rain Child came, too, and together they scooped a grave out of the wet mud with their hands until Rain Child's fingers bled, while Clever watched them. They put Only in it, and piled a cairn of stones on the top.

"She was your sister," Howler said. "It is right that you do this. Don't let others tell you what matters."

"No." Rain Child scratched the top of Clever's head, muddy fingers in muddy fur, and shivered.

"Come along, child." Howler put his hand on her shoulder. "We had best start some fire, or we'll all freeze by nightfall."

What was left of the Dry River camp, a name that made the Holy Clowns shout and hoot as they danced about the wreckage, was a slick expanse of mud, smooth as poured batter, studded with small lumps of things that had once been people's possessions. Their feet made tracks in it like tracks in new snow. At the end of the valley, where the river channel narrowed and fell into a trough, everything else had ended, and could perhaps be dug from the dam of debris that had clogged the channel there. But here, where the center camp had been, was only the smooth glaze of mud, and sticking from it, like an offering on an altar, Rain Child's pot.

The ground made a sucking noise of regret as she pulled it from the mud. Its handle and single leg were still there, and it gleamed when she rubbed the mud away. The sand had scrubbed it clean inside and out, left it polished and luminous. When the sun struck it, light flared from its belly like silent lightning.

Rain Child hugged it to her. Old Grandmother Jumping Mouse wheezed and pointed with a muddy hand.

"Throw it away!"

Rain Child hugged the pot tighter and glared at the people encircling her. Toad Nose frowned and the husband of the lightning-struck woman, who had found his dead baby and then his dead wife, looked at it as if it were a snake.

"Give it to the storm."

"The storm didn't want it."

"Why should you have that thing when I have nothing?" He started toward her, and Howler stepped between them.

"Later. Go tend to your dead now. We have a world to remake. Out of mud, like the Beginning."

The Holy Clowns started dancing again, miming digging things up with shovels.

Spotted Colt told them, "Take what we can take back from the river before the water spoils it. Go. Now." He pointed down the channel toward where the debris had lodged. A group of women had started down that way already. "Night won't wait for you."

They excavated tents, thick with black mud, and baskets, sodden and almost unrecognizable. Someone's cradleboard, its beading stripped away. A box with no lid and a leather medicine bag with its charm still inside. A shoe. A dress of white doeskin, fringed and streaked with the remains of red and yellow paint. A length of rope. A buffalo skull. A broken bow. A handful of arrows, intact, their fletching turned to sodden goo. Flute Dog found their tent and tugged and pulled it from the mud.

They found six dead horses and one live one, and a dead baby caught in a tree. Rabbit Dancer circled around and around the tree with spells to send its spirit away to the land of the dead before he would let the parents take it down. Ordinarily, babies were encouraged to come home and be reborn, but Rabbit Dancer said that this one had the storm's anger in it. The father climbed the tree after it while the mother sat down beneath it and wailed, a terrible, howling grief that echoed off the sky. When he handed her the child, she clutched it and her eyes fastened on Rain Child.

Howler jerked his head silently at Flute Dog, and they took Rain Child away with them, still clutching her treasure. Together they dragged Flute Dog's tent back up the stream bank, sodden and heavy with mud. Up on the ridge, Uncle Head Carrier and his son Beaver had got some wet buffalo dung to burn. It gave off a towering column of smoke, like a signal fire. People had made drying racks from tent poles and were drying out hides and clothes around it.

"Take that thing away," Beaver said when he saw Rain Child and the pot.

"You are stupid," Rain Child said to him, but she walked away, wet hair still plastered to her face and her dress clammy with dirty water.

Uncle Howler scooped up an armful of the salvaged dung with a look that dared Beaver to argue with him, and went after Rain Child.

"Stop pouting and help me light this." With a look of sly triumph, he took a buffalo horn with a thatch of slow-burner inside from under his shirt.

Rain Child grinned suddenly.

"Clowns know what to take with them when it rains," Howler said, arranging sticks. He pulled another bag from under his shirt and extracted a small handful of kindling.

"Clowns are Most Wise," Rain Child said. Flute Dog squatted on the ground beside them and together the three of them blew on the fire.

"Why is everyone angry about my pot?" Rain Child asked. "It hasn't done this, it was just a storm."

"Mmm. Maybe, and maybe not. The Thunder Being is angry when he sends a storm like that. I heard him shouting up there."

"What did he say?"

"I don't know." Howler dropped some more tinder on the fire. "But if you hear people shouting in the next tent, you know they are angry even if you can't hear the words."

Clever was snuffling at the pot again, nostrils puffing little clouds of steam against its cold sides.

"What do you think it is made of?" Rain Child asked him suddenly.

"Who wants to know?"

"Well, I do. I think. Clever asked me once." She scratched her head.

"Clever?"

"I think she did."

Howler's eyes narrowed. "Well, you are Dog Sister, so maybe." He looked at Clever. "Do you talk to this child?"

Clever looked sad.

"There is nothing more pathetic than a wet dog," Howler said. "But I don't believe you."

"Why would Clever want to know what your pot was made of?" Flute Dog asked. "A person, certainly. I want to know myself. But not a dog. You were dreaming."

"She said that if we knew what it was made of, we could make more," Rain Child said. "I think she said that. And then everyone could have one." She sniffled. "And people wouldn't be jealous."

"They aren't jealous now, they are afraid," Howler said.

"Do you think my pot made it storm?"

"I think somebody did." The wet dung smoked, but it caught, and he arranged another piece on it.

"If the Thunder Being made a storm because he didn't like my pot, then why did he leave it for me?"

"I don't know."

Clever knew. She had seen the Big Dog, bigger than ever, fighting with the sky, and then she had seen him run away with the pot, the handle in his teeth. She lay down by Howler's fire and stretched out, inching her belly as close as she could get it to the warmth. By the time her fur was dry, she had forgotten that.

"Clever said it was made of melted rocks," Rain Child said. "I remember now."

"You can't melt rocks," Flute Dog said.

"That was what I told her."

"Can you melt rocks?" Flute Dog asked Howler.

"The mountains melted them, a long time ago," Howler said. "That is where obsidian comes from, and the black desert to the southwest of here. So anything is possible. But is it good to know? That is the question."

"I thought that was why the Great Mystery put us here: to think about things," Rain Child said rebelliously. "You said so."

"To think, yes. To pursue like dogs after a rabbit—well, maybe not, when the Thunder Being has just wrecked your camp. The Great Mystery also put us here to listen."

"I don't see how you know the difference."

"I know that some things can be known that should not be known," Howler said. His face was scratched with brambles, and the feathers in his scalp lock were plastered against his dank hair. He stood up, wincing as his knees creaked. "Pah! Cold water is bad for the bones. If you will listen, I will tell you a story about that while you scrape the mud off your mother's tent."

Flute Dog had spread the tent on the ground and was looking at them expectantly.

Howler said, "I will help also, since I have lost my tent. Perhaps Most Kind will give me a place at the back of hers."

A smile twitched Flute Dog's mouth, but she didn't answer him.

"This is about when Coyote asked Rabbit what was in his pack," Howler said.

Rain Child sighed. Coyote stories were always about how not to behave.

"It's not the right time of year for that," Flute Dog said.

"The world is upside down," Howler said mildly.

Flute Dog didn't say anything else. Rain Child took the salvaged scraper that Flute Dog handed her and started work on the tent.

"Coyote was walking along, seeing what he could scrounge—you know the way he does—" Howler began, "when along came Rabbit, boing, boing, boinging over the Grass, his long ears flying out behind him. Coyote saw that he had a little leather pack on his back."

"Ho, friend," Coyote said. "How are you?"

"Middling," Rabbit said, "just middling."

"It's a nice day," Coyote said.

Rabbit didn't answer.

"I see you have a pack on your back."

Rabbit didn't say anything to that either.

The pack on Rabbit's back was not very big, just a

middling-sized pack, such as might contain lunch.

"What's in it?" Coyote thought it must be something to eat, and he's always hungry.

"In what?"

"In your pack."

"What pack?" Rabbit said.

"The pack that's on your back," Coyote said, "and don't tell me there isn't one, because I can see it as well as you can."

"Oh, that pack. That isn't important. You wouldn't like what's in it, anyway."

"How do you know? Is it something to eat?"

Rabbit didn't answer, just went on boinging over the prairie. Coyote had to run to keep up with him.

"Is it back fat? I certainly would like a nice mouthful of back fat, and you know you don't eat meat. You wouldn't want it."

Rabbit didn't say anything.

"Well, then, is it tobacco? I sure would like a smoke. Come on, don't be stingy."

Rabbit didn't answer.

Coyote got mad. "Hey! Long Ears! Answer me! What's in the pack? If it isn't tobacco, is it a medicine bag? Come on, give me some—you're small and I'm big. You don't need all that." He smacked at Rabbit with his paw as they ran.

Rabbit didn't say anything. Coyote got madder and nipped at Rabbit's tail. "It isn't manners not to answer somebody when he asks you a question politely."

Rabbit just kept running. All he would say was, "It's nothing you would want."

"Well, let me see that nothing."

"No. You'd be sorry. And then you'd be angry with me." Rabbit shook his head.

"No, I wouldn't. I just want to see it." Coyote is made of curiosity. And besides, he still thought it was something to eat.

"I already told you, you wouldn't want what I have in this pouch," Rabbit said.

"Yes, I would!"

Rabbit didn't answer, just bounced on over the prairie, as if Coyote wasn't there, the pack flopping on his back.

In a rage, Coyote snapped at the pack and got it between his teeth. He jerked it and shook it, and it split open. The pouch was full of fleas, so many that no one could count them. They all jumped on Coyote, and Coyote ran off howling and yowling and scratching himself, black with fleas.

Rabbit yelled after him, "I told you so!"

But Coyote was too far away to hear him and he was making too much noise himself.

Rain Child chuckled, but she said, "It wasn't knowing what was in the pack that got him in trouble; it was opening it."

"They were the same thing. There is no way to know fleas without being bitten."

"If it wasn't Coyote, someone else would have let the fleas out," Rain Child said. "Something like fleas doesn't stay in a sack."

"That's what worries me," Howler said. "That may be what's wrong with your pot here."

"It's not!"

Howler didn't say anything else, just went on scraping Flute Dog's tent, and when it was clean, he helped them put it up. On Spotted Colt's orders, the Dry River people had moved their camp away from where it had been before the flood, up the slope to the top of the ridge. From the edge of the new camp, they could look down at the trampled mud that had been the old one, where the river still ran noisily with brown water.

Flute Dog let Howler come in and sleep with them, on beds cut from grass that was still wet and only half dried by nightfall. The chill soaked through Rain Child's blanket and she slept fitfully, feeling damp and hard-done-by. She had never seen a storm like that one, where the sky had just blackened the stars without warning, although Flute Dog said she had been born in such a storm.

Clever crept under the blanket next to her and Rain Child cuddled close, grateful for her doggy warmth. In the next bed, her mother was asleep with Uncle Howler beside her. It was warmer that way, Uncle Howler had said, and Flute Dog hadn't argued with him. Rain Child thought her mother was glad to have him there. The angry people who thought it was all the fault of Rain Child's pot didn't come any closer when they saw Uncle Howler.

In the morning, not even Howler could keep them away. They came in a delegation led by Spotted Colt, who was flint-eyed and angry. It was clear that this matter was beyond his control. A chief did not possess unlimited power; he was a man elected to lead the people in the way that they wanted to be led.

Rabbit Dancer was beside him, holding his salvaged horseleg staff, with Toad Nose behind, arms folded stubbornly. Rain Child could see Mud Turtle hanging back, his face still grief-stricken and miserable. He looked at Rain Child sadly from the edge of the crowd.

"Everyone is up early, for people who have had to remake the world," Howler said mildly, standing in front of the doorway to Flute Dog's tent. Rain Child looked past him apprehensively. Flute Dog pushed her back out of sight and came through the doorway to stand beside Howler.

"What do you want?" Flute Dog demanded.

"We have come to tell my sister that the foreign child has to leave us," Uncle Head Carrier said, assuming the expression of one who does an unpleasant family duty.

"What?" Flute Dog's jaw dropped. "*What?*"

"She never was a proper child," Auntie Soft Foot said. "And now this."

"Now *what*, Poison Tongue?" Flute Dog darted around Howler and stood nose to nose with Soft Foot, fingers balled into fists. Howler put his hand on her arm and drew her back.

"What have the Dry River people decided without even asking the Holy Clowns?" Howler said, looking very surprised, although Flute Dog could tell he wasn't. "The Dry River people must have acquired great wisdom."

"The Dry River people and the rest of the Holy Clowns have voted," Spotted Colt said quietly. "It seems to them that evil has come with the strange pot."

"And the strange pot with the strange child!" Toad Nose said.

"She probably isn't even a human person," Crane put in spitefully. She had a dark bruise spreading over her left cheek and she walked with a limp. "She's a buffalo spirit and we ought to give her back to them before they get angrier."

Green Gourd Vine, hanging back on the edge of the crowd with Mud Turtle, looked as if she wanted to speak. Spotted Colt turned and looked at her as if he could tell what she was thinking, and shook his head. Green Gourd Vine shook hers back at him and turned away.

"She's nicer than you are!" Hopeful said to Crane, having no tribal politics to consider.

"Whatever she is, she is ill luck," Toad Nose said. "And young women who do not know everything should listen to their elders."

Hopeful gestured scornfully at Crane. "I know more than she does."

"Yah, she has probably poisoned you," Crane retorted. "With her pot. You be careful that child of yours doesn't sicken."

Hopeful's lip trembled. "That is a wicked thing to say!" Her husband tugged at her arm, and Toad Nose stepped in front of them.

"It has been voted on."

"The women didn't vote," Hopeful muttered.

"The Grandmothers were asked," Toad Nose said, shocked. Not to consult the Grandmothers would be unheard of. Young women were something else.

"It has been voted on," Howler said. "To the shame of the Dry River people. Perhaps the Dry River people will wait a few days until they come to their senses, and vote again."

"It has been voted," Rabbit Dancer said. "It has been thought on, and voted."

"What if she gives up the magic pot?" Howler asked. "What if she gives that to you?"

"I do not want it!" Rabbit Dancer looked horrified, as if the pot might be going to leap out of the tent at him.

"I think it is full of trouble, myself," Howler said. "What if we take it into the Grass and give it to the Grass?"

"No! It was voted," Toad Nose insisted.

"Yes, it was voted!" They crowded around him, like dogs who have cornered something and want to fight with it.

"It was voted!"

"She's a child!" Flute Dog said furiously. In the tent, Rain Child rolled herself into a ball and put her hands over her eyes. Hot tears flowed out under them.

"She is *not* a child. She started to bleed over two years ago."

"She should have married by now."

"She is too old to be running with the horse boys."

"She is ugly looking."

"She's a water spirit, Flute Dog was foolish to bring her home!"

"She poisoned the river and the rain."

"She poured it out of that pot!"

They crowded closer, yammering until Rain Child, inside the tent, put her hands over her ears instead, blocking out their cries, that battered against her mother's voice and Howler's.

"Go away!" Flute Dog picked up rocks, washed from the ground by the rain, and began to throw them. "Go away!"

They backed off a little, arms up to shield their faces. "We will go, but she should be gone by nightfall."

"By tomorrow's tomorrow," Spotted Colt said. "We are not wicked, to send her out into the dark with no food."

Flute Dog hit Crane with a rock and she shrieked in fury.

Hopeful said, "Let me come in. Let me in to talk to her."

"You go away, too!" Flute Dog shouted. "All of you! Wicked! Wicked!" She picked up another rock.

They backed away, down the length of the ridge. Flute Dog saw that in the night they had moved their tents so that hers stood alone. Someone had left a skin of water on the ground, so that she wouldn't go to the river. "They think I will curse it," she said furiously, and kicked the skin.

"Not you," Howler said.

"We will go north," Flute Dog said. "We will go north, and we will curse them every step of the way."

"You will go?" Uncle Head Carrier came to Flute Dog's tent and shook his head in disbelief. "Howler says that you will go. Why should you go?"

Flute Dog stared at him in blind anger.

"My brother wouldn't like that, that *you* should leave," Head Carrier said.

"My husband will not like that you banished his daughter!" Flute Dog managed to say. "Maybe he will curse you, too."

"You should not go," Head Carrier insisted. "I have

come here to tell you that, even though it is dangerous, because I do not mind danger."

"Yah, you are afraid of a baby and a pot!"

Head Carrier looked affronted. "Even Soft Foot says you should not go."

"Soft Foot may lick my backside!"

"Now I see," Head Carrier said. "You are bewitched by this monster child. When she has gone you will come to your senses. It would not be good for the herd if you take your horses away."

"You are a fool," Flute Dog said. "And the horses have all run away. Let Spotted Colt come to me and tell me my daughter is welcome here, and I will stay."

But Spotted Colt could not, because it had been voted.

"We will go north," Flute Dog said, holding Rain Child, rocking her back and forth. "We will go north with our horses, and the people in the north will be glad to have us. We will never come to this evil place again."

"Am I a monster?" Rain Child pulled away and stared at her mother. Her face was slick with tears. "I can't see myself, except in the river, and sometimes the water in my pot. It reflects better than a basket, did you know that? But I still can't see."

"You are not a monster. Your hair curls. I think it is pretty." Flute Dog buried her face in Rain Child's hair. "And your skin is paler than most people's. That is very distinguished looking. The people in the north will think you are a sky spirit come to live with them. I just wish I could take your father's bones with us." She broke into tears.

"We can take his skull," Rain Child said. "Then you could talk to him." She sniffled miserably. "If I was dead, they wouldn't even let you put me in the skull ring, would they?"

"If you were dead, I wouldn't put you near them. I

would make you your own place with your father, and when I died, someone could put me there too and then we would be just our family. I *wish* he hadn't died before you were born!" Flute Dog began to sob again.

"I know where the horses are," Rain Child said quietly. "I heard you talking to Uncle Head Carrier. But I know where they have gone."

"All of them?"

"Ours, anyway. In the valley where the three dead trees are. At the west end, there's a canyon halfway down that cuts into the bluff. Painted Water Horse likes that canyon. I don't know why. But whenever Red Sandstone Horse isn't there, he tries to drive the mares up that canyon."

"He probably wants to hide them there." Flute Dog chuckled tearily. "First old Magpie Horse owned the mares, and then Red Sandstone Horse. Poor Painted Water Horse never got to be chief."

"Well, I will be surprised if they aren't in that valley."

"Painted Water Horse killed your father," Flute Dog said, staring into the cook fire. "Then he brought me you."

"I am trouble," Rain Child said sadly. "Uncle Howler won't want you to go away."

Flute Dog widened her eyes. "And is Uncle Howler my husband?"

When Flute Dog had packed everything except the tent they sat in and their blankets, she made a sleepy tea and gave it to Rain Child to drink, and then sang to her, as if she had been a baby.

Rain Child closed her eyes wearily. She could feel the people out there, waiting for her to go away, resenting her more because Flute Dog was going, too. When she went outside the tent no one spoke to her. They just stared and made crossed-finger signs at her as if she were a witch or a ghost. *I will haunt you*, she thought. *When I die, I will come back here instead of the Hunting Ground of the Dead, so I can haunt you. I will put dead frogs in your soup.*

She dreamed, and her curse frogs crept into the dream, hopping, hopping, puffed up alive again, green as grass. They hopped from green into brown and then into rabbit skins, until they were boinging across the prairie out of Howler's story. There were hundreds of them, each with a little pack on his back. Coyote was chasing them, trying to see what was in the packs, but they just kept bouncing. The bouncing made Rain Child queasy.

"They won't stop for me," Coyote said, skidding to a stop. "You chase them."

"I can't catch rabbits," Rain Child said, but she felt as if somehow she ought to.

"You need to see what's in the packs."

"I don't want to," Rain Child said fretfully. "It's fleas."

"Oh, no. It's something wonderful. Something that will make you a person out of story times, something that will change the world."

"I don't want to change the world." Forgetting what the Dry River people had done, just now in her dream it seemed a fine world.

"Yes, you do," Coyote said. "You want to change those Dry River people."

"Oh." She had forgotten that.

"With what is in those packs, you can be chief over them so they will be sorry."

A rabbit slowed, going past her, so that she could reach out and touch the pack on his back. It was soft, velvety as a deer's new horns. Her fingers slid along the straps.

"I will tell you the story the way it really happened," Coyote said.

Coyote and Eagle were hunting together. Coyote caught grasshoppers and Eagle caught rabbits.

"My chief, we make a fine pair," Coyote said. "Let us always hunt together."

"Very well," Eagle said. "But why is it that I catch all the rabbits?"

"My chief, that is because I am down here on the ground, and I drive the rabbits to where you can swoop down on them with your talons."

"Oh," said Eagle.

Then they came to a deep canyon. "My chief," Coyote said, "I can't fly. You will have to carry me across."

"Very well," Eagle said, and he let Coyote climb on his back. Coyote was very heavy, and he kept leaning down to look where they were going, which made Eagle overbalance. When they came to a river, Eagle said, "You can't fly, but you can certainly swim. I don't need to carry you over this."

Coyote didn't like to get wet, but he swam across the stream while Eagle flew. He didn't swim very well. He kept swallowing water, and he almost drowned. When he crawled out on the bank, he said, "Aaack! That was bad. When we come to another river, you had better carry me."

Eagle began to regret having chosen Coyote for a companion.

A little farther along, they came to a place where the spirits were dancing. The earth was still new then, and there was no sun or moon in the sky yet. Coyote and Eagle sat down to watch the spirits dance, and saw that they had a square box that made light. When they wanted a lot of light, they opened the lid and let a round yellow ball peek out. When they wanted less light, they opened the lid just a little, and a white ball looked out.

"This is something wonderful," Coyote whispered to Eagle.

"I think it is the sun and the moon," Eagle said. "I have heard of them."

"We should steal that box," Coyote whispered.

"No," Eagle said. "That would be wrong."

"But why should they have all the light? They don't take care of it properly. We should give everyone a bit of light. That would be fair." Coyote made it sound very reasonable.

"We could borrow it," Eagle said.

So when the spirits weren't looking, Eagle swooped down and snatched up the box in his talons, and flew off. Coyote ran after him, craning his neck up to the sky.

"My chief," he called up to Eagle. "Let me carry the box."

"No," Eagle said. "You aren't reliable."

"Oh," Coyote said, "but I am ashamed to let you do all the work."

"You would open the box," Eagle said. "Then these wonderful things we have borrowed would get away from us."

They went on, with Eagle flying and Coyote running along the ground under him. "My chief," Coyote called up, "people will talk badly about me if I let you carry this burden by yourself. Let me carry the box."

"I don't trust you," Eagle said. "You are too curious. You will open it."

"Oh, no, I won't even think about it. Oh, let me carry the box. People will say I am lazy and disrespectful for letting you do all the carrying."

"No. This box is too precious to entrust to a person like you."

Coyote went on running after Eagle, calling up to him, "My wife and children will no longer respect me, people will say around the campfire that I am lazy, they will tell stories about me and I will be shamed, when they find out that I let you carry this all by yourself."

Finally Eagle relented. "Will you promise not to drop the box?" he asked, hovering over Coyote.

"Oh, yes, my chief." Coyote sat down on the ground, looking up at him.

"Will you promise under no circumstances to open it, not even a peek?"

"Oh, yes, I promise."

Eagle soared down out of the sky, riding on the thermals, and set the box down with a last flap of feathers at Coyote's feet. "Very well, you may carry it a little way."

"Oh, you can rely on me." Coyote took the box in his mouth and began to run, while Eagle flew over him. He did as he said and didn't open the box, but it drove him crazy, knowing those magical things were in there, and wanting to take them out and look at them thoroughly—inspect them from all sides, nose them to see if they were hot or cold, taste them a bit to see if they were good to eat, bounce them, roll them over the prairie with his paws. But Eagle was up there, watching him.

Finally they came to some woods, stretching clear across the prairie. Eagle soared over them, and Coyote ran through the trees with the box in his mouth. He looked up over his shoulder. All he could see was the green canopy over his head. Eagle wouldn't be able to see him, either. Coyote slowed a bit. He found a thick patch of brush and burrowed into it with the box. Inside the brambles, he sat down and nosed the lid off it.

The sun flew out of the box, setting the brush and the trees on fire with its hot breath. Coyote yelped and ran out of the brambles. The sun whirled away to the very edge of the sky and all at once the world grew cold. The leaves fell from the trees and the grass turned brown and Coyote saw Eagle circling furiously above him in the smoke. He tried to hook the box out of the burning brambles with his paw and put the lid on it, but before he could, the moon flew out, too, and blew away after the sun to the outer rim of the sky. Snow began to fall, putting out the fire in the brambles, and freezing Coyote's toes.

"You idiot!" Eagle called down to him, flexing his talons. "I told you not to look! I should have remembered that you never keep a promise. Now we have winter; just

look what you've done! We could have kept them close to us and had summer all year if you weren't so stupid!"

Coyote sniffed the snow-covered ground. The snow went up his nose and he couldn't smell anything.

"Hah!" Eagle said. "Now *how are you going to eat?"*

Coyote saw that there were tracks across the snow, hundreds and hundreds of them, of mice and turkeys, rabbits and deer. Coyote could see that one of the deer, a little one, was lame. He grinned up at Eagle, his tongue lolling out, red against the snow.

"Every difference has its use," he said.

9

The Wild Dogs

RAIN CHILD WOKE BEFORE DAWN TO FIND FLUTE DOG shaking her. "Get up. We are going."

"It's dark," Rain Child said.

"It won't be," Flute Dog said. "I want to leave before those fools are awake."

Rain Child got up and they rolled up her bed and piled it on the travois with their packed belongings. Rain Child could feel the bump of her pot in its pack. When she laid her hand on it, it felt warm, like a dog. Flute Dog was taking down the tent and Rain Child helped her pile it on the travois, too. A horse snorted in the darkness beside Red Sandstone Horse and Rain Child saw that it was Mud-Spattered Horse, tethered to a stake.

"Where did he come from?"

"Hush," Flute Dog said.

"Are we stealing him?"

"We are borrowing him."

"Does Uncle Howler know that?"

"Not yet." Flute Dog had started packing as soon as

Uncle Howler had gone away last night—to argue with the Holy Clowns some more. "*You* ride him," Flute Dog said.

Rain Child swung onto Mud-Spattered Horse's back and talked to him the way Uncle Mud Turtle had taught her. He tossed his head. Flute Dog, who was the smaller of them now, hitched Red Sandstone Horse to the travois and got up on him. They set out with Clever padding beside them and the travois bumping behind, making a soft *scritch scritch* on the ground. The half-moon still hung on the edge of the sky, and Rain Child kept Mud-Spattered Horse tight beside Red Sandstone Horse as they circled around the sleeping camp, so that the Night Watcher would see only one of them. On the other side his dark silhouette sat beside his fire, waiting for daylight.

When they were clear of the camp, Rain Child looked back once over her shoulder. The tents were just visible in the dawn light, shapes misty and uncertain. The horses left in the horse herd lifted their heads as the outcasts passed. *We could steal some more of them*, Rain Child thought. She looked sideways at Flute Dog and suggested it.

Flute Dog shook her head. "Then they would chase us."

Rain Child wondered how Flute Dog knew Uncle Howler wouldn't chase them. She didn't look back again until they had gone far enough that there was nothing to see, just some black ants on the horizon. She wondered what they would do if there were no horses in the Valley of Three Dead Trees. Maybe they should have stolen a mare instead, although Uncle Howler hadn't had a mare. His had all run away with everyone else's. Rain Child still didn't know why Flute Dog had taken his stallion, and Flute Dog wouldn't say. "We need another horse to ride," was all she said, but if they found their own, then they wouldn't. Rain Child didn't think Flute Dog was planning to let Mud-Spattered Horse go.

The rain had flattened the grass in the Valley of Three

Dead Trees, and downed the limbs on two of the trees, so that they stood like headless sentinels at its mouth. As they rode down the valley, Red Sandstone Horse whickered and danced under Flute Dog, shaking the travois. Flute Dog grinned at Rain Child. When they turned up the canyon mouth, he screeched in indignation.

"He can smell Painted Water Horse up there with his mares," Flute Dog said. "You were right."

"I will go get him," Rain Child said. "Red Sandstone Horse will want to fight him." She handed Mud-Spattered Horse's rein to Flute Dog and set off up the canyon on foot with a coil of rope, keeping an eye out for the snake people who had been disturbed by the rain, and would be out sunning themselves. As she walked, she whistled through her teeth. If they were lucky, Painted Water Horse would have all their mares.

He had five, all but one; but he had one of Toad Nose's instead. Rain Child decided it would be a shame to leave that one, when the poor thing probably couldn't find her way back to the Dry River camp. They were grazing at the high end of the canyon beside a tangle of downed trees, where the shrinking torrent had left a round water hole. She walked up to Painted Water Horse, whistling to him. He pricked his ears and snorted at her proudly.

"Old fool. So you thought you would be a Horse Chief? Red Sandstone Horse will bite you when he finds out." She rubbed Painted Water Horse's nose. He snorted some more and told her about the big storm and how the rain had washed all the trails away, and how wise and clever he had been to bring the mares here.

"Oh, Most Wise. Most Clever." Rain Child slipped the rope around his nose. She grabbed a handful of his mane and swung herself onto his back. Together they rounded up the mares and began to drive them down the canyon.

Red Sandstone Horse was waiting for them. He shrieked imprecations at Painted Water Horse and tried to round the mares up himself, bumping the travois behind him.

"We had better put that on Whitetail Horse," Rain Child said. "He'll knock it to pieces. I ought to put it on you," she informed Painted Water Horse, as she slid off his back.

They shifted the travois, while Flute Dog pretended she didn't see Toad Nose's mare.

"Where are we going?" Rain Child asked finally. It was the question she hadn't wanted to give voice to, in case Flute Dog didn't know.

"North." Flute Dog kicked Red Sandstone Horse, and he danced forward, free of the travois. Rain Child led Whitetail Horse on a lead. Mud-Spattered Horse trotted along in the herd, seemingly happy to be there. You could steal a horse, Rain Child thought. They weren't like dogs.

North. North where? Her mother had said something about people in the north, but Rain Child wasn't sure that Flute Dog really knew where any were. And foreign people were dangerous. The Red Bow people made slaves of anyone they caught. How did Mother know these people in the north weren't like that?

We should just live by ourselves, she thought. *I can hunt. I am a better shot than some of those boys*. It was not approved of for girls to hunt, men said that their woman magic overpowered hunting magic and scared the game away, but women could and did when they had to. Dry River people were used to living apart, sometimes just a husband and wife together in the winter.

That was no different from Rain Child and Mother. Men only thought they were important. They could live by themselves and Rain Child could hunt, and they could raise horses and sell them back to the Buffalo Horn, never to the Dry River people, for the things that they wanted.

"We will live here on the Grass by ourselves," Rain Child announced.

"You will be lonely," Flute Dog said.

"I was lonely with Dry River people," Rain Child said sullenly. "I would rather live with just us. With two of us and Clever, we can take care of ourselves."

"We will see." Flute Dog rubbed her knee where it was beginning to ache in the evenings. What would they do by themselves when she was old?

We will be legend, Rain Child thought. *We will be the Horse Women that no one can catch, who have a magic pot that never breaks. Yah, we will steal their horses.*

They rode northeast until sunfall and camped where the Grass whispered along the bank of a shallow stream that seemed bound for nowhere in particular, so often did it loop back on itself, like a snake sunning. Flute Dog made a stew in Rain Child's pot with onions that grew along its bank, and some of the dried meat from their packs. There wasn't enough to last them very long—much of the food had been spoiled in the flood—but Spotted Colt had made the Dry River people give them all they could, and then some more that he had made Toad Nose find.

For tonight, it was enough to be warm and dry, with their bellies full. Rain Child began to untuck her tail from between her legs. She had felt abandoned and forlorn when the Dry River people drove her out of their camp. But now it felt more as if something around her neck had been untied, loosing her on the world.

The moon was waxing, and at night they sat in the tent with the doorflap open and the fire at their backs and watched it break loose of the horizon and float into the sky. Rain Child felt as if she might float with it.

The weather was still warm and the moon grew bigger and more luminous every night. Flute Dog said that they would find a winter camp in the northern hills, where there were caves that the Ancient people had used. They sang a Riding Song in the daytime and a Moon Song at night, and made stew from camas bulbs and onion and dandelion greens. Rain Child killed a rabbit with her throwing stick and danced a wild Victory Dance over it, her curly hair flying out in a cloud around her head. In the morning a flock of larks flew over them, their song cascading down like drops of water.

When the moon had grown full and shrunk again to a thin fingernail of light, they came to the border of the Dry River grazing ground, to the edge of unknown land. Flute Dog said now they were near where the Ancient people had camped. "Rabbit Dancer told me about them. They lived in caves in the hills and hunted with a throw-spear."

Rain Child imagined them, wild people dressed in uncut skins, children of the First Time, still half kin to the animal people. She could feel their bones just under her feet in the Grass.

There was something different here about the Grass. Or maybe it was just that winter was coming. She no longer had the sense of the Grass lazily sunning itself. It was growing brittle now, and crackled when you bent it in two. Mice ran through it, seeds in their mouths, burrowing into hummocks beneath the brown tufts. Something in this crackling Grass made the horses nervous. They were restless at night, and swiveled their big ears in circles, listening to whatever might call their name. Clever sniffed at the ground wherever they went, but if she could name what she smelled, she chose not to. Flute Dog and Rain Child saw no people, not even ghosts of the Ancients, only sometimes signs that a herd had been grazed this way once, or a camp had been here. At night their fire glowed like an eye in the dark sea of the Grass. They met a herd of antelope once, a buck and three does, but they couldn't get close enough to catch them. At dusk the next day they saw the dim shapes of wolves trailing the antelope. They trotted, tail-down, purposeful, along the riverbank. Clever watched them very quietly.

That night they camped in a valley in whose center a little stream meandered through the bottom of a steep wash. A trail ran down the side of the wash to the water and Rain Child could see that people had come this way before, but not for several moons. There were fresher prints of wolves or big coyotes in the damp ground along the riverbottom. Clever sniffed them and growled.

"Sit by the fire with us and don't take any foolish notions in your head," Flute Dog told her.

At night Rain Child saw the moon slice into the black sky through the smokehole over her head. The horses rustled in the tall grass outside the tent, grazing in a rope pen. Their dark eyes glinted with starlight. The Grass had looked very deep and very black to her when she had gone out to check on them, as if she and Mother were in a boat floating over its surface. She squatted to pee and gazed up at the stars hanging like chips of ice in the sky. The night was cold, and getting colder. Flute Dog had counted on her fingers and said that tonight was the equinox, when the day and night were the same length, one of the hinges of the year. Time to be in a Winter Camp. Whatever was abroad at night in the winter was always hungry.

In the tent, next to Mother's warm body, with Clever's moist dog breath in her face, Rain Child listened to the year turning. She fell asleep to the voice of the Grass and woke to the sound of horses screaming.

Flute Dog was already pulling on her boots, yanking her doeskin riding dress over her head. Rain Child bumbled into her clothes and flung herself through the door after her mother. Clever shot past her, between her legs, a gray streak of smoke. The sky was beginning to pale enough for them to see dimly. In the trampled grass outside the tent, they found the horses scattered, the rope pen a tangle of line on the ground.

The shrieking stopped and the air was still; as if it was waiting for something. Rain Child put her fingers to her teeth and whistled, and they stood still, heads cocked, listening. Clever was sniffing the ground and growling a low, singsong growl. No horses came out of the dim dawnlight. Flute Dog peered at the tangle of hoof- and pawprints in the soft ground.

"Get your spear." Flute Dog had taken her own as she ran from the tent.

Rain Child rummaged hers out of the jumble of the packs, and put her bow and quiver over her back for good measure.

Flute Dog had already started for the trail that led down the wash side to the water. On the edge she stopped and Rain Child and Clever caught up with her. The trail's lip was nicked with clumps gouged out by running hooves, and as the light paled they could see where a frantic animal had half slid down the slope. Below, by the water's edge, five gray shapes crowded around a downed horse in the mist.

It was plain that Painted Water Horse was dead. His carcass was a bloody mess of torn-open belly and spilled, half-eaten entrails that steamed in the cold air. Flute Dog shouted and the gray shapes lifted bloody muzzles and bared their teeth.

"Wolves!" Rain Child said. Beside her, Clever's growl shook her whole body. Rain Child nocked an arrow into her bow and sent it into the middle of the pack. A dark shape yelped and ran off.

Beyond Painted Water Horse, Flute Dog and Rain Child could see Toad Nose's Mare trembling, her lead rope tangled in a thicket by the river, too afraid to tear her way out. Flute Dog started down the trail, spear leveled. Wolves never tangled with two-legged people unless they were defenseless. She picked up a rock and threw it.

The wolves backed away a little, but they didn't run. She shouted. One of them, the leader, advanced on her, and they saw that he wasn't a wolf at all. His pale coat was the color of sand, with darker splotches on his feet and face. Black lips drew back from his teeth in a snarl. A wild dog.

Clever shot by Flute Dog and launched herself at him with a furious growl. They exploded into a snarling tangle while the rest inched forward, eyes on Flute Dog. Clever snapped at the big leader's throat and he sank his teeth into her shoulder. Her teeth raked open his skull, and he let go and closed his jaws around her forepaw, snapping the bone.

Rain Child saw her mother in front of Painted Water Horse, jabbing her spear at the others. They were dogs, too: a white spotted one with a torn ear, a black dog, and a reddish-brown one with a fraying shred of rope around its neck. The one with the torn ear advanced on Flute Dog, hackles up.

The hair on Rain Child's neck stood up. Wild dogs were dogs driven off or abandoned by people who didn't have enough to feed them, or escaped from tribes that kept dogs for food. Some, with more coyote blood than dog blood, ran away to the wild of their own accord, but rarely did the wolves or coyotes adopt them. Instead they found each other, made their own packs. They were fearless, Uncle Howler had told her once. Wild dogs knew what wolves did not: that people could be eaten as easily as anyone else.

Rain Child nocked another arrow and aimed it at the dog with the torn ear. It grazed his side and he backed away, snarling. She heard Clever's leg bone snap.

Clever and the big sand-colored leader thrashed in a furious cloud, kicking up dirt and small stones. Foam dribbled from Clever's mouth and her breath rattled past her jaws, but she had sunk her teeth in the leader's flank and hung on, hopping on three legs, her right forepaw dangling. The leader had his teeth in the back of her neck, feet scrabbling for purchase. Rain Child abandoned her bow. She shortened her grip on her spear and drove it into the leader's exposed shoulder, a glancing blow for fear of hitting Clever. The point raked a bloody slice down his hide and he let go of Clever. Rain Child went at him with the spear again, shouting at Clever to let go, too, but Clever wouldn't. Rain Child kicked her, shortening her grip on the spear again, jabbing it in the leader's snarling muzzle. Clever let go, limping to her feet, mouth bloody.

"Yah! Get away!" Rain Child shook the spear at the leader, eyeing her bow on the ground. How quickly could she pick it up and nock an arrow? Faster than the leader could decide to go for her throat?

Clever limped between Rain Child and the pack leader, and Rain Child dived for the bow. She nocked an arrow and let it fly. The leader yelped and retreated. He knew about arrows. Rain Child sent another arrow into the pack and the black dog dropped, bloody foam dribbling from its mouth. The rest ran away into the brush.

Flute Dog pushed her way into the thicket and disentangled Toad Nose's Mare. Rain Child looked at the muddy slope up the wash and lifted Clever, cradling her in her arms. She trudged to the top while Flute Dog led the mare. The other horses had begun to come back, circling the tent and the tangle of the rope pen with wild, white-rimmed eyes.

Flute Dog whistled them up and tied them to the picket rope, driving the stakes deeper into the ground with a stone maul. "We will have to take turns at night," she said grimly, "sitting up."

Rain Child was splinting Clever's leg with two green sticks and strips cut from the travois bindings. Flute Dog didn't say, "The leg will likely get diseased and the dog die anyway," and Rain Child didn't look up as Flute Dog went into the tent and came out again with her butchering tools. There were some things you already knew. Flute Dog took Rain Child's bow and went down the trail into the wash again. Rain Child heard her howling a mourning song while she worked.

Clever's neck was torn, and a strip of flesh hung loose from her matted, bloody ruff. Rain Child dosed it with a smear of yarrow and pine pitch from the small store of medicines that Flute Dog had salvaged from the water, and tied a length of soft hide around it so that Clever looked like a hairy woman in a new dress. "Foolish," she said into Clever's bloody fur. "Most foolish. That dog was bigger than you are."

Clever felt very sorry for herself, but proud. She looked mournfully into Rain Child's eyes and licked her hand.

In a while Flute Dog came back up the trail with Painted Water Horse's meat, dragging it on his hide, grunting and puffing over the ridge. She had scrubbed her face in the water, but her eyes were red. "I don't know why I'm crying," she said furiously. "That horse killed your father. Then he found me you," she added sadly. "He was always a Finding Horse and a Losing Horse. Now he has found us a lot of meat." She sniffled and rubbed her arm across her face.

The other horses snorted and swiveled their ears at the smell of Painted Water Horse on his own hide.

"Those dogs will come back if we don't burn the bones," Rain Child said. She got up. "I'll do it."

"Be careful," Flute Dog said. "They're as like as not to hunt in daylight."

Rain Child got the ax and the slowburner in its buffalo horn and made her way down the trail again, the bow over her shoulder. The flesh between her shoulder blades itched. She could feel the sand-colored pack leader watching her from wherever he had gone. Wild dogs were a wrong thing, a contradiction, Contrary Dogs, moving backward in their world. Contraries were holy when they were people, dangerous when they were dogs. *I'm a Contrary too*, she thought. A wild person. Her jaw jutted out. *I am not afraid of that dog. I am more contrary than he is.*

Painted Water Horse lay naked where Flute Dog had left him, his ribs an open cage, the legs shorn of hide and hoof, his head staring at her, surprised. Flesh clung to the bones in bloody tatters, and blood soaked the ground. Rain Child piled buffalo dung, the staple fuel of the Grass, inside the carcass, and what brush she could find around it, and lit it from her slowburner of shredded sage bark, blowing on the fine, dry twigs to light them. When they were blazing she prodded them into the heart of the ribcage where she had packed the dung.

The smell of blackened meat and fat rose from the wash. Flute Dog ignored it and went on methodically cutting up the horseflesh and laying it out in strips. It would dry in the sun and then they could pack it on the travois. They couldn't afford to waste meat.

Clever hobbled out of the tent, her front leg stiff in its splint, nose twitching. Flute Dog shied a rock at her, but gently. "No! When it is dry. Or tonight, when I've cooked some. Not now." They couldn't afford to convey to a dog that horses were game, either. That was what the wild dogs had known. And a dog who knew that secret couldn't be kept.

Rain Child stayed in the wash until the carcass was burned to grease and blackened bone, and then she poured water on it so some stray spark might not set the Grass alight. It took a long time. Flesh was hard to burn, and took the white-hot heart of the fire to consume it.

It was afternoon by the time she had finished. When the fire was out, she took the dog she had killed and dragged it down the stream bank, to the place where they had seen the prints of the pack coming to water, and left it there, stretched out in the torn-up grass and river stones, flies collecting in its mouth. The wild dogs were nowhere to be seen but she could feel them, hidden in the Grass, waiting.

As Rain Child came back up the trail, Flute Dog was arranging a makeshift drying rack of travois poles. Rain Child began to build a wood fire, a big one, beyond the rope pen, laboriously cutting wood in the wash where the only trees grew, their feet in the water of the stream. She laid another opposite it, and two more at each side, so that tent and horses were enclosed within their four points, the magic number, the four directions.

"Dogs aren't afraid of fire," Flute Dog said when Rain Child had dragged the third pile of logs and brush past her, towing them on the travois hide.

"They will be afraid when I set their tails on fire. Anyway, these have been wild a while. Maybe they have forgotten." They had forgotten to be tame, forgotten the companionship of the hunt and the fireside. Or maybe they remembered, instead: a booted foot in the ribs, a stick on the back. *You are a wild dog, too*, they said to her out of the Grass.

"I am not."

"Your people drove you out."

"We wanted to leave, Mother and I and my pot."

Rain Child looked around her. She could hear them, could feel their feral faces and brown eyes watching her out of the prairie grasses, but they weren't there. Her long shadow flowed across the prairie: a tall, storklike person with a tiny head, bending to the ground. Past it the tall, huge-footed horses were painted flat across the grass. The dogs were transparent shadows in the pale light beyond.

Clever saw them, too. Flute Dog had put a rope around her neck, and tied her to the tent pole, when she had tried to go out and chase them. They were foreign dogs, or worse yet, dogs that belonged to nobody and ought to be chased.

"They will eat you, Little Sister," someone said, and Clever saw the Big Dog standing by the drying rack. His coat was pale now, the color of the sandy pack leader's, and his hair ruffled in the wind like the waves in the

Grass, so that it was hard to tell where the Grass stopped and he began.

Clever looked very sad and showed him her splinted leg. The hide bandage around her neck kept her from chewing the splint off, which she wanted to do. "I am supposed to chase those dogs away."

"I have been watching them," the Big Dog said, as if that made it all right.

"They are wild," Clever said disapprovingly. Coyotes were wild; dogs were dogs, even when they were part coyote, or they left with the coyotes. These were both and neither, which upset the balance of things. "Are they yours?" she asked the Big Dog.

"Not exactly. Not yet. They still belong to two-legged people."

"Which two-legged people?"

"The man who beat him with a shinbone. The man who set her to fight a wolf to see if she could kill it. The woman who tied her with a rope and never fed her. Those things stay twisted in the heart, and they own you."

"Oh. They ate our horse."

"Everything is edible." Clever saw now that the Big Dog had a blackened bone in his mouth. He lay down beside her and cracked it, licking the marrow out. The smell enticed her. "Have you found the rocks that pot is made of yet?" he asked.

Clever tried to think about the pot. She remembered hunting rabbits, and then the rain. "The pot made all the other two-legged people angry," she said finally. "I don't know why."

"Where is it now?"

"On the fire."

The Big Dog went to the cook fire and stuck his nose in the pot.

"They will throw rocks at you," Clever told him, but Flute Dog didn't look up from her drying rack, and Rain

Child was across the square of fires, kindling the last one. The Big Dog tasted the stew in the pot and licked his muzzle.

"There are some rocks near here that are the right rocks, I think," he said. "Your person needs to get them very hot in a fire. A charcoal fire, in an oven," he added.

Clever yawned. She didn't understand him very well, although he was still speaking Dog. The words shimmered at the edges with meaning she couldn't comprehend. She closed her eyes, thinking of rabbits, and of how she would bite the wild dogs' throats out if they came near her horses again.

The Big Dog touched his nose to hers and Clever saw suddenly how small she was, much smaller than the wild pack leader. The Big Dog's own wild smell overwhelmed her. She whimpered. The Big Dog sniffed at her splinted leg and licked it. "Stay in the tent until that heals," he said. He walked into the prairie and turned into grass.

Flute Dog found the burned bone that the Big Dog had dropped, and blamed it on Clever. "Although I don't see how you got down there to get it," she told her, hands on her hips, puzzling over Clever. Clever looked happy and wagged her tail to tell Flute Dog that she hadn't stolen the burned horse bone at all, it had been the Big Dog, the Other Dog, the Ghost Grass Dog.

"Never mind," Flute Dog said. She took a shovel made from a buffalo blade bone and went down into the wash to bury the charred remains of Painted Water Horse's carcass.

The wild dogs came back in the night and ate the body of the dead dog instead. Or at any rate, they dragged it off. Flute Dog supposed they ate it.

"Maybe they buried it," Rain Child said sleepily, when Flute Dog told her in the morning. She had sat up half the night watching in case the wild dogs came back, and instead they had gone up the wash on silent feet.

"Have you ever known a dog to do anything with something dead besides eat it?" Flute Dog asked.

"Maybe they are people bewitched into dogs." Rain Child didn't really think so, but there was some enchanted quality about them, dangerous as they were.

"Dogs bewitched into behaving like people, more likely," Flute Dog retorted.

"Then maybe they buried it," Rain Child insisted. She liked the image of that. Dogs digging a hole, conducting a dog funeral, with dog prayers. Maybe they buried a bone and a dead rabbit in the grave with it, if it had been an important chief dog.

Flute Dog looked at her oddly. "We will not be able to stay out here by ourselves if you go mad," she observed.

Rain Child giggled. She felt light-headed and as if she might see unexpected visions. "If we stay out here by ourselves, I will go on a vision quest," she announced. "And then I will find a guardian spirit who will help me hunt."

"You might," Flute Dog conceded.

"I will." Rain Child liked the idea. She took hold of it the way she would a turtle snatched from the river and looked at it from all sides while it paddled its feet in her hand. It was definitely an idea that was going somewhere. If she let it loose it would walk up over the low, grassy hills to the north and take her with it. "I will do it now," she said.

"And leave me to fight wild dogs?" Flute Dog inquired.

"No, I won't go so far I can't hear you. Just to the fire, there. And then I can watch for the dogs and my guardian spirit too."

"Then I suppose you don't want any breakfast."

Rain Child's stomach rumbled, but she said, "No." She

had hold of the idea now, or it had hold of her. You couldn't see visions on a full stomach. Anyone knew that. "And now is a good time because we have to stay here while that meat dries."

"I see." Flute Dog chuckled. "You can just tell your guardian spirit that you managed to squeeze him in between drying the meat and making some new shoes, when you had a morning free. That is why women don't go on vision quests," she added under her breath.

But Rain Child refused to be deterred. She dug a hole with the buffalo blade shovel and made a tent over it with blankets and brush from the stream bed. While Flute Dog watched her skeptically, she piled rocks in the nearest fire pit and handed the shovel to Flute Dog.

"When they are hot, you bring them to me," she told her mother imperiously, and stripped her clothes off. She disappeared into the tent with a waterskin.

"Very well, Most Wise, but don't stay until you faint," Flute Dog said, when she brought her the first rock on the blade of the shovel. The sweat bath at least would do her good. Misery and blame and bewilderment were things a prudent person sweated out of themselves occasionally in the steam, in order to live in balance.

Rain Child took the shovel from her and laid the rock in the bottom of the hole. She knew what her mother thought. Her mother thought she was trying to be too like the men and that was what had gotten her driven off from the Dry River people. If they were going to be women alone, Rain Child thought, she would have to be like men. Maybe someone had known that ahead of time. When Flute Dog had brought all the rocks, Rain Child closed her eyes for a moment, praying over them.

Grandfather, let me see what I need to see.
Make me pure of heart.
Give me eyes to see.

Let me know the earth, the air, the water,
and the fire.
Let me look in the six directions.

She took the waterskin and poured a fourth of it out onto the hot rocks. The steam billowed up in her face, scalding and heavy as a wet cloth. She breathed it in while the sweat rolled down her skin.

Grandfather, make me mindful.

She poured more water on the stones. Before she could ask for a guardian spirit to speak to her, she had to be pure, and purity meant knowing yourself, your dark secret unpleasantnesses as well as your virtues. You had to promise to change the unpleasantnesses, but to do that you had to look at them.

You who live on the edge of the Universe, hear me.

She poured out the third portion of the water. The steam glowed like the inside of a shell in the pale light that came through the hide. Rain Child's leg bones began to feel bendable, like cooked cartilage, and her arms heavy with the weight of the heat. She tore shreds from a handful of sage she had picked along the wash edge, and scattered it on the stones.

The scent rose from the sage and the hot stones like a Fool Dancer, dancing wickedness out and knowledge in. Rain Child's head swam and she sat down with a thud, counting her dark places—pride, temper, stubbornness. Her strange skin and stranger hair—but how could she change those? She looked at the ends of her hair and saw that the steam had curled them tighter, like wisps of brown cloud.

"Nothing wrong with that," a voice said out of the

steam. "Does Horse try to change his hooves to be like Deer? You aren't paying attention to the right things. Think on why you're here. Think on Fear."

Rain Child's head felt light now, as if it was just a skull in a skull ring. She poured the last of the water on the stones and thought on Fear. She thought on the Dry River people and her pot and why they had driven her off. By the time she knew for certain that it had to do with fear, and that it was theirs and not hers, the steam had dissipated, condensing like raindrops on the hide walls. Rain Child stood up and stretched, her knees buckling a little.

The light was bright and blindingly white when she opened the blanket flap and stepped outside. She spread her arms wide for balance and wavered down the trail to the stream to plunge her whole body into the shallow current and let the icy water jerk her back into the world.

The sun sparkled in the water drops in her eyelashes, making bursts of light across the sky, which was a deep blue, like the heart of a turquoise. Rain Child burst from the water and danced a quick step up the stony bank, past Painted Water Horse's burned bones under their mound of earth and stones, past where the dead dog had been. She could see the marks where its pack had dragged it away.

Maybe Father can ride Painted Water Horse in the Hunting Ground of the Dead now, she thought. That thought cheered her further, and she scrambled up the bank and danced into her clothes while her mother watched her.

Rain Child scooped up her pot by its handle. "I need that." The pot still had mush in it from Flute Dog's breakfast, and she scraped it out with her fingers and dropped it into Flute Dog's bowl. Then she took the pot down the trail to the water and washed it carefully, rubbing every last bit of mush away with her fingers. When it was clean, she filled it with more sage and a small, shiny pebble she saw glinting in the water. It was white quartz, worn smooth by the current, so that it looked like an egg. If she put it in the pot, it might hatch something.

At the top of the trail, Flute Dog said, resignedly, "You are going to do this, aren't you?"

"I am." Rain Child stood with her pot swinging from the fingers of one hand, the other tucked against her hip, elbows out. Her feet moved in the dirt as she spoke. She felt giddy.

"I will be here when you come back," Flute Dog said. She watched Rain Child go, sighing. It wasn't that women didn't seek visions. Often enough they did, although not ritually, like the men. *Maybe I am just afraid of what will come*, she thought. What sort of creature might be guardian to a child like that, born of a rainstorm? For the first time she felt uneasily that Rain Child wasn't really hers, just someone borrowed, like her pot, a vessel holding who knew what.

Rain Child sat down cross-legged in front of the farthest fire, her pot between her knees and the flames. Something was wanting to talk to her. She could feel it. It wouldn't come right away, though. You had to sit and wait for it, and pray. She tried to concentrate on the stone in the pot as a focus for her prayers. The milky stone glowed yellow as yolk in the slanting sun.

It was dark when she looked up. The fires outlined the square she had drawn about their tent and the stone was moonlit and mysterious. Flute Dog was putting more fuel on the fires. The wood was gone. She came to Rain Child's and laid an armload of dung on it without speaking to her. Rain Child stared at the flames. To look at her mother would distract her.

When she looked up again, the stars had moved across the sky, and the chief of the wild dogs was staring at her from the other side of the fire, head outlined in the whispering grass.

"Are *you* my spirit guide?" Rain Child asked it suspiciously. She had hoped for Bear or Elk. She had forgotten she was Dog Sister.

"I will eat you if I can," it told her.

"I have a spear here, and my bow."

The dog didn't move. It looked at her out of the grass.

"And fire."

"We know fire."

Rain Child poked a glowing ember out of the fire in front of her. The dog backed away. Something else whispered through the grass. Rain Child squinted her eyes, but she couldn't see what it was. It seemed to be made of the grass, but she caught a whiff of coyote. The dog chief turned, snarling, the hackles rising on his pale back. The grass rustled again and he gave a sharp bark. He ran away along the edge of the camp, circling outside the fires, the gash Rain Child had made in his shoulder a dark red line along the pale fur.

"You shouldn't talk to people like that," someone said, and Rain Child squinted her eyes some more. She could just make out his shape now, pale as the pack leader had been, or the whispering stalks of grass. He came closer and sat down beside her by the fire and she saw that it was a big coyote, gnawing on a bone.

"Who are you?"

"I'm your spirit guide. Didn't you ask for me?"

Rain Child knew that you were supposed to take what the spirits sent you. "I suppose I did."

The coyote lay down and cracked the end of its bone open between its front paws. The bone looked charred.

"Where did you get that?"

"Oh. Just down there. It was just coming along."

"Were you with those dogs?"

"Certainly not." The coyote looked virtuous, as virtuous as a coyote can look while chewing someone's leg bone.

This was not how Rain Child had imagined talking to her spirit guide. She had imagined a cloud of white light, a misty form in a bright aureole, and a deep, soothing voice that would call her "My child." Her guide would tell her what taboos to observe in her life, and give her a token, a magical item with which to begin her spirit bundle.

She would paint her guide's sign on her tent and her horses, and when she found things that spoke to her of the things her guide had told her, she would put them in the bundle with the token. Rabbit Dancer's bundle had a stone egg and a piece of petrified wood, and a rock with a lizard's shape etched into it. All these things Elk, his spirit guide, had shown him, and told him about the Old Times.

Rain Child knew, because she had sneaked into Rabbit Dancer's tent to look. The Dry River tribal bundle held the sacred tobacco pipes, a medicine rattle made of a buffalo bladder and tail, elk teeth for wealth, a braided strip of otter skin for finding water, an eagle's claw, and the arrowhead that had killed Dark-of-the-Moon, the first chief of the Dry River people.

Rain Child studied the coyote. It looked solid, but there were stars caught in its tail. "Why am I different from everybody else?" she asked it.

"You are the New Person," the coyote said. "The New Person who is always coming along."

"I have this pot," Rain Child said. "You can't break it, or burn it in the fire."

"Oh?" the coyote said, not really looking at the pot. "It must be a New Person pot then." He gave particular attention to the bone, as if the pot didn't interest him.

"My people were afraid of it," Rain Child said. "They drove me out, my mother and me. We are going to be Horse Women with a Magic Pot and live by ourselves on the Grass."

"Oh, that isn't a good idea."

"Why not?"

"Well, how are you going to eat? And take care of

yourselves? Oh, no, you should be with people. There are some to the north of here," he added.

"I can hunt," Rain Child told him. "Even if I am a girl."

The coyote nodded. "Girls are more dangerous."

"Well, then."

"Something might hunt you."

"Why do you say I am a New Person?" Rain Child asked, ignoring advice she didn't want.

"There's always someone new. Your people are new everywhere since they have horses. Haven't you noticed that? And horses are new."

"Was the stranger woman who was my first mother a New Person? Mother says she looked like she was from the Cities-in-the-West, and they aren't new."

The coyote sat up and leaned over to nose Rain Child in the belly. "How do you think babies get in there? Do you think women find them under greasewood bushes and push them up in there?"

"Oh," Rain Child said. "Who was he?"

"Buffalo, maybe," the coyote said, nosing her hair. "But I don't think so."

"Who would know? Can you take me to someone who would know?" In the stories, spirit guides often took their chosen ones to the other world.

The coyote didn't look as if he was going to. He lay back down and cracked the end of his bone with his teeth. "The Moon might know," he said, after he had licked the marrow out.

"The Moon?" Rain Child looked up at the thin hook hanging in the sky.

"She knows woman business. Who fathers a child is woman business if anything is."

"How do I ask her?"

"Well, you can say prayers. She likes that. Or you could give her something."

"What?"

The coyote looked in the pot. "That stone, maybe. She likes things that look like her. She's really very vain."

Rain Child wasn't sure she should be listening to disrespectful talk about anyone as important and powerful as the Moon. "What taboos must I observe?" she asked him.

"Don't talk to wild dogs."

"Just that?"

"Oh, and you must find out what that pot of yours is made of."

"How?"

"The Moon says it's rocks. If you find the right rocks, she might be pleased and tell you about your father."

Rain Child nodded, liking that. Now she had a taboo and a task to perform. Surely they would give order to her life, even if a coyote had brought them. After all, she was Dog Sister. That would be why she was not allowed to speak to the wild dogs, they were too like her, a boundary too easy to cross. Things that were sacred to you were often also the things that were forbidden. The spirit world was one of opposites, opposed and related things, repelling and attracting each other at once. To keep the balance between them was the people's task.

"I am told that the right kind of rocks are to the north of here where some people are that your mother thinks you should live with," the coyote said. "Ask your dog which are the right ones."

"Clever knows?"

"Any nose knows. Any worthwhile nose."

"Oh." Rain Child's nostrils flared. She could smell coyote and the sage in her pot, and a faint scent that came from the pot itself and made her think, for some reason, of blood. But she couldn't smell the night the way the four-footed ones could.

"I will do as you say," she said humbly.

The coyote turned into grass and disappeared in the waving stalks.

She hadn't asked it why she was supposed to find out what the pot was made of, although she wanted to. But if you were given a task, you didn't ask your spirit guide why. It was the girl or the boy who met a magical being and trusted it and did as they were told who came home victorious, and the ones who didn't listen who were blinded, or eaten by monsters. All the stories made that clear.

The dawn wind blew around her and Rain Child shivered. She stood up, her legs rubbery, clutching her blanket. She went back to the tent to tell Flute Dog what the coyote had said, and that they would go north now the way Flute Dog wanted to, and find those people Flute Dog wanted to live with.

10

The Third Wonderful Thing

THE WORLD GREW COLDER AS THEY WENT NORTH, AND they rode bundled in hides and heavy boots and gloves.

"The hungry time is coming," Flute Dog said. They began to be glad they had Painted Water Horse. The wild dogs thought so, too, and followed them. Rain Child rode with her bow and quiver slung over her back.

It was one thing for the coyote spirit to tell her not to talk to the wild dogs. It was another to avoid doing so. Rain Child could feel them, always a little way behind on the trail. Clever knew they were there, and growled at the night out the door of the tent. Her neck healed with only a thin ridge of scar and a white patch in her ruff when the hair grew back in. It made her look as if she had been hit with a snowball. Rain Child and Flute Dog took turns sleeping outside the tent, rolled in blankets next to the fire, bow and spear handy. The dogs didn't come close enough to kill a horse again. The horses were angry and suspicious now, the dog scent in their noses no longer benign, and Red Sandstone Horse snorted and stamped his heavy hooves when he smelled dog. The dogs listened.

Instead they watched the herd and its two-legged guardians from a distance. Rain Child would see them running along a ridge line at dusk, their tails held high, so that she always knew it was them, and not wolves or coyotes, who wore their tails low. Unexpectedly, they rode into a spate of autumn days so crisp and blue and yellow that they were like fruit held in the hand. The sun bathed the Grass with honey light and the birds danced on the wind like butterflies. Rain Child and Flute Dog shed their heavy blankets and rode barelegged again, skirts hiked above their thighs, backs turned to the sun that was like a warm hand on the shoulders. They came to a river that pooled into a circular pond fringed with willows, where the current barely moved, eddying lazily over smooth stones in the bottom.

It was only mid-afternoon, but "We'll stay here," Flute Dog said, and Rain Child didn't protest. The water looked warm and glossy, like a pool that has lain in the sun. Her skin itched with a week's trail dirt and her hair felt greasy and lank. She watered the horses in the downstream end of the pond and loosed them to graze on the tufty grass that grew along the bank. Clever went along to keep an eye on them, and Flute Dog rummaged in the packs on the travois for the tent hides. When she began to drag the poles toward a flat spot, with pointed looks at Rain Child, Rain Child sighed and went to help her. The pool waited, shimmering like honey in the sun.

When the tent was up, Rain Child went back to the pool with a ball of yucca soap and her hairbrush. She waded in and sank like a turtle into the warm water, only her nose and eyes showing, while the current eddied over her skin. It was just deep enough to float on her back, and she closed her eyes and spread her arms out across the water. The water rocked her like a cradleboard.

Behind her closed lids, things drifted in the blackness

and the sharp red glare of the sun, dark shapes of buffalo and men on horses, their dogs trailing them. The pot rolled along behind the dogs, and she thought of the story of the Rolling Head that ate everything in its path. Finally the wife of the man the Head had been when it was human tricked him by running across a river and pulling the bridge away behind her. The head fell into the water and a pike leaped up and swallowed it. In the black and red behind Rain Child's lids, the pot rolled into the water and a coyote jumped from the surface and ate it.

Rain Child opened her eyes and saw the chief of the wild dogs watching her from the reeds that grew along the bank under the willows. His sandy head caught the low sun and his ears glinted with its light along the edges. His brown eyes watched her as if he were trying to figure out something.

Rain Child took a stone from the bottom of the pool and threw it at him. He ran away with a yelp and she looked around her cautiously. She couldn't see any more of them. Annoyed and uneasy, she stood up and waded out of the water, wrapping herself in the robe she had left on the bank. She hefted her spear, inviting him to come back and start something, but he was gone.

"There are dogs by the pool," she said to Flute Dog when she came back to the camp.

"How many?"

"Just that sandy colored chief. He was watching me in the water."

"Go see about the horses."

The horses were grazing peacefully in the sunset, noses rustling the grass, lips twisting tufts of it together for their sharp teeth to bite off. They didn't smell dogs or Red Sandstone Horse wouldn't be dozing in the last of the sun. Rain Child rubbed his nose and he snorted at her.

"Pay attention," she told him.

There was no sign of dogs in the morning, either, but when they stopped two days later on a ridge overlooking a bank tunneled with rabbit holes, they saw them dodging through the dusk with a rabbit between them. The sandy dog chief carried it and the others tore at it as they went along.

Clever pricked up her ears, thinking, *Rabbits*. The image of the Big Dog came into her head and went out again as Flute Dog and Rain Child unpacked the travois and unloaded Rain Child's pot. Clever had almost forgotten whatever it was that the Big Dog had said to her about that pot. Flute Dog cooked dinner in that pot. It was a dinner pot. Clever sat down expectantly by it.

Rain Child lay on her stomach and peered down at the bank where the rabbit holes were. There was no movement. She ground her teeth and muttered a curse on the wild dogs for scaring the rabbits into their burrows, and then remembered that she wasn't supposed to talk to them. Cursing them might count. She took the curse back, silently unsaying it, syllable by syllable.

When the sun dropped behind the western mountains, the air snapped around them, crisp as a rim of ice on the stream. The golden days disappeared in a breath of frost.

Rain Child crawled quietly backward to the tent and put her leggings on. She got her bow and her throwing sticks, and eased down the hill in the gathering cold, with Clever, the dinner pot now forgotten, at her heels.

"Stay!" Rain Child snapped at her, and Clever gave her a wounded look. *Me? Scare rabbits?* She tucked herself in closer to Rain Child's heel to prove her good faith.

They sat down together behind a clump of rabbit brush and watched in the stillness while the moon, icy as a fishhook, came out of the darkening sky. In its faint light Rain Child saw a pair of rabbit ears poke out of a burrow. She eased herself to her knees and wrapped her fingers around her throwing stick. (She had a good shot from here, and the stick didn't make such a mess of the rabbit.) Rabbit hopped a hop from the burrow mouth, a cautious hop, accompanied by much swiveling of long ears and twitching of whiskers. Rain Child eased her arm back. Beside her, Clever tensed, breath held. Rabbit took another hop away from the burrow, and a rabbit head behind him stuck its ears out the door.

Around them, more rabbits appeared in the dusk, silently, like apparitions, nibbling shining grass in the starlight. Rain Child eyed their positions while Clever quivered beside her. If she took one from the edge of the group, she might get a second before they scattered. But one on the edge was harder to hit. Be greedy or not?

Not, she decided, feeling virtuous because now she had a spirit guide, even if it was a coyote. *More rabbits*, Clever thought at her, but Rain Child ignored that.

She eased her arm all the way back and let the curved throw stick fly. Clever shot out of the brush with the stick, swirling among the panicked rabbits. A rabbit fell over, its neck broken by the stick. As Rain Child ran for it, Clever emerged from the mélée with another kicking in her jaws.

"Good girl!"

Clever gave the rabbit a good bite and it hung limply.

Rain Child picked hers up by the ears and held her other hand out to Clever, the throw stick tucked under her arm.

Clever danced away from her.

"Share!" Rain Child said sternly, and Clever hung her head.

"Give it here."

Clever looked mournful.

"Oh, very well, Most Fierce, you can carry it. But if you run off you'll be sorry."

Clever raised her ears happily and trotted along beside Rain Child. They took the rabbits to Flute Dog, and Rain Child skinned them while Flute Dog stirred onions in the bottom of the pot with a lump of fat from Painted Water Horse. Rain Child gave all the entrails to Clever and pegged the skins out to soak in the stream that ran at the bottom of the bank. "Some people need mittens," she told Clever when Clever looked interested in the skins, too. "Some people are not covered with fur."

She made a fire and stuck the skinned rabbits on a stick balanced across two stones, while her stomach growled and Clever drooled. The rabbit scent and the onion smell twined together in a braid in the air.

The wild dogs smelled it and crept closer from their hiding place by the stream. The gray dog that Rain Child had hit with her arrow cringed and held back; a splinter of the shaft still hung from his festering shoulder. The others looked uncertainly from him to the sandy-coated leader, whining softly in their indecision. It had been a long time since they had been fed cooked meat, or smelled it. With the smell came memory, of hot food and a warm place to sleep, of a fist in the muzzle, a foot in the ribs, of stones thrown, of the soft scent of the night calling to instincts dulled in a smoky camp.

The gray dog licked his shoulder, twisting around on bony ribs. The sandy leader ignored him, and skulked along the riverbank. He ignored the rabbit skins pegged out in the stream, the wild eyes and starveling coats of the pack behind him. The cooking smell filled his nose.

Rain Child sat by the fire nursing the rabbits. The rabbit grease dripped onto burning wood, permeating the night with its smell. The sky was cold and starry, like spangles of ice on a black blanket. It looked as if it went on forever, reflected in the Grass below, anchored only by the meat smell, the home scent of a campfire. In the Old Times, the spirits had sent certain people, who had been good or bad, up into the sky to be stars. Rain Child wondered if they had sent any into the Grass. To be stones, maybe, like the piles of stone that people left to mark their passage here. If she were at home she could ask old Rabbit Dancer or Uncle Howler about that. If they didn't know, it would be something to think on. It was the duty of the Dry River people, Uncle Howler had told her, to think on mystery things.

I will think on it anyway, Rain Child thought to herself. *I will be Woman With a Pot Who Thinks About the Grass and Knows Who Lives There*. She wondered if she could ask the coyote spirit about that instead, when he came back.

It wasn't the coyote who came streaking out of the brush, but at first Rain Child thought it was, just for the boldness of it. The sandy pack leader burst out of the Grass into the circle of the firelight like a seed pod popping open, a wild pale dog seed spit out of the dark night. Before she could jump up or Clever could bite him, he had pulled a rabbit off the stick and vanished with it, leaving the other spattering grease in the fire and ashes.

Rain Child howled with indignation, poking it out of the fire with the stick.

Flute Dog burst out of the tent. "What is it?"

"That dog! He stole my rabbit right off the stick! I'm going to kill him!"

"Come back here!"

Rain Child didn't answer. She had picked up her spear and run after the dog.

"Clever!" Flute Dog shouted, but Clever didn't listen, either. She ran after Rain Child.

Rain Child stumbled along the stream bank, trying to look for holes before she stepped in them. She could hear the wild dog ahead of her scrambling through the brush, slowed by the rabbit in his jaws. Flute Dog was still shouting for her to come back, but Rain Child's rage didn't listen. The dog turned away from the stream, up a dry wash that angled to the west. It had been full of water at some time, but not lately, because brush grew along the bottom of it. Rain Child followed him, blundering through the bushes and dark with Clever on her heels.

* * *

Clever felt very excited. She had forgotten what the Big Dog had said about not chasing these dogs. This one had stolen her rabbit before she had got even a bite out of it and she and her two-legged person was going to catch him. Then they would bite him. Clever could see down the wash with her dog-dark eyes. The pale dog was ahead of them, slowing now because he was trying to eat the rabbit as he ran. Clever barked at him to let him know they were coming.

"Hush!" Rain Child panted. She stumbled on up the wash, banging her toes on the tumbled stones. She could see a flicker of movement in the night, and hear the dog crashing through the bushes. She gripped her spear tighter.

The bed of the wash ended abruptly in a fall of rock where the banks had caved in, and trees and other river flotsam had piled up on top of them, making a dam, a wall of rubbish as high as Rain Child's head. The chief of the dogs scrabbled at it, trying to climb it. Rain Child ran for him and fell facedown over something half-buried in the bed of the wash. The spear spun out of her hand.

Clever kept going.

Rain Child hobbled to her feet. Her foot felt as if it was broken. "Clever!"

Clever looked back dubiously.

"Wait!" Rain Child lunged forward, falling down, and grabbed Clever by the ruff, dragging her back, encircling her with one arm.

The chief of the dogs turned at bay before the tumble of trees and rock with the rabbit still hanging from his jaws. He gave two quick gulps and most of it vanished.

"That's my rabbit!" Rain Child shouted at him, sitting on the bottom of the wash, forgetting she wasn't supposed to speak to him.

The chief of the dogs pricked his ears toward her and cocked his head. He swallowed the last of the rabbit.

Rain Child got on her hands and knees, glaring at him,

while Clever growled. The chief of the dogs growled back. Rain Child's spear was just out of reach. She edged toward it and the dog chief raised his hackles and growled again.

"Be quiet!"

He looked startled and his tail drooped. Rain Child snatched the spear. She could just stand, but her foot throbbed horribly. She leaned on the spear like a walking stick.

"You're the other half of me," she said to the chief of the dogs, because she had already done what she had been told not to. "I am Dog Sister. If you eat me, you'll eat yourself. Now go away."

The dog chief whined. Clever thought about biting him. Then she saw just over the rim of the wash the Big Dog, with the stars showing through his coat. He opened his mouth. The chief of the dogs cringed down low. Then he turned and scrabbled up the pile of rubbish that blocked the wash, paws digging frantically into the stones and brush until he clawed his way over the top.

Clever heard him running into the Grass.

Rain Child shook her spear at the dog as he scrambled over the top of the wash. She turned away, limping, and stumbled again on whatever it was she had fallen over. This time she could feel blood running across her foot. Cursing, she knelt down to look. The skin was scraped away from her instep, but it wasn't much of a cut. But it wasn't a stone she had fallen over, either.

The sharp corner of a box protruded from the bed of the wash, floated downstream on some flood, unearthed again maybe by the last rain, or the Grass wind. It was wooden, partly rotted away. The corner join separated when Rain Child tugged at it. Intent now, she scooped the earth away from its sides, scraping it with a flat stone, digging at it with her spearpoint, prying at it with both hands. It was big, the size of a buffalo skull, but the buried wood was soft and the sides fell apart as she dug it loose from the earth. She laid the pieces out on the ground, peering at them in the darkness, looking to see what had been inside.

Clever looked over her shoulder, the other dog forgotten now. Maybe there was something to eat in this box. Rain Child pawed through the remains of what felt and smelled like old ground meal, and a wet mass of some kind of leaves. Her fingers found something else and she dug it out: a string of dirt-encrusted beads. She rubbed one clean with her thumb and it glinted in the starlight, round and shiny as a green berry. Rain Child held out the beads to look at them. The strand was long enough to fit around her neck, and a little man hung from crossed sticks at the bottom of it. The little man was no longer than her thumb, and he couldn't be very comfortable, hanging from those sticks like that. Rain Child thought he must be some kind of magic.

Clever nosed the beads.

"Look what I found," Rain Child said to her.

Clever snuffled at them, but they weren't food.

"I wasn't supposed to talk to that dog," Rain Child was saying, "but I was angry about the rabbit. And now look. If we hadn't chased him, we wouldn't have found these. I will take another sweat bath and say I'm sorry." Rain Child hung the beads around her neck. She felt around and carefully scooped up all the broken pieces of the box, making a sling of her skirt to carry them. She looked across the wash, leaning on her spear, in case the dog chief was waiting to follow them.

"Do you smell that dog anywhere still?" she asked Clever. Clever seemed to have forgotten him, so Rain Child imagined he wasn't coming back. She caught a faint whiff of coyote scent. The night seemed darker and even more mysterious with the beads around her neck. New things were coming. That was what the coyote had said. Rain Child set out back down the wash with Clever at her heels.

The Big Dog trotted along beside them, but as they neared the camp, Clever saw him fade into the starlight until there was nothing left of him.

In their camp, the horses stamped and snorted in the darkness, eyes white-rimmed at the lingering dog smell. The tent was like a cone of light among them, illuminating their hides with fireglow. Pale smoke drifted through the smokehole at the top, wreathing the tent poles.

Rain Child hobbled past the dying cookfire outside and ducked through the flap to kneel excitedly across the hearth from Flute Dog.

"Look what I've found!"

"Eat." Flute Dog had heard them coming back and gone to sit inside to prove she hadn't been worried. She pushed a bowl of rabbit meat at Rain Child. "Before dogs steal this one." She gave Clever a haunch to chew on.

Rain Child was spitting on the beads, polishing them with the hem of her dress. The pieces of the box lay on the floor beside her.

"Before *your* dog steals it," Flute Dog added, lifting the bowl out of Clever's reach. Clever had gulped down her haunch and was looking hopeful. "What is that?"

"They are beads. Look!" Rain Child held them up to the fire. In the light they shone like pieces of hot coal, red and yellow and sunset-colored, with bits of blue strung between them.

"Is that turquoise?"

"No." Rain Child tasted the blue beads and the red ones, and bit them. She rubbed their surface with her finger. "No, they're too shiny. And this broken one is sharp." She ran a fingertip over a cracked red bead. "Ow! See?"

"What is that hanging from them?"

"It's a little man."

"I don't like that." Flute Dog held out her hand for the beads, tentatively, the way she might ask someone to hand her a snake. She peered at them, squinting her eyes together. The little man on the crossed sticks looked back at her, enigmatic. "I never saw anything like that before."

"I know," Rain Child said as Flute Dog spat on the beads and rubbed them on her own dress as if some hidden message might come clear. The little man gleamed dully once he was clean.

"Let me see that box." Flute Dog examined the pieces of it, too, suspiciously. "Look where the sides were held together, cut into themselves. Our people don't make things like this."

"I know," Rain Child said happily. "It's another New Person thing, I'm sure of it."

"A New Person thing?" Flute Dog put the beads and the box down. "What New Person?"

"The coyote said I am a New Person," Rain Child told her. "And my pot is a New Person pot."

"I told you not to go looking for visions," Flute Dog said tartly. "I told you. And look what came."

"We must accept that which the Mystery sends us," Rain Child said, in perfect imitation of Uncle Howler.

Flute Dog chuckled, and then looked away abruptly. "Why did the coyote say you were a New Person?" she asked carefully, after a moment.

"He says I am the one who is always coming along. He says we are new since we have horses. I didn't understand exactly."

"One never does, with spirits," Flute Dog said. "It's all right."

"He said that I must find out what my pot is made of. And I have to give the Moon my white stone and then she will tell me about my father."

"Your father was named Young Owl, and he is living in the skull ring in the valley of the western trail just below the winter lodge of Dark-of-the-Moon."

"My first father," Rain Child said stubbornly.

"Well, he must have been a man of the Cities-in-the-West," Flute Dog said.

"Why? If he was, then why was the Stranger Woman out in the Grass in a storm all by herself?"

"I don't know."

"You didn't think on it? Ever?"

"When you want something very badly, and someone sends it to you, you do not ask questions about it," Flute Dog said tightly.

"Oh." Rain Child shifted her weight, putting her hurt foot to the fire.

"What have you done to your foot?"

"I fell over the box. It was buried in the ground."

"Let me look at that. Tcch!" Flute Dog took the waterskin from its hook on the center pole and poured some in her cupped hand. She washed Rain Child's foot with it and clicked her teeth again. Then she fetched her medicine bag and began to rummage through the contents.

"It's all right, Mother."

"It is not." Flute Dog produced a small buffalo-horn vial capped with a lump of clay, and stuck her finger in it. "Hold still."

Rain Child wriggled as Flute Dog smeared greasy ointment into the cut. "It's just a lot of blood," she protested. "It isn't deep."

"That no doubt is why you are limping."

"I bruised it. I fell over the box."

"Indeed." Flute Dog added a dab of some other ointment from a different vial. "I expect that little man pulled you down. I don't like him at all."

"I don't either, to tell you the truth," Rain Child said. "But I want the beads. They are New Person beads."

"He may be a New Person himself, for all you know."

"No," Rain Child said firmly. "I know what I'll do with him. I'll give him to the Moon with my white stone. She'll like him, and I can keep the beads."

"Mmmm," Flute Dog said, but she didn't argue.

The next night they camped near the river whose course they had been following, and Rain Child waited until the moon was shining in the water. Then she stood on the bank and tossed the white stone into the hook of the moon's reflection.

"The coyote said to give you this, Mother," she told it. "From your obedient child."

She fumbled with the beads, sawing her belt knife through the thong that knotted the little man into their pattern. "And I thought that you might like this little man. I don't know who he is, but he might like living with you better than being tied to sticks." Rain Child balanced him in the palm of her hand. He looked back at her, unwinking, inscrutable. She tossed him and he arced head over heels on his sticks and disappeared with a plop into the Moon's watery arms.

"Very nice," the Moon said, examining the stone. It reflected her aqueous light in a halo around her hair. "Dear boy, you are sometimes quite thoughtful."

Coyote looked modest.

"And what is this?" The Moon dipped her slender fingers in the river and brought out the crucifix. She was thin and hawklike tonight and her eye was avaricious. "Gold. My goodness."

"It's a New Person thing, isn't it?" Coyote asked. "I was right."

"And what will you do if they want it back?"

"I'm not afraid of them," Coyote said. "I stole horses from them."

"You may regret that." All the same she tucked the little gold crucifix into her bodice.

"The person who had this thing is dead anyway," Coyote said, shrugging. "The sun shone too brightly on him and he died. A cousin of mine ate him."

"There will be more."

"I have a plan about that."

"A plan." The Moon snorted. "You had a plan to fly

with the Raven Clan. You had a plan to play with Grizzly Bear. You had a plan to drown Water Turtle and eat him."

Coyote looked offended. "This plan will work."

"And what *is* this plan, Most Likely To Be Grizzly Bear's Dinner?" She made a display of listening, tapping long ivory nails on the sky.

Coyote's eyes glowed amber with enthusiasm, his moods as mercurial as the moment. "Well, that hard stuff that the child's pot is made of—that iron stuff. I have watched these pale new people that are in the Cities now, and they have other things made out of this iron. Like those stick things that shoot fire and rocks." Coyote paused and tucked his tail tightly around himself with a reminiscent twitch. "Those are very dreadful. That shiny skin they wear that bounces arrows is made out of iron, too." He looked somber. "And I have seen how iron knives break flint knives."

"Well, that is why they are all over the place, annoying people in the Cities," the Moon said dryly. "Because they can."

"And in the south. Jaguar says they are there too, and it is very bad."

"Bad for whom?"

"For the people there. These pale new ones don't have any manners."

"Coyote is going to teach the pale people manners?" The Moon hooted delicately, fanning her pointed face with a slender hand.

"I have perfectly fine manners," Coyote said haughtily. "And in any case these are my people here. If I want to trick them, or they wish to give me dinner, that is my business. They do not belong to these pale people who are coming in and stealing things."

"The stolen horse belongs to the thief," the Moon said.

"So," Coyote said, ignoring her, "I am going to teach the child there to make iron. Then my people will have iron *and* horses, and all the young men can get big reputations telling these pale people to go home again."

"The way you told them at Red Earth City?"

"That was before we had iron."

"You don't have iron now."

"We will." To Coyote's mind, it was the same to say a thing as to do it.

The Moon rolled her silvery eyes. "Why the child? Why not the medicine men, or the Grandmothers?"

"Aha!" Coyote looked superior now. "I know something you don't." His expression grew happily secretive.

"I have just come from the other side of the world," the Moon said. "Where in a small town a small girl has just been born who will cause an emperor to die. What do you know that I don't?"

Coyote sidled up to her, even though she was angular and cross tonight. "Most Far-Seeing, you know all. But sometimes I see things closer to the ground. Where Most Exalted sees the hinges of the world, I see the small ear of grain in Wood Rat's house. The small insect that crawls on the tail of the pet monkey of the third wife of the Jaguar King."

"The Jaguar King has no wives now," the Moon said. "They are all dead."

"All right then," Coyote said. "But I saw the child's mother run away from the Cities-in-the-West with a full belly, and I saw the child when it came and I am no fool."

The Moon peered down at the cone of light that was Flute Dog's tent in the center of the Grass.

"Of course I am certain that Most Astute saw this too," Coyote added with elaborate politeness. "Naturally."

The face of Rain Child hovered before them, hair curling in wisps around those odd eyes, bent over the strange string of beads.

The Moon looked annoyed. "I was in China just then," she said haughtily.

"Now this child will make iron for my people."

"How do you know she can?"

"Because they can," Coyote said with painstaking patience. Sometimes it took a very long time to explain his ideas to other people, who didn't see possibilities the way he did.

"That doesn't mean *she* can make it."

"Her father's people make it. Like calls to like. Don't you know anything about magic?"

"I know magic may bite the magician. And I know this isn't magic. Contrary to your way of thinking, there is no way to get anything important that does not involve work."

"I am not afraid of work!" Coyote said indignantly.

"Tell that to some turtle riding a horse." The Moon smiled sadly. "Dear boy."

"I work very hard." Coyote contrived to look hurt. "I will teach the child to make iron and then we can all chase the pale people into the Endless Water."

"*You* don't know how to make iron."

"Ha! You told me. Get rocks very hot, hot with charcoal."

"It isn't like that." The Moon flailed her arms in exasperation and a bank of little clouds skittered across the sky.

Coyote scratched behind one ear. He knitted his brow. His big ears pricked forward earnestly. "Explain, Most Wise."

"It has to be the right kind of oven. I have watched them make it. And the right rocks. And anyone can do it, but they have to learn from someone who has done it before."

"I don't believe that. Are you telling me that just anyone, with no help from the spirits at all, can make this stuff that that pale person shot my tail off with, and I can't?"

"Your tail is not so valuable as all that."

Coyote craned his head around, inspecting it. The fur

had mostly grown back but he remembered the sting. "I want to be able to shoot one of those sticks." His eyes gleamed. "Hoo! That would surprise Grizzly Bear!"

"It would even the odds, certainly." The Moon sighed, breathing out a wisp of cloud. "I am not sure. It's a bad idea to interfere in human people's business."

"And what happens if we don't? Tell me that. Pale people running around telling everyone what to do, shooting people's tails off. Giving us no respect."

The Moon shook her head. "Everything goes out on the tide one day. You can't stop it."

"I can try," Coyote said stubbornly.

Cold weather closed around Flute Dog and Rain Child like a hand. They rode farther each day, trying to outride it, Rain Child with the beads about her neck. The wild dogs followed them, but they never came into the camp again, skirting instead about the edges, lean forms skulking in the dusk. Finally Rain Child took to leaving a duck or a goose for them when her snares caught more than she and Flute Dog and Clever could eat.

"They will follow us now," Flute Dog said.

"They are following us anyway."

"Are you going to take them into the tent for the winter? That is where they will be next."

Rain Child shook her head stubbornly. She didn't know why she fed them. She just knew that somehow, with the gift of the beads, they had become hers, or she theirs.

They came to the caves in the cliffs, where Flute Dog said Rabbit Dancer claimed the Old Ones had lived, just as the first snow began to fall. Flute Dog examined all the caves, cautiously, spear in hand in case anyone was living there already, and they swept out the biggest one with the levelest floor with a broom of sage. It looked very much as if Mountain Cat had lived there once, by the single dusty print they found near the back. He had left a little pile of bones that had once been his dinner, but they were old and dry, and there was no sign that he had been back in over a year, so Flute Dog and Rain Child moved into his house. The cat scent was so old that the horses didn't mind, and they let them come in and sleep at the back, where Flute Dog and Rain Child fed them on piñon nuts and cut grass dug from under the snow.

After the snowfall, the land looked to Rain Child like an uninhabited white blanket, rippled here and there with the fingers of the wind, but otherwise barren of the landscape of her childhood, the puffs of smoke that would mark a neighbor's winter lodge, or the drying racks and tanning hides of industrious winter wives. She lifted the blanket that Flute Dog had hung across the cave mouth, tied to sticks wedged into the crevices of the rock, and stood watching the empty white prairie until finally she could see the people who were living in it—the rabbit whose bounding feet had left gouges in the snow near the frozen stream, the quail who had picked her way across the crusted surface, the tiny skittering feet of a mouse looking for withered chokecherries; and beyond those, the pad prints of the wild dogs. They would be denned somewhere, dug in for the winter under a bank or among the roots of a stand of cottonwoods. There were only three left. The gray dog with the arrow in his shoulder was gone since the last dark-of-the-moon. Rain Child wondered if they had eaten him too, finally.

Rain Child made a rabbit fence out of hair from the horses' tails, and stretched it between two stands of trees where it hung like an invisible skin separating one world from the next. Then she and Flute Dog and Clever drove the rabbits into it, and killed them with their throwing sticks and clubs while they thrashed in the net. Rain Child left the skins and entrails for the wild dogs and hung the rest up in the trees where they couldn't reach it and Clever couldn't either. Flute Dog didn't say anything.

When Rain Child made a sweat bath to make amends for breaking her taboo, the coyote didn't appear to acknowledge her apology, and she wondered if he had abandoned her for being disobedient. Then the next night at dusk she saw him standing just under the dead tree that grew on the slope below the cave, his tongue hanging out, red against the snow. He looked at her a long time, then trotted away into the twilight, and she saw him later running with the wild dogs, and knew that in some way they were his now, just as they were hers.

Mindful now of his orders to find the rocks that her pot had been made from, she took Clever with her and dug stones from the bank below the caves, and the rough slope above it, but Clever didn't seem to know which rocks were which, and the Moon, although appealed to, failed to send her any sign, either, about the rocks or her father's origins, the mystery that lurked always at the back of her head despite Flute Dog's insistence on Young Owl's paternity.

It was something to think on during the long winter. When the weather was clear, she took the horses to dig their own grass from beneath the snow, and thought on it lying along the back of Toad Nose's Mare, soaking up horse warmth. If the dogs could run away from their two-legged people to be wild, and then begin to follow people again—although Rain Child was still pretty sure that they would eat her willingly if she gave them the chance—then maybe that was what she was fated to do—go from the Dry River people to another. Could the Stranger Woman have been pregnant by a man of these northern people that her mother was taking her to? Were *they* her true people, and did the coyote want her to have the gift of more pots to take to them, to be sure of her welcome?

Rain Child thought on that, envisioning them in her

mind, a dark, serious people, with bright eyes, and soft hands. They would be amazed by her gift of horses and magic pots, and they would take her and her mother in and make them wise women among the people.

It wasn't until the day of the first thaw, when she saw the boy looking at her from the reeds along the stream bank, that she thought of the possibility that they might be as wild as the dogs, and as dangerously afraid.

On the day that the thaw came, the sun's glittering breath filled the air with such possibility that the horses' nostrils widened and they chased each other like colts across the slushy snow. Rain Child and Flute Dog woke up and stretched and ran their hands with dissatisfaction through their smoky hair. Rain Child went to fetch bath water.

The ground was wet and squishy between the caves and the stream, and there were a few new blades of grass poking themselves through the slush and mud. Here outside the air smelled dizzy with excitement. Clever zigzagged back and forth in front of Rain Child, nose to the ground, inhaling the world. On the stream bank, Rain Child plunged her pot through the splintering ice. The current lapped her toes and her teeth chattered, even in this changed, softened air. When she looked up, the boy was there, peering through the dry reeds on the other bank.

They stared at each other for a long moment, Rain Child bent to the stream, open mouthed, the boy parting the brown, clattering reeds with his hands. His hide shirt was painted with a bear's paw, his long hair dressed in two braids and a scalp lock tied with a bundle of hawk feathers.

They looked at each other until abruptly Rain Child saw his eyes go wide, his face terror-stricken. She heard the scuffle behind her, and Mud-Spattered Horse, who had followed her, scrambled down the bank and butted her with his head, fumbling at her dress for piñon nuts. Rain Child pushed him away with her hands but the boy had already bolted from the reeds and run.

11

The Messenger of the Bear

SUNFALL BOY WAS RUNNING. RUNNING AS FAST AS HE could, stumbling in the slushy snow that his hide boots churned up, running from the monster that had materialized along the stream bank and eaten the girl. He was shame-faced, running, because he ought to have fought the monster and saved the girl, but he had not. And in the back of his mind he saw her, pushing the monster's head away, laughing, and that memory kept him running, his quiver and waterskin bouncing on his back. Monsters trapped unwary strangers thus. They made themselves seem something they were not, they kidnapped maidens and waited for a warrior to try to save them. And in any case, Sunfall Boy was not a warrior yet.

He slowed a little, his breath coming in gasps, as he reached the trail that wound through the foothills. It wasn't a trail that just anyone could see, but it was the way of his people to the High Place, the stone where a young man sat and waited for his vision spirit to come upon him. Sunfall Boy's father and his father's father and *his* father's father had walked that trail. Any man of the Bear knew the way.

Tonight Sunfall Boy would sit on the High Place and pray. He would stay until his vision spirit came to him, and then he would go home a man. Surely it was not expected that he kill monsters before then. And in any case he had only his hunting bow with him. It was known that monsters could not be killed with human weapons but only with magic. When his vision spirit came, then he would know what to do.

Sunfall Boy did not question that his vision spirit would come. That was not to be thought of, although in the back of his mind he did think of it, and of Stone Hand, who had sat on the High Place for as many days as there were fingers on his hands, and come home disgraced. And of Peewit, who had sat there until he died of hunger lest he too be a disgrace, a thing who was neither warrior nor soft man, but fit only to carry the Bear's burdens when his people traveled. That would not happen to Sunfall Boy, who was the son of the sister of the Bear.

Sunfall Boy climbed. The ground glowed with a soft light that the Sun made with his breath along the late snow. It lit the path with a streak of unearthly fire, and Sunfall Boy climbed it. All along the way the pads of a wolf or a big dog ran beside him and Sunfall Boy gripped his bow tightly in his hand.

The track wound higher, and halfway up Sunfall Boy stopped to catch his breath in the shade of a windbent spruce tree. Spread out below him he could see the way he had come, his dark tracks churning the snow, and the river in the distance. He shivered in the wind. The mountain loomed above him, dark patches of thawed earth and rock showing through the snow, the trees a dark green blanket on its slope.

As the trail climbed into a stand of aspens, just beginning to show pale uncurling leaves, Sunfall Boy stopped to sing. This was the Singing Place, the first stop on his journey. He had never been up the mountain before, but he knew. Everyone knew. Each boy of the Bear learned the songs and the trail from his toddler days, when old Eyes of Bear scratched it for them in the dirt and in the ashes of campfires.

You who live in the mountains, hear me.
You who live in the sky, hear me.
You who live in the red heart of the fire, hear me.
You who live in the rain, hear me.
I am a child of the Bear.
I come to the mountain to learn.
I come to the mountain to see.
I come to the mountain to ask.
Hear me.

Sunfall Boy waited in the silence that shrouded the aspens as the last notes of his song died away. The air shimmered with it, with possibility. Sunfall Boy set off up the trail again, winding higher, eyes searching for the landmarks that old Eyes of Bear had imprinted on his mind—the white stone beneath the lightning-streaked aspen; the outcropping of rock with the mark of the Bear on its face; the high meadow with the bowl-shaped depression in its heart.

On the meadow's edge, the pads that had dogged the trail beside him turned away into the scrub pine. On the far side, above the bowl, the mountain sloped up to the High Place—a flat slab of granite balanced on the topmost brow of the earth, its surface jutting over the valleys and ridges to the west.

Sunfall Boy took a deep breath, his heart pounding at the sight of it. *I am here*, he told it.

It had taken him all day to climb the mountain, and the afternoon sun struck the High Place just as he spoke. *You are here*, it said back to him.

Sunfall Boy touched his forehead in acknowledgment.

He walked down into the heart of the bowl and stopped again to pray.

You who hold me cupped in your hand,
send a message to me.

The marks of his feet were dark holes in the snow behind him. An eagle soared on the air above, stitching a pattern across the bright blue sky. Sunfall Boy climbed out of the bowl and up the last slope to the High Place. It was higher than it had looked. He stood on the ground, peering up at it, jutting above his head. Eyes of Bear had not told him how to get up there.

Sunfall Boy walked around all three sides of the High Place and peered over the cliff that fell sheer beneath it. The best spot to climb appeared to be on its north face, where three stair-step boulders protruded, each as tall as Sunfall Boy, stacked one above the other. He slung his bow over his shoulder with his quiver and waterskin, and dug his toes into the face of the first boulder, hands clawing at its top. He scrambled up it and found another foothold in a crevice where the second boulder jutted from the rock. He pulled himself up over that and stood spread-eagled, fingers clutching the rock face, with only enough room to stand on tiptoe. Craning his neck, he could see the top of the last stone step, with the flat surface of the High Place hanging just above it. He felt the stone with his fingertips and found a niche where the withered tuft of some alpine flower had grown. His fingers dug into the soft earth at the flower's roots and he put his right foot against the rock face. His left hand found a grip and he scrabbled upward, hooking his elbows on the top of the third step, kicking his feet. He wriggled up again, got his torso onto the top ledge, and then grabbed at the surface of the High Place. Another wriggle, and he was up, a fish person stranded in bright air, lying facedown on the stone.

He lay a long time panting, his cheek against the faintly warm surface of the granite shelf, feeling the spirits of the boys who had come here from Time Way Back, to sit on the High Place and learn their destiny. He wondered if Peewit had lain in just this spot, and sat up abruptly.

Sunfall Boy went to stand at the edge of the High Place, where he could make his prayers to the setting sun, as Eyes of Bear had instructed him. He laid down his bow and quiver and waterskin, all that he had brought with him, all that tethered him to the world below, and lifted his arms to sing the Sun down behind the western ridge. It was strange to be higher than the sun.

Old one, who was here from the First,
Send me a message with the Sun.
Send me a teacher with the Moon.
Send me a voice from the stars of the Wolf Trail.
Instruct me.

Sunfall Boy sat down on the High Place, folded his legs into the proper position for thinking, and waited. The sky dimmed above him and in the distant valleys and white folds of the foothills the coyotes began to sing the evening in: first a yip, then an answering warble, then a chorus, undulating across the hills. The Elk River pack began their song, then the Sand Hill pack answered. Beyond the first ridge the Porcupine Mountain pack began to yelp too, and the dusk was filled with voices.

Sunfall Boy smiled. Coyotes were dirty and crafty and dangerous, but they were the voice of Evening. When their song faded and night dropped around him, he closed his eyes to shut out the cold, warming himself with the prayers that Eyes of Bear had taught him. With the dark, the eagles and the hawks descended to their nests and the people who live in the night came out, blinking and stretching. They scuttered through the moonlight, hurrying about their business at his feet, in fear only of the silent wings of owls. The ones who came to sit on the mountain did not hunt.

Sunfall Boy sat there through the dark and into the dawn of the next day, as the birds woke, and the thawing world shook itself, splashing dripping water from its shoulders. His stomach growled and he ignored it. Fasting was part of the Seeking. Water he was allowed, but only as much as his waterskin held.

The sun arced his way across the sky while Sunfall Boy waited. At noon he drank a swallow from his waterskin. He waited into the night and through the circle of another day and another night. At dusk on the third day his vision spirit came to him.

It called his name, a wild cry that broke open the egg of the sky around him and shattered its silence. Sunfall Boy leapt up and turned to the sound. It came again, an undulating shriek that stood the hair on the backs of his hands on end. Sunfall Boy stood gaping.

The spirit stood at the center of the bowl, its tracks obliterating his own. It lifted its hideous bony head and cried again.

It was the monster from the stream, white as the snow, and spattered with brown spots like thawing ground. From its rear depended a tail like the torrent of a waterfall, and from its neck a mane of human hair. Its back was as high as a man. More wonderful and terrible yet, on it rode the girl, captive no longer, but holding a rope in her hand that tied its head to her bidding.

Sunfall Boy stood and stared, his mouth gaped open. The monster cried again and he knew that it spoke to him.

Sunfall Boy raised his arms in a gesture of respect. "What do you come to tell me?" he called to it, trembling.

The girl on its back replied, but her words were magic words, with meaning only to those who knew how to hear it. Sunfall Boy couldn't hear them. The girl spoke to him again, but he only shook his head, hands out to show her they were empty of understanding.

The spirit monster also cried out again, and now Sunfall Boy heard another voice answer, from far away in the scrub pines that edged the meadow. He jerked his head around and stared into the dark greenness of their boughs. A head came out of the branches.

The spirit called, the girl put her fingers to her mouth and whistled, and someone trotted out of the scrub pines. The someone was shaped like the spirit, but was the color of sunlight. The first spirit trotted toward it, but the second one tossed up its head and raced across the meadow, snow and splatters of churned-up mud flying from its feet.

It was running toward him. Sunfall Boy held his breath. It raced across the meadow, its white tail streaming like a comet, and now it was so close that he could see its eyes, dark eyes rimmed in white, and see its red open mouth and feel in his heart the pounding of its heart under the sunlit skin. It wheeled, sending up a drift of flying snow, and stopped in front of the High Place, breathing hard, its head raised, ears pricked forward at him.

"I am here. Teach me," Sunfall Boy said, paralyzed. It had come to him in the High Place. Whatever it was, it was for him. A monster certainly, but his monster. His vision.

The spirit made a noise in its throat, a sound somewhere between the growl of Mountain Cat and the high voice of Prairie Hen. It nodded its head as if for emphasis.

Sunfall Boy saw the white spirit with the girl on its back coming toward them. The girl maybe was the intermediary, the translator between Sunfall Boy and these spirits who had never before been seen in his world.

"Where do you come from?" he asked it, and hoped the girl would answer him. She slid from the back of the white spirit and approached the other, a coil of rope over her arm. She spoke to it in a chiding voice, the way a mother will scold a loved child, and Sunfall Boy watched it hang its head. The girl put the rope around its neck. She saw Sunfall Boy watching and said something to him, but he could hear no words in it, only a song like that of the birds or the coyotes, beyond his understanding. He hung his head, too, sorrowfully.

The girl frowned at him. She leaped upon the back of the white spirit, holding the other by its rope.

"Don't go," Sunfall Boy said to her. "I am trying to hear you."

The girl shook her head. They turned and flew away across the snow, into the woods on the other side. As they vanished, Sunfall Boy saw a pack of wild dogs come out of the pines and follow them.

He sat back down on the High Place, his heart pounding, facing the meadow now, his back to the fall of ridge and valley. He would pray, facing the direction from whence had come his visitation, and then he would go back to the camps of the Bear and tell them about it.

"She went up the mountain," Rain Child said. "And that boy was there."

Flute Dog stroked Whitetail Horse's nose. "Foolish. Foolish Go Up the Mountain, a cat might have eaten you."

"Those dogs were following her," Rain Child said.

"Maybe they were following the boy. Was it the same boy as the one at the stream?"

"I think so. He was just an ordinary sort of boy. A little older than me maybe. He had braids and a bear's footprint painted on his shirt, and a scalp lock like the ones our men wear. Those people we used to live with, I mean," she corrected herself.

"Time we had people to be our people again," Flute Dog said, deciding. "I think this boy comes from Grass folk. I met a trader once from the north, he said they call themselves the tribes of the Bear, and they hunt buffalo. We'll pick up his trail and maybe he will take us to them."

"He'll be a long way down it," Rain Child said. "He looked like he'd seen a water demon. His jaw dropped down to here—" she put her hand at knee-level—"and his eyes got big." She ringed her own eyes with circled fingers and laughed. "Like an owl."

"He was afraid of the horses. But if they are Grass people, they will very quickly see what horses are worth. Those people of the Northern Grass hunt their buffalo on foot."

"They will like my magic pot, too," Rain Child said thoughtfully.

"I am beginning to be afraid of that pot," Flute Dog said. "It keeps giving you things."

Rain Child grinned at her. She flipped the bright beads around her neck. "And what is wrong with that?"

"You'll find out when you find out what it wants for them," Flute Dog said darkly. "When we come to the people of the Bear, I don't want you to show them that pot. Not just yet."

"Mother—"

"Or those beads."

"Mother!"

"You listen to me."

Rain Child folded her arms sulkily, but when Flute Dog didn't say anything else, she got a bag from her pack and put the beads in it, and put the bag in the pot.

Sunfall Boy came back, striding across the frozen grass, his black hair flowing behind him like a dark wind, because he had seen his vision spirit. He wouldn't braid his hair again until he had been given a name.

The people of the Bear were waiting for him, and he stopped suddenly, stubbing his toe, because a woman somewhere behind the crowd of men was wailing. Her voice rose and fell like the coyotes' dusk song, anguished.

As he listened there came two short, sharp shrieks, and then the wailing began again.

"Who has died?" Sunfall Boy whispered to the men who walked across the thawing ground to meet him.

Striped Badger spoke. "The Bear is dead."

Sunfall Boy stared. It must be true. Striped Badger's face was streaked with ashes. And only the First of the Bear Dancers, the fearsome clowns who could turn into bears while you watched them, could bring news such as that. Sunfall Boy sucked his breath in. Long Walker had been the Bear since before Sunfall Boy was born, but he was not yet an old man, even so.

"How did it happen?"

"We trailed a buffalo cow and her calf. He fell as we were closing the circle."

Sunfall Boy nodded. Cows with calves were more dangerous than the bulls. She would have charged as soon as she saw him fall. "When?" he asked.

"Three days past."

"Did you kill the cow?"

Striped Badger nodded. "We brought him back in her hide." Sunfall Boy could see it drying, pegged out on a rack. It would be a tribal relic now.

The rest of the men crowded around them. Long Walker's wife came out from behind the tents, the tips of her fingers on both hands dripping blood, the women trailing behind her. Sunfall Boy saw that his mother, Blue Runner, who had been sister to the Bear, had scratched her cheeks until they were laced with red welts.

Striped Badger cocked his head at Sunfall Boy. "Well, nephew. Did you see your vision?"

They waited silently, ash-smeared and solemn, to hear what he would say. A vision's words were always important. Now they took on the weight of destiny.

"I saw something no one has seen before in this world," Sunfall Boy said.

"What direction did it come from?" Striped Badger asked him.

"From the east."

"Out of the sun?"

"Out of the twilight."

"Did it speak to you?"

"No words that I could understand. It spoke in magic."

"When?"

"Three days ago."

Striped Badger stopped, standing in a circle of stillness, the center of silence, balanced in it like a leaf on water. The people of the Bear held their breath.

"Tell us of its outward form."

Sunfall Boy tried to see it again in his mind, the waterfall of tail, the heavy feet, the high, bony head. "It was most wondrous. Like an elk without horns, with round hooves that had no split in them. From its back it hung a tail like a fall of long hair, and more hair grew along its neck. Its ears were pricked like a dog's, and it made noises in its throat."

"What kind of noises?"

"A snorting noise. And a chuckling noise. And then a scream. Like this." Sunfall Boy threw his head back and screeched, the sound an overlapping reverberation like the shriek of bone on rock.

"He has seen the messenger of the Bear!" Sunfall Boy's mother said.

Sunfall Boy's father kept his eyes on Striped Badger. "Did he not say the spirit came to him three days ago at dusk? And when was the death of the Bear?"

"Three days ago at dusk," Striped Badger said. "I can count."

The rest murmured and counted on their fingers, nodding. Long Walker's widow reached out and touched Sunfall Boy's forehead with her bloody fingertip. The people of the Bear nodded again. The wife of the Bear did not possess the status that his sister did, but just now her fingers carried power.

"What did the spirit do?" Striped Badger asked Sunfall Boy carefully. Sunfall Boy's eyes had grown wide. "What did it tell you?"

"There were two of them. And a girl. She rode on the Spotted One's back and spoke words I did not understand. She caught the Yellow One with a rope."

Striped Badger pointed at a little boy. "Go and wake up Eyes of Bear." The child scooted off.

Eyes of Bear was very old and he slept most of the time. He had said a charm over the buffalo cow skin and gone to sleep again while the Bear's widow cut off her fingertips. Everyone waited now to see what he would say. They held their breath collectively as he tottered over the grass to the crowd around Sunfall Boy.

"He has seen his vision," Striped Badger said, nodding at Sunfall Boy. "Tell him, Nephew."

Sunfall Boy tried to tell it all again, but his voice squeaked in his throat while Eyes of Bear looked out at him from under his blanket, his sunken eyes and bony nose looking terribly like a turtle. Sunfall Boy wanted to giggle.

Striped Badger was watching him and Sunfall Boy took a deep breath and started over. He told Eyes of Bear about the monsters, and the girl who rode on them, and how their voices had rung off the stones of the High Place, and spoken to him in magical sentences. He made the monsters' sounds again, and tried to remember what the girl had said, but the girl's words were like bird language in the air and he couldn't retrieve them. He shivered, telling it, the urge to laughter gone from him while Striped Badger and Eyes of Bear listened solemnly.

"The messenger of the Bear," Sunfall Boy's mother, Blue Runner, said again, and no one shushed her because she was a sister of him who had been the Bear. Her husband, Weasel, nodded, even though he was unimportant.

The rest nodded because everyone agreed. Sunfall Boy was young but he was touched by magic. And there were older men to guide him.

Eyes of Bear reached out a trembling hand and laid it on Sunfall Boy's head. Sunfall Boy's eyes widened further. They were going to do it. This was not something he had thought of, except maybe very secretly, in his tent in the darkness. But Long Walker had been young, and the Bear did not always speak next to a sister's son anyway. Long Walker had been no kin at all to the Old Bear before him. Thinking on "what if" did not catch fish.

But now it was clear that the spirits that had come to him had risen from the Bear's dying body, and their message, and all its mysterious content, was his life work to decipher.

Eyes of Bear's fingers caught up Sunfall Boy's scalp lock, where it fell unbound from the crest of his head, still crimped from its wrappings. He took a thong from his own hair and tied it, with some difficulty, into Sunfall Boy's. His fingers were bony, with knotted, gnarled joints, and they shook as he worked. When the scalp lock had been retied, his took up the rest of Sunfall Boy's hair, which, unbraided, reached his waist, and began to plait it.

"Go now into your manhood and in the darkness of your tent your mother and your wife may call you Sunfallen now, because you have stood above the sky and seen miracles. In the daylight, in the sun that is still in the sky, we will name you the Bear."

Sunfallen saw the eyes all watching him like a gathering of dark, bright birds. He thought: *They are waiting for me to tell them what to do.* The thought caught in his throat like a fish bone. *I don't know what to do!*

"First we must see the Old Bear onto his bier," Striped Badger said quietly, and Sunfallen looked at him gratefully. The title of nephew which Striped Badger accorded him was a courtesy only, but among the people of the

Bear, any young person was niece or nephew to an older and wiser one. In that way, untried footsteps were guided.

"Yes," he said. His voice squeaked and he cleared his throat. "Yes."

They sang as they raised the bier at sunset with Long Walker's body atop it, shrouded in his ceremonial bearskin and the painted buffalo hide that had been his tent. The plank platform rested on poles, higher than a man's head above the ground, its corners tied with buffalo tails and tassels of scarlet leather. The buffalo cow's horns, still red with Long Walker's blood, adorned the head of the bier. Around Long Walker's neck, under the painted shroud, was his necklace of bear claws.

The Bear Dancers cavorted solemnly about the bier, faces somber, heads capped with bear's ears. They faced the bier, stamping on the ground, the bearskins that hung from their shoulders wagging. When they turned around, Sunfallen's breath caught in his throat. The fires that were lit in the four directions, outside the circle of the dance, caught the dancers' faces and glinted on the teeth that protruded from their mouths, the bear teeth, sharp and yellow. The bear claws clacked as they waved their hands and the bear tails waggled behind. Striped Badger spun around in a circle, patting his big feet on the ground in time to the slap of the drummers' hands. Another bear bumped into him, and they faced off, growling, waving their paws at each other. The people chuckled. Striped Badger stamped his feet and pulled something suddenly from beneath his bearskin. The second dancer jumped back, peering at it with elaborate curiosity. Everyone leaned forward to see what it was.

Striped Badger had made it from a piece of buffalo skin and sticks—tall, bony, a comically elongated buffalo or maybe an elk with no horns. Instead, it had a long tail, as long as Striped Badger's arm, and a tuft of hair that grew straight up from the top of its head like a quail's crest, with circles for eyes, giving it a startled look.

"What is it?" the other Bear Dancer asked.

"What is it? What is it?" Striped Badger cocked his head at it, holding the thing out in front of him, looking at it all ways, from all directions. "We don't know what it is. What shall we do with it?"

"We'll think on it," the other dancer said, bending over, hands on his knees, to peer at it. "Think on it, think on it!"

"Think on it!" Striped Badger shouted, flinging the thing suddenly at Sunfallen. "The Bear will think on it!"

Sunfallen caught it in both hands. Its round monster eyes looked back at him mysteriously.

The ground thawed as Long Walker's body decayed on its bier. The Grass sent up new green shoots between the stiff brown remnants of last season and the ice broke on the streams. The children caught turtles in rush baskets and gathered icy hot cress by the handfuls from the tumbling water, starved over the long winter for something fresh and green. The sky shimmered and the air rumbled with the season's first thunderstorm. Sunfallen's people began to prepare for the spring hunt.

"It is necessary for the Bear to make his kill first." Striped Badger spoke quietly to Sunfallen, as he always did, lest someone hear him and the Bear be shamed at having to be told things he did not know.

"I know that," Sunfallen said. "I have been waiting for the trail to dry."

"They will not be denned now," Striped Badger said.

"I know that too. Is it right for the Bear to make his kill of a sleeping bear?"

"It has been done," Striped Badger said dryly.

Sunfallen sniffed. "Not by me."

Striped Badger smiled. "The Bear has made a wise choice." He meant the Bear Spirit which had chosen Sunfallen to lead his people, not Sunfallen himself, but it was open to misinterpretation. Sunfallen looked suitably modest.

"We will go in the morning's morning," Sunfallen informed him. Eyes of Bear had consulted the stars and said that that day would be propitious. The hunt had lain in the back of his mind like a cold handful of snow, the past moon since he had become the Bear, and it was a relief finally to let it loose. It was more than possible for a Bear not to return from his hunt if the Great Bear's choice had been misconstrued.

Sunfallen's words went through the camp on a Speaking Wind. The tribe of the Bear got up and made ready to do great things. A ritual bear hunt took more preparation than a hunt for food, and that in itself was an elaborate undertaking. For this, the Bear's first hunt—from which he would return with the claw necklace which he would wear for the rest of his life—great getting-ready was required. The camp filled with the smell of fat cooking for body paint; women bustled back and forth with medicine kits and journey bags of dried meat; children were sent on endless errands for water and bow strings and talismans affixed with bear magic unused since the Hunt of Long Walker. The men rebound spearpoints and fletched their bear arrows with new feathers, and everyone gave everyone else orders.

At dusk the Bear and his party took a sweat bath in a hide and willow-pole lodge built from scratch. As they emerged they offered smoke to the bear's skull who sat at the lodge's door.

"Come back into your body and grow fat," Sunfallen said to it, blowing smoke across its bleached and empty eyes, and its snarling teeth. "Come back into your fur and your teeth and claws, into your breath and heat. Rise and walk across the land so that we may track you."

The Bear Dancers cavorted past the skull, dancing their own way out of the sweat lodge, and everyone felt the magic that floated in their wake on the clouds of steam. Mothers gathered children to them and told them to stay inside their tents tonight. The camp dogs whined and skulked along the edges of the midden, starting at twilight sounds, and when it was dark, they crawled into their masters' tents and buried their noses in the bedding. In the night outside, the bear skull rose and shook itself, and its body came out of it like smoke, a ghost body, steam-born from the heat still living in the stones of the sweat lodge. It stood on its hind legs and looked around, and then it lumbered away into the night, leaving the dry skull behind it, overturned on the ground.

In the morning the tracker came back to say that he had found signs of a big grizzly, a morning's walk from the camp. He brought Sunfallen the scat and Sunfallen sniffed it and nodded.

Sunfallen washed away and repainted the red stripe that ran along the part in his hair. He painted his eyes with red circles made from scarlet earth and tallow, and his cheeks with blue stripes made from duck dung bought from people who lived by the lakes. The yellow paint of bull berries outlined a red sun and the blue bear's paw across his bare chest. On his arms and thighs were rings of white clay. All paint came from the earth and its creatures, and tied a man to that world so that he walked among it and through it in harmony.

Striped Badger took Sunfallen's hair and tied it into two knots on his head, one on each side, like bear's ears, and drew a single bear claw through the bundle that knotted his scalp lock. His mother, Blue Runner, gave him a new knife with a flint blade honed to a fine edge and a handle made from a bear's jawbone, with the teeth still in it. Weasel had made it, but Blue Runner gave it to him because her giving carried more power. All power came down through the mother, even though it was given to the son. Thus a chief's sister's son, child of his mother's daughter, had more standing than his own. (All the same,

Sunfallen was glad that Long Walker hadn't had any sons.)

The hunters left as the sky was just paling into an opalescent mist. Sunfallen took Striped Badger with him, and Weasel, his father, and six more, including the tracker, whose name was Dog Nose.

Dog Nose trotted along, head bent and nostrils flared wide like his namesake, a little man with brawny shoulders and silent feet. He could spot tracks that no one else could see, and it was rumored among the people of the Bear that he could smell the game in the wind. Certainly no one ever crept up on him even in the dark that he did not know who it was.

"He came past here, see," he said to Sunfallen and the hunters, but no one did. Farther on, where the trail zigzagged up a hill into a berry patch, they could see for themselves where the bear had fed among the torn vines. Dog Nose bent his head to the ground. "There." He pointed to the faint impression of the grizzly's pads in the soft earth. "He is feeding, not in a hurry."

"He is very big," Weasel said uncomfortably. "I saw a black bear's trail just the other day."

"This is the one the Bear has sent us," Sunfallen said, although he would have preferred a black bear, too. His father had excellent reasons for the suggestion. Grizzlies were unpredictable, big and smart and inclined to charge at people. They knew it was a male by the size, and Sunfallen was relieved by that. Even though females were smaller, they were more dangerous than males in the spring. Most would still be denned this early, sleeping while their cubs grew large enough to venture outside.

"We will find him when he has gone to earth," Striped Badger said. He made it sound like a simple matter, and Sunfallen brightened. It was always easier to be confident in Striped Badger's company.

Sunfallen clenched his fingers around his spear and then deliberately made himself loosen them. If you were afraid, Bear would eat you. He rubbed the smooth wood with his thumb. His quiver, heavy with flint-pointed bear arrows, was a comforting weight on his shoulder, but Sunfallen knew he must make the kill with his spear. Arrows, even bear arrows, might slow a grizzly but not kill him unless one made that lucky shot to the heart—and even then there were tales of grizzlies who had kept charging with arrows in them later found to have pierced their hearts through.

The trail meandered through the woods and stopped at another berry patch. From there the tracks angled downward toward a stream, and they saw where it had fished. The stones on the bank were marked with the silver smear of scales and a scattering of bones rippled in the shallows, caught against a mossy rock. The bear had padded farther along the bank, caught another fish, and moved on. Up a hillock beside the stream they marked where the grizzly had dug roots in a clearing, and then where it had torn out a groundhog's den, raking up the earth with claws as long as a man's fingers. Dog Nose declined to follow too speedily from there. The signs were fresh, and a freshly wakened bear is always hungry, ravenously hungry, and eats anything.

At midday the tracks turned upward again into the trees. The bear lumbered purposefully now, the marks of its feet farther apart.

"He is going to ground to sleep off the noonday sun," Dog Nose said softly, and they picked up their pace, keeping silent. The woods around them were still as the small things that had flattened themselves into invisibility at the bear's passing retreated once more. Halfway up the slope of a low hill, they found the carcass of a fawn among the sodden leaves of last winter's growth. It was newborn and there was little left of it but the bones.

Striped Badger clapped Sunfallen on the shoulder, his fingers gripping him tightly in a gesture of reassurance. "A full belly will make him sleepy."

Sunfallen could feel the sweat prickling his palms, and he wiped them on his leggings, shifting the heavy bear spear from hand to hand.

"He is big," Weasel said heartily now. "He will make a fine necklace."

"If you have necks left to put it around," Dog Nose hissed. "Be quiet! Do you think the bear puts stones in his ears to sleep?"

They dropped into silence as Dog Nose led them along a trail that they could all see now. The bear has passed over soft, damp ground, its big feet sinking into it heavily, leaving the mark of pads and claws like a handprint in the earth. Dog Nose held up a warning finger. At the foot of a bank they could see where the bear had dug its den under the roots of an upturned beech tree, disguising the entrance with clumps of moss and debris of dead branches.

Striped Badger took a wad of slowburner from the buffalo horn slung around his shoulder and selected a dry stick from the debris near the den. Weasel and the rest nocked their arrows and made a wide half circle around the den mouth. Sunfallen nocked his bear arrow and half drew the bow. He waited, trembling. Striped Badger thrust the burning stick into the den with a shout and leaped back. They heard the grizzly snarling and thumping inside, and then it exploded from the bank, eyes flaming with a surprise that turned to anger in an instant. It rose on its hind legs to stare at them furiously for a moment, as the hunters let loose their arrows. Three shafts stung it in the chest and shoulder and it came down on all four feet with a roar.

There was no time to loose a second arrow. The bear charged, and Sunfallen, his heart in his throat, stepped in front of the rest, spear leveled. Striped Badger and Weasel ran at the bear from the sides. The bear wasn't looking at anyone but Sunfallen. Its teeth were in Sunfallen's face, its huge paw swiped Sunfallen and sent him flying, claws raking blood from his ribs, and came after him. Sunfallen tumbled head over heels, losing his bow and quiver. He got to his feet with a fiery pain in his ribcage, clutching his spear in both hands as the bear came. He leveled the spear and thrust it at the bear's heart as it roared across the ground at him. The bear towered above Sunfallen, blocking the sky. Its eyes glowed red in its snarling face. The rest could not shoot for fear of hitting Sunfallen. They danced around the bear, pricking it with their spears to distract it, but none could make the kill but the Young Bear. If he missed, and Great Bear ate him, then he had been the wrong man. That was how they would know.

The bear's breath smelled of fish and the blood of the fawn. Its teeth were longer than Sunfallen's arm, its tearing mouth wide enough to fall into. He braced the spear against his thigh and rammed it into the bear's heart. At first he thought it would not go in, that the bear was made of hide so thick that it could not be pierced. Sunfallen leaned all his weight on the spear shaft and felt it break the hide. He drove it deeper as the bear's paws swiped at him, raking deep tracks across his face. His eye filled with blood.

Out of his other eye he saw the Bear stand on its hind legs, taller than the sky, saw the bones beneath the shaggy silver-grizzled hide, saw the heart of the beast within its cage of ribs, and the point of his spear embedded in its red core.

The Bear spoke to him. It said, *What I am, you are. What I have been, you will be. Remember also that what I am now, you will come to.*

Sunfallen drove the spearhead deeper still and the red blood gushed from the brown fur. The bear stood on its hind legs again, front legs pawing at the air. It fell slowly, tumbling through thick air, dropping silently to the leaves on the forest floor, blood running out between its teeth.

What I have been, you will be. The voice spoke to Sunfallen out of the dazzle of light that came through the treetops, and the red glaze of the blood in his eye.

Striped Badger knelt by the dead bear and pulled Sunfallen's spear from its chest. "A clean kill," he announced to the hunters ringed around them. "The Bear has chosen."

Sunfallen stood still, weaving on his feet, the pain in his ribcage making him dizzy. The face of the Bear looked back at him out of the sundazzle, and then faded, and he wiped cautiously at the blood in his eye.

"Let me look at that." Striped Badger pushed Sunfallen's hand away gently and wiped the eye with a handful of moss from his medicine kit. The blood welled up again swiftly.

"I can't see out of it," Sunfallen said. It was beneath the dignity of the Bear to whimper.

"Small wonder. He as near as anything took your eye out." A deep gash angled sharply from temple to eyebrow, stopping short of the eye on the bony ridge of the brow, above Sunfallen's nose. "Here, now, is this better?" Striped Badger held the moss to Sunfallen's eyebrow, soaking up the blood as it came.

Sunfallen squinted. "I can see."

"Well, that is fine, then," Striped Badger said cheerfully. "Goose From the North, who was Bear before Long Walker, who was Bear before you, lost a finger at his Hunt. His bear bit it off."

"I am fortunate indeed," Sunfallen said with dignity, and Striped Badger grinned at him. Sunfallen grinned back. The relief of having it over with thudded in his chest.

"Hold that moss to the cut," Striped Badger told him. "And you"—he pointed at two of the junior hunters—"get some ropes around this bear."

Sunfallen's bear was the biggest anyone had seen and it took all of them, hauling on four ropes, to drag it back to the camp. Striped Badger and Eyes of Bear both said it was a mark of favor from Great Bear. Blue Runner fluttered around Sunfallen, dabbing at his eye with salve until he told her to leave it alone. Weasel told everyone about the bear.

"It was taller than I would be standing on your shoulders."

"I can see from the carcass. A bear of legend." White Grass Mouse, who was Weasel's year-brother, nodded admiringly.

The smell of roasting meat rose from the cookpit at center camp, where the women turned the huge carcass on a wooden spit. The hide was already scraped and rubbed with the brains, rolled up to work overnight. Sunfallen sat by himself, fingering the claws about his neck wonderingly. Striped Badger and Eyes of Bear had cut them loose as soon as they reached the camp, and drilled and strung them so that they were around Sunfallen's neck before nightfall. That was important. Now he would never take them off. Long Walker's necklace still clung to his decaying body. When Long Walker was bones, the necklace would be burned with them.

Sunfallen could see Striped Badger watching him, amused, watching the mothers whisper to their daughters and give them little pushes toward Sunfallen, just enough so that they would walk past, not meaning to attract his attention, of course, but if he should happen to see them . . .

I will have to marry, Sunfallen thought. There would be trouble until he did. Sunfallen had no sisters, so his wife would be more powerful than Long Walker's had been. Ordinarily, Sunfallen would be told he was too young to marry if he took that notion in his head this year or the next. But now he was the Bear. That made the difference.

Two girls walked past him, laughing softly, whispering to each other, their dark eyes watching him out of the corners. *How will I pick one?* he thought, panicked.

Blue Runner came from the fire pit and sat next to him.

"You must talk to me about these girls," she said to Sunfallen. "You must talk to me first."

"I don't know about any girls." Sunfallen fingered the bear claw necklace, the claws that had been on the bear only that morning.

Blue Runner studied her son with a certain suspicion. "Young men your age always know about girls."

"You said I was too young," Sunfallen pointed out. "When you found out I had gone walking with Little Yellow Bird."

"That girl is not the girl for you."

"Why not?" Sunfallen asked, just to be argumentative. Little Yellow Bird was so shy she had hardly spoken a word, and since Sunfallen was shy too, it had not been a success.

"Her father owns a tent so old you can see through the hide, and one dog with fleas. The Bear must choose a wife carefully. From among girls of good families. A girl with the proper spirit," Blue Runner added, which meant doing what her mother-in-law told her to. Little Yellow Bird would have done that.

"I will be careful to know your opinion, Mother." Blue Runner would let him know it whether he asked or not.

She beamed at him approvingly, her face lit by the glow of the fires that dotted the camp and shone from within the tents of the Bear. In the flicker of red flame, she looked young, as she might have looked when her brother had gone to hunt his Bear, and she had stayed at home and married Weasel, who had been picked out by her own mother. Sunfallen wondered who she would have married if she had done the picking. He had never dared to ask.

It was hard to learn to be the Bear. Eyes of Bear, turtled into his blanket with only his bony nose sticking out, recited the prayers that gave Great Bear thanks for his meat and his fur and his wisdom, and asked him to intercede with Buffalo to bring the great herd to the hunting grounds. His thin fingers told off the prayers on the claws of Sunfallen's necklace so that Sunfallen had to crane his head around, pressing his chin into his neck like an owl, to look at Eyes of Bear while he did so. Then Sunfallen was made to take all his clothes off and stand in the slushy melting snow while Eyes of Bear and Striped Badger and the rest of the Bear Dancers washed him and painted him with a fourfold design of claws that splayed out across his chest like a strange flower. He could see the girls watching him from a little distance, ready to giggle and run if Eyes of Bear growled at them. The paint sticks tickled his chest and thighs and when he saw the girls looking at him he felt himself getting bigger, which made Striped Badger guffaw.

"Tell that one to put itself away," Eyes of Bear said severely.

"It doesn't do what I tell it."

"A young man's never does." Striped Badger nodded his round face up and down happily, apparently pleased with his protégé.

When they were done with him, Sunfallen tied his breechclout back on hastily, but it was a point of pride with the young men to go nearly bare even in the snow, so he left his leggings and shirt off.

Then they began to teach him. Eyes of Bear opened the tribe's magic bundles and took out the sacred objects and laid them out on a skin one by one while Sunfallen held his breath. These were the heart of the tribe, its breath in its mouth. Every man had his own bundle, his personal talismans and love charms and feathers or fur that symbolized his vision spirit. He kept it hung around his neck, or tied in a special beaded, feathered, fringed case in his tent, with his paints and his pipe. These, the Bundles of the Tribe, gave to the tribe itself what each man's bundle gave to him—life and wealth and guidance on the road from birth to death.

The largest of the Bundles lived in a quilled case of white calfskin, fringed with drilled shell beads and painted with the linked spirals that showed how all life was connected to itself, how nothing stood alone from the rest of creation.

"This is the antler of the deer who spoke to Thunder First Father and gave us hunting magic." Eyes of Bear balanced a small, worn point of horn reverently in his palm.

Sunfallen nodded solemnly. The antler glowed dimly with remembered life.

Eyes of Bear produced a small round blue stone from a pouch of red cloth. "This is the stone that was given by the mountain to him who was Bear in the days of the Great Moving, and cloth woven by the people who live in mud houses in the west. And these are the health and wealth and swiftness of the tribe, and the water-finder." He laid out a buffalo's hoof, a string of elk teeth, a quill-wrapped bundle of eagle feathers, and a braided strip of otter skin.

Sunfallen made a gesture of respect at them all. They were old and luminescent with power.

Eyes of Bear unwrapped the lesser bundles then, naming the powdered herbs and bits of wood and bone that lay inside. Each had a history, each had been given to or found by a man whose deeds were now remembered in the Song of the Heroes or the Song of the Buffalo Warriors.

Each name and song was Sunfallen's to learn, a sign to carve onto his heart, Eyes of Bear said. By reciting the names and the deeds and the descent of each generation, the history of the tribe was known.

At dawn on the next day, Grandmother Scarlet Water came to tell him the descent of the mothers of the Bear.

"The names of the Fifty-Eight Grandmothers are Lightning First Mother, Sunrise daughter of Cloud, Blue Stone daughter of Sunrise, Long Day daughter of Lily,

Swimmer at Night daughter of Follow who was sister to Lily, Chipmunk daughter of—"

"Stop! My head is full!" Sunfallen waved his hands at Grandmother Scarlet Water as she leaned on her stick, one quivering arm holding her up while the other counted, clawlike, the names of ancestresses in the air.

"They must be learned." Striped Badger clapped him on the shoulder encouragingly. His broad smiling face nodded up and down. "The Bear must know."

"I can't remember them all."

"That is why we will say them over four times a day. Then you will learn them."

Sunfallen groaned. The Fifty-Eight Grandmothers comprised the lineage of the tribe of the Bear, the Bear's endless mothers, clear down now to his own mother Blue Runner, daughter of Blackbird, at the end of them. With each new Bear, there was yet another mother to learn. He wished he had been born in Time Way Back, when there weren't so many.

"Chipmunk was daughter of Chokecherry Girl and the man from over the Mountains," Grandmother Scarlet Water went on relentlessly. "Her daughters did not live and the next Bear was son of Bird daughter of Raven. Then came the Antelope Sisters whose mother was Bird."

They went on and on, endless mothers, bringing into the tribe new incarnations of the Bear, marrying strangers, dying in childbirth, one vanishing magically into the sky. That story fascinated him, but Grandmother Scarlet Water wouldn't say how she did it, just that it had happened. It was not her job to explain, only to remember and list.

When he had learned the Fifty-Eight Grandmothers, and the Song of the Deeds of Burned Buffalo, and the Song of the Coming of the Cub, then Eyes of Bear brought out the calendar hides of the tribes of the Bear and showed him the procession of years across them, not as far back as the Cub or Lightning First Mother, but back as far as the year of the Great Fire when Burned Buffalo son of Porcupine became the Bear. There were more hides than Sunfallen had learned to count, each neatly rolled and tied with a red cord and stowed in the keeping of Eyes of Bear. There were so many now that they had their own tent, and their own dog travois to carry them when the tribe moved on. Eyes of Bear unrolled each and spread it before Sunfallen.

"Here is the buffalo hunt of Goose From the North in his first year, when the white bull calf was found. And here is the great drought that came the year before, and then the great rain that the white calf brought."

It was all painted on the hide, in concentric circles beginning with the earliest events at the center, the brown grass broken by the drought, and then the white calf running in a circle around it sunwise, and then the long jagged blue lines of the rain. The years of the tribe spiraled out from the heart of each hide. There was no set number of years that a hide might hold, for only great and momentous events were recorded. Some who had been Bear in uneventful days had no record of their tenure left at all.

I will do some deed to be painted on my hide, Sunfallen thought. Otherwise the only memory of him would be his mother's name in the Counting of the Grandmothers. Even the white buffalo calf's hide was preserved as the box that held the magic bundles of the tribe. "Why don't we remember the names of the Bear?" he asked Striped Badger indignantly.

"Because Bear has only one name, and that is Bear. He only borrows yours for a while.

"It is necessary to attend to the lesson at hand." Eyes of Bear put that hide away tenderly and unrolled the next one.

Sunfallen looked rebellious. "I am tired of learning the names of dead people."

"Let the boy rest for a while," Striped Badger said. "He is young."

"He is the Bear," Eyes of Bear said. "He must learn."

"But not all at once. If you trample the young grass, it does not grow so well."

"And if there is no rain, it does not grow at all. But very well." Eyes of Bear rolled the hide up grumpily. "We will begin again tomorrow."

"My head aches," Sunfallen said plaintively.

Striped Badger smiled. "The cure for that is fishing."

"I don't like fish."

"The point of fishing is not to eat fish." Striped Badger took him by the hand and pulled him to his feet. "The point of fishing is to lie on the riverbank and think and look at the sky. Come along." He went to his own tent and fetched a basket of bone hooks and a roll of fine line made from hair and put them in a bag. He prodded Sunfallen down the muddy trail to the stream. A beaver working on a young birch heard them coming and trundled away.

"I will never learn all these things," Sunfallen said, as they settled in a spot Striped Badger selected, where the low sun streamed in yellow strands under a willow's rustling pale green fronds, and the stream eddied into a small blue-black pool.

"You will learn more," Striped Badger said placidly, knotting line onto hook while Sunfallen dug worms from the cold mud of the bank with the tip of his belt knife. "They will all be graven onto your heart when you are done with it, the things that are the Matter of the Tribe. But Eyes of Bear is an old fool who remembers not his youth. My father's father told me that he was wilder than any boy of his year and sat in a tree and refused to recite the Song of the Road to the High Place when the other boys were learning it, and thumbed his nose and made rude noises at his teachers."

"Eyes of Bear?"

"Indeed. It is a shame he has forgotten that."

Sunfallen tried to imagine Eyes of Bear young enough to stand up straight without his stick, his skin smooth and unwrinkled, hiding in a tree. He couldn't. It was cold sitting on the muddy stream bank, and Sunfallen thought longingly of a fire and hot soup in his tent, but Striped Badger seemed content here, fiddling with his hooks, whistling a little between his teeth like a courting flute. Sunfallen eyed the pool pessimistically. He never caught anything. A little way upstream the beaver had half finished his dam.

Striped Badger handed him a hook and line and Sunfallen poked a worm onto it and dropped it into the cold waters of the pool. It undulated in the water, making concentric rings that rippled the surface. The other worms tried to wriggle away and Sunfallen put them in the bag with the hooks. "Tell me why I have to learn these things. And don't tell me it is because I am the Bear. Why is it important?"

"It is always important to do honor to the Grandmothers." Striped Badger was baiting his own hook. "When there is great power in a thing, it is wise to make polite gestures to it."

"All right," Sunfallen conceded. "But why do I have to know every drop of rain that has fallen since Coyote pulled the ground up from under the lake?"

"How do you know not to stick your hand in the fire?"

"Because I have been told I will be burned if I do."

"Indeed. Because some other person in the First Times stuck his hands in the fire and was burned. Thus we see the use of history."

Sunfallen chuckled. A fish tugged at his worm and he wriggled the line so that it squirmed interestingly.

"If fish had history, they would not eat worms off hooks," Striped Badger said.

12

The Fourth Wonderful Thing

THE NEXT DAY, WHITE GRASS MOUSE CAME TO SUNfallen to say that he and Weasel had killed a buffalo cow but Surprised Raven and his brothers had taken it. Whistle came to complain that Nighthawk Woman had left a dead snake in her path, and Nighthawk Woman said that Whistle had put a spell on her.

Sunfallen wondered what he was supposed to do about these things, and it came to him that these people wanted him to settle their troubles—to give the buffalo cow to the rightful owner and remove any curses. Whistle clutched the snake for proof of Nighthawk Woman's wickedness, and White Grass Mouse waved the bloodied arrow with which he personally had killed the buffalo cow.

Sunfallen looked around him for guidance and Striped Badger stepped out of the shadow of the tent, where they had caught Sunfallen before he had even properly dressed or had his morning mush.

"I believe I saw that Surprised Raven's wife has begun to butcher that cow," he murmured.

"See?" White Grass Mouse bristled indignantly. "I left Weasel there to keep him off, but they pay him no mind!"

"Is she dividing the meat?" Sunfallen inquired. He thought he saw the way that Striped Badger would have him take this.

"It doesn't matter," White Grass Mouse said stubbornly. "That thief is saying that my arrow missed. He went and pulled an arrow out of a tree and said that was mine. But this is my arrow." He shook it under Sunfallen's nose.

"Stop that," Sunfallen said, pushing it away. "I can see it without your putting it up my nose. Is Surprised Raven's wife dividing the meat?" That was the law in the case of a disputed kill.

"Yes," White Grass Mouse said grudgingly. "But that doesn't matter. It is a matter of honor. Not only my honor, either," he added. "It is Weasel's honor."

"What about Surprised Raven's honor and that of his brothers?" Sunfallen put his hand over his mouth as if he were deep in thought. White Grass Mouse was making him laugh, jumping up and down as if he had fallen into a box. And Sunfallen wasn't going to fall into the trap of considering his father's case differently from any other man's. He was the Bear now. Eyes of Bear and Striped Badger had made that plain to him. He was no man's child but Great Bear's.

"Surprised Raven has no honor," White Grass Mouse said sulkily.

"Is that wise to say?"

"The Bear speaks and I obey." White Grass Mouse's mouth pursed into an annoyed pucker. "But that was Surprised Raven's arrow in the tree."

Behind Sunfallen, Striped Badger murmured softly, "The Bear learns that often there is more and more to a story, like a skein of rope unfolding."

"Surprised Raven also was shooting at this cow?" Sunfallen asked.

"Yes. But he missed."

"No doubt. But it is wrong for the tribe when the hunters fight and call each other bad names."

"I didn't."

"You called him a liar. And he said your aim was bad. So I command both of you to stop."

White Grass Mouse sniffed. "The people of the Bear are free people."

"Then they should refrain from asking the Bear for judgment," Sunfallen said.

White Grass Mouse went away grumpily to claim his share of the cow, and Whistle stepped into his place. She was about fifteen summers old and newly married. Sunfallen looked desperately at Striped Badger, who appeared to be counting the clouds, judging by his position, hands behind his back, neck craned skyward. Sunfallen, who had settled himself on a hide box outside his tent and wished violently for his breakfast, sighed. He eyed the snake.

"Right in my path. Outside my tent." Whistle held it by the tail, a limp green grass snake.

"And you say Nighthawk Woman put it there?"

"Who else? Snakes don't come to my tent to die." Whistle looked venomously at Nighthawk Woman. "Ever since I married this woman's nephew."

"Ever since you married my nephew, my knees hurt!" Nighthawk Woman said. "Just like that! Overnight! I told him not to marry her, and now see what she does to me."

"Why did you tell him not to marry her?" Sunfallen asked, distracted by curiosity. He had a vague recollection of his mother talking of bad blood between those families, but he hadn't paid attention. It was no business of his. Now it seemed that he must poke his nose into every squabble.

"She's a witch," Nighthawk Woman said.

"Snake tongue!" Whistle said. She threw the actual snake at Nighthawk Woman. It landed with a dead thud across her instep and Nighthawk Woman flung it away from her, dancing on her toes.

"Be quiet!" Sunfallen bellowed at them, and saw Striped Badger's eyebrow go up a notch. "You are making my head hurt. Take that snake away."

Whistle picked it up by the tail again, with dignity. She jiggled it a little at Nighthawk Woman, glaring. "Here," she said to a small boy, who was watching the proceedings with interest. "Put this snake on the midden."

The boy looked as if he didn't want to miss anything, but when an adult asked something, you were supposed to do it—particularly if the Bear was watching you—even if the Bear had only been Sunfall Boy a handspan of days ago. The child took the snake and headed for the midden, amusing himself by dancing as he went and holding it high by the tail so that it bounced. A dog got up and followed him.

The boy disappeared around the last tent, into the handful of windbent trees that lay between the camp and the midden.

"Now what do you want?" Sunfallen demanded of Whistle and Nighthawk Woman.

"I don't want to live next to someone who can catch snakes. Tell her to move her tent."

"Tell her to take off the spell she put on me."

"There isn't any spell that will make you not old and ugly. Yah!" Whistle made a face at her.

The boy came running back, still clutching the snake by the tail. His eyes were wide as an owl's. He stopped in front of Sunfallen and opened his mouth.

"You were told to get rid of that thing," Sunfallen said.

The boy dropped the snake where he stood. "There is a herd of horrible things in the valley beyond the midden. They are coming this way."

"Horrible things?"

"I expect *she* brought them," Nighthawk Woman offered, jerking a thumb at Whistle.

Sunfallen snapped his head around and looked at her. "Be quiet now," he said very softly, and Nighthawk Woman closed her mouth. "What sort of things?" he asked the boy.

"Big as elk," he said. "But they have long faces, and hair like a person's growing down their necks. White ones and red ones and spotted ones. There are women riding on their backs. They shouted at me when they saw me and I ran so fast."

"Demons!" Nighthawk Woman said.

"Yah! They have come for you," Whistle told her.

Nighthawk Woman shrieked.

"Be still!" Sunfallen looked at Striped Badger. "I think they are my vision spirits." He was a little afraid now that they had followed him to camp. He had not expected that. "Were they real women on their backs?" he asked the boy.

"They looked real to me. There were two of them," the boy said. "They had a dog with them that barked at me. I was afraid of them, though."

"Perhaps the Bear should put his shirt and leggings on," Striped Badger suggested.

Sunfallen looked down at his breechclout, which seemed an inadequate garment in which to greet magical women riding spirits. Striped Badger was right. "Go away now," he said to Whistle and Nighthawk Woman. "My order is that Nighthawk Woman has to move her tent—*if* there are any more snakes," he added, as Nighthawk Woman opened her mouth indignantly. "And Whistle is to treat her husband's aunt with respect and remember that she herself is young and ignorant."

"Very well," Whistle said, because current events were much more exciting than her quarrel with Nighthawk Woman. "But can't we stay and see the monsters?"

"They may eat you," Striped Badger suggested.

Nighthawk Woman left hurriedly, but Whistle shook her head. "They did not eat the Bear, so why should they eat me? I will stay."

Sunfallen abandoned the conversation and went into his tent. He took out his best leggings, the ones with the fringe and shell beads on the sides, and his good shirt of doeskin, painted with blue lines of water and red suns in a pattern that he liked. Water and light were the elements of life. Surely they would give him power when speaking to these spirits. He wondered uneasily what they had come to tell him to do.

The rest of the people in the camp had seen them too, by the time Sunfallen came back out of his tent, regal in his bear claw necklace, a buffalo robe across his shoulders. The spirit women and their creatures had stopped just this side of the woods between the camp and the midden. The spirit animals were eating grass, like deer, which eased Sunfallen's mind somewhat.

The people of the Bear fell silent as Sunfallen approached, and waited for him to tell them what these things were, and what they ought to do about them. Surprised Raven had his bow in his hand, an arrow nocked to the string.

"Put that down," Sunfallen said quietly. The women on the spirit animals waited silently, eyes on Surprised Raven's bow. Sunfallen could see their shoulders loosen as Surprised Raven let his arm fall. They had no magic weapons, then, and were afraid of a bow.

There were eight of the animals, counting the two that the women rode on, and one dog, a very ordinary looking one. The spirit animals, on the other hand, looked like nothing on earth that Sunfallen had ever seen, except in his vision on the High Place, and no one really expected that sort of vision to solidify and come to your camp. Visions were things of the mind, like dreams, just as real as the world of dirt, but separate. Not since Time Way Back had a vision spirit actually materialized in the flesh.

"The Bear welcomes you," he said, to see what they would do.

The women cocked their heads at him, listening, but

they didn't appear to understand. They were an old one—not a grandmother, but the age of his own mother—and a young one, about the age of Whistle. They wore ordinary-looking clothes, dresses of doeskin, hiked up about their thighs where they straddled the spirit animals, and somewhat trailworn. The parts in their hair were painted red, as Grass women almost all did, and their hair was braided in two braids each that hung over their shoulders. The old woman was ordinary looking. The younger one was the one he had seen at the High Place, and even now, here in the flesh, this one was different. Her skin was paler than most people's, as if the sun had somehow bleached her like old bones, not darkened her, as it did to other people. Her hair, where it escaped from her braids in thin wisps, curled like a buffalo calf's around her face, and he could see that the ends of her braids curled too. It wasn't black, like ordinary people's hair, but brown, like a mouse or a ground squirrel. He half expected her eyes to be light, too, like a coyote's, but they weren't. They were brown like his own.

The older woman made a gesture with one hand that caught his eye and puzzled him.

"That is the Sign Talk of the Grass," Striped Badger whispered in his ear. "Which the Bear knows."

Sunfallen looked at her again, and she made the gesture again, and now it made sense, as if he had come blinking out of a dark tent, blinded, and she had come suddenly into focus.

"We come from the south," she said.

Spirits generally came from the north.

Sunfallen lifted his own hands while everyone watched him. (They noted with relief that he was being advised by Striped Badger.) "I am Sunfallen the Bear. Have you come to talk to me?" he asked with his hands.

The women looked puzzled now. The older one fluttered her hands at him. "We are from the Dry River people to the south," she said.

Ah. Sunfallen had heard of them. Heard strange tales of them, in fact. He hunted all round the edges of his mind to see if he could find these tales. Something heard from a trader in the winter, but he hadn't been listening. He had been a child, only those few months ago.

"The trader," he said to Striped Badger. "The man from the south with the turquoise beads. We bought meal from him."

Striped Badger nodded to show that he remembered.

"He told a tale. I remember sitting with my father, listening, half asleep. About some new animal. I thought it was fancy. Just something to earn his dinner with."

Striped Badger's eyes widened. He remembered. "The Bear is wiser than his years," he said quietly.

"He said people in the south ride its back to hunt the buffalo. He said also that pale-skinned monsters have brought it here." The story was beginning to materialize in Sunfallen's head, mixed with the dream he had been dreaming while the trader talked with Weasel his father. Then Sunfallen had gone back to the Boys' House where he lived with the other unmarried boys and dreamed more dreams, about riding on an elk, very far up in the air, a monster elk with fiery red eyes. Then, in the way of boys, he had forgotten all about it.

Now he lived in a tent newly painted and sewn by his mother, as befitted the Bear, and the name of the animal came to him suddenly. "Horse," he said.

The strange women looked at him, startled. "Horse," the young one said back to him. He wondered if she was one of the pale-skinned monster people the trader had talked of, but she wasn't all that pale. Very likely the trader had exaggerated, in the way of storytellers.

"Horse," the older woman said, and she made a new gesture with her hands to show that that would mean horse in Sign Talk.

"Why have you come here, with these horses?" Sunfallen asked her. His eyes strayed again to the younger one.

"We have come to give them to you," the older woman said.

There was a murmur, compounded of both fear and greed at that. It ran like a ripple through Sunfallen's people.

"Why?"

There was no answer.

Sunfallen pointed at the younger woman. "I saw this person on the High Place and she spoke to me, but I did not understand her then."

"Do you understand me now?" the younger one asked with her hands.

"Maybe," Sunfallen said. With spirits you never knew, because they might speak in riddles or a kind of code. "Are you a spirit?" he asked her.

The young one looked at the other. A fleeting look of mischief crossed her face. The older one shook her head. The younger one chuckled. "No," she told Sunfallen.

Sunfallen felt disappointed.

"I am daughter to the Dry River people," the young one said, making a face at the name. "They were wicked people and drove my mother and me away. I am called Rain Child. This is my mother, Flute Dog. We have come to live with you."

Even if they weren't spirits, Sunfallen thought, surely spirits had sent them. "Why did those people drive you away?" The stories were full of people who had seen spirits and had neglected to listen to them, or had treated them with disrespect. Then the spirits took away their gifts. He eyed the horses hungrily. They were beautiful beyond imagining.

Flute Dog frowned at her daughter. She made soothing gestures at Sunfallen. "My daughter was born to a stranger woman from the Cities-in-the-West, in a cave where I found her. As you can see, she does not look like other people, and my people, who are stupid and ill-mannered, were afraid of her. Also, they thought that we owned too many horses for women who were not married, and so they were jealous."

Sunfallen knew that what one man may foolishly reject may bring luck to another. He also knew that luck ran both ways, and these women looked willful. Still, the spirits had sent the girl to him in the High Place, so they had a plan for her. "Why have you brought these horses to us?"

The older one looked weary. "It is time that we lived among people again."

The younger one looked crafty. "Also, it is not right that the people of the South Grass hunt all the buffalo meat they need in one killing, while the people of the North Grass must go hungry, tracking their meat on foot."

There was a murmur of agreement at that among the people of the Bear. Not fair at all, they felt. They eyed the horses possessively, already assessing their usefulness.

Sunfallen stared at them, with their wide, round hooves, not split like Deer's, and dark, liquid, intelligent eyes. "Are they very fast when they run?" Sunfallen asked. "Can anyone ride one?"

"Come and see," the girl said suddenly. She slipped down from her spotted horse and led it toward him by the rope around its head. Surprised Raven scuttled backward out of their path, and mothers grabbed their children by the shoulders, pulling them close. Only Whistle stood her ground and touched its flank as they went by.

Nighthawk screeched and pulled at her nephew's sleeve. "Make her get away from it!"

Sunfallen resisted the urge to step backward himself, which would be beneath the dignity of the Bear. Striped Badger also stood his ground at Sunfallen's elbow, but it was to Sunfallen that she brought the horse. It looked at him soberly and nodded its head twice.

"Horse," he said to it, so it would know he knew its name. "I am the Bear." He needn't tell it his true name. That way he would have a power over it that it would not have over him.

The horse, whose face was white with red spots spattered across it, made a loud snort down its long nose and Sunfallen jumped.

"It's all right," the girl said with her hands, laughing.

"I know that." Sunfallen looked at the horse. It snorted again and bobbed its head up and down. It made a strange chuckling noise in its throat, like an old man with a high-pitched laugh. Sunfallen's shoulders tensed, waiting for it to make the shriek he had heard at the High Place, but it butted its head into his chest instead. Its head was hard and bony. Sunfallen staggered back in spite of himself.

"He thinks you have something to eat in your shirt," the girl said. "He likes melons and squash, and maize cakes."

"Tell him there is nothing in my shirt but me," Sunfallen said.

"They don't talk."

"They don't?"

"They are animals, like deer or dogs. They talk to each other, but not to us. He will like to lick the salt from your hand, though."

Sunfallen was not at all sure that he would like that, but she was plainly expecting him to try it.

"Like this," she said, holding her hand out flat, palm up.

Sunfallen did so, too. The horse nuzzled his fingers with soft, clever lips, and then licked his palm. Its tongue was as big as a buffalo's and it emerged from a mouthful of long, yellow-white teeth. The tongue was warm, like a dog's.

Rain Child looked sideways at the boy while Mud-Spattered Horse licked his hand. He was plainly the chief of these people, but the older man standing beside him had some power. The older man had a dreamy look, as if he were always thinking important thoughts about something far away. He was watching her and pretending not to.

"Do you want to ride on a horse?" she asked the boy, to get him away from the other man. The boy looked startled, and she waved her hands at him again to be sure he knew what she meant. The boy looked from the ground to the top of Mud-Spattered Horse's back. He looked as if he thought it was a long way. Mud-Spattered Horse was also likely to throw him, which would not start things off the way that Mother wished. Rain Child grabbed Mud-Spattered Horse's withers and swung herself onto his back again. She smiled down at the boy. "I'll bring you a horse. Wait here."

Rain Child picked out Blue Squirrel Horse, who was the littlest of the herd, as well as the gentlest. She whistled to her and Blue Squirrel Horse followed Mud-Spattered Horse over to where the boy was still standing, looking as if giant turtles had just landed from the sky in front of his tent. Rain Child untied a spare bridle from around her waist and slipped it into Blue Squirrel Horse's mouth. She led her over to the stones of the camp firepit, beckoning the boy to follow. "It is easier to get on their backs from a rock, until you have practiced it."

Sunfallen nodded. He had seen the girl swing herself onto the animal's back and suspected correctly that this was not something one wished to practice in front of people. He stepped onto the edge of the fire pit and felt the horse's warm gray-speckled back. It made a friendly noise at him out of its nose. Sunfallen swung one leg over its back, balancing on the tip of the other toe. The girl came around to the horse's other side, leaned over from her own horse, and pulled him up, her hands around his waist. The horse began to walk suddenly and he grabbed at the hair on its neck with both hands.

The girl leaned over and put the horse's rope rein into one of his hands, taking it in hers and uncurling the fingers to do so. "Hold that," she said. "That is how you tell her where you want to go."

Sunfallen was not afraid of heights. He had climbed trees all his life. He had sat on the top of the High Place. But none of those things had got up and moved. He held the rein and gripped the horse's mane with both hands at the same time.

"You are doing it very well," the girl said encouragingly with her hands. Sunfallen didn't know how to answer her without taking his own off the horse's neck, which he was not going to do. The horse walked behind the girl's, passing by all the people of the Bear, who goggled at their leader like frogs, eyes raised, mouths open.

The girl led the way out of the camp, past the trees in whose shade the other horses were cropping grass, and the midden with its heap of bones and ash. The gray dog trotted at the spotted horse's heels, stopping to investigate the midden until the girl shouted at her. Sunfallen felt the horse move between his legs, felt the long muscles stretch and release, and the heat of the warm hide soak into his. A breeze danced by and lifted the horse's forelock in its passing, and he felt his scalp lock flutter on his head to the same tune.

There was such power in this animal. If it was not a spirit itself, then surely it was a thing of magic. It moved beneath him like the slow thunder of the buffalo when they ran across the plain. And all that power danced to the tug of a thin rope rein. Sunfallen relaxed his fingers and tried to hold the rein the way the girl had shown him, loosely in his fingers. His other hand kept its grip. The girl smiled and maneuvered her horse into place beside his. Sunfallen looked at her curiously now, and smiled back at her. Maybe, like the horse, she was not a spirit herself, but spirit-sent.

Up close, her curling hair looked like wisps and

strands of fine cloud. Her nose was short and turned up at the end and her skin was the color of the sand along the riverbank. He had had no notion that people came in different colors, like dogs.

His horse began suddenly to trot and Sunfallen grabbed at its mane with both hands. Its backbone felt as if it would drive itself up between his legs until he was neatly sliced in two halves, and then he would fall away, one on each side of the horse, and the horse would just keep going.

"Tell it to stop!" he shouted at the girl, but she didn't understand him. Her horse began to keep pace with his. Sunfallen bounced up and down like a sack being shaken out, but the girl didn't. She sat glued to her horse, smiling at him. Suddenly she clucked to his horse and put her heels to the flanks of hers and both horses lengthened their stride.

The ground fell away beneath Sunfallen at an alarming rate, but the bouncing and shaking had stopped. This running was like being swung in a cradleboard from a high tree, exhilarating and frightening, terror laced through with a fierce excitement.

The sound of the horses' hooves on the ground echoed the booming in his head. The speckled horse beneath him lengthened its stride further and they flew across the Grass like a huge bird, like a stooping hawk. The girl turned sideways to him, swaying on the spotted horse's back. She dropped her rein, and her hands asked him, "Is this better? A gallop is easier on the backside than a trot."

Sunfallen nodded, too petrified to lift his hands to answer. He smiled, to indicate to her that he was not afraid, only preoccupied with studying this new experience.

The horses flew across the Grass with the little gray dog at their side, her body stretched out in a full run. Her ears streamed behind her and her tongue hung out like a flag. A rabbit burst from the ground at their feet and the spotted horse leaped sideways in midair with a snort, but Sunfallen's horse kept on running. He looked back to see what had happened to the girl, but she was still on the horse, soothing it with a small hand and laughing. Then the spotted horse thundered after them again and drew even with Sunfallen's. It occurred to him, and he knew sheepishly that it was true, that the girl had given him the slower and safer of the two.

"It takes practice," the girl said, reining in her horse, seeming to know what he was thinking. Sunfallen's horse slowed too. "Among my people we ride from the time we are babies." She stuck two fingers in her mouth and whistled sharply, and the gray dog abandoned the rabbit and came back to them.

"I will learn." Sunfallen felt entirely confident of that, now that they were ambling at a walk again. It didn't matter that this was a slow horse. He had done what no one else had had the courage to do in getting on it in the first place, as befitted the Bear.

The little gray dog gave a short, sharp bark and they turned her way to see three dogs running along a ridge that crested where the valley began to walk up into low hills, tearing at a bloodied rabbit as they went.

The girl leaned down easily from the spotted horse's back and scooped up a stone. She threw it at the dogs and shouted at them. "Go away, Mannerless! You can't come here!"

"Are they yours?" Sunfallen asked.

"No. They are wild."

He looked over his shoulder. The dogs were still trailing them as they rode. They kept their distance, but it was plain they were following the horses.

The girl laid her rein on the spotted horse's neck and it turned, with the gray horse following. "We will go back to your people before they think I have stolen you," she said to Sunfallen with a smile and a look over her shoulder again.

When they rode back into the camp, Flute Dog had dismounted and Striped Badger was talking solemnly with her, all four of their hands waving very fast, while the people stood around and stared at the horses. Whistle had snuck over to one and was rubbing its soft nose with her palm.

When Sunfallen and Rain Child dismounted, the people swarmed around them, bringing Flute Dog and Striped Badger in their wake.

"This is a very good place we have come to," Flute Dog whispered to Rain Child. "These people are very intelligent. They are not afraid of new things."

"I could show you where to put your tent." Whistle, on Rain Child's other side, waved her hands. "The horse animals could graze there, too," she added, looking longingly at them.

Other people sidled up and patted Rain Child's arms and hair, pulling the wispy curls around her face out straight and letting them go to see how they sprang back.

"Stop that," Whistle said, "she isn't a toy."

Rain Child went with the girl, who looked to be her own age, to a spot beside the tent that Whistle shared with her husband, and unloaded their own tent off the horse travois. The Striped Badger person who had been talking to Flute Dog helped them set it up while Sunfallen the Bear gave people orders about a feast and a buffalo cow that some people had been arguing over (Whistle explained to her) and set them all to work.

When the tent was up, Flute Dog and Rain Child went inside it and shut the doorflap. They could hear the people standing around outside, waiting for them to come out again.

"Phoo," Rain Child said. "They are like a litter of puppies. They are everywhere."

"They're curious." Their voices sounded outside the tent, mysterious and untranslatable as birds. "Leave that pot and the beads in here," Flute Dog said. "Hide them."

Rain Child pouted. She wanted to wear the bright red and blue beads. Sunfallen the Bear would like those.

"They are trouble. Like those dogs. These people will think *you* are trouble, again."

"Maybe I *am* trouble," Rain Child said resentfully.

"No, trouble only comes to you." Flute Dog sighed. "I'm not sure why. But leave it in the tent this time."

Rain Child sulked, but obeyed. They could smell meat cooking and hear a bustle of activity and a buzz of voices, bee voices zooming about the tent. When they emerged, the girl Whistle was waiting for them with her husband, whom she introduced with hand gestures as Swallow. He was a little, quick man with bright eyes, not much taller than Whistle. Whistle had a round, interested face and hands with long, clever fingers. An older woman hung back two paces from them, glaring.

"That is my husband's aunt," Whistle said, working the relationship out on her fingers for Rain Child. "Bad Dream Woman."

The older woman took a swift stride forward and boxed Whistle's ears. Swallow pushed them apart. "Her name is Nighthawk Woman, and my wife is being very bad." He shook a finger at Whistle, but his lip twitched.

Flute Dog drew the older woman aside. Rain Child saw her hands saying something about young girls and manners. Mother was tactful when she wanted to be. Nighthawk Woman subsided somewhat. Her hands said something back about stranger people with big animals next to her tent, and not being asked about it. Flute Dog nodded sympathetically.

Whistle linked her arm through Rain Child's, chattering with her other hand so fast that Rain Child couldn't make out what she was saying. Hand talk was the universal trade and treaty language of the Grass but it varied in the nuance of its gesture from tribe to tribe. The buffalo cooking in the fire pit made Rain Child's mouth water. It had been a long time since she had eaten buffalo meat, the proper food of Grass people. She said a little silent prayer of gratitude to Painted Water Horse for keeping them alive (and to the wild dogs, too, she supposed, who had helped with that) and looked longingly at the cooking meat.

Whistle and Swallow led her to the fire pit and sat her down in what Rain Child knew was the place of honor at the end of the fire. The Bear's people were beginning to jostle each other for position in the circle on either side. Whistle plopped down next to Rain Child, ignoring the disapproving looks of her elders. Flute Dog sat on her other side and patted the ground for Nighthawk Woman to sit with her. Nighthawk Woman did, looking as if she thought someone might bite her. The Bear appeared, very resplendent in his bear claw necklace and a shirt of doeskin whitened and painted with running figures that Rain Child thought were horses.

An old man doddered along beside him, so old that he had lost most of his teeth and his hair was nearly white. Grass people took a long time to gray and mostly didn't live long enough to get there, so this one must be ancient indeed. "A blessing on you, Grandfather," Rain Child said politely with her hands.

"I am Eyes of Bear," the old man informed her, nodding his head. The rest of him nodded, too, like a willow frond in the wind. She was afraid he was going to fall over.

Between them, Sunfallen the Bear and Striped Badger set him down on a pile of skins close to the fire and settled a buffalo robe about his shoulders.

"He is very old," Whistle said unnecessarily. "Last Full Moon he went to sleep sitting up and no one noticed until he snored." She hid her hands under the shadow of her knee so only Rain Child could see.

Whistle's husband, Swallow, carried on the tide of

people to the other end of the fire pit, watched her uneasily. Whistle was young and unreliable.

Sunfallen the Bear stood in the center of the circle, enveloped in the smoke and smell of the cooking buffalo, and raised his arms. Everyone more or less quieted down and watched him expectantly. Striped Badger sat down beside Flute Dog, smiling, inserting himself between Flute Dog and Nighthawk Woman with a bland nod at Nighthawk Woman.

"He is making a speech," Striped Badger said to Flute Dog, unnecessarily. The Bear spoke loudly, his face shining red in the cook fire, waving his arms, this time for emphasis, pointing south and then west. His eyes were bright and excited like a cat's that sees something to stalk. One hand crept up to touch the bear claws at his neck as he spoke.

"He is telling us again how he saw your daughter and the spirit animals when he went to sit on the High Place and receive his vision."

"We aren't a vision," Flute Dog said uncomfortably.

"Oh, yes. A vision is what comes when you call it."

Flute Dog looked dubious.

"Perhaps a vision does not always know what it is," Striped Badger said. "I must go now." He stood up suddenly and when Flute Dog looked he wasn't there anymore.

She blinked. Sunfallen the Bear had stopped talking, and now he was surrounded by real bears, or no, men in bearskins, who had come out of the smoke of the fire and the smoke that magic made in the corners of your vision so that you didn't see things until they were ready. The first bear stepped into the cleared space around the cooking buffalo, lifting first one foot and then the other in an exaggerated flat-footed way, waggling his rump from side to side so that the bear tail waggled too. When he turned his face to Flute Dog, though, it was fierce, a snarling row of teeth and eyes that caught the fire's reflection and spat it back. The bear head nodded once at her and she saw that it was Striped Badger inside. He made her think of Howler, and for a moment her chest ached suddenly.

The Bear Dancers jumped up and down, landing on their broad flat feet, facing north, then east, then south, then west. They tilted their heads to the sky and faced up, and bent their heads down between their knees and faced down.

Sunfallen the Bear wasn't part of this dance. He sat on the skins beside old Eyes of Bear and watched. The bears lined up in front of Flute Dog, and Striped Badger said out of the Bear mask, "The What-Is-It has come to see us."

"The What-Is-It has come to visit," the other bears said.

"The Bear thought on it and it came to him, so great is the Bear!"

Sunfallen shifted uncomfortably on his seat and Flute Dog thought they were baiting him, even though she couldn't understand. That was the function of clowns, to make people uncomfortable so they would think. Particularly important people.

Striped Badger waved something with a long tail and round, staring eyes. It might be a little horse made of skin and sticks, by someone who had never seen a horse. It was pop-eyed and splay-legged and its mane stuck straight up in a tuft like a jay's.

"What is it?" the Bear Dancers chanted. "What is it?"

Striped Badger danced it around the circle, shoving it unexpectedly in people's faces. He stopped when he came round again to Flute Dog.

"What-Is-It is a horse!"

Flute Dog recognized that word. He threw the little thing triumphantly at her. She resisted the urge to duck and caught it in her hand.

"What-Is-It came with the Women from the South! What-Is-It is a horse!" The other Bear Dancers began to chant that now.

"What does What-Is-It do?" Striped Badger bent down suddenly, his face a finger's length from Flute Dog's, but she couldn't answer him. He hopped over to Sunfallen.

"What does What-Is-It do?"

"He runs very fast," Sunfallen said. "With two-legged people on his back."

"What-Is-It could hunt buffalo?"

"I think so. Once one has learned to stay on his back," Sunfallen said, remembering. "It takes practice," he added modestly. "I nearly fell off."

Striped Badger seemed pleased with that answer. It behooved those in power to remember their frailties.

"We live now in a new time," Striped Badger said.

Old Eyes of Bear woke up. "A time of legend," he announced.

Striped Badger got down on all fours and another bear climbed on his back. Striped Badger began to walk and the other bear fell off, comically, feet splayed in the air, paws paddling. Flute Dog chuckled. Other bears began to ride each other, grunting and snorting and prancing. Everyone laughed.

We are important, Flute Dog thought. If the clowns took notice of you, you held some great matter in your hand. Laughter opened the heart, Howler had said, and let light into it. She closed her eyes for a moment and when she looked up again the bears had vanished. Women were cutting into the meat on the fire, heaping it on plates. One of them brought a platter and set it down before Flute Dog and Rain Child, as Striped Badger came back, without his bear suit. He wasn't there, and then he was. He offered her a piece of back fat on the tip of his belt knife. A small naked girl brought her a turtleshell bowl full of water, her mother standing proudly behind her, urging her on.

Flute Dog waved her hands to tell her "Thank you," and the mother beamed.

Striped Badger offered Rain Child a piece of back fat, too, but his eyes were on Flute Dog.

"I like it here," Rain Child said, her mouth full of buffalo fat and roasted onions. "But that man is paying too much attention to you."

"That man is a holy clown," Flute Dog hissed back. "He is important."

Rain Child eyed him disapprovingly.

Any newcomer changes the balance of things, the web that knots the tribe together. When the new women came with horses, the tribe of the Bear shifted, its pattern forming and reforming like ripples on water until it would coalesce again finally as something entirely new. Striped Badger could see that.

Striped Badger paid just enough attention to Flute Dog to honor the newcomer, and not enough to cause talk. He knew what caused talk. It was the function of the holy clowns to have their eye on such things, because talk, once started, gained a life of its own, and sometimes went places that were not good for the people. It was the function of a clown to make people think, and preferably before they talked.

On the other hand, Striped Badger was a bachelor, and most people thought it was high time he got married. He was thirty summers old and then some, and even allowing for the serious nature of a Bear Dancer, which made a man delay these things, it was time to stop walking out with each new crop of girls and choose one. The Horse-Bringing Woman was old, of course, but she was still good looking. And she had all those horses. It was appropriate for a man of power to marry her and help her decide who should own them.

So the People of the Bear talked a little, but quietly, while Striped Badger undertook to teach Flute Dog their speech by pointing out things in the camp and speaking their true names.

"Tent," he said, while she repeated it after him, wrapping her tongue around unfamiliar words. "Hide." He thumped the drying cowskin. "Man. Sleeping old man," he added, pointing at Eyes of Bear dozing in a patch of sun.

"Man."

"Ugly old man." Striped Badger pointed at himself, grinning.

Flute Dog repeated it and he laughed, translating with his hands.

"Not ugly," her hands said indignantly. "Most handsome." She chuckled. It was pleasant to have someone to joke with. She had missed Howler.

"Gray horse," Striped Badger said, pointing at the herd. "Red horse."

No one had said anything yet about who would own all these horses, but Flute Dog knew she and Rain Child couldn't keep them to themselves. The people in this place had begun bringing them presents every morning—things to eat, like a sweet onion or a piece of liver from the newly killed deer. Or little pretty things like a fresh flower or a smooth stone from the river; things a person would like to have, to put in her collection. Flute Dog and Rain Child had begun teaching a few of the more adventurous among them to ride. That was how it was done.

It was understood, of course, that the Bear would be the first to learn, but Rain Child had also picked Whistle, which caused an angry buzz of talk. The old woman was behaving as she ought, the talk said, but the young one was ignorant.

"Whistle isn't afraid of the horses," Rain Child said stubbornly. "That fool who wanted to ride yesterday was breathing so fast I thought he would die." That was White Grass Mouse. "And Surprised Raven thinks he knows everything before you can tell him, and Toad Nose's Mare scraped him off under a tree limb. I laughed so hard. He was very surprised."

"I will talk to Striped Badger," Flute Dog said, "and see if I can make him understand. But Whistle is not important and you will make enemies if you upset the order of this place."

"Whistle is my friend," Rain Child said stubbornly.

"And so? This friend has to ride a horse?"

"You won't let me have my pot, either." Rain Child's lip stuck out.

Flute Dog rolled her eyes. "And how many places would you like to be driven out of? Perhaps Most Important doesn't need a home, but her mother does. Her mother is old."

"I'm sorry," Rain Child said contritely. "Anyway, the Bear's mother brought me a ball of soap for my hair this morning and I let her ride Blue Squirrel Horse and she was very happy. And why do you have to talk to that Striped Badger person about me? I don't like him."

"He's a good man," Flute Dog said. "He is teaching the Bear because he is young."

"*He* can ride," Rain Child said, brightening. "Sunfallen. *He* isn't afraid anymore and he leaned down and picked up a stone from Blue Squirrel Horse's back today. I am going to put him on Mud-Spattered Horse tomorrow. And how is your Striped Badger person doing?"

"He fell off," Flute Dog said with a sigh. "And Whitetail Horse bit him. He was very nice about it."

Rain Child was secretly pleased by that. Why should Flute Dog let that man court her—and Rain Child was not Most Stupid, she knew he was courting her—when she never would have Uncle Howler? Mother was too old to marry anybody now; it was disgraceful.

She went into her tent in a defiant mood and put on the necklace of blue and red beads. They gleamed like fire around her neck, like Northern Lights. And Mother was wrong. Whistle gasped when she saw them and fingered them enviously when Rain Child told her she might.

"Where did you get them?"

"I found them. My vision spirit took me to where they were."

Whistle shivered with excitement. It was like talking to lightning to have a friend like Rain Child, who had been strange places and seen strange sights, and ridden horses since she was in her cradleboard. All the young women envied Whistle.

"I think Blue Runner wants you to marry the Bear," Whistle whispered to her.

"Oh no." Rain Child was shocked. No mother had ever wanted her to marry her son.

"Oh, yes," Whistle giggled. "You are very important." She lowered her voice. "Everyone thinks your mother is going to marry Striped Badger. Blue Runner couldn't stand it if anyone had a more important wife than *her* son did."

"I don't like Striped Badger," Rain Child said firmly. "Mother is too old for that."

"No, she's not. And he is very important, too, so it all makes sense. If he marries your mother, it will be very good."

"For who?"

"For all of us," Whistle said practically. "Eyes of Bear is right. You and your mother are people out of legend. Among us, the only person more important than the First of the Bear Dancers is the Bear himself."

"What about Eyes of Bear?"

"Well, he is older than the dirt, so you would have to wake him up when you wanted to do it."

"That is disrespectful!" Rain Child eyed Eyes of Bear uneasily, in case he could hear in his sleep, but she giggled, too. He stirred and she grabbed Whistle. "Whitetail Horse needs a run and so does Toad Nose's Mare if I am going to let Surprised Raven ride her again. You can take Toad Nose's Mare for me."

Whistle bounced excitedly. She had never expected anything to fall into her life like the horses. It was like riding on the back of the wind. She knew she wouldn't be given one, but maybe her husband Swallow would, which was almost as good. Then she could still ride it. She swung herself up on Toad Nose's Mare's broad black back and wrapped the rein around her wrist so she couldn't drop it.

Striped Badger and Flute Dog were riding along the stream bank when Whistle and Rain Child passed them at a trot. Clever detoured long enough to sniff at them as they went by, and then darted ahead to Rain Child. The wild dogs were still out there and Clever felt the urge to find them, to bite them. Or maybe not. She was coming into her season and the scent of the sandy coated lead dog hung in her nostrils.

Rain Child trotted past her mother and the Striped Badger person, the red and blue beads bouncing on her chest. When she was two lengths ahead of them she kicked her own horse into a gallop, hoping that Blue Squirrel Horse would run away with him, but she didn't. Rain Child drew Whitetail Horse up and looked back over her shoulder. Her mother and the Striped Badger person were still talking, heads bent toward each other, while their horses paced sedately. They waved at her.

13

The Last Wonderful Thing

RAIN CHILD AND CLEVER WERE ASLEEP WHEN THE COYote came nosing into their tent. Clever, curled in a ball in the crook of Rain Child's bent knees, sat up with a sharp yip, ears pricked, as a smoke coyote came flowing past the door flap and solidified. Rain Child blinked at it. Flute Dog was up and gone—talking to that Striped Badger person, probably, Rain Child thought, while she was left by herself to fend off spirits.

"Black rocks," the coyote said.

Rain Child heard the pot answer him.

"Your pot will teach us to make iron," the coyote said. It was a word Rain Child didn't know.

The pot sang its name. The pot had been calling to her, whispering from its hiding place in her packs. She wanted to rub its smooth sides, show it to Whistle, cook buffalo stew in it, be the Magic Woman With a Pot again.

"Magic Woman With a Pot was driven out of her home graze." Rain Child heard Flute Dog's words hanging in the air of the tent, right where she had left them last night.

Rain Child ignored them. Blue Runner had given her a new dress, of soft white buffalo cowskin, embroidered all over with porcupine quills. Hah!

Rain Child sat up and reached for her clothes. The coyote faded into smoke again as she pulled on her old dress and boots. She dug into the packs and laid her palm on the pot's round side, feeling it sizzle under her hand. She felt inside it until she found the red and blue beads, which she had hidden from Flute Dog just in case, and put them on, tucking them under the neck of her dress. Then she took her belt knife, a waterskin, a bag of dried meat, the buffalo horn with its nest of slowburner and Mud-Spattered Horse's bridle from its peg on the center pole. She put the pot over her arm.

"Shovel." The word came into her mind, so she took that too.

The coyote was back as she swung up onto Mud-Spattered Horse, pack on back, pot over her arm, and the shovel in her other hand. He materialized out of the grass in a whisper of wind, and Clever touched noses with him.

"I don't know where to go," Rain Child said. If he was her spirit guide, then he would tell her.

The coyote loped away through the tall grass and Rain Child and Clever followed. They went away from the camp toward a series of low, dark hills that lifted their heads from the Grass in the distance. The coyote set a steady pace, a coyote trot that ate up space and held the sun pinned in the sky so that it seemed never to rise any higher. Rain Child could feel the blue beads like drops of water around her throat.

The coyote stopped at an outcropping of dark stone, where brush-covered hills began to climb the sky, with a ridge of scrub trees at the top. "Now you dig up the rock and burn it," he told Rain Child.

"You can't burn rocks," Rain Child said.

"Everyone says that," the coyote said, exasperated. "Pay attention to me and I will tell you how to do it."

"What rocks?"

Clever was sniffing at a lump of gray stone embedded in the rising ground.

"See? Your dog knows the right ones. Any nose knows. They are what the stars are made of."

"Stars?"

"Yes. Sometimes a piece of them falls to the ground. But their heart is hidden in this stone, too."

It seemed as likely as anything else. If there were pale monsters and talking coyotes in the world, why not star hearts? Rain Child slid off Mud-Spattered Horse and tied his rein to a big rock (he didn't like the coyote) and poked at the ground around the stones with her shovel. The roots of the Grass were laced thick around it, like fingers, and she had to saw at them with her belt knife, for fear of snapping the shovel blade. Clever and the coyote sat down side by side and watched her. When the grass was cleared, Rain Child worked the shovel into the earth beside the stone. The sun had begun to move again and it stood heavy in the sky over them, its heat burning through the air onto her back. The sweat ran down her neck and ears and she drank deeply out of the water skin. The stone was still embedded in the ground.

"He won't come," Rain Child said, gasping. "His feet are in the heart of the earth, I think."

The coyote began to dig around the stone too, scattering showers of dirt behind him. He was bigger than he had been, but the stone looked bigger, too. "Oof, you are right," the coyote said between breaths, his tongue hanging out one side of his mouth. He redoubled his efforts in a spray of earth. The pot sat enigmatically on the ground beside Rain Child's pack, lopsided and silent.

"Push on it now," the coyote said, and Rain Child pushed. The stone rocked a little, but it didn't move. The coyote dug furiously at its base with his long-clawed forepaws. She shoved it again and again, rocking it back and forth in the earth. Finally it pulled loose and sent her sprawling.

The stone was huge and gray, dark with damp where it had been buried in the ground, its rough sides a mix of different colored flecks, crusted with earth and the curling form of an indignant worm.

"Well, that's too big to burn," the coyote said, inspecting it and swallowing the worm. "You'll have to carry it to the top of the cliff there and drop it off, to break it."

Rain Child picked herself up, rubbing a skinned knee. "I can't lift that. You should carry it."

"I am thinking how to make the fire," the coyote said. "That is my job, thinking."

"Then think how to get this rock up a cliff," Rain Child said.

The coyote closed his eyes for a moment, then opened them. "Put the rock on your dress and drag it up the cliff."

"Take my dress off?"

"There's no one here."

"You're here."

"Oh, me." The coyote waved a paw as if to dismiss that. "I'm a coyote."

Rain Child looked at him dubiously. He wagged his tail. It looked ludicrous, like a buffalo dancing. "Stop that." She turned her back on him and pulled her dress off. She spread it on the ground and rolled the stone onto it, puffing.

She tugged at the dress. "You might help pull."

Clever and the coyote each took a corner and Rain Child pulled in the middle. The dress slid along the ground. A deer trail went up the hill between the outcropping rocks and they took that, going up backward, bumping the dress and stone along. The sun burned down on her bare skin. Her hair was wet and plastered to her face, curling around her forehead. The red and blue beads about her neck snapped and sizzled, making a little shower of sparks before her eyes. She pulled, and the dogs, or whatever they were, pulled, their teeth making holes in the dress. When they came to a flat shelf partway up the hill, they stopped to rest. The coyote looked over the edge.

"Here," he said. "We can drop it down onto those stones there. That ought to do it."

Rain Child peered over. From the ledge they stood on it was a sheer drop to where they had been, several times the height of a man, paved with a flat rock at the bottom. It made her a little dizzy.

"Come on," the coyote said. He nosed at the stone.

They tugged Rain Child's dress to the edge and rolled the stone off it, over the lip of the shelf. It hung in the air for a moment, as if thinking about falling, and then plummeted. It made a satisfactory crash on the stone below them and split into a lot of pieces.

Clever danced on the edge with excitement, barking.

"Stop that, Foolish." Rain Child frowned at her, but it was hard to be dignified when you weren't wearing any clothes. She snatched her dress up and put it back on, and as she did she caught a glimpse from the corner of her eye of a young man with a wild dark face and pointy ears, watching her. She snapped her head around and there was no one there but the coyote. He was studying a bug on the path.

"Are you ready?" he said. "Good. Now we'll make the oven."

"What's an oven?"

The coyote decided the bug was edible and ate it. "To melt the rocks. I know all about it. The Moon told me. You make it out of clay."

"We don't work clay." That was for people in the Cities-in-the-West, who lived in mud boxes. What use was clay on the Grass? Clay broke.

"An oven is a little house made out of clay, shaped like a big hornet's nest. It has a mouth and a smokehole at the top. You put the rocks inside with charcoal and they melt. That is what the Moon says."

"The Moon changes shape every night," Rain Child retorted.

"You must trust me," the coyote said grandly. "I am your spirit guide."

Rain Child thought. What if she really could make iron? *Iron*, the pot sang to her from the ground below. Iron would make a knife that no one could break. She and her mother would be safe forever, if they had that. And if they wanted to, they could own all the horses in the world, even the Dry River people's.

"All right."

As soon as she said that, the coyote set off down the trail again without even waiting to see if she was coming. At the foot of the hill they collected pieces of the stone and put them in Rain Child's pot, and then she got on Mud-Spattered Horse and followed the coyote to where he said a stream would be, with clay in its banks. She hoped he knew. He always talked as if he knew everything.

Clever followed her person and the Big Dog, excited, hopeful that something—she wasn't sure what—was going to happen. When they got to the stream, Rain Child tethered Mud-Spattered Horse to graze, while Clever watched the Big Dog digging in the sand by the bank, nosing and tasting the mud until he found a patch that held his footprint perfectly. Rain Child scooped it into her pot and carried it up the bank. She tipped it out on a flat, bare spot and went back for more. She didn't know that clay must be tempered with sand or mica to keep it from cracking, or that air bubbles will cause it to explode. She didn't know it needed to be fired. Rain Child came from the Grass.

She patted it into shape, coiling a long snake of clay the way the coyote told her to, building a little house that did look like a hornet's nest, with an open mouth at the bottom and a little chimney on top. It took more clay than she would have thought, and she went back to the stream again and again with the pot, lugging its weight up the bank. Mud-Spattered Horse grazed in the shadows of the trees that lined the stream, and Clever dozed in the sun, her legs in the air and her head on the Big Dog's flank.

When Rain Child looked up, thinking that she was hungry, the coyote appeared with a fish in his mouth, and they made a fire with Rain Child's slowburner and cooked it in the bottom of her pot.

"How did you catch that?"

"Oh, it was just coming along," the coyote said.

Clever didn't say anything.

It was like living in a story, Rain Child thought, where the animals talked to you and magical, mysterious things came to pass. She wasn't surprised to see, when she went back to coiling her clay house, the noses of the wild dogs peering through the trees at her. She saw the shadow of the coyote flow toward them and then after a while she looked up again to see herself ringed with dogs: the three wild ones, Clever, and the coyote, all sitting on their haunches like a meeting of medicine society chiefs.

Then the sun, which had stayed pinned to the sky, slid down the western horizon in what seemed the space of an instant, and Rain Child saw that it was just a puddle of fire floating on the edge of the Grass. She stood up, panicked in the twilight. The story she had lived in all afternoon broke open and left her alone with Clever on the Grass, a very long way from camp.

Rain Child slung her pack onto Mud-Spattered Horse's back, hooked the empty pot over her arm, and swung herself up.

The coyote reappeared, just a smoky wisp in the dusk. "We aren't finished," it said.

Rain Child didn't answer him. She put her heels to Mud-Spattered Horse's flanks and they ran for home.

Flute Dog was waiting for her, pacing outside their tent. "Where have you been?"

Rain Child tried to think where she had been. "I went riding, to the hills there." She pointed.

Flute Dog snatched the pot off her arm and pushed it through the tent door. "I told you not to bring that out! And where is my shovel?"

Rain Child saw the shovel in her head, lying on the ground where they had pried the stone loose. "I'll get it tomorrow."

"What were you doing with it?"

"I thought there might be something to dig," Rain Child said.

Flute Dog felt her forehead. "Do you have a fever? She isn't right in the head," she said to Striped Badger, who Rain Child now saw had been standing there all along.

Striped Badger smiled at Rain Child. "Maybe there are things in her head we don't understand. What did you find out there in the Grass, child? Another magical pot?"

You told him. Rain Child glared at her mother. "No," she said to Striped Badger. "There wasn't anything. And that's *my* pot."

"Of course." He sounded as if he were speaking to a baby. Rain Child felt cross and tired, and her fingers ached where she had scraped them raw digging clay. She went into the tent without saying anything else, rude as that was.

"Perhaps one day Flute Dog will let me look at the magical pot from the south," Striped Badger said. He knew it was magical. It glowed with the kind of light most people couldn't see. And why else would she hide it? "I am interested in such things." He smiled gently.

"Perhaps," Flute Dog said noncommittally.

Striped Badger didn't pursue the matter. He had seen the child in the foothills. Whatever magic she was embarked on, he would know; it was his function to know things for the rest of the people. He went back to his tent to paint his face and put a new feather in his scalp lock. The mother had agreed to let him show her a place where the moon reflected in the running water of the river, that was very beautiful at night.

Striped Badger took his love flute out of its otterskin case and tucked it through his belt. It was a splendid one, carved from cedar and painted with red and white flowers, bound with thin lashings of rawhide thong. He delved into the hide box beside his bed and brought out a handful of small leather bags, his store of charms: a white shell wrapped in rabbitskin to let him see in the dark, and a polished stone from the river drilled and strung on a string with three red seeds to call the buffalo. In a bag sewn with bits of turquoise and green jasper he kept a dried weasel foot in a nest of white hair that had come from one of the mountain sheep that lived in the cliffs to the west. Love magic lived in the foot and the white hairs, a spell to charm any girl the owner could touch with it. Striped Badger had never known it to fail. He had in fact lent it to other men (for a satisfactory price) when he had felt it necessary to remain undistracted by matters of love. He tucked it into the pouch at his waist, and went to inspect his reflection in the stream.

Rain Child saw Flute Dog brushing her hair and braiding sweet grass into it and snorted. "You ought to be embarrassed."

"Because I'm walking out with a man?" Flute Dog asked her.

"You never did before."

"I never lived alone a year in the Grass with no one but a surly daughter to talk to," Flute Dog retorted. "And we are not so easy among these people that we don't need help."

"Yah, they think spirits sent us. They give us presents!"

Flute Dog brushed her hand down her own new dress, smoothing its soft folds with the stubbed finger of her left hand. "Do I look all right?"

"For what? *I* heard he courts *all* the girls."

"Then you aren't in any danger of having him for a father," Flute Dog said.

"You could have married Uncle Howler. Why didn't you?"

"Maybe I was foolish."

When she had gone, Rain Child lay down on her bed and tried to sleep instead of looking at the stars through the smokehole to see how long it had been since her mother had gone out with that man.

Flute Dog and Clever came home together, both looking happy. Rain Child rolled over and looked at the tent wall, pretending she was asleep. Clever got into bed with her, nosing her way under the blanket. She smelled of wild grass.

As soon as it was light, Rain Child crept out of bed, leaving Flute Dog snoring lightly in the cool morning, and got Mud-Spattered Horse's bridle.

"Good morning."

Rain Child jumped, biting her tongue.

Sunfallen the Bear smiled at her outside her tent. "Did I scare you? I didn't mean to."

"Um."

"Where are you going so early?" he asked with his hands.

"Um."

Sunfallen raised an eyebrow. Rain Child wished she could do that.

"I'm just going to look for a better graze to take the horses to. The grass here is nearly grazed down."

"I'll go with you," Sunfallen suggested.

Rain Child felt like someone trying to hide a large object behind her back. "The Bear doesn't have other business?"

"Eyes of Bear is teaching me a long song about the first of our people," Sunfallen said plaintively. "A very long song."

Rain Child smiled. "It must be very tiresome to be the Bear."

"Only sometimes," Sunfallen admitted. "It is a great honor. We all believe that you were the Messenger of the Bear, when you came to the High Place."

"I was looking for a horse."

"The Messenger doesn't always know. That is what Striped Badger says."

"Oh." Rain Child felt uncomfortable. Everyone wanted her to be a messenger. The presents were nice, but somehow that made her uneasy.

"It is very pleasnt, however, that the Messenger is so beautiful," Sunfallen said. "The Messenger who came to the last Bear was a giant turtle."

Rain Child was startled. "Am I beautiful? More than a giant turtle, maybe. I've always been told I am odd-looking."

"That's what's beautiful. And much more so than a giant turtle."

"Well, that's not hard," Rain Child said severely, and he laughed.

He looked at the horses."They are very mysterious animals. Do you think we'll be able to ride them well enough in two moons to take them on the Fall Hunting?"

"To drive buffalo?" Rain Child bit her lip. "That's dangerous. That's how my father was killed."

"Striped Badger thinks we should, because we'll get more meat. Last year two of our babies died, and a brother to Eyes of Bear. That's the sadness of winter."

"Striped Badger will change his mind when he falls off his horse in front of Bull Buffalo's hooves."

"It's hard on the people to see how to kill more buffalo, and still be told, *Not now*."

"Harder to lose their hunters." Rain Child gestured urgently with her hands. "My people ride from the time they are babies. How long have we been here?"

"Less than a moon." Sunfallen hung his head sheepishly. "I am impatient. And the Horse Girl is wise."

Tell that to Striped Badger, Rain Child thought, but she didn't say it. Sunfallen smiled at her and she noticed how the light rippled in his eyes like water. If Mother wanted that man, then she could have him, Rain Child decided. Mother was old. She might not have another chance.

"I'll take the horses to their new graze with you," Sunfallen offered again.

"Not this morning." Rain Child shrugged her arms through her pack straps so that it hung on her back. "But tomorrow. Tomorrow we will go." She wanted the day to finish her oven, the thing that the coyote had told her to cook rocks in. She wanted to see if he would be there again when she got there. She could see Clever's nose poking through the doorflap. When she saw the pack and bridle, Clever hopped through it and sat expectantly at Rain Child's feet.

"Then maybe you will let me show you a place where the moon dances on the water at night. It is very beautiful to look at."

Rain Child's eyes opened wide. *That's where Striped Badger took my mother. This boy is courting me.* She narrowed her eyes again so she did not look like Frog Lady, all surprised. Behind Whistle's tent she could see the edge of Nighthawk Woman's face, peering out. The Bear's people would all know that the Bear had asked Rain Child to go walking with him by the time Nighthawk Woman went down to the stream with her waterskin and back. Was Blue Runner really trying to marry her to him? And what did *he* want? He didn't look like a young man who would marry just to please his mother. *Her* mother, on the other hand, probably wouldn't notice.

Rain Child's eyes danced. "I would like that." She started toward the horse herd with the pack on her back. "My mother also says it is very beautiful."

Sunfallen followed, chuckling. "I saw Old Striped Badger slinking home. Maybe he is younger than we thought. Your mother, too."

How odd. Since Rain Child herself had been old enough to marry she had not thought of her mother doing that. *How very odd.* She caught Mud-Spattered Horse and swung herself up on his spotted back, the pack thudding against her ribs.

"I have been practicing that," Sunfallen said.

"Good. You can ride Mud-Spattered Horse tomorrow, and try it on him." Rain Child put her heels to his sides and they trotted away before Sunfallen could ask her what was in the pack. The pot made it bulge and bounce suspiciously.

Clever loped beside them, her tongue hanging out.

"And where were you last night?" Rain Child asked her.

Clever didn't answer.

"I know," Rain Child said severely. "Now there will be pups, won't there, and is *he* going to help you raise them?" She thought it was funny, all the same. There were lots of stories in which hapless maidens married spirit beings—Blue Racer Snake, Bull Buffalo, even Fire—but she had never heard of anyone's dog doing it. "I suppose he took you to see the moon on the water," she said severely.

The coyote and the wild dogs were all waiting for her when she got to the place where they were building the oven. They sat down in a circle to watch as soon as she brought more clay from the riverbank. Rain Child reached into her pack and got out the bag of dried meat she had stolen from Flute Dog's stores. She threw a piece to each of them, Clever and the coyote and the three wild dogs. They gulped it down, jaws closing with a clack. Even the white dog and the red one with the rope around its neck had come to sit in the circle with the sandy-coated lead dog. The scar on his shoulder where she had gouged him with her spear had healed.

"Now we are going to finish this oven house," she explained to the dogs as she worked, hands slapping the wet clay, rolling out a long coil. The clay was cool to her fingers, like frog skin. It had begun to seem normal to talk to them all; after all, she was Dog Sister, Uncle Howler had said so.

"And where do I get charcoal?" she added as she patted the coil into place, looking severely at the coyote.

"Steal it." The words formed in her head, but she knew who had spoken. Rain Child snorted. The little pieces that formed in the heart of a hot fire were valuable because they burned hotter and with less trouble than wood or dung. They made good black paint, too. But even the wood to make them was scarce. Mostly on the Grass they burned buffalo dung.

"Well all right, then." The coyote sounded disappointed. It was always more fun to steal things. "We'll make it. You cut down a tree and we'll cover it with earth and bake it, and that will make charcoal. I have seen the men in the east do this," he added proudly.

"I will cut down a tree." Rain Child looked at him. "Why do I have to do all the work?"

"You have hands," the coyote said.

When Rain Child had finished her oven the sun was still warm in the sky, and so she lay down next to it in the dust and dozed like the dogs, sleepy with accomplishment. She dreamed of horses, of riding on Mud-Spattered Horse with his hairy flanks warm between her knees, and woke in the dusk instead to find a young man beside her, with his hand between her legs. She sat up and he vanished as she looked at him, turning sideways and disappearing into nothing, as if he had been only a flat sheet of hide. Rain Child snapped her head around, but there was no one else there. The oven sat enigmatically on the riverbank, a squat, silent presence, and even the wild dogs had gone. She whistled to Clever and flung the rein over Mud-Spattered Horse's neck. As she rode she thought of the feel of that hairy hand between her legs, and of Sunfallen the Bear who had wanted to show her the moon on the river.

"See how she smiles in the water?" Sunfallen asked. The moon was a series of white crescent ripples on the current's flow, and they were sitting above it on a flat rock where they could watch and listen to the water burble over stones.

Sunfallen took his flute out of a quill-embroidered case and put it to his lips. The love flutes of the Grass had sad voices, plaintive with longing. No one but Little Striped Bird had ever played one for Rain Child before, but she knew what you were supposed to do: sit gracefully, head cocked a little to the side, listening, hands beautifully folded, counterpoint to his fingers on the flute. The music coiled around her head, breathing soft notes like singing smoke or a flight of invisible birds.

"Where do you go in the daytime?" Sunfallen asked, when he took the flute from his lips.

Bewitched in the music, she almost told him. The words fell over the edge of her lips and she breathed them back, startled. "I will tell you when it is finished," she said. "It is a surprise. Something good." The skin itched on her thighs where the hand had been. It had had, she thought, long black nails.

"You are a mystery," Sunfallen said. His eyes gleamed in the moonlight.

Rain Child felt embarrassed. "I am a mystery to myself, too," was all she could think to say.

The next day she let him come with her to find new graze for the horses. The Bear's people didn't move on as often as the Dry River folk, having had no horses to feed until now. Rain Child and Sunfallen stayed with the herd, who were flighty and unreliable in new surroundings, and Rain Child showed Sunfallen how to lie along Mud-Spattered Horse's broad back and doze in the heat, while Mud-Spattered Horse ambled slowly, biting off mouthfuls of grass.

Sunfallen played his flute to the sky, while Rain Child closed her eyes and listened to the dreaming notes that flitted into the sun.

When they reappeared in camp in late afternoon, Striped Badger told them the Bear had no business disappearing all day when there were serious matters to attend to, and gave Rain Child a black look. Sunfallen made polite apologies but Rain Child and Striped Badger could both tell he didn't mean them. Striped Badger pursed his mouth. Rain Child decided that she had been right all along, and Flute Dog didn't need that man. She saw him afterward, conferring with Blue Runner, Sunfallen's mother. Blue Runner laughed at his serious expression.

Rain Child went behind her tent and kept going, keeping the tent between her and Striped Badger. She needed to look at her oven. She had a thing they didn't know about, and Striped Badger would be sorry when Rain Child gave magic pots and knives to everyone but him. She caught a horse out of the herd and melted into the Grass.

The oven felt almost dry to her, its surface dusty looking now instead of slick. It would be ready by the time they had made the charcoal, she thought. Rain Child had never done any of these things before, but the coyote sounded as if he knew all about it.

Blue Runner was foolish. She might not see that fewer people were bringing her presents now, and were giving them to the Horse Girl instead, but Striped Badger did. Striped Badger looked into the Grass. That was one of the things he could do. He could see into the heart of the Grass and tell what was happening there. Right now the Horse Girl was doing something that made the stalks stand straight up like hair on the back of his neck when lightning was coming. A handful of tiny frogs had littered the path by the river this morning, dead and drying in the sun, and an owl had come out in the daylight. Signs like these meant something. Those dogs that had come with the Horse Women had been around the midden, and one of them tried to come into Nighthawk Woman's tent, as if they had decided to be tame. More significantly, Sunfallen the Bear was mooning around the courting rock instead of tending to business. Striped Badger considered whether that might mean there was a spell on him.

Striped Badger closed his eyes and felt the air with his tongue for signs. Very often he could taste things before they happened. A bug flew into his mouth and he swatted it off his tongue and swore. The air looked green to him, the way it sometimes did before a summer storm, but there were no clouds and the day was windless. Something was moving through the Grass, though. Striped Badger looked more closely, but it was invisible. All he could see was the path it made, something heavy and lumbering, trampling down the stalks. When he went back to his tent, the snake bones that he kept for calling rain climbed out of their bag and slithered away, flicking their dry white tail in the dust. Striped Badger took out his shell that gave him eyes-in-the-dark and put on his bear robe and went to follow whatever was making the tracks through the Grass.

In the morning, Rain Child went back again to where the oven sat drying. The coyote and the wild dogs were waiting for her. She had brought Clever's dog travois and an extra harness rolled up and tied across Mud-Spattered Horse's back, with Flute Dog's ax.

"I was going to tell you to bring that," the coyote said, when he saw the ax. "Did you bring anything to eat?"

Rain Child took a bag out of her pack. She threw each of them a piece of stolen meat.

The coyote caught his and gulped it down whole. The dogs retreated to the trees with theirs.

"Next time, put in a piece of back fat," the coyote said.

Rain Child inspected the trees on the bank above them. A dead sycamore, stark and forlorn, was caught in the heart of the green limbs. It would be easier to cut down, and it would burn better than green wood, too. She started up the bank.

The ax handle bit into her palms and raised a blister and the sweat poured off her forehead into her eyes. The coyote watched her from the trees, occasionally offering advice.

"You're nearly through that other side. Don't let it fall on our oven."

Rain Child gave him a long look, and whacked the tree one last whack with the ax. It toppled, falling through the green branches of the canopy with a screeching like hooves on stone. When it had shuddered into stillness, Rain Child began to lop the limbs off it, chopping the dry trunk into lengths that would fit on the travois.

She loaded them onto the hide and whistled for Clever. Then she looked at the coyote.

"This is more than she can pull. You'll have to help." Rain Child held out the second harness.

"Me? What about those dogs?"

"They're wild." Rain Child stood waiting until, seeing that she wasn't going to give up on the idea, the coyote ambled over and sniffed the harness. Rain Child tied it around his chest and middle.

"This is very undignified."

"I have heard stories," Rain Child told him.

"This is only because I wish to help you," the coyote said. "If I wanted to, I could speak a magical word and all this wood would be down there by the oven."

"That might be easier."

The coyote leaned into the traces, looking irritated. Between them, he and Clever, who knew how to maneuver a load, got the travois out of the trees and down the bank to the clearing where the oven was drying.

Rain Child unhitched the travois. "You'd better dig the fire pit," she told him. "You dig much faster than I do. On account of not having hands."

The coyote laughed. For just a moment his face had even white teeth and dark soaring eyebrows. Then it was long-nosed and hairy again. He began to paw at the dirt, spraying it up in a shower behind him. Clever watched a moment, head cocked, and then began to dig beside him. Rain Child gathered an armful of tinder, dry moss, and thin branches and the trimmings from the dead tree, and sat studiously sorting it into little piles, her bare shins crossed on the sandy bank. After a while the wild dogs came out of the brush and dug too.

They looked like the formation of a dance, or clowns in dog hides, and their excavations dug a circular pit as wide as Rain Child was tall and as deep as the length of her arm. When they were done, the coyote scrambled out of his end, panting, and the dogs leaped over the sides and were gone again. Clever was still nosing the damp earth at the bottom, batting her paw at a grub that hurried out of the way.

The coyote sat down beside Rain Child. His tongue lolled out over his teeth, red and dripping. "Woo! That is hard work. Now you bury the wood in dirt."

"In dirt."

"And build a fire around it. If the air can't get to it, it will bake everything away but the charcoal in the heart."

That sounded improbable, but Rain Child called Clever out of the pit and rolled half the logs off the travois bed into it. She climbed down inside with them when the coyote told her to, and began to arrange them neatly in a stack, according to his instructions. Afterward she packed the damp earth the dogs had dug out around and over the wood until it was buried, and cut just a tiny hole into the bottom and another at the top. She piled her tinder around and over the buried wood.

"I have seen this done in the east," the coyote assured her.

Rain Child climbed out again and pulled the rest of the logs off the travois bed, arranging them on the tinder. She knelt on the edge of the pit with her horn of slowburner and touched its coil of sage and cedar bark to the dry stuff in the pit. It flared up and licked at the logs. The damp earth felt clammy on her knees and the smoke that rose from the brush was acrid, like leaves burning.

"Be sure it catches the logs," the coyote said.

"I can light a fire." Rain Child blew on the little flames that wavered in the branches.

The coyote sat down on the opposite edge of the pit, admiring their handiwork. "You'll have to stay with this all night, you know."

"What?"

"I remember now, it takes a long time to burn charcoal. Days, I think."

"I'm not going to sleep out here at night," Rain Child said.

"Then who will watch our charcoal?"

"You can watch it."

"The wind might shift. It might rain. We should put up a canopy over it."

"I don't have a canopy."

"You'll have to go get one and come back."

Rain Child thought about sitting with Sunfallen on the courting rock. "I have to see a young man who is courting me tonight."

The coyote looked scornful. "Which is more important? Your foolish young man, or this charcoal that will make iron?"

Rain Child gave him a long look. "Put up the canopy yourself. You have hands when you want to."

"I don't know what you're talking about."

"Yah, you do too." She glared at him. "You watched me when I had my clothes off, and when I went to sleep you put your hand up my dress."

The coyote laughed suddenly, showing a mouthful of long pointed teeth, a mouthful of even white ones, black muzzle, no, red lips, wild yellow eyes under dark-winged brows. The tail was a brush of stars on the ground behind him and he was a naked young man, a little hairy, with russet skin and long black braids. He stood, balancing himself gracefully on the edge of the pit. The flames were roaring in the tinder around the buried wood now. They threw dancing patterns on his skin.

"You don't want *that* young man," he said, wheedling.

"I'll show you something better than the moon on the water."

"What?"

"It's in the woods there."

"I'm not walking with you," Rain Child said, indignant. "You slept with my dog!"

"What difference does that make?" Coyote produced a long flute from somewhere and put it to his lips.

"It makes a difference to me! And I don't want to marry a spirit, anyway."

"Nobody said anything about marrying," Coyote said sulkily.

Rain Child began to laugh. "If this is how you court girls, no wonder you can't get any!"

"I get lots of girls."

"Dog girls." She made a face at him.

Coyote leaped over the pit, his feet just clearing the flames. "You are a New Person." He poked at the curls of hair around her forehead with his fingertip. "You should come with me. We could live in the Grass, and have New Person babies."

Rain Child backed away from him. "Until you lost interest." He was as changeable as the weather, first a coyote, then a young man, wild, then seeming tame, which she knew was illusion; maybe he was something out of her head and didn't exist at all.

Coyote put the flute to his lips and began to play, and Rain Child saw herself dancing with him in the moonlight, a coyote girl with big pricked ears.

She picked up Mud-Spattered Horse's bridle and got on his back before she danced off into the Grass, chasing rabbits.

14

Fire

STRIPED BADGER DIDN'T SEE THE YOUNG MAN, NOT being able to see as far into the Grass as he thought; he saw only the girl talking with a coyote, but that was enough. He lay a long time on the ridge above the stream bank, flat on his belly in the brush while the fire burned around the buried wood and the smoke stung his eyes.

He thought a long time about what she might be making. He still wasn't certain whether it was a thing or a magic, and sometimes the two were the same, anyway. He wasn't certain what he had followed through the grass either. He had thought at first that it was the girl or her spirits, but it had gone off past this place, rolling over the Grass, flattening everything in its path like a great wind. In a little the Grass sprang back up again, but Striped Badger could see its passage on the stalks like a black mold. The girl hadn't seemed to see it, but she might belong to it anyway and not know that either.

When the girl rode away with the gray dog at her heels, the coyote faded into the afternoon shadows like a long sigh. The fire burned on in the pit, the buried mound of earth giving off reeking yellow smoke that boiled away in great clouds over the trees. As the Grass darkened with evening the flames glowed redder, like the heart of some fearful beast. Striped Badger said a charm to keep off malevolent spirits. Finally he crept down the ridge and crouched on the edge of the burning pit, trying to see through its buried heart to ask it what it was for. It didn't answer him. Striped Badger stared at the oven, sitting by itself a little distance away. He had seen things like that in the Cities-in-the-West. He was not an ignorant man. He had been to the Cities-in-the-West in his youth, when the buffalo had grazed far out of their usual range and the bravest young men had followed them. A thing like that was an oven, to cook things in. What would the Horse Girl want to cook? And did Sunfallen the Bear know about this? Striped Badger didn't like the idea that Sunfallen the Bear knew things he did not tell his mentor. Sunfallen was too young to know which things were important.

Striped Badger took a long stick and prodded the mound of baking earth, gasping at the horrible smoke that rose from it. Nothing happened, but he thought, *I can't stay here*. His throat burned and his eyes were watering. He would come back when the Horse Girl did. She apparently knew better than to choke herself to death with her own magic.

She was sitting on the courting rock with Sunfallen the Bear when Striped Badger came back to camp. He frowned at them, but it was dark and they weren't looking at him anyway. Sunfallen was playing his flute, a pining, lovesick melody like a dying cow. Striped Badger marched across camp to Flute Dog's tent to see what the mother thought about it and if she was inclined to go walking with someone old enough to play a flute properly, but she wasn't there.

Striped Badger went to the fire circle in center camp in disgust. He was not used to events that evaded his direction, to run their own course. Things like that were dangerous, when people were ignorant.

Flute Dog wasn't at the fire, either, but Nighthawk Woman and Blue Runner were, heads together at the married women's end of the circle, weaving baskets from a common store of rush.

"—very peculiar looking," Nighthawk Woman said.

Blue Runner said, "She is a magical creature, what do you expect? When First Boy married Bear Woman, did someone tell him she was peculiar looking? He will listen to his mother."

Striped Badger sat down a little past them, beside old Eyes of Bear, who was apparently asleep. Their voices carried like flute notes over the drumming of a handful of young men at the other end of the fire.

"Ah," Nighthawk Woman said, "young men never listen to their mothers or their aunts. It is a great shame. My nephew, for instance—"

"Sunfallen always listens to me," Blue Runner said.

"Well, she is ugly," Nighthawk Woman said flatly. "A stranger, and that odd skin, like a toad's. She pays too much attention to that Whistle. Now my nephew's wife is getting a big head, riding around on those horses, and when I told her she wasn't twisting her rope tight enough, she just laughed at me."

"Is it that new girl?" Wide Muskrat, Surprised Raven's wife, waddled around the fire to the women's end, her breath whistling through a missing tooth.

"No, that Whistle," Nighthawk Woman said.

"She thinks the Horse Girl is a bad influence on her niece," Blue Runner said indulgently.

Wide Muskrat settled herself conversationally next to Nighthawk Woman. "She's very pale. I asked the mother if she had been grown in the dark, maybe, but she said no."

"We're all grown in the dark," Blue Runner said.

"And we don't look like grass that's been under a rock," Nighthawk Woman retorted.

"I just thought maybe . . ." Wide Muskrat trailed off. "I was just trying to make conversation, to make her feel at home, and she took offense."

Nighthawk Woman sucked a tooth. "She's ignorant. She doesn't know how to act here. That's why it would be such a shame if the mother of the Bear let her son marry that daughter."

"Marry the daughter! I should say not! You know my daughter Sweetie can grind meal finer—"

"Mmmm," Blue Runner said noncommittally. Sunfallen must be married to the Horse Girl without arousing the other mothers' animosity. It was a difficulty.

Striped Badger leaned toward Eyes of Bear. "He is sitting on the courting rock with that girl," he said loudly to Eyes of Bear, who snored gently into his necklace of stones and owl feathers. "He ought to be learning the Song Cycle of the Fall Buffalo, with the hunt coming on soon, but what can I do with him? After all, he is the Bear." He heard Blue Runner put down her basket in a rustle of rushes. Wide Muskrat whistled through her teeth, and Nighthawk Woman hissed at her, "See?"

Blue Runner stood up, shaking off the other women's attention like a dog shedding water. She wrapped her blanket about her shoulders and strode through the camp in a direct line to the river. She stopped there, just short of the courting rock. The Bear was sitting on it with the Horse Girl, their heads together. Blue Runner took a deep breath, thinking what to say to him, about duty and proper behavior, that wouldn't merely make him stubborn, when Striped Badger caught up with her, puffing.

Blue Runner looked at him disapprovingly, as if it was his fault. "This is what comes of *you* courting the mother, and lying about in the woods legs-in-the-air."

"That's not the same thing at all," Striped Badger said,

breathing hard. "Before the Mother of the Bear speaks too hastily, she should stop and consider."

"Consider what? Striped Badger's wish to own horses?"

"The Bear is young. Perhaps it would be best for him not to marry at all just yet." As long as he wasn't married, all the mothers would bring presents to Striped Badger. "Certainly not this girl, since she is a bad influence. He needs direction," Striped Badger suggested.

"And where is the direction that you are supposed to give him?" Blue Runner shook her finger under Striped Badger's nose. "If you weren't legs-in-the-air with the mother, he would be tending to his duties, and considering marriage with proper restraint. My son is the Bear. It is not right that some other man marries this girl."

"You will have pale ugly grandchildren with buffalo hair," Striped Badger said snappishly.

"If my son has horses, I will learn to love pale ugly grandchildren with buffalo hair."

Her voice carried through the leaves and Striped Badger saw the couple on the rock turn their heads. "Come and let us consider what is best to do." He took Blue Runner's arm and tugged at it.

Blue Runner looked at him suspiciously. "You don't want him to marry the girl. Do you think you can marry both of them?"

"The Mother of the Bear does me a grave injustice." Striped Badger nodded his head solemnly. "Because she is worried. The Bear is young. If you tell a young man what he is to do, he will desire most in the world not to do just that thing. It is the way of young men. There are other ways to handle this difficulty."

"What ways?" Blue Runner tapped her foot, her arms folded across her chest.

Striped Badger tugged on her arm again, disengaging it from the other. He pulled at her, trying to lead her away from the trees. He heard a giggle behind them on the riverbank and ignored it. "Sunfallen is young," he said again in her ear, "but he is the Bear. He knows his duty."

"His duty is to marry and have children. But not until he learns the sacred songs so he does not make a fool of himself, and he is forgetting that part."

"Certainly, Most Wise. And is his duty also not to cause dissension within the camp of the Bear?"

"There will be dissension if he forgets the Fall Buffalo Song in the middle."

Striped Badger sighed. Blue Runner was an intelligent woman, and not a malleable one. Most particularly not when it came to her son. "Turn the thing around and look at it from another side," he said, wiggling his hands as if he were revolving a basket. "Sunfallen must not do anything that will break peace among our people. If courting this girl causes angry talk, because he neglects his duties, even though the Mother of the Bear is gracious, the other women will be somewhat louder . . . and they have daughters with prospects to think of. Do you see what I am talking about?"

Blue Runner's expression was impatient. "Why should Striped Badger not just tell them to hold their tongues?"

"Because they will be jealous."

Blue Runner looked disinterested in that.

Striped Badger shook his head. "The Bear knows. He has been taught, and he will remember. Sometimes it is necessary to forgo what one wants, for the peace of the people."

"Your mother doesn't like me," Rain Child said mournfully.

"Yes, she does. She only gave me a scolding for not learning the Fall Buffalo Song. She told me to sing it for her, and I sang the third part twice instead of the fifth part." Sunfallen sounded cheerful about that. He was the Bear; he could do what he wanted.

"Neither does that Striped Badger person."

Sunfallen sighed. "I have told you: Striped Badger won't harm you. He just thinks he knows everything."

Rain Child chuckled. They were beginning to understand each other half with hand talk, and half with words. She wiggled her fingers under his nose. "Every man thinks that."

"It is a fine thing then that women are so humble," Sunfallen said, with a solemn face. "Like my mother."

Rain Child yelped with laughter, then slapped her hand over her mouth.

"Yah, we are supposed to be secret here," Sunfallen said. "Why not stand up on this rock and howl and dance around, in case there are people who haven't noticed us yet."

"I'm sorry," Rain Child whispered. She thought of Long Face and Little Striped Bird, who had asked her to go walking with them, among the Dry River people at home. Long Face had pretended afterward not to know her and Little Striped Bird had wanted to be paid to marry her. This boy was chief of his people, and he was courting her. "Why are you courting me?" she asked him abruptly. She stumbled over the words and said it again with her hands.

Sunfallen grinned. Her accent was horrible, like someone with a mouth full of rocks. And "courting" wasn't what she had said. It was another word, less nice, and he would bet she had learned it from Whistle. When she said it with her hands, it came out "courting."

"Because I like you." He said it with his hands, too, to be sure she understood. He was overcome with an urge to do the word Whistle had taught her, too. His fingers stroked her cheek.

"I am ugly," Rain Child said, not looking at him.

"You are not!" Sunfallen was indignant.

"Everyone else says I am. Your mother wants me to marry you because I have horses."

"And are you going to feel Most Pitiful all your life,

listening to Everyone Else? Everyone Else is an old woman with time on her hands."

"I don't look like other people."

"That's because you are not like other people." Sunfallen buried his face in her neck and bit it, gently. She was like the horses to him, wild and strange, with eyes that had seen things he couldn't imagine. His mother thought it was his duty to marry her. He thought it was an unimaginably wonderful thing to do.

His fingers on her cheek made invisible ants run down her arms. Rain Child felt the way she had when Long Face and Little Striped Bird had asked her to go walking with them, or when the coyote man had put his hand between her legs. She felt floaty, as if the two of them drifted a handspan above the rock, cradled in air.

"Where do you go in the daytime?" he said into her ear. "Take me with you."

She wanted to tell him, but the coyote had said it wasn't time. "I will, just not yet. It's something wonderful, but I have to finish it before I can show you." She floundered around with the words. She didn't know how to say "wonderful" and settled for the hand gesture that meant "great" or "important."

"Then surely the Bear should know about it." Sunfallen nuzzled her neck.

Rain Child pulled away from him and crouched on the rock, ready to stand up. "Is that all you want, to know where I go?" Her eyes narrowed at him.

"No!" Sunfallen said hastily. "No, come back. I don't care where you go." He put his arms around her shoulders and pulled her back down on the courting rock with him so that they both collapsed in a heap, skinning their knees.

She twisted in his grip. "Let me go, or you'll be sorry."

He let her go. "I'm sorry now that I asked where you went," he said penitently. Her temper bloomed around her like a black and blue cloud, but he thought it was mostly hurt feelings. "Most Beautiful, I don't care where you go. I am sorry I asked."

Rain Child sniffed. Sunfallen hung his head. Rain Child hung hers. He picked up his love flute and began to play. The moon rippled in widening sheets on the river's current. She and Rain Child both looked at him out of the curtains of their hair. He put the flute down and grinned at Rain Child.

If Rain Child had known how many people were trying to watch her through the hide of Sunfallen's tent, she might not have had as good a time. As it was, the difference between Sunfallen and Long Face or Little Striped Bird was like the difference between dancing under the Spring Rain Moon and eating green berries. She didn't think Sunfallen knew any more about how to do this than Little Striped Bird had, but he was cheerful about it, where little Striped Bird had been merely determined and in a hurry. Sunfallen spent a lot of time playing with her, investigating her body, fascinated by what it did when he touched it, and he seemed happy to let Rain Child investigate his. She had seen naked men before, of course, but never one this close who was hard and wasn't trying to put it inside her right away. Rain Child was intrigued, and it felt good when someone wasn't in a hurry.

From his perch in the foothills, the coyote could see them, and their adventures made him grin widely and run off to find the wild dogs, one of whom was female. Striped Badger, closer to the tent, couldn't see them, despite his best efforts. He said several powerful charms and squinted his eyes but all he could see was the rising sun and the six bear paws painted on Sunfallen's tent.

Blue Runner, in her own tent, could see everything in her head, and was thinking of how many buffalo they would need for the feast when he formally married the ugly girl, because now that was certain. When couples went walking together, what they did in the trees was no one's business but theirs, but if a boy took a girl to his tent, that was another matter. Blue Runner knew of someone who had married a man she didn't like at all, because it had been raining and she had been foolish enough to go in his tent with him.

Flute Dog was worrying about much the same thing, wondering if it was the same here as among the Dry River people. (It was.) And how they hadn't been here very long and did Rain Child know her own mind? Flute Dog bit her nail. Clever was curled up on the foot of her bed, oblivious, but thinking about it made Flute Dog think of Striped Badger anyway, despite what she tried to think about. She hadn't gone in his tent with him, but she had gone in the trees and he had been very understanding about Rain Child and Whistle and the horses, and it had felt very fine to be with a man, with the camp full of people nearby, and know that she wasn't alone on the Grass anymore. She had looked for him when she had come back from seeing to a gash on Blue Squirrel Horse's hide where Toad Nose's Mare had bitten her, but she couldn't find him, and when she asked Wide Muskrat, Wide Muskrat just sniffed at her and whistled through the gap in her teeth. Flute Dog wondered where he was and shifted restlessly in her bed.

No one else noticed whatever emanated from the air over Sunfallen the Bear's tent. They were just another boy and girl, even if he was the Bear, and there was enough of that in the wind all the time in the summer when the weather was good.

But when Rain Child slipped out of Sunfallen's tent just before dawn and rode Mud-Spattered Horse to where the charcoal was baking, the coyote leered at her. He knew.

"Yah, go and stick it in a knothole," Rain Child said rudely.

The coyote sniffed elaborately at Rain Child's dress until she swatted him away with her hand.

Clever, who was pregnant and so not interested in males for the time being, was nosing instead in Rain Child's pack, hoping to eat the scraps Rain Child brought for the wild dogs before they could.

"And there isn't anything," Rain Child said. "Do you think I am just here to feed you?"

Clever and the coyote both looked mournful.

Rain Child looked at the fire burning in the pit. "You've nearly let it go out," she said accusingly.

"I watched it all night," the coyote said, but she could tell he hadn't.

Rain Child gathered another armful of brush from the dry stuff on the hillside, and found a small downed tree. She dragged it back to the fire pit and shoved it onto the embers, wiggling its length into the pit and jumping on the end to snap it off. It broke and she staggered after it. "No one can trust you," she said disgustedly to the coyote, while she shoved the broken end into the other side of the fire, coughing. Smoke still rolled off the baking earth in horrible yellow clouds. "How long does it take?"

"Mmmm," the coyote said. "Days?"

"You don't know?"

"Of course I know." He stuck his ears up straight, looking alert, like someone hunting. Rain Child snorted. "Two days," he said. "We'll let this new fire die down and then we'll open it up."

Rain Child rolled herself in her blanket and lay down on the ground. "I'm going to sleep. You and those dogs can watch the fire." She yawned.

The coyote leered at her again and sniffed her blanket.

Rain Child took her belt knife out of her sash and closed her fingers around the handle. "If anyone touches me, I'll cut his ears off," she said sleepily.

Clever watched the Big Dog sniffing at the fire as the smoke gradually died down. The wild dogs had come out of the trees and were sitting in a ring around the firepit, attentive, as if they were watching a rabbit burrow. Rain Child was sleeping.

The fire was still burning, but the horrible smoke had died down. Clever had caught a wood rat, which she had bolted down before the coyote or the other dogs could see it, so her stomach was full. She no longer wanted to bite the sandy-colored pack leader, who sat on the edge of the fire pit, rough-coated and thin, an outcast dog with no person. Clever felt superior.

The Big Dog sniffed at the fire again, jumping back when the embers singed his snout. He put a paw out cautiously, prodding the baking mound of earth. Then he poked Rain Child with his ashy nose.

"Go away!" Rain Child batted at his muzzle with her hand.

"Wake up."

"Sleep," Rain Child said. She turned over and pulled her blanket over her head.

"Lazy, that's what happens when you're legs-in-the-air all night," the coyote said disapprovingly.

Rain Child opened an eye. "Don't lecture me about sex. My dog's pregnant."

"They will be very beautiful puppies." The coyote looked modestly at the ground. "You should be grateful."

"They will be thieves." Rain Child tried to go back to sleep. It might be a dream, that she was arguing with a coyote. The whole thing might have been a dream. If she slept a little longer, perhaps she would wake up in Sunfallen's tent, or even her own, and not out here in the hills with wild dogs and a coyote that talked. She pulled the blanket over her head again.

The coyote pulled back, sinking his teeth into the blanket's edge. He tugged hard, trying to unroll her. Rain Child gripped the blanket with both hands. The coyote yanked on the edge and she flailed her arms around, looking for the belt knife. She found it, and sank the blade into the ground just beside his paw. The coyote bit her.

"Yah!" Rain Child sat up suddenly, dropping the knife and rubbing her wounded hand. The coyote tugged at the blanket again.

"Let go. You bit me. I'll probably get blood poisoning."

"It's time to make iron," the coyote said. "Aren't you excited?"

Rain Child rubbed the sleep out of her eyes. Her hand stung.

"If you can make iron, everyone will love you," the coyote said, looking crafty. "These Bear people will give you presents and marry you to their chief."

Rain Child got up. She was still in the hills, and the coyote was still talking to her, so she supposed he wasn't a dream. Dreams didn't generally bite you. "All right. What are we supposed to do now?"

"Now we dig our charcoal out of this pit. Then we melt our rocks with it."

"Are you sure this will work?"

"Mmmm. You will have to dig the charcoal out. I burned my feet already."

Rain Child thought of telling him to be a human person then, but thought better of it. He was probably less trouble as a coyote. She took her wonderful pot and filled it with water from the river and dumped it on the embers of the fire. Steam rose up in a hissing cloud that made her gasp. It was a hot day already, and sweat drenched her shoulders and face. She took Flute Dog's shovel, which she had brought back, and began to dig through the earth that covered the mound. The earth had caked hard as adobe brick and she dug at it and chipped at it with the shovel end and finally with the ax until it cracked open. More dreadful smell came out of the crack. Rain Child held her nose and the dogs all retreated into the brush.

"Phoo! It smells like bad eggs in there."

"Is it charcoal?" The coyote leaned eagerly over the pit. Rain Child chipped at the earth some more and prodded the blackened mess underneath it with the ax head. Some of the wood was unburned and some half charred. A thick, sticky layer of goo puddled in the middle. There were a few blackened lumps of what might be charcoal. Rain Child lifted them out on the shovel blade and peered at them.

"Is this how it's supposed to look?"

"Mmm."

Rain Child squatted and poked the lumps of charcoal with the end of a stick. "I don't know."

"Oh, I'm certain it will work," the coyote said.

"How do we burn it?"

The coyote scratched behind one ear, looking thoughtful. "They put the charcoal in the oven with the rocks, and seal it up," he said. "I think that's what they do."

Surely a spirit would know these things. He must be testing her. It was important to do what spirits told you to. All the stories made that clear. When you met a spirit and disobeyed it, awful things happened, but when you obeyed, then you were lucky for life.

Rain Child carried the lumps of charcoal to the oven on the shovel and piled them inside it, singeing her fingers arranging them. She tucked more tinder around the charcoal to start it burning, and lit that with her slow-burner. Then she took the pieces of rock they had broken off and laid them gingerly on the charcoal.

"Is this right?"

"Put your pot beside the oven, so it will know what to do," the coyote said.

Rain Child arranged the pot where the oven could see it. Her fingers left black prints on its surface.

"Now seal it up with more clay."

"It will go out."

"No, you leave a hole open in the top. Like the smoke-hole in a tent. And a small one at the bottom, the way we did with the charcoal."

"Oh." Rain Child went to the river and came back with a load of mud on the shovel this time. She didn't want to take the pot, in case the oven forgot what it was doing.

"Now we will change the world," the coyote said, while Rain Child was filling the oven mouth with mud.

"Will iron change the world more than horses?"

"Iron and horses go together. They are linked things. One calls the other."

"Why?"

"I don't know. I just hear them. Because they are New Things. The way you are a New Thing."

"I don't want to be a New Thing," Rain Child said, slapping clay into the oven's mouth, as if she could stop it from naming her. The cool slickness of the new clay soothed her burned hands. What she had put on first was drying already, dusty under her fingertips.

She poked more into the chimney, leaving a hole she made with a stick. "There. It's sealed." Smoke trailed through the tiny hole at the top. "Yah, I am dirty." She looked at her hands and the dark smudges on her arms and dress.

"There are ashes on your nose," the coyote said.

"I'm going to wash. If you had any proper manners, you would turn your back."

The coyote bent his head down and put his paw over it.

Rain Child laughed. She was cooking up a new world. A new everything was baking in that oven. She snatched up her blanket and dropped it over his head, and ran for the river before he could untangle himself.

The water was cool and slick when she waded into it. Rain Child pulled her dress over her head and dropped it on the bank. She ducked her head beneath the surface and rose sputtering, shaking out her hair. The drops flew into the sun like beetles. She paddled out lazily into the center. It was just deep enough that she could manage to float there, fingers plucking the rocks in the stream bed to keep the current from carrying her downstream. On the bank she could see a shimmer that she thought was the oven's heat, making the air wavy so that the trees looked like ripple trees in its current.

She sank under the water again and when she surfaced, the coyote was there, too. She splashed river water at him with her hand, and he reared out of the water on his hind legs and came down on his forepaws so that a wave of water rolled over Rain Child, drenching her. She laughed and pulled his tail, and he dove and surfaced beneath her, lifting her on his back and tipping her headfirst.

Rain Child curled in a ball and rolled under the water. The light revolved above her, filtered through the green veil of the river. On the bottom tiny fish darted between the stones, and an old turtle, surprised and disapproving, stroked away in a hurry and disappeared in the rocks by the bank. She could see the coyote's feet paddling above her. She reached up and grabbed one and pulled him down. His yellow eyes stared at her through the ripple of the water, his gray ruff floating about his throat like water weeds. His paw in her hand was long-nailed and hairy; no, it was russet colored, long fingers like fish—

Rain Child dropped it and the coyote leapt into the air like a grasshopper, spraying water, and rolled her over again on the rocks as he landed. Rain Child came up snorting water. She was reaching for him when the air shimmered again, this time like someone shaking out a blanket. There was a dreadful crack and boom and the treetops shook.

Rain Child and the coyote stopped in the stream, staring. A cloud of birds was exploding from the trees and Rain Child saw two of the wild dogs scrabbling and floundering up the bank, trailing blood.

"Clever!" Rain Child waded out of the river and scrambled up the bank. With another horrible bang, a piece of the oven flew past her head and a shower of stones rained down on her.

The ground around the oven was littered with shards of

clay and stone, and what was left of it was in flames that had caught the brush nearby. Clever came limping toward her from the trees, trailing one foot.

Rain Child looked around her for the coyote, who just stood staring.

"It blew up," he said.

"Where's my horse?" Rain Child put her fingers in her mouth and whistled, but Mud-Spattered Horse didn't come. Sobbing, she pulled her dress on over wet skin, tugging and fighting it. She whistled again for Mud-Spattered Horse, but he was gone. Rain Child could see him in the distance, a hysterical fleeing figure across the Grass, hooves thudding the earth, mouth wild and foam-flecked. She ran into the Grass after him, with Clever limping behind her. On the bank the tops of the trees had caught now.

Striped Badger felt the explosion before he heard it. He felt inexplicably that someone had folded in the fabric of the universe, bent time back upon itself. Then the sound rolled through the air like flood water in a dry wash, lifting everything in its path. Striped Badger flattened himself in the brush on the ridge above the riverbank, into a patch that proved to be nettles, but he was too afraid to move. Only when the brush went up in flames and he saw it coming his way did he jump up and run. As he looked back over his shoulder, he saw the coyote fleeing the fire, too, and the girl and her dog running into the Grass.

The dull boom of the oven blowing up rose like a black bird from the riverbank. It circled on coal-colored wings and flapped across the Grass, trailing a gray shadow below it. The animal people felt it. Wood Rat looked out of his burrow and went back in again and told his wife that the two-legged people were blowing up the world with lightning. A hawk, circling over Wood Rat's house, was blown out of his air current by the shock wave and flapped and floundered in a most undignified fashion while Wood Rat looked out of his door again and laughed at him. The antelope heard it and leaped straight up like grasshoppers and before they could ask what the matter was they were in the next valley.

Bull Buffalo heard it at a distance and stopped chewing, lifting his ponderous head in the direction of the sound. He could feel it in the ground, a deep rumbling under his feet. "This is not a good place," he told his cows, and they began to move, slowly and with dignity, because they weren't very frightened yet, but steadily, so that soon they were a black paint poured over the Grass, flowing away to the south.

A man who was coming along from somewhere in the south heard them before he saw them, a steady rumble through the core of the earth. He put his ear to the ground and heard the sound come closer, and heard the dark flapping in the air that was the crow-shape of the explosion spreading over the Grass. He turned out of the way of the buffalo and waited in the lee of an outcrop of stone while they went by.

The stone, one of the teeth that occasionally pushed through the jawbone of the Grass, heard it too, and so did the skulls in the skull rings where the dead lived.

"My daughter has made a great magic," the skull of Young Owl said.

"It is the end of the world," said the skull of Dark-of-the-Moon.

In the camp of the Bear, the sound was faint, but Eyes of Bear heard it and waked from his nap. He stood outside his tent, sniffing the wind.

Inside the tents, stones cracked on cold hearths, and waterskins split, dribbling their contents unnoticed on clothes chests and stores of herbs, on paint cases and flutes and newly stretched drums, leaving them a sodden mess in pools of mud. Women cleaned up the water and found that the tents were full of mice. Men out hunting felt the game reverse themselves, walking backward, vanishing into the sky.

"Where is the Bear?" Eyes of Bear said to Blue Runner as she passed.

"Gone!" she snapped. She was carrying a muddy wooden box to the river to wash it. Strands of sodden sinew trailed from its open mouth.

"Oh, that is not good." Eyes of Bear shook his head.

"I was cooking in a buffalo paunch and it tore. And he has gone with the girl, playing the fool somewhere." Blue Runner looked exasperated. "They are children."

Eyes of Bear wasn't listening. He was still sniffing the air. "Fire," he said finally.

"What?"

"The Grass is on fire."

Blue Runner sniffed. "I don't smell anything. It is your hearth fire, maybe. You have tipped your bedding into it again."

Flute Dog and Whistle ran past them, trailing coils of rope in each hand.

"They know," Eyes of Bear said. "The horses know."

Blue Runner whirled around, staring into the Grass. The sky was a bright blue, sharp as turquoise, but it faded, paled, overlaid with a haze that thickened as they stared at it. Blue Runner could suddenly see a glowing edge along the distant ridge line.

Sunfallen could see it, too, as he struggled through the Grass, driving Gray Squirrel Horse with his heels. She hadn't minded being borrowed, but now that she smelled smoke, she wanted to turn around. Sunfallen pummeled her ribs with his feet.

Gray Squirrel Horse threw up her head and whinnied, ears pricked forward. Sunfallen saw a galloping shape hurtling through the Grass at them, but then it passed in a drumming of hooves, and he could see that Mud-Spattered Horse had no one on his back.

He had only been trying to see where Rain Child went. Striped Badger had told him a tale last night about a girl who sneaked off to meet a monster who was her lover, and then came back and foisted her monster child on her human husband, but Sunfallen didn't believe a word of that. He just wanted to see where she went. He had borrowed Gray Squirrel Horse and followed the trail through the Grass.

It wasn't hard. Rain Child's tracks were fresh and the Grass was bent where the horse had lumbered through it. *Anyone could find you*, Sunfallen thought, amused. And then there had been the sound, and the dark crow-shape rolling through the air.

Sunfallen could see the flames now and Blue Squirrel Horse began to swerve. Sunfallen clung to her mane. The air was thick with smoke. He heard a yelp and saw the little gray dog running on three legs, trailing a bloody paw. He panicked, screaming Rain Child's name.

Sunfallen called her name again, and she stumbled out of the Grass, face black with ash and the ends of her hair singed off.

15

A Hard Person to Steal a Horse From

THE PEOPLE OF THE BEAR BROKE CAMP AND RAN, LOADing their boxes and blankets and bags of belongings onto dog travoises, and their own backs. Rain Child, sobbing, put Clever into the horse travois and hitched Clever's little travois to Toad Nose's Mare.

"What happened?" Flute Dog asked her over and over, but Rain Child wouldn't answer her.

Sunfallen had only asked her once. Now he was busy with herding his people out of the path of the fire. The wind came most often from the northwest. If it didn't turn, the fire might go east for days, blackening the dry fall grass. The Bear's people went west, babies weeping on cradleboards on their mothers' backs, leaving even the old Bear's bier behind them.

Striped Badger felt their anger as they walked, and wove it with his hands, turning it into a garment he could wear. They were already glaring at the Horse Girl as if they knew she was to blame without Striped Badger telling them. Sunfallen looked grim. That was good, too.

He would see that he should have consulted Striped Badger more than he had, and then people would continue to give presents to Striped Badger out of respect. And Blue Runner would be quiet, and ashamed for being ambitious.

The fire was still burning to the east, and Sunfallen thought it safe to camp for the night as dark fell. He didn't ask Striped Badger.

Striped Badger found him binding up the foot of the Horse Girl's gray dog. The dog looked out from the crook of Sunfallen's arm and growled at Striped Badger.

"It is ill luck to have left the old Bear's bones," Striped Badger said.

"Worse luck to have met the fire." Sunfallen tied a thread of sinew around the dog's paw to keep her from chewing the bandage off. Rain Child sat next to him, stroking the dog's head and looking miserable.

"And ill thought to spend your time on a dog!" Striped Badger snapped. The dog looked back at him with baleful eyes.

"Dogs are part of the world," Sunfallen murmured. "Part of the circle."

Rain Child bent her head. Striped Badger glared at her and walked away.

Flute Dog found him stalking the perimeter of the camp, staring at the faint red glow that could still be seen in the distance.

"Are you going to sleep tonight?" she asked him.

"I am going to watch the fire."

"We have Night Watchers for that." Her fingers touched his arm.

Striped Badger sighed. It would not be pleasant when it was time to fix blame for the fire, even though the child was only a foster one. "The Night Watchers cannot see what I see," he said gently. "They cannot see the spells in the wind. But I know them by their names."

"Oh." Flute Dog didn't know what he was talking about. Perhaps she wasn't understanding him. Their language was hard for her to wrap her tongue around.

"In the morning," Striped Badger said. "In the morning it will be known." He went on pacing along the outer ring of tents.

The man who was coming along from the south saw the fires of the Bear's people to his left and the bright line of the grass fire to his right. His horse was weary and he was hungry. He had eaten the last of the buffalo calf he had killed on the trail and the nest of quail eggs he had found. And he had seen horse dung in a patch of grazed grass. He turned his horse's head toward the cones of light that were the strange tents.

When he got close enough that he thought the Night Watcher might notice him if went any farther, he dismounted in the grass and rolled himself in his blanket, his horse's rein tied to one wrist. Strange people were generally more welcoming if you didn't arrive in the dark.

In the morning he yawned, sat up, and ran his fingers through his hair, combing the burrs out. He waded into the stream he had been following and washed, drying himself on his blanket. When he felt clean, he took out his paint box and painted a red line down the part in his hair and two white spots on his cheeks, marks he had made so often he could do them without a bowl of water to look in. There didn't seem to be anything else to do to get ready, so he swung up on his horse's back, let him drink in the shallows, and rode slowly into the dawn-lit camp.

Something important was happening. He could see that before they even saw him. Then the Day Watcher pointed and shouted, and a handful of men trotted between the outermost tents. The horse herd was grazing just past the last tent, on a tight picket line, and in the light the newcomer could see them clearly. He took note of the brown-spotted stallion among them and grinned.

"I am a friend," he said with his hands, and the men looked at him suspiciously, as if they doubted it.

"Take him to the Bear," one of them said to the other. It

sounded like unintelligible squawks, but they motioned him forward.

"He has another horse," they told a boy sitting angrily on a pile of bearskins, before a fire. The newcomer understood that word. The boy wore a necklace of bear claws. There was a crowd of people around him, as if they were in the middle of some important business.

Flute Dog was standing with her arms crossed just in front of the boy on the skins, and she opened her mouth in a round shape like an egg when she saw him. Howler grinned again.

"I am a hard person to steal a horse from," he said.

"Is this person from your people?" the boy on the skins asked, with his hands.

"Yes." Flute Dog blinked at Howler as if she thought he might disappear.

The Bear's people stared at the stranger.

A large man with a round face and an important expression pointed at Howler. "You will have to wait," he said to him.

Howler saw Rain Child now, crouched on the ground beside her mother. Her face was cut and bruised, and there was a burn on her hand. Her hair curled in dirty twists around her forehead. She was glaring at the round-faced man.

Rain Child's eyes widened when she saw Howler, but her attention didn't waver from Striped Badger. She jumped up and spat words at him furiously. "Yah! You are ignorant! And I am not a witch!"

Blue Runner's eyes slid back and forth between them. Striped Badger could see her thinking.

"I am not so ignorant that I didn't see you dancing naked with a coyote in the hills," Striped Badger said. "And now look what has come from those hills. Fire." He nodded, as if agreeing with himself.

"I was going to make another pot," Rain Child said contritely. "Like my magic pot. We must not have done it right."

"We?"

"My spirit guide—he came to me in the Grass and said to make a new pot by melting rocks."

The crowd around her laughed and then fell silent under Striped Badger's gaze.

"Witchcraft," Nighthawk Woman announced.

Several people nodded solemnly at that.

"Nothing of the sort." Whistle rolled her eyes at Nighthawk Woman. "Do we ask *why* when a spirit speaks?" Rain Child thought of Hopeful, trying to keep the Dry River people from driving her out. Were these people going to do that, too?

"A child has no business talking to spirits," Striped Badger said importantly.

Flute Dog's hands balled themselves into fists.

Because they were talking mostly with their hands, Howler could partly follow the talk. "Spirits come to those they wish to speak to," he said, with his own hands.

The Bear's people regarded the stranger cautiously now.

"And who are you?" Striped Badger demanded. "And why shouldn't we kill you?"

"Because we are an honorable people!" Sunfallen snapped. It was the first thing he had said. He said it again with his hands.

"This person is relieved to hear that," Howler said. He stared at Striped Badger. "I am First of the Holy Clowns, the Fool Dancers of the people who came out of the Dry River in the Long Ago."

"And I am First of the Bear Dancers of the people of the Bear," Striped Badger retorted. "What do you want here?"

They stood silently a moment, sizing each other up. Howler said, "I am looking for my horse, which has strayed away with these women's horses."

"Those are *our* horses now," Striped Badger said. "But you can take this girl child away with you."

"Liar!" Flute Dog spat at him. "Wicked! I am sorry I

walked anywhere with you. I hope it turns pale and falls off!" She said it with her hands, to be sure he understood her.

Sunfallen's eyes snapped. "Am I invisible? Have I become an air person? It is not proper for you to speak so to Striped Badger. Or for Striped Badger to decide this matter." He stood up and Striped Badger noticed that he had grown a good deal over the summer. He was looking Striped Badger in the eye now, which made things harder.

"She has bewitched the Bear," Striped Badger announced. "She has put a spell on him like the spell she put on the rocks that caught fire. Now all the buffalo have gone."

Surprised Raven pushed through the crowd, and his brothers followed him. "In the winter we will be hungry. Is your magic pot going to feed us then? *Or* your horses?" What use were magic animals when there was no food?

"This is for the Bear to decide." Weasel shouldered importantly past Surprised Raven. He was the father of the Bear, after all. He hadn't liked having Striped Badger more important than he was.

"He is a boy." Blue Runner stuck her chin out at her husband. "We need to think about this."

"I haven't seen any magic pot," White Grass Mouse said, taking Weasel's part. "Likely it is just a child's story."

"It was there!" Rain Child insisted. "The coyote gave it to me, but it burned up with the fire, I think."

"The coyote," Striped Badger said. "Is it good to talk to Coyote?"

"Coyote talks to whom he wishes." Howler interrupted them and they stared uneasily at the wild-eyed stranger. "This child is Dog Sister. She was nursed by a dog when she was born and they speak to her. If Coyote speaks to her he has reason, and perhaps it would be wise to listen."

Striped Badger put on his bear face and turned to stare at

the stranger. The stranger didn't flinch. The stranger looked as if he couldn't see the bear face over Striped Badger's own face. Striped Badger bared his teeth fiercely.

The stranger put his fingers to his head like horse's ears and whinnied. A horse in the herd answered him. Everyone laughed except Striped Badger.

"The Grass is on fire," Striped Badger said. "We will think on what to do with you, and the one who talks to coyotes, when it is out." He turned on his heel, nodding at Surprised Raven and his brothers to follow him. Blue Runner went, too, while Weasel stood uncertainly, looking from Sunfallen to the stranger.

Nighthawk Woman sniffed. "Do we need one who talks to dogs?"

"Spiteful Old Woman Who Talks to Hornets," Whistle said. "They will nest in your bed!"

"She cursed me!" Nighthawk Woman howled.

"Be quiet! Wishful thinking is not a curse," Sunfallen snapped at her. "I am the Bear and I will think on all of this." He looked miserable, his glance straying from Rain Child to the stranger, and then to the way that Striped Badger and his mother had gone. The wind whipped his hair, still blowing from the northwest. He looked down it to the wavering line of red on the horizon. It seemed dimmer, as if the fire were going out, or traveling the other way, into some other people's graze. It was not the first time he had seen the Grass burn. Lightning-struck fires came sometimes in dry weather, and drove people and buffalo alike like scattered ants. And the people were always hungry afterward.

"Go and see where the fire is going," he said to Weasel and White Grass Mouse.

Rain Child was sitting miserably in the dirt again. "Go away!" he shouted, and everyone else went away but Flute Dog, Rain Child, and the stranger. "I am going to see if Eyes of Bear can see the wind," Sunfallen said wearily to Flute Dog. His hand started to brush Rain

Child's hair and she flinched away from him. "Take care of her."

"What of the messenger which the Bear saw?"

"It may be that the messenger was a false one," Striped Badger said gravely to Surprised Raven.

"The messenger was not false!" Blue Runner said, and they looked at her sternly, because they were men talking together and she was not.

"I am Mother of the Bear, and Sister of the Bear," she reminded them.

"Perhaps the message was not false, and yet the messenger was," Striped Badger said. "That would be a mystery, but it might be true."

"The horses are a good thing," Surprised Raven said firmly. "I want one myself. I don't see why I have not been given one yet."

"Perhaps the horses are the messenger, and not the girl," Blue Runner said. That made everything explainable. And much easier.

"She might be a witch," Weasel conceded.

"I think she is." White Grass Mouse nodded his head. "But Striped Badger is full of himself."

"That is not new. That is why he is First of the Bear Dancers."

"Your wife listens more to him than she does to you," White Grass Mouse said.

"I gave him a good buffalo blanket. Out of respect, because he is teaching my son," Weasel grumbled. "But my son is not listening to him now. I think she *is* a witch."

"The wind is turning."

"*She* must have turned it."

"The fire has burned enough that if it blows back our way now, it will go out."

"She could do that."

"Why?"

"To put us off the trail," Weasel said darkly.

Flute Dog and Howler took Rain Child to Flute Dog's tent.

"I am sorry," Rain Child sniffled into her hands. "I don't think the coyote knew it would blow up."

"Very likely not," Howler conceded. "Coyote is the part of us that dives off cliffs without looking to see how deep the water is."

"You saw my pot. With a knife made of that, I wouldn't be afraid of anyone."

"Except fire."

Rain Child snuffled, digging in her pack. "Look. He gave me this too." She spread out the red and blue beads on her palm.

Howler inspected them.

"There was a man on crossed sticks hanging from them," Flute Dog said. "I didn't like it and I threw that away."

"I have heard of him. That was wise, I think."

"What is he?"

"He is the pale people's dead god."

"A dead god? Like a ghost?"

"Sort of. I don't understand very well. A trader told me about him in the fall. Before I left to look for you. There are wicked things happening in the Cities-in-the-West."

"Why did you look for us?"

"I wanted my horse."

"We took Toad Nose's Mare, too, and he didn't come looking for us," Rain Child snuffled.

"Toad Nose doesn't like you as much as I do. Or your mother, even though you left without telling me. And now I find she's been walking with some bear person. It's a good thing you can't speak their tongue very well yet, or I wouldn't know that." Howler shook his head sorrowfully.

"I was lonely," Flute Dog said under her breath. "And how did you find us?"

"The wild dogs told me. I met them in the Grass and one of them spoke to me."

They looked at him, trying to decide if he meant that. With Howler you never knew. Just now he seemed more mysterious than ever.

"He spoke Dog, of course," Howler said. "But he seemed to know where he was going. He seemed too bold for a wild one, too, as if he wanted to be tame. And too fat, as if someone had been feeding him."

"Um," Rain Child said.

"Suppose you show me what you did to melt these rocks," Howler said to Rain Child.

"It was the coyote. He said to build an oven. Out of clay. Oh, first we cooked a tree to make charcoal."

"To make charcoal?"

"The coyote said the Moon told him that the rocks had to be melted over a very hot fire."

Howler looked at Flute Dog over Rain Child's head.

"Well, she is either crazy or she has been talking to spirits," Flute Dog said.

"Sometimes it's hard to tell the difference," Howler said.

"I am not crazy." Rain Child stood up. She felt wobbly in the knees. She hadn't felt right since Sunfallen had taken her up on Blue Squirrel Horse with him and ridden her out of the fire. She hadn't known that Striped Badger had been there too until they saw him hobbling into camp on burned feet, in a temper. Mud-Spattered Horse had come home before they had.

Rain Child put the beads around her neck. Everyone thought she was a witch, anyway. She looked at Flute Dog to see if she was going to say anything, but Flute Dog didn't. "The coyote said I was a New Person," Rain Child said to Howler.

"That's very likely," Howler said.

"She is not!" Flute Dog said. "I saw her first mother."

"From the Cities-in-the-West, you thought?"

"Yes. Maybe. She had cloth clothes, like they wear. It was a long time ago and I don't remember."

"And if a woman such as that had a child of a pale man, what do you think she would look like?"

Rain Child goggled at him. Flute Dog compressed her lips. "No," she said, and snapped them shut again.

Howler didn't argue. It wasn't a thing that would be good for these people here to know, anyway. But he was a Holy Clown, and a clown's job was to think, and to make other people think, too. To think on the fact that if the pale men could get babies on human women, then maybe the pale men were human, too—just dangerously different.

"That Striped Badger person is trying to make me leave," Rain Child said. "Everyone always wants me to leave."

"You do seem to bring on bad weather and fires," Howler said.

"I don't. They just follow me."

"It's those dogs," Flute Dog said, looking for something to pin the blame on.

"It isn't," Rain Child said.

"You've been feeding them."

"They follow me, too."

"She is Dog Sister. Maybe the dogs have kept her safe," Howler said.

"From what?"

"From whatever is trying to happen to the world."

Flute Dog looked around her nervously, as if whatever it was might be coming along just now. Outside, Weasel and White Grass Mouse came out of the Grass, running at a steady pace. Weasel had Rain Child's pot by the handle.

"That's mine!" Rain Child dove through the door at him and Howler grabbed her by the arm. "It is!"

"And these people are not in a mood to be charitable." Howler held onto her.

Weasel and White Grass Mouse's faces were blackened with soot, and their hair clung to their heads in sweat-dampened strings. They stopped before Sunfallen's tent, puffing. Sunfallen had already come out of it, with old Eyes of Bear tottering behind him.

"Is the fire turning?" The wind had held steady, but you never knew. Fire changed the wind sometimes, sucking it into a roaring spiral, spitting it out somewhere else, alight.

"It ate the Gorge of the Dead Buffalo Cow, and it is feeding on Two Rock Valley now. When we got to Where the River Goes by the Hills, where it started, a bush caught fire again and its flames chased us. We found this." Weasel swung the pot by its handle.

"That is dangerous. You had better give it to me." Striped Badger appeared from nowhere, hand out. Weasel hesitated.

"That's mine!" Howler didn't manage to get his hand over Rain Child's mouth in time.

"It is what started the fire, we think," Weasel said.

"You are stupid. How could a pot start the fire? It was the oven we tried to cook the rocks in," Rain Child said indignantly.

"Who is 'we'?"

Rain Child bit her lip.

"This girl and the coyote," Striped Badger said. "This is very bad."

"Where is the fire going?" Sunfallen asked.

"Still away from us, but the wind is angry. It keeps turning. It may turn back. There may be enough burn to keep the fire from coming this way now, but we aren't sure."

"We will move again," Sunfallen said.

Eyes of Bear peered rheumily into the smoke and nodded.

"Leave that one here," Striped Badger said, pointing at Rain Child.

"Maybe," Eyes of Bear said.

"No!" Sunfallen glared around him, daring anyone else to make the suggestion. "Give me that!" He took the pot and put it among his own things, still mostly packed on the travois that his dogs pulled. Flute Dog had rigged other travoises with spare tent poles and blankets, for the horses to drag, but Sunfallen had put the oldest people's belongings on them and left himself only his dogs.

"We will decide these things later," Striped Badger said smoothly, deciding that he had miscalculated. The young Bear was still infatuated with that dangerous girl. He smiled gently at her mother, but Flute Dog glared back at him. Usually women trusted Striped Badger's judgment. This one had been too long in the Grass by herself. If he could detach the young Bear from the girl, then perhaps she could vanish quietly, in a way that would satisfy the mother. It would be important where these horses went to live, and Striped Badger had seen how they obeyed the stranger women's words and the little flicks of their hands and heels.

"The Bear is right, of course," Striped Badger said soothingly. "We cannot turn the child out in the Grass, even if she is a witch."

"Why not?" Blue Runner demanded. Striped Badger had been trying to do just that for two days.

"We are not monsters." Striped Badger shook his head gently. "Perhaps Eyes of Bear and myself can drive the wickedness from her, instead."

Rain Child started to retort and Howler's fingers dug into her arm. He wasn't sure what was being said, but he knew that Rain Child shouldn't answer it when she was in a temper.

"The wind is turning," Sunfallen said angrily. "Move!"

Fire heard. He saw the people spread out like ants in the Grass, fleeing westward, and spat his hot breath at them. It roared down the canyons and clefts in the Grass's surface, which is flat only from a distance, licking the river bottoms and washes, boiling the leaves of the trees that clustered along the watercourses. They shriveled and blackened, crumbling to ash that blew on the whirling torrent of the flame-driven wind, settling in distant tinder. They leaped to life again there, a flowering of flame in dry leaves, in the tall stalks of the Grass, in the scrub of the wash sides and the berry vines of the foothills.

The animal people fled before them, leaping, bounding, scurrying, burrowing, desperate to outrun death or dig deep enough to crouch, choking on the smoke, while it passed by. The deer and the antelope fled wild-eyed, the rabbit people dashed blindly though the tall stalks, and the birds exploded into air, beating up on the wild wind. The insect people burst from the Grass in dark clouds. The wild dogs trailed the human people on burned paws, linked by Rain Child to a life once forgotten.

Sunfallen's people hurried now, frightened as the wind turned and the flames, spark borne, leaped over the burned lands and ignited new fires behind them. Flute Dog and Rain Child put old Eyes of Bear on a horse, and Rain Child got up behind him to hold him on, and no one argued with her. Sunfallen gave Weasel and Blue Runner a horse to ride, even though Weasel often fell off, but Sunfallen himself walked beside his dog travois, as befitted the Bear. Striped Badger and Howler walked, too, and found themselves walking side by side, coughing in the smoky wind.

Howler covertly eyed Flute Dog, riding on his stolen horse behind old Grandmother Scarlet Water, who looked as frail and angular as a praying mantis, bundled in her buffalo rug with just her head and bony hands stuck out. Her fingers were clenched in Mud-Spattered Horse's mane, and her eyes rolled from side to side as Mud-Spattered Horse lumbered along, dragging a load of tents and piled bags and boxes on a travois.

"The old lady thinks the horse is going to leap into the air with her," Howler said to Striped Badger with his hands.

Striped Badger eyed him appraisingly. "They stole your horse?" He made it a question. That might be useful, but this man would also probably want to have the horse back.

"Yes."

"Which horse?"

"The one she's riding," Howler said.

"It is not a good idea for women to have so many horses," Striped Badger said judiciously. "I have already thought of that." He wondered if it would be possible to kill this man, but thought that he would want to have a few charms set first to keep the man's spirit from coming back. It was dangerous to kill clowns, even for another man of power. "I have been thinking about marrying her," he added. "But that girl is a disadvantage. She is disrespectful."

Howler opened his eyes a little wider, but he didn't answer that. "She is young and ignorant," he suggested.

"Where did that pot come from?" Striped Badger looked disinterested, while he waited to see if the newcomer was going to answer him.

"She found it." Howler thought a moment. "And then they ran away, I think because the pot talked to them. I have been looking for it. It is a shame that she was the one to find it. I feel that it has much power. If someone could make more of that substance . . . someone who knew how to tame the spirits of the stuff, of course, as the child does not . . ." He let the sentence trail off, his hands drifting aimlessly in air.

"You have not tried?"

Howler looked away. He seemed ashamed. "I am afraid of it," he said finally.

"Ah. Well, it takes much power to control these things." Striped Badger looked smug. "It is no disgrace for a man to know his limitations."

"No indeed."

They left it at that for a while, hurrying along while floating ash powdered their hair. Sometimes a wind-borne spark would set a little piece of the Grass alight around them and someone would frantically stamp it out. In fall the Grass was brittle and soaked up fire as if it were hungry.

Sunfallen sent runners ahead to test the Grass westward of them and they came back to say that it was very dry, too, but the Buffalo River was flowing strongly, and it might be too wide for the fire to jump. It had already jumped the Little Snake River, where they had been camped. Sunfallen shouted an order and they swung the line of march south, the quickest way toward the Buffalo. North of them they could see that a stray spark had set the Grass alight there, and it was too big already to put out.

"Hurry!"

Mothers picked up small children, and everyone shouted at the dogs to pull harder, bumping the travoises along the path the horses had made through the Grass.

Rain Child held on to Eyes of Bear and kicked Whitetail Horse hard in the ribs. Whitetail Horse, already wild-eyed with the smell of smoke, flung up her head and snorted. Eyes of Bear slid dangerously to one side. Rain Child grabbed him by his shirt and hauled him back up. He was muttering something; she wasn't sure whether it was a prayer or a spell. He stopped when Whitetail Horse broke into a trot. The travois thumped behind her.

"Uncle, if you can keep the fire away, I will slow down."

"I don't know. You called it. It does not want to go away." Eyes of Bear leaned his head back against Rain Child's chest. "Maybe it is following you."

"I am sorry. How do I tell it to go home again?"

"You can't tell fire. It does not listen." He coughed.

No one tried to talk to the little fires in the Grass anymore, either, unless they were nearby. There were too many of them. They struggled on, coughing, toward the river. The animal people fled, too. A mother wolf with a singed tail plunged through the scrub, her half-grown cubs behind her, and Sunfallen nearly fell over a porcupine trundling along. A doe shot past them, mouth foam-flecked, eyes staring, too frightened to pay mind to the wolves. They took no note of her either. Fire made all things equal. The air was thick with buzzing, zooming things, some blinded by the smoke, some homing on the water with instincts not given to two-legged people. In a prairie dog village where there was still only a whiff of smoke, Flute Dog saw their heads popping in and out of holes, undecided whether to run or dig. She shouted and waved her arms to drive the horses away from the holes. A crow flew overhead cawing, and an owl, disturbed in its roost, flapped past in a rustle of great wings. A jumping mouse leaped from the grass into the neck of Sunfallen's shirt, and, panicked, bounced off again in the other direction.

Surprised Raven and White Grass Mouse circled the band in opposite directions, making certain no stragglers fell behind. Their faces were streaked with ash so that they looked as if they were painted for a dance. When they met at the heel of the band, Dog Nose came running from the east to say that the wind had turned the fire again, for a little, anyway. His skin was blistered and they gave him the last of their water.

"What is this substance of which this pot is made?" Striped Badger asked Howler as they walked.

Howler coughed, spitting ash. "The child says it is called iron. I have heard of it—some trader told me a tale of pale people living in the Cities-in-the-West now who make this stuff."

Striped Badger frowned. "I have heard these tales, too, of pale people. And horses. I have heard that they brought the horses."

"That may be. Ours were brought by the Horse-Bringers of our people, and tradition says they came from a river near the Cities-in-the-West. You know how it is with stories."

Striped Badger did. Stories might be both fact and legend, and true and not true.

"If iron is the pale people's magic, and *if* they brought the horses—then iron must be a great thing, I think," Howler said, furrowing his brow in thought.

"Not a thing for a child to put her fingers in, certainly." Striped Badger looked sad. "You see what came of it."

"And it is a cook pot."

"Does it call food?" Why else would a pot be magic?

"*I* know how she tried to make it," Howler said, looking secretive.

"But you have decided not to make it." Striped Badger put it tactfully. "That was wise. But still, you might sell the recipe for this iron. I am First of the Bear Dancers. I am permitted to buy magic from strangers."

"That would need a very great price."

"It is unwise to keep magic you cannot use."

"I will think on it."

Striped Badger smiled.

The river watched the fire coming, floating on its back, its broad face to the sky. It could feel the ash speckling it and the heat of Fire's breath on its eastern bank, but the river didn't care. It bubbled serenely while the human people threw themselves into it like ants, splashing water on hot skin, coughing smoke. They knelt in the shallows at the ford, sucking down water, and only began to drag the travoises through when Sunfallen shouted at them.

16

Contrary

STRIPED BADGER DANCED ALONG THE BANK, TURNING handstands, using his bear face, shooing people into the water. When they were all across, he began to walk backward into the river. Midway he stopped, took off his wet shoes, and put them on his head.

"Striped Badger is walking backward!"

The people on the far side turned, dripping, to watch him, to see what he would do next. On the other side of the river, he stood on his hands again, grabbing at his shoes as they fell off his head. Everyone laughed. He righted himself, hopped on a rock, and climbed onto Mud-Spattered Horse behind Flute Dog and old Grandmother Scarlet Water. He got on backward, facing Mud-Spattered Horse's tail. Flute Dog tried to push him off.

"Striped Badger is being a contrary."

"His shoes are on backwards now. He is coming when he is going."

"Some great magic will happen."

Sunfallen's people, and Sunfallen himself, watched

him with a nervous excitement. A contrary made strong magic, because he ran counter to the order of the world. He was the lightning in the storm, capable of striking anywhere. Striped Badger got down from Mud-Spattered Horse and began to walk backward again, away from the river. Sunfallen's people followed him.

When they had put a good distance between themselves and the river, along stony ground where grass grew only in ragged clumps, Sunfallen let them stop. Striped Badger put his tent up inside out and sat before it on his head, with his legs folded in the air.

Flute Dog pulled Rain Child into their tent and made her stay there.

On the other side of the river the fire roared through the scrub and grass, but there was not much food for it where the ford washed through stony shallows, and it died trying to cross the water. The burned land behind it smoldered evilly, and in the dark they could see red embers glowing amid the destruction.

"All it will take is a strong wind," Sunfallen said uneasily, but the wind was still. And when it did come up in the night it carried thunderheads on it. The sky opened with a crack and boom, and a flash of lightning showed the scarred land across the river sheeted in rain. Sunfallen's people retreated into their tents while the rain poured down. They saw, fearfully, Striped Badger, walking on his hands in the lightning.

In the morning, the far bank of the river was sodden and ashy, but no fire burned, and none could be seen on the horizon. Clever saw the Big Dog poking among the ashes, but no one else seemed to notice him. They were too preoccupied with Striped Badger, who had put his clothes on inside out, and was walking backward in circles around his fire.

"It is very hot," he said, as each person passed him, "but the flames will cool my hands."

"What great magic is Striped Badger making?" Surprised Raven asked him respectfully.

"Who knows?" Striped Badger said. "Who knows yet? Who can make the things the pale people have? The magic things?"

It was a rhetorical question, not meant to be answered, and Surprised Raven knew that. He wondered what magic things the pale people had.

"Sticks that shoot fire," the newcomer told him with his hands. That made no sense. But the newcomer was very friendly, and respectful toward Striped Badger. Surprised Raven thought he must not be as powerful, but of course as a clown he would recognize Striped Badger's power.

The people of the Bear moved on again at first light, into land that would be better graze for the horses, following signs of the buffalo who had scattered before the fire. Dog Nose said the signs showed the buffalo had been running very fast. It was not likely that they would settle until they had gone a long way, and even then they would feed in small nervous bands. The great herd that blackened the whole of the Grass from horizon to horizon would not come together again until spring.

"We will be hungry all winter," Surprised Raven grumbled.

Striped Badger ate a handful of dirt and rubbed his stomach.

"Striped Badger is thinking on a great magic," Weasel said to Sunfallen. "Do you know what it is?"

"Um," Sunfallen said, because Striped Badger wanted Rain Child's pot and he knew that was going to make trouble. "I don't have time for magics. We must hunt or go hungry." Striped Badger's antics made him uneasy, and also annoyed him because hunting seemed more important than anything else right now. But Striped Badger was holy and that meant what he was doing was important, so Sunfallen couldn't say so. He saw Rain Child sitting dejectedly outside Flute Dog's tent, mending a bridle rope. She looked up as his shadow fell on her.

"Striped Badger has asked me for your pot."

"That is my pot." She muttered it under her breath so that he could hardly hear her.

"He says he will make a magic with it that will bring the buffalo back."

"How? It doesn't call buffalo. It's a pot."

"Maybe you didn't use it right," Sunfallen said. "Striped Badger believes it will give us food. He is going to make more of them."

"It is my fault the buffalo are gone. I can't stop him," Rain Child said sullenly.

Sunfallen sighed. Everyone was angry with her, and with him because of her, and they wouldn't listen to him if he went against Striped Badger. Even his mother, who had insisted that he marry the Horse Girl because he was Most Important, now didn't want him to. For the first time since he had become the Bear, Sunfallen felt precarious. When a Bear proved to have been the wrong choice for his people, he could not be deposed, so usually he died.

Sunfallen got the pot and gave it to Striped Badger, who was cooking his food over a bucket of water.

"He took my pot," Rain Child said to Howler.

Howler smiled.

"He's going to do something evil with it!"

"He's a man of great power," Howler told her, so that anyone standing nearby could hear him.

"So are you. Why did you let him take my pot?"

"Oh, I haven't got the power that one does." Howler shook his head.

"I will need help," Striped Badger said to Surprised Raven and his brothers. "I will need someone to carry things for me." He stood upright so they would know he was not speaking contrariwise, but meant what he said.

"What sort of things?"

"Oh, rocks, and my magic pot."

"*Your* pot?"

"It is safer with me. I know how to keep it under control." Striped Badger felt satisfied with his bargain. The new man had wanted only his horse back when Striped Badger married Flute Dog, and to let the girl child stay in the camp. That was probably wise, anyway, or the mother would object. The girl had ceased to be dangerous because Sunfallen wasn't listening to her anymore. When Striped Badger had made iron, it would be plain that the choice of the Bear had been wrong, too, the message as well as the messenger a false one.

"What are you going to do with the pot?" Surprised Raven asked him.

"That is a secret for now."

"Striped Badger is going to make iron," Howler said.

"Iron?" Weasel squinted his eyes at the stranger's gesture.

"Iron." Howler said it out loud, and added the gesture he had just made up for it, which meant literally something like "Hard Gray Stuff That Does Not Break."

"The same as the pot that started the fire?"

"Oh, Striped Badger knows how to do it properly. After all, he is First of the Bear Dancers, not a child."

"What good will more pots do?

"Well, first of all, that pot is a cook pot, and so of course it calls food. I myself have seen it make a stew of prairie hens in itself. Striped Badger believes it will bring the buffalo back."

"Striped Badger is going to call the buffalo back with iron." Weasel nodded energetically at Blue Runner to indicate that he had accurate information.

"Can he do that?" Blue Runner demanded.

"The stranger man says he can. He says he has seen the pot call buffalo."

"Then our son ought to have that pot, and not Striped Badger."

"Striped Badger is his adviser." Weasel looked puzzled.

"Striped Badger likes presents too much." Blue Runner set her mouth in a thin line. "Striped Badger was happy to be the Bear's adviser when it was plain he could not be the Bear. Now people are talking about a false message."

"How could horses be a false message? Who has ever seen horses before?"

"Horses are very common where I come from," Howler said to White Grass Mouse.

"But they are not magic?"

"Magic?" Howler furrowed his brow. "Well, they are *useful*."

"What are you doing?" Flute Dog demanded. "Now everyone is saying we are not important, and Striped Badger should be the Bear!"

"I am giving them things to think on," Howler said.

"They will drive us out again, and that boy with us!"

"Not until Striped Badger has made his great magic."

"*Him*. What magic?"

"Iron. Pale people's iron."

"You saw what happened. Who thinks that can be done?"

Howler's lip twitched. "Coyote."

"The pale people who are living in the Cities-in-the-West have sticks that shoot fire," Surprised Raven told his wife.

"How do they do that?"

"They are made of iron—the stranger man has seen them. Striped Badger is going to make some of those sticks."

Surprised Raven's wife opened her eyes very wide. "Will you have one?"

"I think so. Striped Badger has asked me to help him." Surprised Raven looked important.

"You should have one of them," his wife told him.

Striped Badger felt everyone admiring him. It was like a cloak of buffalo fur settling around his shoulders. It made him feel elegant.

"Are you certain of these things?" Eyes of Bear asked him, but Eyes of Bear was getting old and couldn't see the things in front of his nose. That was why it had been given to Striped Badger and not to Eyes of Bear to make iron.

"In the morning I will show you," he told Eyes of Bear. "Is it a lucky day in the morning? That will be important."

Eyes of Bear looked at his stick where he kept his tally of days, and at the stars which had begun to show in the deep blue sky over his smokehole. "Someone's plan will go well," he told Striped Badger.

Sunfallen slept restlessly. In the morning Striped Badger was going to make the magic he had bought from the stranger. He had sent Surprised Raven and his brothers to a distant gray line of hills to cut a green tree because the stranger said that the life at the heart of the tree gave life to the magic. Eyes of Bear said they were living in a time of legend. Rain Child would hardly speak to him. Striped Badger was elaborately respectful but gave orders to Sunfallen's people as if Sunfallen were mute, or dying. The stranger was everywhere, conferring head to head with Striped Badger, talking to Surprised Raven or to Weasel, paying his respects to Eyes of Bear. Weasel said he was a great man among his own people, but plainly no match for Striped Badger, which was why he had sold him his recipe for making iron.

Sunfallen dreamed that Striped Badger picked a stick out of the fire and pointed it at him. The end of the stick blossomed in flame and the flame flowed over Sunfallen, setting his hair alight. Striped Badger wore his bear face. Everyone pointed at Sunfallen and the necklace of bear claws fell away from his neck.

When he finally stumbled from his tent, sleepless, in the morning, the sky began spinning and he vomited in the dry grass outside.

Striped Badger was already setting out, with Surprised Raven and his brothers to help. Striped Badger said that everything must be carried by human people, not by dogs or horses, and so they staggered under the weight of the freshly cut tree and hide boxes full of rocks and dried buffalo dung. Also, said Striped Badger, the rocks must be brought to the place where the iron was to be made, not just picked up along the way as the girl had done, being lazy as women were. The rest was secret.

A hole gaped open in the ground near center camp where Surprised Raven and his brothers had dug the rocks, since the stranger had said they must come from a place where power resided.

A crowd had gathered, even so early in the morning, before it was full light, whispering and pointing at the hole in the ground, as if they expected fish to crawl out of it. Striped Badger wasn't sure how everyone had come to know about his magic. He had intended to take only Surprised Raven and his brothers with him, but everyone had been talking to the stranger man, and somehow they all knew all about it by now. They were plainly prepared to follow him—old Grandmother Scarlet Water had her walking stick, and Whistle's sister had her new baby on her back. He even thought he saw the wild dogs, a handful of baleful eyes gleaming from behind a tent. The stranger was there, talking to Eyes of Bear, his walking stick in his hand.

"Oh, no," the stranger's voice carried through the early morning chill, "the horses must not come. This is a very dangerous task. It would not be safe for them. That was the child's second mistake."

Striped Badger tried to think what the stranger had told him was the other mistake, but everyone was crowding around him and it was beneath his dignity to ask. He nodded brusquely at Surprised Raven and his brothers, and they set out. Striped Badger pretended not to notice the gaggle of people following him. He was aware of Flute Dog and Rain Child trailing at the back of the crowd, and of Sunfallen at its head. The boy looked ill. Striped Badger allowed himself a moment of satisfaction. One did not wish evil on an innocent, of course, but it was plain that they all had mistaken the message of the Bear, himself included. It would be up to him now to rectify mistakes, lest the Great Bear grow angry and vent his anger on the people. The new message would come in the magical substance he would make. No one but Striped Badger had the power to tame it, that was clear. Even the stranger who had sold him the recipe was afraid of it.

"It wants to be made, though," the stranger had said. "That must be why the pot was sent to the girl, so it would come to you."

Striped Badger stopped when the sun was halfway up the sky and surveyed the landscape. This iron could be made only in an open space, on bare land. It was too powerful for ordinary ground. He pointed at the people following him.

"Now you will have to stand back," he told them. "These are serious matters. If the magic escapes, it might harm you."

They nodded respectfully. Even the stranger kept a good distance.

The land Striped Badger had chosen was barren, a rocky wash that had been dry for years since its river had changed its course one capricious spring. Surprised Raven and his brothers cleared the sides and bottom of the few scraps of scrub that grew between the stones, prying them loose with their digging sticks. The wild dogs stuck their noses out from behind a big stone and Surprised Raven threw rocks at them. They made him nervous, although Striped Badger refused to see them. The brothers maneuvered the tree into the bottom of the wash under Striped Badger's direction and began to chop it up.

The people all watched with interest as the wood chips flew. What was Striped Badger going to do with the tree? Would he burn it? Now they piled the cut wood in the bottom of the wash, layered in opposite directions, like basketwork.

Striped Badger got down in the wash with the wood and inspected it importantly. He poked the sticks here and there, straightening them with some ceremony. He paced around them with his hands behind his back. Then he flipped on his hands and walked around them that way, too. Finally he nodded at Surprised Raven.

"Now we will need water."

Surprised Raven and his three brothers looked as if they thought the privilege of making Striped Badger's great magic was taking more work than they had thought. But they set off for the river while everyone waited for them.

It looked like a dance, Rain Child thought. Some of the people had walked back to camp while Surprised Raven and his brothers were gone and brought back blankets to sit on, and food. Whistle's husband Swallow was drumming on a little drum while Whistle kept time with her bare hands on her knees. Children chased a leather ball, and three small boys were fighting each other with sticks. No one talked to Rain Child or Flute Dog, except Whistle, when her husband wasn't looking. Howler was sitting off by himself, just watching.

Sunfallen kept looking at Rain Child, but she wouldn't look back at him. He was going to tell her that they weren't married after all, because of the trouble she had caused, and she kept thinking miserably about why she had gone in his tent with him, and that now she was ashamed. Blue Runner and Weasel sat on either side of him as if they thought something, maybe Rain Child, was going to bite him.

Surprised Raven and his brothers came back with big waterskins, very hot and tired, and Striped Badger had them pour the water in the wash and make mud. Rain Child glared at Howler. It was plain now that he had given the way to make charcoal and iron to Striped Badger, even though it belonged to her.

Surprised Raven and his brothers were stirring up the mud, and Striped Badger finally began to help, too. Small children who ran up to play in the water were shooed off. When they had a mud wallow that would have held a buffalo, Striped Badger told them to pack the mud around the wood. Surprised Raven and his brothers looked like mud men now. Rain Child remembered Green Gourd Vine telling her about the Mud Men who lived where she came from. They were clowns too, of a kind, and they got into all sorts of trouble and had to be shown how to do the simplest things. "Coyote even had to teach the Mud Men how to copulate," Green Gourd Vine had said. "At festivals they pretend they have forgotten again. It's very funny." Rain Child thought about Coyote trying to teach Surprised Raven and his brothers to copulate with Striped Badger, and giggled. Several people turned around to glare at her and she put her hand over her mouth.

They packed the mud all around and over the wood until they had a mound that looked like a giant egg. Then they packed the buffalo dung over that.

Striped Badger set Rain Child's pot on a quilled mat in front of the mound to watch.

"You're supposed to leave holes so the air can come in and the smoke can get out," Rain Child said scornfully, because they were doing it wrong.

"It is an ill thing for a witch to be disrespectful of her betters." Striped Badger pointed a mud-covered hand at her.

"But you—"

"It will be hotter this way," Striped Badger said. "I thought of that myself."

Howler looked admiringly at him, although Rain Child was sure that Howler had told him what to do. Howler had talked often with Green Gourd Vine, whose people baked things in ovens all the time. Howler would know all about it. Rain Child wished she had known he was coming. Then she would have waited for him so he could show her, instead of that coyote.

Striped Badger was lighting the buffalo dung with a slowburner. Buffalo dung didn't make great flames, but it burned hot and steadily. It began to bake the clay hard around the wood. Rain Child wondered if Surprised Raven and his brothers knew that after Striped Badger had made charcoal, they were going to have to go get more water to make the oven to cook the rocks in, and why he had dug up rocks from center camp to use. They were the wrong sort, she could tell that by looking at them, unless that coyote had been wrong. That might be the case, she supposed. The stories were full of Coyote trying to outsmart someone, or to save trouble, cooking his maize before he planted it, for instance (Green Gourd Vine had told her that story), and making trouble for himself instead. She thought for a moment that she saw him among the people sitting around Eyes of Bear, but then he was gone, and no one else had noticed.

Everyone was talking, and then the Bear Dancers began to dance, with their bear heads on.

"What is in the earth?" they asked.

"What is buried in the earth?"

They trundled toward Sunfallen, bear paws slapping the dirt, and pointed at him with long brown claws.

"Where is the Bear?" They looked around as if they couldn't see him.

Blue Runner started to stand up and Weasel put his hand on her arm, reaching around Sunfallen.

"The Bear is here," Sunfallen said gravely.

They looked around wildly again as if he were invisible.

"Where is the Bear? What is baking in the earth?" They hopped away, and everyone murmured and looked sideways at Sunfallen. Rain Child saw Howler watching him, too, although he was pretending not to.

Sunfallen stood up and now no one would look at him. They kept their eyes averted as if he were a ghost, a lost spirit waiting to haunt them. Striped Badger was chanting over the mound of earth.

As the clay baked, the wood inside the mound began to hum. It made a low buzzing note, like bees. Rain Child could hear it. Striped Badger heard it, too. He bent over the mound and put his ear to the fire, not so close as to get singed, but close enough to hear better. He nodded with satisfaction and paced back and forth in front of the mound, with his bear face on.

Howler stood up. He stretched, nodding politely at the people watching. Someone offered him a waterskin and he drank thirstily. Someone else gave him a piece of dried meat. He eyed the mound of hardening clay. The clay hummed. Striped Badger looked pleased. Howler edged just a little bit away from it. Rain Child's eyes widened. She tapped Flute Dog on the arm. When Howler moved away again, they did, too. She looked uneasily at Sunfallen, still standing as if he were frozen, behind Striped Badger.

The humming in the mound turned to a whine, like the sound of hornets. A crack opened in its surface, narrower than a finger, and yellow smoke spewed out of it. Everyone coughed and held their noses, and everyone but Striped Badger and Sunfallen moved back of their own accord now, because of the smell. Surprised Raven and his brothers paddled away, faces still hidden under their bear masks, bear tails waggling. Rain Child laughed, although she knew she wasn't supposed to laugh at that.

Then Howler appeared in the smoke. He whispered something in Sunfallen's ear and handed him his shield, which he must have stolen from his tent. Sunfallen's eyes widened, too. He gave Howler a long look, and then stepped up to the singing mound of clay and stood alone in front of it, behind Striped Badger, with his shield in his hand.

Striped Badger felt the people moving away behind him, and looked at the yellow smoke, gratified. The smoke made him gag, but he choked the cough back, because it was plain now who had the power to control new magic, to bring new times to the Bear's people. The mound sang louder. It sang, *Striped Badger is Bear for the people, Striped Badger is the choice of the Bear.* Striped Badger heard it plainly.

A whining jet of gas escaped the mound. It sounded like the scream of an eagle. Striped Badger gave praise to the Bear, standing before the mound, arms uplifted, while the rest cowered behind him. The jet of gas burst into flame. With a roar, the mound shook, like a great egg hatching. It erupted in the air. Flame billowed from its depths, and a great wind burst out, a wind that carried hardened shards of clay and smoldering pieces of the buried wood and stones from the river bottom.

Sunfallen flung up his shield as the jagged shards flew around him. Striped Badger, surprised, staggered backward, arms flailing, his hair on fire, an arrow of stone-hard clay embedded in his chest. He fell and the contents of the mound rained down around him, spewing fire. Yellow smoke and gas boiled out of the opened mound. The cloud enveloped Striped Badger and hid him from their eyes.

Sunfallen lowered his shield. His stomach rose in his throat. He fought it down again. "The Bear has taken the First of his Dancers to live with him," he said.

They carried Striped Badger's body back to the camp and left the hole in the ground. When Rain Child picked up her pot and slung it over her arm, no one argued with her. When Sunfallen walked beside her, no one argued with him, either. And everyone made a very wide, respectful space around Howler.

When they reached the camp, Sunfallen sent Surprised Raven, and Weasel to be fair, to the distant line of gray hills again to cut poles for Striped Badger's bier.

"I would put him in a hole in the ground," Blue Runner said, and Sunfallen told her to be quiet.

"The Bear learns," Eyes of Bear said. "The Bear does not need a counselor anymore." He did not appear to be grieving over Striped Badger.

"What of the pot?" White Grass Mouse eyed it, hanging from Rain Child's arm.

"The pot is itself. We are not meant to have more than one of it. It is a piece of another world, and not for us."

"The girl said that Coyote told her to make more of it." White Grass Mouse found it hard to let go of the idea of many magic pots that would make him stew.

"Coyote is that part of us that thinks with our stomachs," Eyes of Bear said. "He is greedy. You know that. Where were you when I taught the boys of your year?"

"I was listening," White Grass Mouse said sulkily.

"*You* knew what would happen," Rain Child said.

"Not exactly," Howler said. "Mostly I let that one think of things for himself."

"But you knew from Green Gourd Vine what would happen. *I* said he was doing it wrong, but he didn't listen."

"It is given to us to think for ourselves," Howler said.

"People never do."

"That is why there are clowns."

"He was a clown. I don't think you should marry my mother. You know too much."

Howler looked surprised. He opened his eyes in exaggerated circles and his mouth made a round O. For just a moment Rain Child thought she saw Coyote, a flash of gray ears and pointy teeth. Then it was just Uncle Howler. "But I am on the side of good," he said to her.

Rain Child eyed the wild dogs, curled in a heap by his fire. It seemed to her now perhaps accidental on which side a person landed, like falling off a cliff. It depended on how you defined good, she supposed. Striped Badger would have understood that in the last second before his magic blew up.

"And they want the horses," Rain Child said indignantly to Howler. "I have had to promise Sunfallen that we will divide them, and keep no more than one each. If they are not allowed to make pots, why is it all right to make horses?"

"Horses make themselves. And anyway, those are Coyote's true gift to us. He just tried to give us too much. There is a story about that."

"There's always a story," Rain Child said grumpily, but she pushed the dogs aside and made herself comfortable. The wild dogs, as well as Flute Dog, her mother, had moved into his tent.

"This story," Howler said, "is about when Coyote decided to visit some people he had just made, and impress them."

These people's camp had gotten very big because they were doing what Coyote had told them to and were having babies. Coyote thought he would go and see them, but he wanted them to see what an important person he was. Mostly when he showed up as himself they threw rocks at him.

So he found a brush deer, and said, "You can be my horse." He made it into a very nice horse, painted white with a red blanket on its rump and a red ring around its left eye.

"What do you want me to do?" the horse asked.

"When I get on your back, I want you to prance around and neigh a lot." Coyote stood on his hind legs and pawed the air to show the horse how to do it.

"You need some clothes," Coyote said next. He took some bark and made it into feather trappings for the horse, and a fancy bridle. He tied the feathers on the bridle and in the horse's mane and tail. Then he took some big leaves and made them into a catskin cloth to sit on while he rode.

"Well, that's all right," he said, "but I need clothes, too."

"Then you had better not be a coyote," the horse said.

Coyote changed himself into a human young man, very handsome, with braids down to his waist. He took some dirt and made it into paint, and painted his face and chest with blue and yellow designs. He made a shield out of a shell and painted it blue and yellow, too. He took an old buffalo shoulder blade and made an eagle-feather fan out of it.

"I had better wear a breechclout, too," he said. "Or the women will be chasing me." He made a breechclout out of some more leaves. Then he made leggings and a pair of fancy beaded moccasins. He looked at himself in a pool and thought he looked very fine. But he thought maybe he could use some more decoration. So he added a necklace of turquoise and jasper and bear claws, and a robe embroidered with porcupine quills that he borrowed from Bull Buffalo.

"That will do," he thought. "I will show these people something they have never seen before."

When it was morning, he started for the people's camp. He was so heavily decorated that he could hardly move, but he managed to get on his horse and set out. After a while he came to where the men were playing the wolf-and-rabbits game. He rode up, pretending not to notice them. They all looked at him and said, "Who is that person? He is very fine."

Coyote tightened his hold on his horse's reins and squeezed him with his knees. The horse reared up and neighed. The women were playing a game with a leather ball. They all stopped and looked at Coyote, too. "He is very handsome," they said to each other.

Coyote made his horse rear up again and they all watched while it pawed and neighed. "He is very fine," the women all said. "Maybe he will marry one of us."

Coyote rode closer so they could get a better look at him. But just then the smallest rabbit in the game, who was a little boy, ran under his horse's nose and frightened the horse. The horse shied and tumbled Coyote off his back. It galloped away and turned back into a brush deer. They saw it running off.

Some of Coyote's fancy clothes fell off, too, and they recognized him. They all ran after him and the rest of his clothes fell off. He turned back into a coyote and ran off into the brush, barking. All his clothes and decorations were strung out through the brush. The people picked them up and saw that they were just leaves and bark. But after that everyone always dressed the way Coyote had dressed.

"So now they will all ride horses, even though the iron didn't work?" Rain Child asked. "But those pale people are somewhere, and they still have sticks to shoot fire at us."

"They'll shoot themselves, too," Howler said comfortingly. "A thing like that's bound to make trouble. No one but Coyote would try to give it to someone."

EPILOGUE

IT HAD ALL BEEN MORE COMPLICATED THAN COYOTE had thought. He sat on the mountain to the west, looking at the hole that Striped Badger had blown in the ground, impressed in spite of himself. He was already pretending he hadn't really wanted to make iron, and thought that he had done a fine job keeping them from killing the little horse girl, and Sunfallen the Bear, who was going to be important to his people in a number of ways.

He watched the ghost form of Rain Child's mother drifting across the Grass, and saw the pale shape of her father tumbling after. It hadn't taken the Grass long to eat him, either, and now they both blew over it on the wind. Coyote could see the father's people in the Cities-in-the-West, building new walls and buildings, spreading out, taking for themselves whatever there was. He could see the things they had taken moving inside them, changing them, until they were alien and new and their homes Over the Water didn't know them anymore.

* * *

"But what about Rain Child?" the girl on the bench asked. "Was she happy?"

"She married Sunfallen the Bear."

"What about her beads and her pot?"

"They are in the medicine bundle of the tribe of the Bear."

"And the horses?"

"The horses made more horses. It was a long time before the white men got that far into the Grass and annoyed those people, so they had time to be a great people."

"Was Rain Child's father really a white man?" the other girl asked skeptically.

"Does it matter? We are what we are given to be."

"Then why did Coyote give her all those things, if she was just an ordinary person?"

"He wanted her to be more. But people aren't always accommodating that way. That is part of the law of Unintended Consequences." The old woman looked slantwise at the girls. She took a roll of knitting out of her bag and began to work at it. The needles flashed in the sun and the reflection from the fountain. The yarn was dirty and looked as if she had been carrying it around for a long time.

"You've dropped a stitch," the girl said severely.

The old woman picked it up on her needles. "See? You don't know how it's going to turn out when you start."

AUTHOR'S NOTE

I WOULD LIKE TO THANK LUCIA MACRO AND ELIZAbeth Tinsley, for their patience; my husband, Tony Neuron, for the wild dogs; and the following sources, for the traditional stories retold in this book: *American Indian Trickster Tales*, edited by Richard Erdoes and Alfonso Ortiz, for the stories of the upside-down maiden, the sun and moon in a box, and the bag full of fleas; and *Reading the Fire: The Traditional Indian Literatures of America*, by Jarold Ramsey, for the tale of coyote's visit to his people.